**W9-BJZ-590**

CROWN
OF
SHADOWS

CROWN OF SHADOWS

C. S. FRIEDMAN

DAW BOOKS, INC.
DONALD A. WOLLHEIM, FOUNDER
375 Hudson Street, New York, NY 10014

**ELIZABETH R. WOLLHEIM
SHEILA E. GILBERT
PUBLISHERS**

For Nancy Friedman

Because the only thing better than hanging fifty feet over a smoking volcano with nothing but a thin sheet of plastic between you and it—with a pilot whose idea of fun is to tip the helicopter over on its side without warning and cheerily yell, *"Don't worry, you won't fall out!"*—is having someone to share that with.

The author would like to thank the following people for their help in making this book possible:

Neil Rackham, for sharing his volcano;
Gene Fisher, for sharing his horses;
Helen Zebarth, for fielding some very strange medical questions;
and Shirley Maddox, for the most precious gift of all: time.

Prologue

There was lipstick on his cheek. He could feel it when the wind brushed by, a spot of waxy moisture on his cold-parched skin. Red, he thought. Crimson. He recalled it vaguely, distantly, in the same way he remembered its wearer. Lips. Breasts. Thighs. Parts of a body, divorced from the whole. Flesh without a soul. He tried to remember her name and found that he couldn't. Was that his fault or hers? What kind of woman would cast her net for the heir of Merentha, when the very name of his family had become an epithet for disaster?

Ahead of him the castle loomed, cold stone arches framing the night in moonlit numarble. Once there would have been lamps in the windows, a crackling fire in the great hearth, the smell of mulled cider seeping out into the courtyard. Once there would have been servants aplenty, running up to greet him as he made his wee-hour approach to the great estate. Once Samiel himself might have stood in the doorway, scowling at his younger brother as he dismounted, prepared to lecture him until dawn on matters of propriety. Or Imelia might have been waiting, equally concerned but gentler in her castigation. Or Betrise, broad-shouldered and belligerent.

Not any more. Not ever again.

All gone.

He dismounted—or tried to—but he was drunk enough that he stumbled as he struck the ground, and he barely kept himself from getting trampled as he disentangled his booted foot from the stirrup. He leaned against the animal for a moment, breathing heavily. This was always the worst time, these first few minutes when he came home and and it hit him how absolutely alone he was. While he was in town he could pretend that nothing was wrong—wining and dining and womanizing with a vengeance, forcing his flesh into that ac-

1

customed mode as if somehow the spirit could be forced to follow suit—but when he came to the castle gate all his illusions dissolved like smoke, and he was left with nothing. Absolutely nothing. The emptiness inside him was so vast that no woman's caress could begin to fill it, the memories so horrible that no amount of alcohol could ever dull their impact.

He managed to get the horse stripped of its saddle and set it free to roam. He knew he should do more for it, but that duty—like everything else—was too much for him now. There were hay and water in the stables, and the horse knew how to get to both. The great wall that had been erected around the estate during the war of 846 was now crumbling, but it would still serve as a pasture fence. That was enough. It would have to be enough. He lacked the strength—and the will—to do any more.

Why was I left alive? he despaired. It wasn't the first time he had asked that question. Samiel could have carried on. Samiel would have mourned and raged . . . and then he would have picked up the pieces of his life and carried on, somehow. Building new memories. Learning to forget. They'd had such strength in them, all of his family . . . all except Andrys. The playboy. The gambler. The black sheep of the family. Why had he alone been spared? Why was it that on that terrible night when his family had been slaughtered, he alone had been allowed to survive?

You know why, an inner voice chided. *You don't want to understand it, but you do.*

He forced his mind away from that question as he fumbled with the latch. Too painful. The only way he could get through the empty days was to try to forget, to fight the memories back in whatever way he could. Even if that meant alcohol. Even if that meant blackout. Even if that meant other drugs, illegal drugs, that might calm the terror in his soul for a moment and grant him a simulacrum of peace. Anything that worked.

He was dying.

He considered that thought as he walked through the great hall of the castle, staring up at the portraits that flanked him on both sides. A man could die slowly, if conditions were right. The life could seep out of him gradually, a little bit each day, until at last there was nothing left of him but a shell of flesh, cold and colorless as a corpse. He looked up at the portraits of the other Survivors—seven of them, whose names and dates he had learned like a catechism in his youth—and shivered. Seven men who had survived the death of their families, and lived to renew the family line. How had they done it?

Why had they done it? How could a man put such a thing behind him, and take a wife and sire children and start all over again, as if nothing had happened? He laughed shortly, mirthlessly. Whatever magical strength they'd had, he sure as hell lacked it. He lacked even an understanding of its nature.

You picked the weakest one this time, he thought. As if the family's destroyer could hear him. *The least deserving.* Maybe he could hear, at that. Maybe he was aware of all their thoughts, and had chosen Andrys to survive because somewhere, deep inside him, he saw—

What?

Don't kid yourself, he thought bitterly. *There's nothing of value in you, and he knows it.* He looked up at the portraits of the other seven, one after another, and saw all too clearly what quality he shared with them. If only he didn't see! If only he didn't understand. . . .

With a moan he staggered to the liquor cabinet and poured himself a drink, from the nearest full bottle at hand. Sweet cordial, his late brother's vice. He threw it back quickly, wincing as the syrupy stuff slid down his tongue, trying not to taste it. Alcohol was his elixir now, his solace, and its flavor was irrelevant. If he could figure out how to pour it straight into his bloodstream, he'd do that and save himself the glasses.

A shadow seemed to move suddenly in the corner of the room. Startled, he dropped his glass. It shattered on the numarble floor, spraying the sticky cordial on his feet; the sugary smell of norange liqueur filled the room. A small accident, but it was suddenly more than he could handle. He felt the tears start to flow free, and with them memories from earlier in the day. Her voice. Her body. Her scorn. God in Heaven! How much more merciful it would have been if he had been utterly emasculated, instead of this half-life in which the memory of slaughter might or might not unman him at a crucial moment. In which he could perform just often enough to get his hopes up, just well enough for him to convince himself that maybe, just maybe, the healing had finally begun . . . and then suddenly the room he was in would be splattered with blood, and the body he caressed so desperately would seem like that of a corpse, bodily parts disassociated from one another and from their owner. . . . He wrapped his arms around himself, shivering. It had to end. God, it had to end. One way or another. How long could a man go on like this?

Until you end it, an inner voice whispered. *There's no other way. And how much would it hurt? You're already dead, aren't you? Like*

the rest of your family. He killed them fast and he killed you slow,
but he killed you all the same.

"Oh, God," he whispered. "Help me. Please"

The memories were coming now, like they always did at night.
Seeping into his brain like some dank poison, corrupting his senses.
Was that real blood, there on the carpet? Was that the smell of death
in the air? He whimpered softly and tried to fight it, but he lacked
the strength.

*Blood. Splattered everywhere. Drops of crimson glistening in the
lamplight like a thousand cabochon garnets, scattered across the rug
and the floor and the clawed feet of the great table. Blood that
dripped from—*

Dripped from—

"No!" he whispered. "Please. Not that."

*Blood that pooled at the feet of the great chair, blood that coursed
down in thin rivulets over the fine novebony carvings, blood that
dripped from his brother's head where it had been thrust upon the
sharp strut of the chair, impaled as if on some warrior's spear. . . .*

His eyes squeezed shut, his body spasmed into a foetal knot of terror. The memories hurt. God, they hurt! Wasn't there any way to
stop them? "Anything," he whispered, shivering violently. "Not
again. I'll do anything. Stop them!"

*The room was a study in carnage, disjointed fragments too horri-
ble to absorb: Imelia's body, laid out across the great table. Gutted.
Betrise's long hair strung out like silk in a pool of blood, yards from
her body. Dianna. Mark. Abechar. All the Tarrants, every single one
of them except him—every brother and sister and cousin that had
ever laid claim to the name, down to the last helpless infant in its
own crimson puddle—and watching over all of it, as if from some
grisly throne, his brother Samiel. Samiel, elder and heir. Samiel, self-
proclaimed Neocount of Merentha. His eyes were rolled back in their
sockets now, as if what they had gazed upon were too terrible for human sight; the blood smeared on his face made his contorted expression doubly unreal, a parody of human terror.*

*For a moment Andrys was too stunned to react. Then sickness
welled up in him, sickness and terror and raw, unadulterated horror.
Doubling over, he vomited. Again and again until there was nothing
left in him to bring up, and even then his body continued to spasm.
As if somehow the effort might squeeze him dry of fear, as well.*

*Only then did he become aware that there was someone else in
the chamber: a tall figure, dark and silent, who stood halfway across
the room. Malevolence was so thick about the figure that it was al-*

most visible, and the cold that emanated from it chilled the tears on Andrys' face. Though the shadows of the room obscured its expression, its purpose was clear. Man or demonling, it was his family's murderer. And it was watching him. Waiting.

Panicked, he fell back as far as the wall behind him would permit. Knocking over a chair as he did so, which skittered across the blood-slicked floor and at last fell across his sister's outstretched form. "Who are you?" he cried. His voice was strained and broken, like his nerves. "What do you want?"

For a moment the figure was still; in the chill silence of the room Andrys could hear his own heart pounding wildly. Then the dark form stirred, and in a voice as smooth and as refined as silk pronounced, "I am the first—and only—Neocount of Merentha."

Fear made Andrys' bones turn to jelly; he would have fallen, had not the wall held him upright. "The first Neocount is dead," he gasped. "Dead!" Nine hundred years in the grave, he wanted to say. To shout. But the words wouldn't come out.

"Hardly," the figure responded. "But that was the story your father preferred, and so it passed for truth in your schooling. The illustrious Reginal Tarrant! He thought that if he kept you ignorant he might somehow make you safe." The shadowed head turned to the side briefly as it gazed upon Samiel's ruined head, then back again. "It didn't work, of course. It never does."

The figure took a step toward him. Terror caused Andrys' bladder to spasm suddenly, and hot urine trickled down his leg. He wished he could die right here and now, and not wait to be killed like . . . like that. Like Samiel, and Imelia, and Mark. Dear God, not like that, please oh please. . . .

But the figure stopped, as if knowing that another step would be one too many for Andrys' frayed nerves. "He knew the truth." The figure indicated Samiel. "The firstborn has always known the truth. That was one of the conditions I set for this family, when I first decided to let the line continue. And when he placed the coronet of this county on his head, when he laid claim to the title that wasn't his to take, he knew what the price of that would be."

It took him a minute to understand. To believe. "Is that it?" he choked out at last. "All this . . . because of that? Just for a title?"

He could sense anger stirring within that dark, faceless form: not hot, like human rage, but as chill and as biting as an arctic wind. "I gave this family life," the figure pronounced acidly. "And I dictated the conditions under which it would be permitted to endure. I spared your ancestor when it would have been just as easy to kill him, not out of human compassion but because I was curious to see what the descendants of my blood might accomplish. And so I left you my lands, my keep, my wealth, my library—whose true value is beyond your imagining—all these things and more, a treasury beyond measurement. Only two things were forbidden to you . . . and one of those you insist on claiming. Eight times now." A sweep of one black-cloaked arm encompassed the carnage. "Consider this a reminder."

"You killed them all for that?" he whispered feebly. "Because of Samiel's mistake? All of them?"

For a moment the dark figure regarded him in silence. Andrys was acutely aware of the filth that soiled his shirt front, the urine that had plastered one pants leg to his flesh. Shame flushed his cheeks, hot blood suffusing death-white flesh.

"His mistake was defiance," the figure said coldly, "which I will not endure. As for my methods . . . I find that the harder the lesson is driven home, the longer it is likely to last. Remember that, when you raise your own heirs."

Heirs? For a moment he couldn't remember what the word meant, or how it might apply to him. His heirs? He had no children yet. And never would, if this creature killed him—

Then it sank in. All of it.

Images of the Survivors rose up before him. Haunted figures whose biographies were shrouded in mystery, who had survived to continue the family when all others died of sickness, or in war, or (the records were unclear) in some terrible accident.

Or were slaughtered.

Like this?

Oh, my God, Andrys thought desperately. Let this be some drunken dream. Let me wake up in the back room of some tavern to discover that I passed out and had a nightmare, just a nightmare, please, God, just that. . . .

"I see you understand," the figure observed. "I trust you will not be so foolish as to repeat your brother's mistake."

He turned away from Andrys then, meaning to leave him alone with the carnage. To make his peace with his fate, if he could. But as he turned, a shaft of moonlight fell across his features, illuminating them. Illuminating a face—

"No," he whimpered. "No!"

Illuminating a face so like his own that he screamed, he screamed, he started screaming and he couldn't stop, because suddenly he understood—he understood—he knew what kind of dark *vanity might drive a man to murder his entire family except the one child who was most like him, knew it without being able to put a name to it, knew it even though his soul burned from the understanding of it. And he knew that every time he looked in the mirror from now on he would see that face, not his own, that those eyes would stare out at him from his own reflection, terrible empty silver eyes so like and unlike his own, eyes that had looked out upon the vast expanse of Hell and found its terrors wanting—*

Moaning. Weeping. Balled up in a tight little knot, tears streaming down his face. Crying uncontrollably, as he had done for so many nights now. Would it never end? Would there never come a point when the memories would fade, in intensity if not in detail? When he could gaze upon the face of the first Neocount of Merentha—the *only* Neocount of Merentha—and not relive the gut-wrenching shock of that horrible revelation?

Never, an inner voice whispered. *Not until you put an end to it.*

"Oh, God," he whispered. "Please. I can't take it any more."

It was then that the voice came: a whispering thing no louder than his tears, but it made his spine shiver as though ragged fingernails were playing across his flesh. A demonic voice, without question; no fleshborn creature could make such a sound.

"*Andrys Tarrant,*" it murmured, in tones that made his flesh crawl. "*Is that what you really want? Oblivion? Or would you rather exult in life again?*"

He raised himself up on one elbow, and with his other arm wiped the wetness from his face. Opposite him stood a figure that was somewhat human in shape, though anything but human in substance. Its surface was a tapestry of sharp edges and ragged darkness, and thin tendrils of fog curled about it like questing serpents. Its eyes took in the lamplight and broke it up into jagged bits, reflecting it back in a thousand burning sparks.

For a moment he stared in awe at the thing his fear had conjured. Never in his life had he manifested something so concrete, so dangerously fascinating. Considering how much he'd had to drink, he was amazed that the creature was coherent.

Then he realized how much danger he was in. And from somewhere he dredged up a prayer of protection, that he muttered under his breath as he retrieved his glass and launched it at the demon thing, as hard as he could. Willing the creature to respond to him, in the way that the faeborn so often responded to members of his family. Filled with a sudden fury that the thing would pick this moment to accost him.

The demon didn't move. The glass passed through its flesh and hit the far wall, where it shattered. Sweet cordial dripped from the wainscoting.

"You didn't create me," the creature informed him, "and you don't have the skill to banish me." Its voice was like cracked glass, jagged and brittle. "I came to talk to you. Of course, if you feel a need to destroy more glassware first. . . ." It nodded toward the bar. "I'll wait."

The demon's tone—cultured, sardonic—utterly disarmed him. "What do you want?" he stammered.

"I came to help you. To save you."

"No!" He knew the ways of demonkind enough to grasp that it was looking for an opening, some way to get to him. Even in his drunken state he knew the danger of that. "Get away from me!"

"You're empty, Andrys Tarrant." The gleaming eyes fixed on him. "So very empty. You try to fill the hole inside you with alcohol, with drugs, you try to bury it beneath a thousand and one couplings, but it won't go away, will it?"

"Leave me alone," he whispered hoarsely. "I know what you want. I won't cooperate. I won't—"

"Even though I can heal you?" the demon demanded. "Even though I can fill that emptiness inside you, and give you life again? Do you really want me to leave?"

He shut his eyes, and his shaking hands curled into fists. Lies. They had to be. Lies and deceptions, custom-tailored to his needs. He couldn't afford to listen to this creature, or to hope. The cost was too high. The minute he agreed to let this *thing* minister to his needs he would find himself sucked dry of blood or brains or dreams or some other vital substance . . . because that was how demons worked, wasn't it? Once you gave them an opening, you were as good as dead.

But what did he have to lose?

From a distance—as if from another man—the words came to his lips. "Go on," he whispered. "Tell me."

"You have an enemy. I'm going to destroy him. For that I need an ally. A *human* ally. In short, I need you. And I'm prepared to barter for your service, by giving you a way to earn your peace."

"My family was murdered. You can't change that. Whatever you're offering—"

"How about revenge?"

The words stopped him cold. "He would kill me," he breathed. Aware of a spark of hope that had suddenly been kindled with that word. Afraid to feed the flame. Unwilling to smother it. "I wouldn't stand a chance."

"He'll never kill you. Human life is cheap to him, but killing you would mean destroying his family line—forever—and he would never do that to one of his own creations. No, Andrys Tarrant, you're the one man on this planet that he won't ever kill. That's why I need you."

"Then he'd torture me—"

"Worse than he has already?"

Andrys lowered his head. And trembled.

"He's powerful," the demon said. "Perhaps the most powerful fleshborn creature that this planet has ever produced. And evil, without question. But he's also proud, and infinitely vain—and that will be his undoing." The brittle voice altered, becoming smooth. Seductive. Liquid tones, that lapped at his brain like a drug. "You know what I want. Now let me show you what I have to offer in return."

Fear wrapped a cold hand about Andrys' heart. A hundred generations of Tarrants clamored for him to flee.

But—

But—

What did he have to lose?

"Go ahead," he whispered.

—And it occurred to him that maybe with demonic help he *could* get the bastard who'd slaughtered his family, could make him pay . . . but not with a quick death, oh no. Nor with simple pain. With something equivalent to what he had done to Andrys—some slow, living death that would rot away his soul until there was nothing left but a core of despair, stripped of all its pride and its vanity and its strength and its power and all its hope. . . . He pictured the proud Neocount of Merentha made helpless by *his* actions, assigned to a living hell by the force of *his* hatred, and felt something stir inside him that had been dead for too long. Purpose. Direction. *Hope.* His blood ran hot with it, and he trembled as unaccustomed vitality poured into his brain. As his body flushed with the thrill of his intentions.

And then it was gone. As suddenly as it had begun. The hope, the certainty, the sense of power—all dissolved into the night, as if they had never been. All that remained was a spark of heat in his groin, as if he had just withdrawn from a woman. And an emptiness so vast it seemed ready to swallow him whole.

"Well?" the demon demanded. "Do you want to live again? Or

shall I leave you to crawl your drunken way into an early grave, and exchange this hell for the one that follows? Which is it?"

His hands shook as he tried to think. Bargaining with demons was suicidal, he knew that. No one ever won that game. And he was hardly in shape to make life-altering decisions.

But . . .

He wanted the feeling of purpose back. He wanted it back so badly he could taste it. He would have traded his soul to have it again . . . and the demon wasn't asking for that, was he? Only for his assistance in ridding the world of a murderer. In cleansing the Tarrant name once and for all.

"I can call it off," he said at last. "Whenever I want. When I say it's over, you go and leave me alone. Agreed?"

The cracked face twisted. The faceted eyes glittered. It was more than a smile, less than a grin—and it made the air vibrate with hatred, until Andrys' soul was filled with it.

"As you command," it whispered.

Demon's Wake

One

She walks in the moonlight, her footfall on the weathered planks as soft and as silent as a ghost's. All about her the sailors are busy cleaning up the detritus of the storm: mending sails, untangling lines, freeing those items which were, for safety's sake, bound to the deck. Intent upon their tasks, they do not notice her. The wind is crisp and clean and she imagines that she can catch the scent of land in it. So close, so very close. . . . For a moment she trembles, and almost turns back. One more month, the priest said. Maybe less. But then she remembers what that month would be like—what all other months have been like on this ship—and she stiffens with new-found resolve. No more, she tells herself. No more.

The sea is quiet now, having spent all its anger in the three days before; in the moonlight she can see no white upon the water's surface, only black glass waves and an occasional sparkle of starlight. Quiet, so quiet. Death must be like that: black and still and utterly silent, a smooth realm that ripples ever so softly as each soul passes into it. Free of turbulence. Free of pain. Free of fear and its attendant demon, whose silver eyes must even now be searching her cabin, wondering where she has gone.

The thought of him makes her breath catch in her throat, and her whole body shivers in dread. No, she whispers. Never again. She steps up onto the railing, her dark toes gripping the rounded wood. The sea is beneath her—

"Mes!" A sailor's voice, behind her. For an instant she imagines she knows which one it belongs to—the blue-eyed Faraday boy, suntanned and lean and oh so innocent—and then she leans forward ever so slightly, into the night, and lets go. "Mes! No!" Footsteps approach her even as her toes lose hold, the long fall into darkness beginning just as he reaches the place where she stood—and then more footsteps, more cries, as the others come running. A world away, they seem to her. A distant dream. She is aloft, a creature of the air, aflight above the waves. Falling. Beneath her the water seems to gather in anticipation—not glass now but velvet, cool and welcoming—and then the moment is past and she breaches the surface, the cold waves give way to her body and she is beneath them, struggling in the icy depths, shocked out of her dream state by the frigid reality of the sea.

Panicking suddenly, choking on seawater, she fights to get back to the surface. There is no thought of suicide now, only the blind, unthinking terror of a suffocating animal. Water pours down her face as she finally lifts her mouth above the surface of the waves and gasps for air, and not until she has drawn in two or three deep breaths does the sense of panic release her. Shaking, she coughs up some water she has swallowed, and her frozen body treads water without thought, grateful for the respite.

Above her the sailors are moving quickly. One has shed his heavy woolen jacket while another has grabbed up a life ring. Will they come down here, after her? Rescue her, and force her to live again? That is a concept even more terrifying than death, and she begins to swim away from them, her heart pounding wildly in her chest. Which does she fear more?

And then she sees him, standing among them. So dark. So still. He is like the sea itself—like death itself—and despite the distance between them she can feel the chill invasion of his thoughts in her head: seeking, analyzing, weighing. Hungering. She watches as he puts a hand on the naked shoulder of her would-be savior, and despite the distance between them she can hear his words as clearly as if she stood on the deck beside him.

"She has chosen," the Hunter tells them, and there is power in his voice; they cannot disobey. "Let her go."

The silver eyes are fixed on her: watching, waiting. He can sense the presence of Death about her, and it fascinates him. Frightens him. For all his power, for all his centuries of wordly experience, this moment is beyond him. For all the choices which his power makes available, this one option is forever closed to him.

She finds new strength in that, and ceases paddling. The waves are gentle, and caress her face as she sinks a few inches. She can taste salt on her lip, and a spot of blood where she bit herself in her *panic. Can he smell that? Does it awaken enough hunger in him that he regrets the promise he made so many months ago, that if she chose to die rather than serve him he would honor her choice and let her go? The complex interplay of cruelty and honor in him is something beyond her understanding. What kind of demon clings to a simple promise when his only source of nourishment is sinking beneath the waves?*

Suddenly resolved, she dives below the surface. The sea closes over her head, dark and insulating. Deep down she swims, as far as she can manage, until her lungs are bursting with their need for air. And then she breathes in deeply, welcoming the cool darkness into her body. Saltwater fills her lungs, and maybe in another time, another place, there might have been pain. Not now. The spasms of her lungs are a glorious song of freedom, and even as the darkness closes in about her, she thrills in the sensation of dying.

No fear this time. So sorry, Hunter. No fear to feed you this time, only the bittersweet embrace of death. Hardly an appetizer, for one like you. So sorry. . . .

Most Holy Father,

I write to you from the deck of *God's Mercy*, which sails westward with its companion ship toward the port of Faraday. In our struggles to return home to you we have now been at sea ten months as Prima measures time, and not a week of that has been easy sailing. The Eastern Gate proved impassable, its eastbound currents too swift and its guardian volcanos too active to permit us passage. Despite his many misgivings, Captain Rozca led us south, into truly unknown waters, where even his limited experience was of little value to us. He hoped to win us passage west between the Fire Islands, which would bring us into the tropical currents and ease our passage home. Alas, Novatlantis was unobliging. Barely had we begun on that course when there was an eruption of such magnitude that it deafened us from miles away, and the sailors struggled in choking fumes to save their sails from the molten hail that fell on us. There were many injuries that day, and there would have been more had not Gerald Tarrant braved the unnatural darkness of the ash-blackened sky to work his cold craft in our favor. From its hiding place within his

Worked sword coldfire flared with the force and brilliance of lightning—

"Shit," Damien muttered. "Can't send that." He read the paragraph over again, then balled it up in his fist and threw it aside. It landed in a pile of similar discardings, now littering the floor of his cabin. He lowered his head to his hands and tried to think.

Most Holy Father,

These are the details of my voyage to the eastlands, which I undertook in God's Name and for His eternal glory.

It took five midmonths for the *Golden Glory* to cross Novatlantis, a journey which God permitted us to make without injury to any of our people. We knew that in the past five expeditions had preceded us along that route, but we knew nothing of their fate. To our surprise and delight we found a nation thriving on that distant shore, which was wholly dedicated to the One God and His Prophet's teachings. Upon learning that we, too, traveled in God's name, these people welcomed us and showed us a land that seemed nothing short of paradise. Even the fae had been tamed there, in accordance with the Prophet's writings, and I was filled with joy and new hope as I saw with my own eyes what miracles a unified faith might reap.

Alas, the godly image of this land was but a facade. Even as we began to suspect that a darker truth lay at the heart of this seeming paradise, we were forced to flee into wilder places, long since abandoned to the fae and its creatures. We traveled as a company of three: myself, the rakh-woman Hesseth, and the sorcerer Gerald Tarrant. I would be lying if I said that I ever fully trusted the Hunter, or that my relationship with the rakh-woman was entirely comfortable, but we discovered in our quest a common cause which overbore our natural tensions. I think it safe to say that not one of us would have survived the journey without the other two. And indeed, at several points even our concerted efforts were barely enough to save us.

Our journey brought us through many horrors, of which I will spare you description; suffice it to say that the poisoning of this land had begun long ago, and was orchestrated by a master hand. Gerald Tarrant determined that a demonic force allied to human sorcery was responsible, and I saw no reason to doubt him. In order to learn more of its nature (and perhaps discover a weakness in our enemy) we traveled farther south, to a land that was beyond the reach of the One God's faith. There humans and rakh toiled side by side in rare unity, devoting themselves to the destruction of God's nation and the very faith which sustained it. It was a land well fortified against invasion, and we were nearly overcome by its gruesome defenses. In that place Hesseth died, and I will mourn forever that I could give her no proper grave, nor better resting place than a blood-spattered chasm in a vile and hostile land. In that land also Gerald Tarrant was approached by the enemy, who offered such a price for the betrayal of our cause that even his cold heart must have been moved

"Hell." He stared at the last sentence for a long minute, then scratched it out with a sigh. "Can't tell him that, can I?"

He sat back, trying not to think of those days. The fear. The suspicion. If he had known then what he knew now—that Tarrant had sold them out in order to get them closer to the enemy, close enough to strike—would it have made a difference? The enemy had offered Gerald Tarrant true immortality. Could Damien have ever felt confident that the Hunter would refuse it?

Probably not, he reflected. Who could have foreseen that in the end the Hunter's vanity would prove more powerful than his lust for immortality? That the thought of seeing his proudest creation destroyed was as abhorrent to him as seeing his family line extinguished? Both were his children, were they not? The last remains of his life-blood on Erna. Was it any wonder that he loved the Church as much as he hated it, and had crafted a false treachery to entrap the man who stood poised to destroy it?

Immortality. Life as a god, unthreatened by any fear of divine retribution. Damien could never look at the Hunter again without remembering that choice. He could never again pretend that he understood Gerald Tarrant, or the balance of forces which moved him. Not after that.

With a sigh he took up his pen again, and started to write.

We determined that the Prince of this land was our enemy, allied according to sorcerous custom with a demon who served his will. Alas, I wish the truth were that simple. Such an alliance might have provided a more finite enemy, concrete enough to destroy—or at least weaken—in a single battle. What we discov-

ered instead was that the man who called himself the Undying
Prince was no more than one pawn in a vast demonic enterprise,
whose stakes are the very souls of mankind. And though we
freed that land and its sister to the north of the demon's immediate influence, I fear it was only the opening move in a vast and
terrible game.

These are the things we now know about our true enemy, a
demon of such strength and subtlety that he may well prove to
be the single greatest threat facing man on Erna: He calls himself
Calesta in this time and place, but there are men who call him
by other names, and some who worship him as a god. He is a
true demon in power and bearing, meaning that he can interact
with humans as subtly and complexly as though he were human
himself. He is capable of forming illusions so convincing that not
all of the Hunter's power can see through them, and of maintaining such illusions over long periods of time. He is from the demon family called *Iezu,* and like all Iezu he is immune to the
normal vehicles of demonic control; as of yet we know of no certain means by which to contain him. Lastly, he feeds (as all the
Iezu do) upon the emotional energies of mankind, preferring the
sharp repast of human sadism to the gentler emotions which
some of his brethren relish.

It has been said that demons live for the moment, that they
lack any ability to pursue—or even grasp the concept of—long-
term goals. That is certainly not true in this case. Calesta means
to remake our world, and from what I have seen in the eastlands
I can only say, with a shudder, that he is clearly capable of doing
so. We were witness to his effectiveness in the east, where his
machinations plunged a land of devout and hopeful people into a
nightmare holocaust whose horrors defy description. I can only
pray that the steps we took to counteract his efforts remain successful. So many souls, to be sacrificed to the hunger of one demon! Never was there better illustration of why our Church is
needed on this world, and why the sword and the springbolt and
the gun and the shield are no more than shadows of the only true
weapon on Erna, which is faith.

Thus it is that I return to you, my heart heavy with its burden
of knowledge. Be assured that in this war I shall be your most
vigilant soldier, until such day as we find a way to destroy this
demon, or banish him forever from the realms of man.

Your most humble and obedient

"Another report-in-absence?"

It was Tarrant, standing in the doorway of his cabin. Damien glared at him, a look meant to communicate that he needed no reminder about his last letter to the Patriarch, or the trouble it might get him into. He had sent it as a substitute for a personal audience, and when the Holy Father finally got hold of him, there was going to be hell to pay for that.

"Not this time," he said shortly. He finished the letter, signed it quickly, and put it aside. There was no denying that he deserved the Patriarch's wrath. The only question was how long it would last, and what form it would take. And whether or not the Holy Father would understand that their entire world was at risk now, and personal venom must take second place to martial expediency if the Church was to triumph.

"You're delivering it yourself, then?"

"No real alternative, is there?" There was an edge to his voice that he couldn't disguise. "I have to go back. You know that."

Go home, the demon Karril had urged. *Go home as soon as you can. If you stay away, if you give Calesta time to work . . . then the world you return to may not be the same as the one you left.*

That was over a year ago. What if it was too late already?

"You're afraid," the Hunter mused.

Anger welled up inside him suddenly, a rage that was ten months in the making. "Damn right!" he spat. "And there you are right on schedule to revel in it." The pent-up fury of a whole voyage was pouring out of him, and he had no way to stop it. "What makes you better than this Iezu we're fighting? What makes you more worthy of life than he is? I can't seem to remember just now."

If his challenge angered the Hunter—or awakened any other emotion within him—the man damn well didn't show it. "Random invective doesn't suit you, Vryce." His tone was cool, maddeningly controlled. "If the girl's death bothers you that much, then say so."

He drew in a sharp breath. "You *killed* her."

"I offered her a bargain which she chose to accept. It was her own choice, from start to finish. You seem to forget that. I never interfered with her freedom of will, or made any attempt to coerce her into service. You know that. She knew what my needs were and she agreed to meet them. If she had survived this trip, she would have been well rewarded for her efforts. The fact that she chose to end our contract—"

"To kill herself! To take her own life! Those are the words," he choked out, "—not some vapid euphemism. You killed that girl as surely as if you cut her throat with your own hands. *You.*"

"She knew what I was," he said quietly. "As do you. And I suggest you come to terms with that knowledge before we reach port, Reverend Vryce. Our enemy is dangerous enough as it is; if we allow ourselves to be divided, what chance do we have to defeat him?"

He started to respond—and then forced the anger back, forced it out of his mind. Along with the hatred. Along with the disgust. Because Tarrant was right, damn him. They couldn't afford to be divided. Not now.

"All right," he muttered. "So what chance *do* we have? Tell me that."

His only answer was silence. The silver eyes were mirrors that reflected Damien's own misgivings back at him. *So little chance,* they seemed to say. *Why measure it in words?* At last the priest turned away, and he cursed softly under his breath.

"I have never lied to you," the Hunter said.

"No." He drew in a deep breath, and tried to relax his hands; they had curled into fists of their own volition. "No, you never have." After a small eternity he managed to add, "Will you be all right?"

It took Tarrant a minute to realize what he was asking. "You mean without the girl."

He nodded stiffly.

"Ah." A pause. "I had hoped she'd last longer—"

"Just answer the question," he snapped.

"Will I live to see port? Yes. Will I be in prime condition to rejoin battle with the enemy when we get there? Not if I go hungry for a month, Reverend Vryce." He paused. "But you knew that when you asked, didn't you?"

He shut his eyes and exhaled noisily. "Yeah. I knew."

"Shall I take that as an offer?"

He remembered their voyage to the east, and the nightmares that Tarrant had placed in his mind so that he might harvest Damien's fear for nourishment. It was not an experience the priest was anxious to repeat, but what was the alternative? Let Tarrant become so weakened by hunger that when they arrived in Faraday he was all but useless? Encourage him to feed on the rest of the crew?

With a heavy sigh Damien nodded, wincing. "Yeah," he muttered. "It's an offer. Whatever you need—"

"And no more than that," the Neocount finished smoothly. "I understand."

God. Those dreams. A month of them and a man could go mad.

Could the Hunter perhaps drink his blood instead? There was enough of the vampire still in the man that sometimes that was possible. Was temporary physical weakness preferable to mental torture?

He looked up at the Hunter again and tried to gauge the hunger in those pale, cold eyes. It amazed him sometimes how human the man could appear, when the hunger inside him was anything but.

"No dreams of the Patriarch," he told him. "Nor of the Church. Not in any form or manner. Agreed?"

A faint smile tightened the corners of Tarrant's lips; the pale eyes sparkled. "No dreams of the Patriarch," he agreed. "Not of my devising, anyway."

"Yeah." He turned away, refusing to look at Tarrant. Or at the letter. "I can manage those nightmares on my own, can't I?"

Faraday: jewel of the east, heart of all commerce, haven par excellence for all the merchant ships that plied the eastern waters. Unlike the other great ports of Erna this city had not relied upon Nature for its security, but had crafted its own safety with walls and locks and measures and men, creating a complex alarm system which rendered the great harbor as safe as any coastal region could ever be.

Faraday: devastated.

They saw it from a distance at first, then assessed it in greater detail as they approached. The great sea wall which towered thirty feet above the water's surface, protecting the harbor beyond, was now ragged along its top. There were broken spars that jutted out from its surface, wooden shards driven deep between the rocks as a memorial to whatever ship the sea had caught up and heaved against its unyielding surface. Mast-bits floated in a muddy sea, rail-bits, scraps of sail. Something that might have been a chunk of flesh was caught up in their wake, but the scavenger fish had so worried it that there was too little left to identify.

At the top of the wall men scurried about, quickly making repairs. Damien saw them nervously looking east as they worked, as if they could somehow measure the sea's temper. But smashers didn't always give warning, and from the looks of the damage . . . Damien felt his stomach tighten as they came around the end of the wall, past the first smasher lock. He hated the sea. He hated its power, and its unpredictability. Most of all he hated the limits it had placed on man's progress, by forcing him to focus on a land-based expansion.

Rozca's expression was dark as they came around the end of the wall, easing *God's Glory* and her companion ship into the narrow harbor entrance. Damien followed his gaze out into the harbor itself, where broken piers and battered hulls littered the tide. "Shouldn't have happened," Rozca muttered. "Not here."

"You can't stop a smasher."

The Captain snorted and jerked his head toward Faraday. "*They* could. Maybe not stop it outright, but keep it from killing. They've got alarms up on the cliff there—" he waved a hand toward the bluffs that towered over the harbor, "—that sense a quake far away as Novatlantis, and enough good men praying 'em to work that they're damn near perfect. With the watchers up there and sirens all along the coast . . . there's never been a smasher yet that they didn't know was coming. Get your ships out into deep water if you can, tie up the rest to a special mooring that lets 'em go with the waves, set the locks so the harbor can't be drained, and then get the vulk out of the way . . . maybe they can't stop 'em, but they can damned well make ready for 'em. There hasn't been a ship lost in Faraday since the last lock was built, nearly a hundred years ago." He gazed out in the harbor, eyes narrowed against the sunset's glare. Shadowed by his thick brows, his expression seemed doubly dark.

"Not this time," he muttered. "Vulkin' Hell, look at the place!"

They had come past the lock and around the sea wall, so that now their view of the harbor was unimpeded. Damien's hand tightened about the rail as he gazed upon what was once the proudest port of the eastern coast, as he compared it to the harbor from which they had set sail nearly two years ago. Where dozens of sleek piers had jutted out from the shore there were now but a handful, and a good half of those were badly damaged. The shoreline boardwalk had lost whole sections, and with it all the buildings that stood upon it. And the sea—that was filled with debris, enough shards of mast and bits of sail that Damien knew more than one ship had foundered in the rising sea, along with all their passengers.

Tsunami. They were always a danger on this volatile world, and more than once Damien had been on a ship that refused to enter port when the tide was two inches higher or lower than normal, for fear that the dreaded flood waves would follow. But Faraday had made a science of surviving them, and was practiced enough in that art that even the dreaded bore, a towering wall of water whose impact flattened everything in its path, did minimal damage here.

Until now.

A soft indrawn breath behind him, almost a hiss, made him turn back slightly. It was Tarrant. He was up early—the sun had barely set behind the towering bluffs and its light still filled the sky—but perhaps he had heard the commotion from above and wanted to investigate. Or perhaps he had caught the scent of death, and wondered at its source. He shaded his eyes beneath a gloved hand as he studied the devastation surrounding them, and Damien knew without asking that the strength of the man's will was reaching down into the sea, trying to tap into the local fae-currents for information.

"The first wave was a bore," he said at last. "Those which followed were . . . incidental."

"You guessing that, or you Know?"

He shook his head slowly, eyes narrowed against the light. "Water's shallow enough for Working, though barely. I can get a somewhat hazy picture."

"Rozca says the port had defenses."

"It did," he agreed. "They didn't work."

"Can you tell why?"

The pale eyes fixed on him. The whites were reddened slightly, burned by the dying sunlight. It was costing him a lot to be up here, Damien realized. "The question may not be *why*," he mused, "but rather, *who*."

It took him a minute to realize what Tarrant meant. "Calesta?"

The Hunter nodded. "I would like to think that an act of nature could be just that, no more. But this does seem a bit of a coincidence, doesn't it? Such devastation to welcome us home. Certainly our enemy would be pleased to make such a statement."

"But he can't conjure a tsunami, can he?" When Tarrant didn't answer, he pressed, "You said that the Iezu only had power over human sensory input. Nothing tangible."

"So I did. But never doubt the versatility of that power, Reverend Vryce. Or the danger it can pose to those who aren't prepared for it. Iezu illusion cannot create a real wave . . . but it *can* blind the men whose job it is to detect one, and prevent them from responding to it."

"You think that's what happened?"

"I think it's very possible. I think our enemy would consider it a very appropriate welcome for us. A reminder of his power, as well as proof that he's monitoring our passage. Yes. Very appropriate indeed." His expression tightened as he tried once more to access the fae; after several minutes he shook his head in frustration. "Wait until we land, Reverend Vryce. I can tell you more then. Out here . . . the fae is too weak."

Land. Damien tasted the word as the great ship prepared to disgorge its passengers. After eleven months at sea he had almost forgotten what *land* was like, how it felt and smelled, what it was like to have the ground remain steady beneath your feet. And land without volcanoes, no less. After months in Novatlantis it seemed to him that his very skin stank of sulfur; he wondered if mere soap would ever wash it clean. God, that had been a hellish trip. . . .

"You'll be going back to Jaggonath," the Hunter said.

Damien looked up at him sharply. "We have to, don't we? Karril's warning—"

"Was to *go home,* Vryce. I have no idea what that phrase means to you."

It hit him then, suddenly. The one thing he had never dared to ask, in all their months of traveling. The thing he had tried so hard not to think about. "You're going to the Forest."

Tarrant nodded. "As you knew I would."

Oh, yes, he had known it. On some deep, buried level where you hid knowledge you didn't want to deal with. Only now it was out in the open. The Hunter would go to his Forest. Of course. And Damien would return to Jaggonath. Of course. Each of them to test out his domain, each one to ascertain what damage their Iezu enemy had wreaked in their absence. Each one alone, their alliance of two years divided. . . . It should have pleased him, to be rid of the Hunter at last. It didn't.

"You think it's wise?" he asked quietly.

"I think it's unavoidable. Would you help me bring order to the Forest? Your soul would never survive that kind of trial. Yet the Forest is my power base; I must see it secure before I can concentrate elsewhere." A faint smile touched his lips. "And you can hardly present me to your Patriarch, can you? It seems in both our interests that we separate for a time."

"For a time," Damien agreed. It was a question.

The cool, clean profile was still; the silver eyes studied the harbor in silence. At last he said, "We have a common enemy. Given his power, and his stated intentions . . . we would be foolish not to pool our resources."

"Yeah." Damien leaned heavily against the rail. "Only the adjective I was thinking of was *suicidal.*"

Tarrant looked down at him. And for an instant, just an instant, Damien thought he saw a flicker of fear behind that measureless gaze. A flaw in the perfect arrogance.

"Just so," he whispered. "Just so."

Two

Red pills. Shiny, like drops of blood.

White pills. Powder-soft, bitter on the tongue.

Black pills. Velvet glass, a kiss of oblivion.

Andrys laid them out on the hotel dresser, tiny bottles that glittered in the lamplight. His hands, he noticed, were shaking. The air seemed uncomfortably warm.

Easy, Andri. Steady now. You're almost there.

Five days on the road. Not an easy journey, for one who had rarely left his home county. Not an easy task, to go among strangers where one's name was unknown and one's heritage meant nothing and the name of the county that had given one birth was just a mark on the map, no more or less meaningful than any other.

He had never loved Merentha, nor had he hated it. Those terms implied strong emotion, and in truth he had pretty much taken his home county for granted. It was there; the Tarrant estate was located within its borders; his family had once ruled the place. But now that he had left, he found there was an emptiness within him that no wine could dispel. He felt lost in the eastern cities, and sometimes when the night was dark and strange sounds and scents surrounded him he felt that if he just relaxed, if he just closed his eyes and let go, the strangeness of it all would carry him away. Until he was no more than a sigh on this foreign breeze, a whisper of lost hope fading out into the night.

Sometimes he would pray to Calesta, as one would pray to a god. Sometimes the demon answered. Then dreams of vengeance would flood his soul, forcing out the loneliness. Dreams of hate so powerful, so driving, that his body shook for hours even after they had ended, and his mind was numb for what seemed like a small eternity afterward. Those dreams ... they were pain and ecstacy almost beyond bearing, a catharsis so terrifying and so necessary that on the nights when Calesta did not answer him he wept, helpless and hopeless as a lost child. The dreams were all he had now. The hate was all that was holding him together.

That and the drugs.

Alcohol to numb the fear, to ease the pain of remembering. Cerebus for the madness within him, the beast that must have outlet now and then or it would swallow him whole. Slowtime for visions of color and music in a world washed gray by sorrow. And blackout— blessed blackout—little black pills for a taste of oblivion, for shadows of death to fold about him like a cocoon, shutting out all the pain and the beauty and the hope and the fear—shutting it all out, every last bit of that agony called *life.* Long enough for him to rest. Long enough for him to sleep. Blackout for the coward within him, afraid to go on living but more afraid to die.

He stared at the tiny bottles, tempted by their contents. He had come to Jaggonath in the late afternoon, had taken a room and eaten a meager meal and cleaned off the dirt of the road as well as he was able. Now ... his fingers closed about the bottle of black pills and he shut his eyes, as though mere physical proximity might somehow transfer its contents into him. But not yet. Not now. There was still time to scout out the city before nightfall, to get his bearings for the morrow's work. He owed himself that much, didn't he? Regretfully he released the small bottle, leaving it beside its brethren. *Later,* he promised it. *Later.*

It was a vast city, a crowded city, filled with sights and sounds and smells almost beyond bearing. Its undercurrent was a tide of anxiety which he could taste on his lips as he braved the crowded streets, trying to make his way as the locals did, without touching. Cobblestoned streets splashed with mud offered uncertain footing, but at least they were clean; he knew cities where the awkward contraptions used to catch horse droppings weren't required by law, and the smell of those was something that defied description. Here, thanks to a strange combination of civil tolerance and legal regulation there were no aging drunks cowering in doorways, no wide-eyed cerebums twitching their way along the sidewalk as they dreamed their mad dreams of chaos and depravity, not even a wild-haired prophet or two to cry out their warnings of doom and destruction while handing out advertising circulars for the nearest pagan temple. It all existed, here as elsewhere, but in Jaggonath it was shut away behind closed doors. And for that Andrys Tarrant was infinitely grateful.

He soon came to the silver district, so named for the metal that best reflected the sun's white brilliance. Warded windows were filled with treasures, worked in that metal and others: yellow and pink gold, copper and bronze, and the sun-metals: silver, white gold, platinum, polished steel, others. He didn't know the names of all of them and often couldn't tell them apart; when Betrise used to bring out her prize serving utensils, worked in five different white metals, he used to shake his head in amazement that anyone would spend a small fortune to purchase such a thing.

Not that money had been an issue in those days, of course. The first Neocount had seen to that by sinking his wealth into investments that tripled in value before anyone could manage the legal contortions required to get at it. If Andrys had thought about it then, he might have believed that the man was trying to provide for his abandoned son by assuring wealth for his progeny. Now it just seemed like a cruel joke. Money couldn't bring his family back, could it? Money couldn't make this nightmare end. But it did pay for drugs and liquor and occasionally—when he required that kind of cold, impersonal convenience—it paid for women.

He forced his attention where it belonged and studied the objects in the windows before him, trying not to dwell on the implications of what he was about to do. Better not to think about that. Better not to think about anything, just accept Calesta's orders and obey them blindly and pray that somewhere, somehow, vengeance would be achieved. Calesta said that Andrys should come to Jaggonath, so he had done so. Calesta said that Andrys should seek out a silversmith, so he would. Calesta said that he should cause to be made—

A cold shiver coursed up his spine. *Don't think about what he wants with it. When it's ready, that's time enough to know.* He forced himself to study the objects displayed in the windows, searching for something that would help him decide on one shop or another. Each shop seemed to have its own specialty: he passed by displays of jewelry, daggers, decorative goblets, engraved tableware, a thousand and one items suitable for courtship, weddings, formal ceremony. Nothing displayed was exactly like what he needed, but was that a surprise? How long had it been since that kind of work was last done in Jaggonath? Or anywhere, for that matter?

At last, with effort, he winnowed the choices down to five likely candidates. One by one he studied them through their mesh-bound windows, trying to get a feel for the businesses inside. Hoping for some kind of sign or omen that would narrow his choices even further, so that he wouldn't have to go through the same painful interview more than once. He didn't think he could stand that.

He studied two shops in that way, found no such omen, and with a sigh he moved on to the third. This one had a promising display, a unique collection of bowls and goblets with delicate figurines intertwined to serve as stems, handles, and spouts. Each one was individual, he noted, and meticulously detailed. So far so good. He looked past the fine steel knives with sinuous sterling handles, the elegant silver picture frames and anniversary mementos, to see what was within the shop itself—

And his heart stopped for a moment. The steel and sterling bits faded into shadows, as inconsequential as dreams. For a moment he could hardly move, then he walked to where the door was and grasped its handle. The ornate grip felt warm in his palm, and he could feel his pulse pound as he held it. Quickly he turned it and pushed the heavy door inward; bells jingled merrily as he stepped into the shop's cool interior. There were display cases within, tables topped in velvet, a long counter capped in fine white numarble. . . .

And a girl.

He stepped inside, letting the door fall shut behind him. God, but she was lovely! Not in the way of the women who normally appealed to him—those were buxom and full-hipped, flamboyantly sexual— but in a way that made it hard for him to breathe, impossible to think. Skin as fine and as pale as porcelain glowed in the late afternoon light, with the pale flush of a sunburn crowning the cheeks and forehead. Hair as black and as lustrous as silk shimmered in a loose chignon at the nape of her neck. Slender hands with impossibly delicate fingers smoothed the black velvet of a display table. Fragile, she seemed. Slender and pale and so very fragile. Like a china cup that might shatter if you held it wrong. Like a pane of fine stained glass with its delicate webwork of lead veins, beautiful to look at but oh, so easy to destroy. Her presence awakened new feelings within him, disturbing feelings, so different from his usual feelings about women that for a moment he could do nothing but stand there mutely, unable to respond.

"Can I help you?" she asked. It was a reflexive response to the presence of a customer, which she began even as she turned toward him. Then the dark eyes met his—God, those eyes, you could drown in them!—and with a short gasp she stepped back. To his amazement, it seemed as if she were afraid. Of him? He looked around, startled, expecting to see someone else in the room. But it was just the two of them. The response was for him alone.

"I'm sorry," he said hurriedly. Not knowing what he had done wrong, but anxious to correct it. Was it possible that in his fevered entrance he had seemed threatening? She seemed the kind of creature who would shy away easily, like a wild and wary skerrel. "I didn't mean to startle you—"

She drew in a deep breath; he could sense her struggling to compose herself. "It isn't you," she said at last. "It's just . . . I thought you were someone else. Someone I didn't expect here. I'm sorry." She shook her head slightly; the black hair rippled about her neck. "I shouldn't have reacted like that." She smiled then, and her expression softened. "Can I help you with something?"

He fumbled in his pocket for the papers he had brought, and somehow he managed to tear his eyes away from her long enough to make sure they were the right ones. "I need some custom work done. Here." He handed her the drawings, a well-worn package. "It's all there."

She led him to one of the velvet-clad tables and pulled up a chair before it; he sat opposite, and watched her as she studied the drawings. God, but she was beautiful! In another time and place he would already have been making a play for her, if only for the sheer pleasure of the hunt. But in this time and place he felt strangely helpless, and he sat there quietly as she studied the drawings, watching as her slender fingers smoothed the papers flat for better perusal.

"A coronet," she mused.

Something tightened in his throat. "Family heirloom," he managed. "It was . . . lost."

Lost in a pool of blood, shattered by sorcery. Shards of metal swimming in the red that dripped down chair legs, over tiles—

"Hey. Are you all right?" Her hand reached toward him.

He shivered as the vision receded. "Yeah," he managed. "Just a little faint." He forced himself to put his hands on the table, so that he might look a little more natural. "I wasn't feeling well this morning." *There* was an understatement! "I thought it had passed." He managed an awkward grin. "Guess not."

"Can I get you something?" When he hesitated, she suggested, "A glass of water?"

"No, I . . ." He drew in a slow breath, tried to think clearly. "Yes. Please. That would be wonderful."

Water. It meant a moment when she wouldn't be watching him, a moment when he could struggle to pull himself together. Those visions . . . he should have taken something before he left his room, he knew that now. A few grains of tranquilizer to ease the painful interview along. How in God's name was he going to get through this?

You have to, he told himself. *Calesta says this has to be done, therefore you will do it. Period.*

"Here," she said, as she set down a small glass before him. Her voice was gentle, soothing; he could listen to it for hours. "I wish we had more to offer."

"This is fine." The water was cool and refreshing, and the glass gave him something to do with his hands. "Thank you."

When she was satisfied that he was going to be all right, she returned to her seat opposite him. He noticed that her hair had one narrow streak of white in it, falling from a spot just above her left temple. A natural discoloration, or faddish vanity? For some reason he hoped it was the former. She seemed a wholly natural creature, more like the timid nudeer that wandered free on his estate than the painted beauties he usually dated. Though such women had never appealed to him before, this one had him totally captivated.

She was paging through the pile of sketches, studying each one in turn. One meticulous rendering of a county coronet. Ten pages of details, in perfect scale. Other drawings, other items. She shook her head in amazement as she went through them. "You did a beautiful job on these."

"I traced the artist's originals." When she looked up at him in curiosity, he added, "My ancestor saved everything."

How bizarre this conversation was, he thought. How utterly bizarre to be discussing the archival habits of Gerald Tarrant in this cool and offhand manner, as if men hadn't wept and suffered and died for that very coronet.

"In sterling?" she asked.

"If that was the original metal."

She nodded. "Silver was customary up until the sixth century. I take it this is older than that."

He nodded.

"It must have been beautiful," she mused aloud. Her eyes traced the lines of his drawings with obvious relish, and he knew in that instant that she was the artist who would be translating his sketches into reality. The thought pleased him. "Revivalist, right?"

"I think so."

"Neocounty?" She smiled as he affirmed that, too, her dark eyes sparkling. "I've never worked for nobility before."

The words caught in his throat; he had to force them out. "We haven't . . . we don't use the title. Not for a long time."

"Are these from the same period?" She had found the sketches of armor at the bottom of the pile: breastplate and bracers of fine steel with embossed and inlaid motifs. "Armor?"

"I should have removed those," he said quickly. Reaching for the sketches. "That's a different job, I know you don't—"

"But we do. At least, Gresham does. My boss," she explained. "He used to do this kind of work. There isn't much of a call for it, you know. Not enough to base a business on. But I think he would love to work on these." The dark eyes were fixed on him again; he didn't dare meet them. "Unless you have someone else in mind, that is."

"No," he managed. "Not at all."

"Then I'll show these to him. He can probably get you an estimate on all this by . . . say, Thursday?"

Estimate. He felt something knot up inside himself at the sound of the word. *Estimate* meant another interview about these damned pieces, more questions, always more questions . . . and he couldn't begin to answer them because he didn't know why Calesta wanted these things made, only that he did.

"I don't need an estimate," he said quickly. Trying to get the words out before he could have second thoughts. "Whatever it takes. Just make everything as much like the originals as you can. Whatever that costs."

She hesitated. "It's going to be expensive."

"That's all right."

"*Really* expensive. This is all gold here, look." She showed him one of the sketches, her finger tracing the line of decoration on a breastplate. "The materials alone—"

"Money's not an issue. Really."

She sat back, and for a moment said nothing. He could see curiosity burning bright in her eyes, but knew she wouldn't question him about his wealth. Not directly.

"He'll want a deposit," she said at last.

He reached into his jacket to where his traveling purse was secured and removed it. Untying its clasp, he spilled its contents out on the table. They were thick coins, heavy coins, the kind of gold one bought for investment purposes, not the kind one normally carried around town for day-to-day expenses. He had brought them with him so that he wouldn't have to wait for the local banks to clear his account before he could buy anything locally. Now he was infinitely glad he had them.

She whistled softly. Despite himself he smiled, pleased with the drama of the moment. "Will that be enough?"

"Oh, yes. I think so." She picked up one of the coins and studied it with a smile. "Yes, I think Gresham'll take these."

"How much do you want?"

She hesitated, then picked out half a dozen of the coins; one was a beautiful memorial piece which she admired before putting it away. In a smooth, flowing hand she wrote him a receipt. "I'll need some information from you."

"Of course."

"Your name?" she asked. And it seemed to him that there was more than professional interest in her tone. Or was that just wishful thinking on his part?

God, he used to be so good at this! Where was all that skill when he needed it?

"Andrys. Andrys Tarrant." Other questions followed, more difficult to answer. Where did he live? Permanent address? How long would he be in Jaggonath? Business references? Personal? He knew the questions were unavoidable, given the value of the work he was ordering, but some of them were difficult to answer. How long *would* he be here? Calesta had said that the process of vengeance would begin in Jaggonath. How long would that take?

Later, when he was finally out of the shop, he leaned against the brick wall outside and shut his eyes and cursed himself for being a fool.

You're an idiot, Andri, you know that? The afterimage of her face was burned into his soul. *You could have said something useful. You could have made some kind of beginning.* Though the fragile appeal of her was new to him, he was no stranger to games of attraction. If this had happened in the days before, he would have had her address by now and probably a tentative date as well. Had this project so unmanned him that he couldn't even manage that?

Good God. He laughed bitterly, mirthlessly; the sound devolved into coughing. *I don't even know her name.*

It was just as well. What did he have to offer a woman, anyway? Restless, distracted days. Bitter, frustrating nights. No, he had better reserve his attention for the whores who asked for nothing but money, and opportunistic wenches who could be purchased with gifts and small talk. That was his venue now, the comfort and prison of his new existence. Better stick to it.

God, those eyes. . . .

With effort he pushed himself away from the wall and began the long walk back to his hotel. It was just as well, he told himself. Women like that usually had a man already, and if they didn't, there was probably a good reason for it. He had enough problems of his own to deal with, didn't he?

He shivered, wrapping his arms around himself, cold despite the warmth of the city streets. The pills would help him. Little black pills. They were waiting on his dresser, a kiss of velvet oblivion. Under their influence he could forget it all for an hour, an evening, an eternity. The pain. The confusion. The fear.

And the girl.

Trembling, he hurried back to the hotel.

For a long, long time after Andrys Tarrant left, Narilka stared at the door in silence. Her heart had been pounding all the time he had been there; only now, with him safely gone, did it resume its normal beat. Only now could she begin to breathe normally, as if nothing whatsoever were wrong.

That face. So familiar. Those eyes . . . she could picture them cast in a paler hue (silver, cracked silver, the color of ice and sunlight) and that was enough to transform them, because in all other ways—in shape, in expression—they were the same as *his*. Just as this man's hair was the same, (golden brown, fine as silk), only Andrys Tarrant had trimmed his in a stylish cut, indisputably modern, while the *other* had let his grow to the shoulder. And so it was with so many other features: token differences, superficial, which only served to highlight the uncanny, unnerving resemblance between the two men.

The Hunter.

She remembered him from the Forest, that terrible, fear-filled night. Remembered his eyes burning black with hunger, his power so chill and fierce that it froze the very air in her lungs as she drew in a breath to scream. Not a man but a demon—a cold, cruel god—whose eyes were doorways into another world, a world of such terrible alien beauty that even as he threatened to devour her, even as the fire of her life flickered weakly before him, about to be extinguished, she longed to be drawn into his private night forever. Mystical, magical, secretive night. Violet light and unearthly music and tides of fae so subtle that the roar of a single breath would drown them out. . . .

And now there was Andrys Tarrant. Here. In *her* world. Alive in a way the Hunter was not, solid and real in a way he could never be. Capable of living and loving with a human heat—

Gods. She shut her eyes and tried to focus on something else. Anything else. *That's not a healthy reason to want a man and you know it.* She had enough trouble with men already without asking for more, didn't she? The type of man who was attracted to her was usually looking for a victim, not a lover, and she had fended off enough of that kind to last her a lifetime. The last thing she needed now was another bad relationship.

But his haunted eyes (green, not gray, and so alive!) stayed with her for hours, and the memory of his presence was still warm in her flesh when she finally closed up the shop for the night.

Three

The Hunter flew west along the Raksha Valley, following the course of the river Lethe. Westward over Sattin, where they had once booked passage across the Canopy: he and the priest, Senzei Reese, and the lady Ciani. It seemed a century ago. His goals had been so finite then, his self-definition so simple, so clear . . . when had it all gotten so muddied?

He could feel the weight of his compact on his back as the strong feathered wings drew him closer and closer to home. In Mercia, in one thoughtless act, he had saved a civilization from ruin. The powers which sustained his unnatural life would surely condemn him for that, and take action to teach their wayward servant a lesson. The only question in his mind was when, and what form the "lesson" would take. They hadn't done anything yet. And though after a year of being unmolested he had begun to hope that they would continue to honor the compact which kept him alive, he had no illusion that he would go unpunished forever. The Unnamed was not known for compassion.

Soon the Raksha Valley broadened out into the Plain of Sheva, on the very doorstep of the Forest. He came to the ground there and re-claimed his human form, the better to study the currents in that place and see if there were any sign of Calesta's interference. But malignant power was sucked into the Forest here with such force that no trace remained outside its borders. In his months outside the Forest, he had forgotten just how strong it was. He could feel its pull on his own soul as he stood there, as if that whirlpool of malevolence would devour him whole. It had tried, once. He had tamed it. And it took little effort now to resist its call, and to rise up on broad white wings once more, to review his domain.

Dare he hope that Calesta had focused his vengeance elsewhere and left the Forest alone? If so, it was a temporary respite, and the Hunter knew it. *This place is my source, my nourishment. If he means to hurt me, then he will strike here.* Even the fact that he could see no mark of Calesta's interference here didn't guarantee that the demon had been absent. A Iezu demon could easily conjure an illusion to cover his tracks, so that even an adept's Sight would be hard-pressed to make them out. Was there a limit to that skill? How many perfect illusions could a Iezu sustain at once? On that question, Gerald Tarrant suspected, their very lives might depend. If only he had more knowledge of the Iezu. Damn the code of behavior which bound them from interfering in each others' battles, which kept others of that kind from helping him!

There were trees beneath him now, and a tangled canopy of vines and branches so thick that even his special Sight couldn't see through to the ground beneath. The earth-fae which coursed below it sparkled through the canopy like stars, hinting at a power so vast that surely no single demon, Iezu or otherwise, could stand against it. He could feel the force of the Forest's fae coursing through his veins like blood, even from this height, invigorating him body and soul. Let Calesta test him now, with all his power at hand, and that Iezu would see how quickly and how ruthlessly the Hunter dealt with his enemies.

It was nearly dawn when he came to the observatory tower of his keep, jutting up from the tangled canopy like a sleek black spear. The sigils engraved upon its narrow roof reflected the moonlight like fire. He took care to avoid the circle they inscribed, a spot he had painstakingly scrubbed clean of all fae for the sake of Earth-like experimentation. That, too, seemed a lifetime ago. Had it really been less than three years ago that he had lived this isolated life, surrounded by nothing but his trees and his servants and his precious experiments? Would that he could simply reclaim that life, and let the darkness of the Forest heal him of all the wounds the living world had inflicted! But that dream, though seductive, was not feasible at the moment. As long as Calesta lived and hated and plotted his Iezu vengeance, not even the Forest would be safe from his demonic predations.

Afterward, he promised himself. *When all this is over, when Calesta is neutralized and my compact defended and Vryce has gone off to make a separate fate from mine . . . then I will have the time and the leisure to find myself again. To define myself anew, on such terms that living men may never again compromise my spirit.*

Amoril was waiting for him atop the tower. The taste of the albino's subservience, carried to him on the chill Forest breeze, was reassuringly familiar. Despite his hunger to resume his accustomed role in the Forest hierarchy, he remained circling for long minutes overhead, searching for some sign in the terrain below to warn him that Calesta had been active here. He was painfully aware of the futility of the act, given the nature of his enemy, yet he dared not sacrifice any possible advantage in this deadly war that the Iezu had declared. But he saw nothing to excite his suspicions, save a fleeting shadow that tasted of the Unnamed's special malevolence. That his patron-demon had been here was hardly a surprise. It had probably set out a Watcher to alert it to its servant's arrival, and was even now preparing its own special welcome for him. He shivered as the cold winds bore him in yet another circle, and tried not to think about what that welcome might be.

I served you faithfully for nine hundred years, he thought to it. As if it could hear him. As if it cared what he thought. *And but for one moment of carelessness, I have never failed you.* But he knew even that wasn't true, that in his travels with Vryce he had more than once pushed the envelope of the Unnamed's tolerance. God willing, when this all was over he would have a chance to establish himself anew and cleanse the taint of Vryce's human spirit from his soul.

Finally he dropped to the tower and regained his human form, coldfire licking at his flesh as he transformed. The Prince of Jahanna, come home to claim his own.

As soon as he had human eyes with which to see, Amoril bowed deeply to him. "My lord." He evinced no surprise at Tarrant's return, which was as it should be. The man who had been assigned to watch over the Forest had damned well better Divine well enough and often enough to foresee that his Master was coming home.

"Is all well?" he asked shortly.

The albino nodded. "There was some trouble out by Mordreth last month—some of the prospectors decided that if they cleared a bit of the Forest their work would be easier—but we settled all that."

"You made a warning of them, I hope."

"I left them impaled on tree limbs, in such a posture that implied the trees might have more volition than Mordreth gives them credit for." His eyes sparkled redly. "They'll think twice before fetching their axes again."

"Excellent," he approved. And it was. A taste of normalcy, after so many months of tension.

The albino bowed again. "I had an excellent teacher."

Together they descended into the lightless depths of the keep itself, where even the moonlight was not allowed to intrude. Though the Forest outside was thriving, the building's interior had not done quite so well. There was dust in the numarble halls, he noticed, irritated. He thought in addition that there was a faint ammoniac smell, like that of stale urine, wafting toward them from a distant corridor. Had the albino's wolf charges been given free run of the keep? Perhaps Amoril himself had seen fit to mark the building in the manner of his pets; Tarrant wouldn't put it past him. He felt rage rise up inside him like a tidal wave, but then drew in a deep breath and forced himself to let it go, unvoiced. For all he knew the smell wasn't even real, but a sensory illusion meant to foster discord between him and his servants. He wouldn't let it distract him now. Once Calesta was safely out of the picture there'd be time enough to teach Amoril the fine points of a Cleansing, and to see that he received sufficient practice in its use.

"What about the Forest?" he asked, forcing his thoughts onto other paths. "My latest Workings?"

"There was a problem with that disease you introduced into the scuttler population just before you left." It seemed to him that the albino was slightly on edge; was he anticipating retribution for his housekeeping failures, or was something more significant at the root of it? "It mutated spontaneously and was beginning to threaten other species. I isolated and destroyed the infected animals, which will hold the disease at bay for while, but in the long run a more permanent solution will have to be found."

The Hunter nodded, his eyes never leaving his apprentice. "I'll design a counterphage for the new mutation. You have samples of the infected flesh?"

There was a door at the end of the corridor they were traversing; the albino pulled it open for him. "Of course, my lord."

"Such concern over minute biological detail is commendable, Amoril. I'm pleased by your development."

"One learns a lot when one is left alone, my lord."

Black halls, dark curtains, a lightless and soothing domain: he drew confidence from it step by step, and from the chill power flowing about his feet. This place was his strength, he thought. His soul. As long as he had the Forest, no man could stand against him.

And no demon either, he thought darkly. *Not even a Iezu.*

Down through the keep they went, Amoril following his lead in silence, until they reached his library. There, on shelves stacked ten feet high, were accumulated all his notes from the last five hundred years. *Would that I had begun this work earlier!* He withdrew a volume of demonological data and handed it to Amoril. *Would that I had understood, in the arrogance of my youth, just how much memory can be lost after nine hundred years.*

The albino opened the book he had been handed and scanned its contents? "Iezu?" His tone was scornful.

"Calesta. You recall him?"

"Calesta." As he sought the proper memory, Tarrant worked a subtle Knowing and cast it about him. Had the Iezu tried to corrupt Amoril while he was in the east? There was no point in trying to Know that directly; the demon's illusions could mask any trace of contact. But a question like this, so casually voiced, so casually answered . . . one might unravel that with care and uncover a hint of artifice, a fleeting breath of warning. "He was the one who tricked you, yes? Before you went east."

"Yes." Nothing. There was nothing. Despite himself he relaxed a bit. "Go through that volume," he commanded. "Look for his name, or anything like it. Or any mention of his aspect, which is sadism. As for his intentions . . ." He looked at Amoril and relaxed a bit. What had he expected? That the one man who needed him most would betray him?

Take nothing for granted, Hunter—not your lands, not your people, not even your own power. When your very senses can be warped by another, everything must be suspect.

"We're at war," he warned the albino. "So be careful. Unless I can find some means of killing a Iezu . . . things may get very unpleasant."

The albino shrugged. "They're all just demons in the end, right? How hard can it be?"

Oh, my apprentice. How little you understand!

He set three more volumes down, which were likely to contain notes on the Iezu. Considering how many Iezu there were and how long they had been active, it seemed a painfully insufficient collection. He would have given anything for Ciani of Faraday's notebooks right now; she had specialized in that demonic family, and must have uncovered countless bits of lore in her many years of study. But she was in the rakhlands now, and all her notebooks were ash. Not for the first time, he cursed Senzei Reese for his damnable shortsightedness. Better to shed human blood for sacrifice—even one's own—than destroy such treasures as that.

"My lord?"

He looked up, saw that Amoril had not even opened his book. "What is it?"

"I have a gift for you." He grinned, displaying sharpened teeth. "A homecoming present, which I prepared when I Divined you coming. If I may be excused to fetch it?"

Distracted by the task at hand, he nodded.

Perhaps he should contact the lady Ciani. Not with a Working, of course; the fae-wall which the rakh had erected about their domain would prevent him from using the currents to reach her. But perhaps he and Vryce should consider a trek to that land, or at least to its border. It was a good bet that she had useful knowledge, and she should be willing to help him. After all, she had once been his apprentice. . . .

She's also a loremaster, and that kind values its neutrality. How strong are her vows, I wonder? Would she help us win our war if she knew that the fate of humanity might hang in the balance? Or would that be all the more reason not to get involved?

The scent of blood reached him just before the scent of fear; startled, he looked up.

It was Amoril, with a woman in tow. The albino grinned. "I thought you might be hungry after your long flight." He had bound her hands behind her, and held the end of the binding thong like a leash. She strained against it like a wild animal, consumed by the kind of terror no human heart could sustain for long. She knew who he was, then. Good. It would save him the trouble of inspiring fresh fear. Not that he didn't hunger for such sport—God knows, after eleven months on that damned ship he could use a hunt—but for once he didn't want to spare the time.

How good it was to be home again, where women were raised to fear him! How good it was to have five centuries of the Hunter's reputation to draw upon, to lend flavor to an otherwise quick snack. Her fear was sweet and hot and he drank it in with relish. When he was done, he let the body fall and motioned for Amoril to take it away. Let the albino feed it to his pets if he liked; the warm blood would please them.

But even the pleasure of a kill could not distract him for long. He began to go through his notes, page by page, searching for something useful. Anything. He didn't expect to find notes on Calesta himself, or any instructions on how to dispatch Iezu. But somewhere, buried in the recorded discoveries of five centuries, there must be a single useful mote of knowledge. Somewhere.

Believe that, he thought darkly, as he turned the ancient pages, binding fae as he did so to support their brittle substance. *Have faith in it. Because without that one hope, we are surely doomed.*

Four

Nighttime. Dreamtime. The hours when the demons of the mind could take hold, their cold grasp firm until the morning. The hours when the human soul abandoned its struggle against the madness of this world, and the dark things that lurked in the corners of the human heart could take form at last.

Though it was late, the Patriarch was awake. Again. Unwilling to sleep, afraid to rest. Again.

Afraid to dream.

A book lay open before him, but he was no longer reading it. With a sigh he rubbed his temples, as though somehow that could soothe his spirit as well as his pounding head. He really should go to sleep, he knew that. If he didn't retire soon, he would pay for it in the morning. Nevertheless . . . he tried to focus on the book again, and only when it was clear that his eyes were too fatigued for the task did he close its cover with a sigh and lean back in his heavy mahogova chair, abandoning the effort. He felt as if he had aged a hundred years in the last ten longmonths. It was the dreams, of course. If only he could somehow shut them out, if only there were some special drug or process, some prayer . . . but there wasn't, he knew that now. He had searched long enough and hard enough to know.

And even if something could make the dreams stop, would that leave the rest of him unharmed? Man couldn't live without dreams. Not sanely, anyway. That was what half a dozen doctors had told him.

If you can call this sanity.

It had all started with visions of Vryce. Fleeting images of the man, sandwiched between the structured narratives of his usual

41

dreaming. Vryce conversing with demons. Vryce surrounded by corpses. Vryce traveling with a creature so evil that its presence was a lightless blot on the Patriarch's dreamscape, a blackness that reeked of hunger and death and the foulest of human corruption. At first the Patriarch had taken these for simple nightmares, and had thought little of them. Considering his fury over Vryce's behavior and his dismay at the man's choice of traveling companion, it was amazing that he had not suffered from such dreams long before this.

But then there came other dreams, with more familiar subjects. And little by little, against his will, he was forced to acknowledge the truth. That these intrusive images weren't merely dreams but true visions, clairvoyancies that came to him even as the acts they represented took place. When he dreamed one night of the mayor's corruption, it was only to awaken and find that the morning tabloids were afire with news of blackmail and embezzlement. When he dreamed of Nans Bakrow's adultery, it was only to hear three days later that her husband had begun divorce proceedings, for exactly that cause. And when he had dreamed of the Gillis child killing himself—

It still pained him to remember that. The midnight awakening. The rapid dressing. The rush to the Gillis' abode through streets that were alive with demonlings, in the desperate hope that something could be done to avoid the tragedy he had witnessed. All to no avail. By the time he had roused the boy's parents and reached the site of his vision, the young veins had already rendered up their last drop of blood; the boy's lips were blue and cold, his dead eyes open and accusatory. *If you knew,* they seemed to say, *why didn't you come sooner?* Words his parents never voiced, but the Patriarch knew they thought them as well. As he himself thought them, all the hours he lay awake before that dawn, struggling against the bleakness of guilt and utter despair.

Prophecies, his aides and servants whispered. The Holy Father was seeing futures. But they weren't that, not by a long shot. *Prophecy* implied a temporal framework, a balance between the present and future that might—with care—be altered. Were there not thousands of potential futures for each moment in this world, of which prophecy revealed but one? No, *prophecy* would have been a blessing compared to this. This was a nightmare of clairvoyance, a forced voyeurism that made him witness to the evils of his world without giving him the power to change anything. A pornography of the soul, which had made of him a helpless victim.

He had tried drugs. He had tried prayer. He had even tried sleeplessness, hoping that sheer exhaustion would culminate in a collapse so total that even dreams could not reach him. To no avail. And though he rarely dreamed of Vryce anymore, when he did it was with such power that he would awaken trembling, cold sweat trickling down his face. Images of volcanoes fuming, of a black sky raining hot ash, of a ship rent into pieces, casting its passengers into a boiling sea . . . and images of a woman suffering such pain and fear that his heart twisted in sympathetic agony, while Vryce stood by and did nothing to save her. Nay, while he *allowed* the suffering to continue, in consummation of some strange demonic pact which he and the Hunter had established.

God help you, Vryce, if those visions are true. He whispered the words into the night, as the last of the images faded into shadows of fire and ash. *God save you from my wrath.*

A knock sounded suddenly on the heavy wooden door of his chamber. He looked up quickly, alerted by its volume. What could be so urgent at this time of night?

"Come in."

The door swung open hard, banging against the wall behind it. Leo Toth stood in the doorway, breathless, his skin sheened with the sweat of recent exertion. "Street of Gods," he gasped. It was clear he had been running hard; he put out a hand to steady himself as he drew in a deep breath. "Temple of Davarti." And he added, almost apologetically, "You said you wanted to know."

He knew in an instant what the man was trying to tell him and he stood quickly, all thoughts of exhaustion forgotten. There was no time for exhaustion now, nor any other time-consuming weakness. "When?" he demanded.

"Just starting now," the man gasped. "If you hurry—"

"How many?"

He shook his head. "Don't know. Two dozen. Maybe more. I passed them just outside the Sangh Shrine, maybe half a block down from Davarti. I stayed with them just long enough to find out where they were headed, then I ran here." He leaned over to ease the strain on his lungs; his breathing whistled shrilly as he fought for air. "It's a raid, Holy Father, no question about it."

A raid.

With quick, decisive steps the Patriarch moved to where his ritual garments hung and layered a thickly embroidered stole over the beige silk robe he was already wearing. He added to that his most formal headdress, a peaked form layered and crusted in gilt embroidery. No hesitation in these choices, or in his dressing; he had gone over this moment too many times in his own mind to falter now. Other times he had been too late, had learned of the incident after the fact; now, for the first time, he had a chance to change things.

And I will, he promised his God. *I will stop it, and bring them back to You. I swear it.*

He ushered the man out of the room ahead of him and hurried toward the rear stairs of the building, his soul praying with all its strength. *Help me to serve Your Will in this.* Two flights down he came to a narrow hallway, and he practically flew to the door at its end. Beyond that was a small chamber, sparsely decorated, that opened on the stables. Bridles hung on the far wall, their brass fittings polished and gleaming; a liveried man with coffee in hand relaxed over a magazine, clearly not expecting any custom at this late hour.

"A carriage," the Patriarch ordered, and there was no need for him to shout the command; his bearing said it all. Startled, the man dropped his reading material and hurredly set his coffee cup aside; brown liquid sloshed over the edge of it, splashing a copy of *Whip and Bridle.* "Of course, Your Holiness." With a clumsy bow he passed through the far door, into the stables themselves; the Patriarch could hear the snort of horses as he followed.

God willing, the carriage had been kept ready, he thought. God willing, he wouldn't have to wait while the beasts were brought out and harnessed. Lives could be lost in that much time.

But the carriage was ready, and in less than a minute he was inside it. "Street of Gods," he ordered, and such was the fever of haste he exuded that the coachman responded immediately, and the carriage began to move the minute the Patriarch's feet were safely off the ground.

Out of the stable and onto the street. It was dark, very dark, with only one moon visible, and that half-hidden behind a row of townhouses. A suitable night for work like this, he thought grimly. "Faster," he muttered, but there was no need; the coachman had sensed his need for haste and was barreling down the deserted streets with a speed that would have been unsafe—and strictly illegal—in the crowded daylight hours.

The Street of Gods was not one single roadway, but a route that zigzagged through the cultural and financial districts, so named for the preponderance of pagan temples flanking its course. At any speed its turns were difficult and at this speed they were downright sickening, but the Patriarch held on tightly to his seat as the coachman drove his horses down the narrow streets and made no complaint. Time was of the essence.

"There!" He half-rose from his seat as he saw the flames, fury and despair warring for dominion within him. Was it too late already? "Stop there!" There were dozens of people in the street outside Davarti's Temple—perhaps hundreds—but it was too dark for him to make out what they were doing. Brawling? Demonstrating? Or simply gawking, as golden flames licked at the ancient building? As he rushed up to the temple's door—simply pushing aside those who were in his way, there was no time for courtesy now—it seemed to him that some were rushing toward the flames, with buckets in both hands. Good. Something might yet be saved of the building, if they worked hard enough and fast enough. As for the souls within . . . that was another thing.

He burst into the temple, so filled with righteous indignation that the fae surrounding him seemed to take fire, lighting the air about his head like a halo. Within the temple all was chaos, as groups of worshipers tried vainly to defend their pagan holy ground from the invading mob. He picked out half a dozen familiar faces among the invaders, enough to verify that the angry men who were smashing relics and pummeling priests were indeed members of his own flock. And fury won out within him at last.

"How dare you!" he cried, and his eyes blazed with rage. Few men heard his voice above the din of the battle, but those few were enough. One man fell back from the icon he had been trying to smash, and the woman who had been trying to keep him away from it followed his gaze to the Patriarch. The invader beside her glanced up to see the cause of the disturbance, and he, too, was stunned into silence by the raw force of the Patriarch's wrath. One by one heads turned as others responded to him, and a hush fell across the sanctuary like a wave. A few minutes later the only sounds remaining were the tinkle of shattered glass falling to the floor, and the soft moans of the wounded.

"How *dare* you!" he repeated, when their attention was fixed on him at last. With angry steps he strode down the length of the central aisle, toward the dais and its idol. Most of the men in his path got out the way in a hurry, pagans and faithful alike; the few who didn't found themselves thrown aside, hurled into the stunned mob like pieces of repellent detritus.

At last he reached the altar and stood before it; black paint dripped from the idolotrous sculpture as he glared at the blood-spattered mob. In the distance flames were crackling, but the fire seemed to be confined to a small chamber forward of the sanctuary, and a handful of men were already fighting to bring it under control. Despite the ominous sound of its burning and a faint stink of smoke, he judged them safe enough.

"Is this how you were taught to behave?" he cried. "Is this how you serve your God?" His eyes swept over them, picking out details, memorizing faces. More than one man flushed hotly as the accusatory gaze hit home, all passion for destruction withering to shame before the force of the Patriarch's rage.

"Who's in charge here?" he demanded. Silence reigned in the vaulted sanctuary, compromised only by the hiss of flames and the slow drip of blood. "Who's responsible for this?" Still there was no answer. He waited. He knew that the real issue was not who claimed responsibility—if anyone did—but the simple act of forcing them to *think* again, to act like men. To throw off the yoke of this communal violence and remember who and what they were, and what God it was they served.

At last a man stepped forward and faced the Patriarch. His face was streaked with sweat and blood and one side of his face was swollen. "We came to cleanse this place!" He gestured toward the altar. "Look! Look at what they worship! Do you want that in Jaggonath? Do you want it out in the streets, where our children can see it?"

The Patriarch didn't turn to look at the idol, but instead looked out over the mob. The faces of his faithful gazed back at him fearfully, and he thought he saw a flicker of guilt in more than one expression. Good. As for the ones who worshiped here . . . their eyes were filled with fear as well, and something else. Awe. What did they see when they looked at him, adorned in all the glory of his faith? A ruler of priests, fit counselor for kings. Little short of a god himself, by their pagan standards; certainly a god's favored messenger. That such a man should come in person to quell their riot was a thing to be wondered at; that such a man should save their idol and defend their faith was a thing past comprehension.

And that is the difference between us, he thought. *That is it exactly.*

"The law of this land allows men to worship as they wish." He spoke slowly, clearly, with a voice that filled the temple; his very tone was a counterpoint to their rage. "The Law of our Church demands that civil order—"

"One world, one faith!" a man cried out. "That's what the Prophet ordered."

"And he also commanded us to preserve the human spirit!" the Patriarch countered. "That above all else." He looked about the crowd; his face was a mask of condemnation. "Is this how you ac-

complish that? With bestial violence? Mindless hatred? Look at you!"
He waved a hand out over the crowd; several men cringed as the gesture included them. "There are demons feasting tonight, my friends.
Glutting themselves on your hatred. There are spirits being born in
the shadows all around you, who will feed on man's intolerance forever because that is the force that gave them life. Or have you forgotten that? Have you forgotten that our greatest enemy is not a foreign
idol or even a foreign god, but the very force that gives this planet
life? Our most sacred duty is to preserve our human identity, and if
we fail in that, all the prayers ever voiced won't win this world
salvation."

He was aware of a crowd that had gathered inside the door as he
spoke, gawkers from outside the building, drawn to his words like
moths to a flame. Praise God, who had given him the soul of an or-
ator; never was he more grateful for that skill than now. "Yes, the
Prophet dreamed of unity. But you can't *enforce* unity—not with terror, not with hate. You have to *earn* it."

Silence, thick and heavy. A window pane, weakened during the
riot, chose that moment to fall inward; it hit the floor with an accusatory crash and shattered into a hundred pieces.

"Go home," the Patriarch commanded. "Go home! Pray for guidance. Beg for forgiveness from your God, and for a new and purer
communion with Him. You've seen the evil we fight with your own
eyes now; you've felt it in your hearts. May you be stronger than ever
in your faith for having known it."

No one moved. A curtain in the balcony caught fire, and he heard
the men upstairs crying out instructions to one another as they
worked to smother the new flames before they could spread. Still
he remained where he was and stared at his faithful, his very presence a reminder of what their God stood for, and what He expected
of them.

Finally, with a curse, one man stirred. Throwing down the crowbar he carried, he whipped about and strode from the building. Then
a second man. A third. The fourth put down the vase he held on the
stand beside him, oh so carefully, and then stepped into the aisle and
bowed to the Patriarch before he, too, hurried out. The Patriarch
drew in a deep breath, exhaled it slowly. *Thank you, God.* Others
were moving now, exiting the building in twos and threes. The anger
and hatred that had welded them into a mob had dissipated, at least
for the moment; though he harbored no illusion that it was gone forever, the Patriarch was grateful for the brief moment of victory.

Be with them, God, now and always. Guide them. Protect them. Nurture their human spirit.

More were leaving now, too many to count. Now that they were separating it was possible to judge their number, and to asssess the contingent of priests and worshipers who had tried to stop them from defacing the temple. *So few,* he thought, gazing down at them. Most were spattered with blood. and more than one lay moaning on the floor. He noted at least two broken limbs, a handful of equally serious injuries. *So very brave.* It never ceased to amaze him what courage men could show when their faith was threatened. Any faith.

The Prophet was right, when he said that faith was the most powerful force on Erna. He looked at the pagan emblems on the wall and shook his head sadly. *If only we could harness it in unity, as he intended.*

All of his people had left the temple; he made sure of that before he stepped down from the dais, his long silk robes dragging in blood as he made his way out of the sanctuary. One man stepped into his path, and for a moment he thought there might be some kind of confrontation. But the priest bowed deeply, as one might to a great lord.

"Thank you," he whispered. His voice was shaking; his forehead was streaked with blood. "Thank you for stopping it."

The Patriarch looked back at the idol on the altar. A human figure with eight sets of arms and four pairs of male and female genitals crouched upon a square stone pedestal. A face was set into the lowest crotch, tongue extruded, and a tiny human form had been thrust into the mouth headfirst; the twisted legs appeared to be struggling as he watched. There were scars on the statue where crowbar assaults had chipped out pieces of the stone, and thick black paint dripped down its head to pool on the altar beneath it. Like blood, he thought. Just like blood.

He turned back to the priest, revulsion thick in his throat. *I didn't do it for you,* he thought darkly. Knowing that this man would never understand what had happened here today, or its importance. To them it was a simple assault, terrifying but finite; to him it was but one more battle in the war for men's souls.

The siren of an ambulance wagon was drawing near as he exited the temple. He strode through the throng of gawkers as though they were ghosts, and like fearful wraiths they parted, making way for him. His carriage had pulled to the curb a good two blocks away, out of reach of the mob, but he did not signal for it to come closer; after the smoky confines of the pagan temple the short walk in the night air felt good. Hate-wraiths fluttered overhead, spawned by the violence of the night, but for now they kept their distance. In time they would gain more substance and learn to hunt men.

Created by my people, in the name of my God. His face flushed hot with the shame of it. *Will they never learn?*

As he came up to the carriage, the driver looked at him; though he would never dare to question the Patriarch, it was clear he was brimming with curiosity.

"Riot's over," the Holy Father said shortly, as he climbed up into his seat. "Davarti's safe. For now." He lacked the energy to go into more detail, but fell back against his seat as the carriage pulled about and started back. The man would hear enough details when word got back to their own Church; no need to rehash it all now.

How many other riots would there be, he wondered, before this madness ended? The horses pulled the carriage about and started back toward the Cathedral; an ambulance wagon rushed past them, headed toward the temple. How many other assaults on the innocent would his people commit, wielding the name of his God like a standard? A year ago such raids were nearly unheard of; now they were commonplace. Why now, after so many years of peace? What was the catalyst for such a change? He had asked himself that a thousand and one times, and still he had no answer. There was no one thing he could point to, no single person or happenstance to blame. Violence was spreading like wildfire among his people, and he didn't know how to combat it. Where had it come from, this fever of destruction? How could he manage to tame it?

The headache he had experienced previously was blinding by the time they reached the Cathedral's stable; he lay back in his seat with his eyes shut, trying to deny the pain. His soul might be that of God's tireless statesman, but his body was seventy-two years old, and sometimes the strain of all those years was almost more than he could bear. Especially now, with his life's work falling to pieces around him. That made every year count double.

"We're here, Your Holiness." The coachman offered an arm to help him dismount; after a moment he took it. At least this riot had been cut short, he thought. At least this one night he wouldn't dream of blood and shattered glass and broken idols, as he had during the other riots. One small thing to be grateful for.

There was a servant waiting for him outside his chambers. The look on the man's face made it plain that he had bad news to deliver. With a dry smile the Patriarch greeted him. "Some new problem, is it? Don't worry, my son. There's not much you can say to me now that will make this night any worse."

"Vryce is back," the man said quietly.

For a moment he just stared at him. Then, with a deep sigh, he rubbed his temples again.

"Yeah," he muttered. "That did it."

Five

To Andrys Tarrant, Hotel Paradisio, Suite 5-A.

Dear Mer,

Regarding the work you contracted this past Friday at my establishment, specifically the ceremonial breastplate with yellow gold decorative motifs: If it is your intention to wear this item, then I will need to see you some time soon to verify its proportions. If it is meant for display purposes only, such a meeting will not be necessary, although you are, of course, welcome to come see our progress any time it pleases you.

Please let me know which is the case as soon as possible, so that we can complete this project with all good speed.

Yours in service,

Gresham Alder

The silversmith's.

Standing outside the shop, Andrys found himself shivering. Was *she* inside? He didn't know if he hoped for that or feared it—or both in combination—but there was no denying that she had utterly obsessed him. He had dreamed of her practically every night, her dark eyes haunting his nightmare-laden sleep. He had drunk himself into insensibility more than once to try to make her image fade from his brain, but it had only grown stronger. And now he was here, and in all likelihood she was inside . . . and he didn't know how to speak to her. Was it because of her beauty, or his weakened condition, or some strange combination of the two? He had always known how to handle women before, even in the depths of his depression; what made this one so different?

With a shaking hand he brushed back his hair, trying to tame it into some semblance of order. A hopeless gesture. Calesta had ordered him to let it grow, and though the reason for that was something Andrys couldn't begin to guess at, like all of Calesta's orders it was meant to be obeyed. Did the demon really have a greater plan, Andrys sometimes wondered, or was he just toying with a wounded soul, seeing how long it would take Gerald Tarrant's last descendant to break? He didn't dare think about that. He needed the illusion of purpose even more than he needed its substance. The demon hated Gerald Tarrant every bit as much as he did, and had sworn the sorcerer's destruction. That was enough, wasn't it? Who cared what the details of his strategem were, if in the end the battle was won? Who cared if Andrys understood it?

He opened his leather satchel to made sure the painting was still there. It was. Hateful, hateful thing! It made his heart knot up just to look at it, rolled up into a tight little tube as if it were just some innocuous work of art being carted home from the decorator's. Amazing, what kind of power a simple object could have. He hoped he wouldn't have to unroll it. He hoped they wouldn't need to see it. He prayed that someday he would be free to burn it, along with all the hateful memories it conjured.

Someday.

With a trembling hand he reached out to open the door. Bells jingled merrily as he turned the knob and pushed it open, a discordant counterpoint to his mood. He tried to relax as he stepped inside, and tried to force himself to walk in such a way that his movements would seem natural. Women could sense it when you weren't comfortable with yourself, and it made them nervous.

She was with a customer, a woman wrapped in fur and draped in oversized jewelery. She looked up and saw him, and it seemed to him that her smile broadened. *Just a moment,* her expression promised, and he thought that her eyes lingered on him for a moment before she turned her attention back to her customer. He forced himself to look elsewhere, wandering about the shop as he studied the works of art displayed there. Gentle, graceful silver forms: it seemed to him that he could pick out which were hers and which had been crafted by another hand. Delicate webworks, sinuous twinings, leaves and vines and wildlife ornaments so delicate that he feared to touch them. So like their maker, he thought. What would it be like to feel that delicate skin in his hands?

Easy, Andri. Easy. His heart was pounding so loudly he wondered if she could hear it. *Take it slow.* The bells rang as the door slammed shut, and he dared to turn around—and found her eyes fixed on him, those beautiful dark eyes which he knew so well from his dreams. His breath caught in his throat.

"Well. Welcome back." Smiling, she fixed a stray lock of hair in place; was she aware of the sexual interest that gesture communicated? She seemed at once an innocent, untested by the world, and a confident, enticing woman. It was a heady combination. "Have you decided to order some more regalia?"

He leaned against the counter with what he hoped was an easy grace; he had never felt less natural in his life. "Not quite." He glanced back toward the display of her work with studied casualness, then back to her again. "It occurred to me I forgot something the last time I was here."

"Oh? And what was that?"

He met her eyes then, and held them. "You never told me your name."

She looked away, but not before he had caught the flash of interest in her eyes. "Narilka," she said softly. "Narilka Lessing."

Narilka: Lilting, exotic, almost Earth-like in its rhythm. He was about to say something about how very beautiful the name was, how well it suited its owner, when the back door of the shop swung open and hit the wall, shattering the fragile spell between them.

"Nari, could you— Oh, I'm sorry, I didn't realize we had a customer." The intruder was a heavyset man with a thick head of gray hair, a lined face etched in patterns of affection, and a strong, slightly coarse voice. He nodded slightly in acknowledgment of Andrys' presence, a gesture at once proud and professional. "Please forgive me, Mer. I didn't mean to interrupt."

"This is Andrys Tarrant," the girl said, before he had a chance to respond himself.

The man's face lit up at the sound of his name. "Indeed?" He came forward toward Andrys, offering a hand. "An honor, Mer Tarrant. Gresham Alder, at your service."

"The honor is mine," he responded formally. The man's hand was warm and rough-skinned, his grip strong; he hoped he couldn't feel him trembling as they shook. "I got your letter. I'm anxious to see your work."

"Not all that impressive in its current state, I'm afraid. Now, as for Narilka's. . . ." He beamed at the girl, and in that moment Andrys knew with unerring instinct that they had discussed him; the man's praise was his gesture of approval. For an instant he sensed the depth and complexity of their relationship, the degree to which she would rely on him for advice in all things. "Why don't you show him the crown, Nari?"

Her cheeks flushed slightly at the implied praise. "It's only half-finished," she told Andrys.

"I'd love to see it."

She led him through the door at the back of the shop, into the workroom beyond. Two heavy wood tables supported a plethora of tools, stacks of wire, canisters and flasks and narrow burners whose doused wicks gave off a strange acidic smell. One slender vise held a blackened silver ring, clearly in the process of being polished, and another gripped a small figurine whose upper half was inlaid with tiny stones. These things he saw peripherally as he followed the girl through the workroom, mesmerized by the play of lamplight upon her hair. It wasn't until they approached the second table that he saw the object laid out upon its surface clearly enough to react to it.

It was the coronet. Not rounded yet, but laid out flat atop the table, with his drawing spread out above it. Delicate figures of exquisitely fine detail supported the central sun motif, which was the focal point of the piece. There were still empty spaces where other figures would be added, and the whole of it was stained black from the process of its manufacture, but there was no denying that even in this incomplete state it was a masterful work.

For a moment he forgot what it was, what price the original had demanded of his family, and could only whisper, "It's beautiful. Just beautiful." He reached out to touch it but then drew back, wary of the memories such contact might conjure.

"It's all right," she prompted. "It's strong enough."

He forced himself to reach out and touch the slender figures. The metal was cold, surprisingly lifeless. What had he expected? It was only an ornament—half-finished at that—whose place in history was assured by its power as a symbol, not some intrinsic malignance. Why then did he shiver as he touched it?

"Have you thought about the armor?" the silversmith asked him, when he finally turned away from the worktable. When he didn't answer, the man pressed, "Whether you'll want to wear it?"

He hesitated. The truth was, he didn't know how to answer. Calesta hadn't responded to his appeal for information on the matter, leaving him to guess at the demon's intentions. "I'd guess I should have that option," he dared. "Is it too much trouble?"

"Not at all. I just need to check the waist length, to see that the

peplum sits properly. Your drawings were geared toward a taller man
. . . which doesn't mean there's a problem, necessarily. Figure types
vary in proportion as well as height."

It came to him suddenly, unwelcome knowledge that brought
panic in its wake. They wanted him to try it on. Here. Now. *In front
of the girl,* he despaired, as the gray-haired man lifted up the heavy
armor and offered it to him. He couldn't. Could he?

For a moment he couldn't seem to make himself move. The strap
of his leather pack seemed to burn into his shoulder, reminding him
of the hateful thing inside it. Then, stiffly, he released it and let it
slide to the floor. The girl caught it up and for one mad moment he
wanted to grab it away from her, lest that *thing* somehow contami-
nate her as well. He forced himself not to move, to draw in a deep
breath, then to step forward and let metal plates be fitted around his
body. Cold, so cold. The weight of it was heavy on his shoulders and
it crushed his velveteen jacket against his body; even as Gresham Alder explained the nature of the garments he should wear beneath it
he felt himself struggling for breath, trying not to be overcome by the
suggestive power of this fitting.

"Fine," the armorer murmured, as he turned Andrys with steady
hands. A tug at the waist, a pull at the armhole. "It'll be fine." And
then he was facing the man and looking up into his eyes, and the
smith asked, "Would you like to see it?" And he nodded, because he
knew there was no other acceptable response.

The girl had brought a mirror, and now she held it before him.
Trembling, he placed himself so that he could see his reflection. At
first there was only a blur of gray, as if his eyes were unwilling to acknowledge what was before him . . . and then it came into focus suddenly, all of it, and it was too much. Too much! Gold sun splayed
across his chest, gold wires coiling about its rays, pectoral and ab-
dominal muscles sculpted like living flesh. Bold in its artwork, perfect in its craftsmanship, and oh, so familiar! Hateful, terrifying relic!
He felt the metal burning where it touched him, hot through his
clothing, acid-sharp; *his* armor, brought back to life by the power of
gold and craftsmanship. But even that wasn't the worst of it. It was
when he looked at the whole image, from top to toe, from the shaggy
long hair to the black leather boots to the breastplate with the sun in
between, that golden sun so like and unlike Earth's, that face so like
a killer's—

The sickness rose up in him with numbling force, too fast and too
hard for him to fight it; helplessly, he fell to his knees, hot bile
welling up in his throat as his body fought to shake off the power of

that hated image. Then the horror of it was too much at last, and his body convulsed, spewing out the bile and the terror and the bitter exhaustion in one wretched flood of vomit. Seconds only, but it seemed an eternity. He brought his hand up to his mouth quickly, hiding behind it as he wiped his mouth clean with the silk cuff of his shirt sleeve; his cheeks burned hot with shame. He could sense the girl standing behind him, and her proximity increased his humiliation a thousandfold. How could he ever face these people again? How could he ever face *her?*

It was Gresham Alder who knelt by his side, muttering words meant to bridge that awkward moment. Andrys heard himself apologizing profusely, offering to clean up, insisting . . . but his offers were set aside, politely but firmly. *Of course,* he thought bitterly. *They don't want me around here any longer than I have to be.* As the smith helped him to his feet, he dared to meet the girl's eyes—just for an instant—and the pity he saw in them made his shame burn even hotter. No hope of getting to know her now, not after a fiasco like this. That knowledge hurt worse than all the fear and shame combined.

Somehow he pulled himself together. Saying the necessary words as he wrested the cursed breastplate from his torso, making the requisite excuses . . . somehow he managed to take up his bag again and get out of the shop without further catastrophe. He didn't even check to see that the rolled-up painting was still in it, but took off at a run down the narrow street. Feet pounding on cobblestones, shame pounding in his temples. When he reached the Hotel Paradisio, the doorman wouldn't let him in, so wild-eyed and disarrayed did he appear; he had to search through his bag with shaking hands to produce his key as proof of residency, and even then the doorman insisted on escorting him to the door of his suite. Taking care to steer him clear of the other guests. What did it matter? What did anything matter? He fell to his knees as the door slammed shut behind him, hot tears flowing down his cheeks. God in heaven, how long could he go on like this?

"What do you want?" he begged aloud. Willing Calesta to hear him, to answer. "What's the point of this? Tell me!" But there was no response. At last he struggled to his feet and staggered over to his bureau, where a flask of Jaggonath brandy awaited him. Disdaining glasses, he upended it and drank directly from its narrow neck, feeling the powerful liquid burn its way down his throat. Not enough. Not enough. Stumbling over to the table at his bedside, he caught up a small glass vial; black pills winked at him from within, promising the ultimate forgetfulness. It was dangerous to drink and then take these, too, he knew that. But what did it matter? Did he really want to live another day? Did he dare to face *her* again?

Choking with shame, he spilled out a small handful of pills, enough for an evening's oblivion. With a quick motion he tossed them all into his mouth and used the brandy to wash them down. Fast. Before he could have second thoughts. If it killed him, then it killed him. At least this torture would be over with.

"What's the armor for?" he begged. The demon didn't answer him, which raised new doubts. What if Calesta didn't just hate Gerald Tarrant, after all, but *all* the Tarrant clan? Him included? What if this was just some complex game the demon had concocted to torture them all—

No, he didn't dare think that, he didn't dare—

Too much torture, too much too much!

"Calesta," he gasped. "Please. Help me."

But there was only darkness, and silence.

"That boy," Gresham said, "has real problems."

She wrung out the rag in the sink, not saying anything. She didn't trust herself to speak.

"Nari."

Slowly she turned to him, laying the rag aside. The floor was clean. The armor was clean. Her hands had finally stopped shaking.

"Nari. He's trouble."

She didn't dare look at him. She knew how well he could read her.

"You're stuck on him, aren't you?" His voice was gentle but the disapproval was clear. "Couldn't you have picked a sane one, this time? There are a few around, you know.

"Please, Gresh." She leaned against the edge of the worktable; her blouse front brushed the coronet. "Not now."

"Nari. Listen to me." He came up behind her and took her by the shoulders, turning her to face him. "You're like family to me, you know that? And when family gets hurt, it hurts me, too."

She was looking away, refusing to face him; he caught up her chin in his and and gently turned her back to him. "He's good-looking. He's rich. He's got charm that most men would kill for. And he's got problems, Nari. Real problems. Did you see the look on his face when he saw his reflection? Did you?"

"I saw," she whispered.

"I don't know what's going on with that boy, but I'd bet this shop it isn't healthy. Haven't you had enough of that kind? Don't you deserve something better?"

"I saw," she whispered. Fingering the delicate silverwork. He had touched it, too, and his hand had trembled. Why?

Yes, I saw him. I saw eyes wide with the kind of terror most men never know. Looking into those eyes was like looking into a mirror. Like being back in the Forest again, running from the unknown. Alone, so alone. Yes, I know that look.

"Nari—"

"I'm not a child," she snapped. Pulling away from him. "Not anymore. I can take care of myself."

And he would accept that, she knew it. That was the marvel of their relationship. Even though he was concerned for her, even though he thought she was dead wrong, even though he was sure she was heading for disaster. That was the difference between Gresham Alder and her parents. He had seen the change in her, when she returned from the Forest, and he had accepted it. Her parents couldn't. They still wanted to baby her, to shield her from all the evils of the world, and no matter what she said or did, they would never change in that orientation. How could she explain to them that she had already faced the greatest evil of all, the well of terror in her own soul? How could she explain the way in which that confrontation had transformed her, smothering the helpless child who so needed protection, giving birth to someone older and stronger and far more adaptable. What did the petty evils of this world amount to, when compared to the Hunter's Forest? Abusive men were an annoyance, nothing more. Even rapists were a finite terror. And as for men who wore the Hunter's face, whose haunted eyes hinted at wounds so vast that no mere words could set them to healing. . . .

I can handle it, she told herself. Running her fingers over the sterling figures, imagining that she could feel Andrys Tarrant's warmth through the metal. Drawn to his pain, even as powerfully as she was drawn to his person. *And I want to.*

"I'll be careful," she told him. "I promise."

Six

"His Holiness will be with you shortly."

Damien nodded a distracted acknowledgment as the acolyte left him. He had been left to wait in the antechamber to the Patriarch's formal audience chamber, which didn't bode at all well for his upcoming interview. It was a space designed to impress, perhaps intimidate, and it did so with marked aesthetic efficiency. The high, vaulted ceiling was of dark polished stone, unwarmed by paint or plaster; the numarble walls were sleek and minimally decorated. The furniture was stiff and formal, and after sitting in a high-backed chair for several seconds he decided he would much rather pace. All in all it was a markedly uncomfortable place, and Damien guessed that the room beyond, where the Patriarch meant to receive him, was much the same. Maybe worse. Not the kind of atmosphere he'd hoped for, that was certain.

What the hell did you expect! 'Come into my parlor for tee, and oh, by the way, would you mind filling me in on your recent activities!' Fat chance, Vryce. You'll be lucky if he listens to you at all, and doesn't just throw you out before you get a chance to open your mouth in your own defense.

There was a small mirror on the far wall, a minimal concession to visitors who might wish to see if they looked as uncomfortable as they felt. He paused in his pacing to look in it, to see what manner of man the Patriarch would be confronting. The priest who gazed back at him was not the same man who'd left Jaggonath two years earlier, that was sure. Limited rations at sea had thinned his stocky frame until he looked almost trim, an unfamiliar somatype. With a weathered hand he stroked the short beard that now marked his jawline, and wondered if he shouldn't have shaved it off. His skin was

59

markedly darker than it had been two years ago, a tawny brown that spoke eloquently of long months beneath an equatorial sun. There was gray in his hair now, a few strands at the temples and scattered bits of it in his beard. Gray! It was an affront to everything he perceived himself to be, the first hint of decay in a life too full of challenges to slow down for anything as mundane as *aging*. He had almost pulled the hairs out when they first appeared—back when there were fewer than a dozen—but the sheer vanity of such an act reminded him of Tarrant, and so he'd let the damn things stay.

You could use the fae to maintain youth, he told himself. *Others have done it. Ciani did it.* At times, now, he could see how tempting that path might become, as age continued its inexorable assault on his flesh. But the Patriarch's words, voiced so long ago, came back to him at such moments. *When the time comes to die, as it comes to all men, will you bow down to the patterns of Earth-life that are the core of our very existence? Or submit to the temptations of this alien magic, and sell your soul for another few years of life?* The acceptance of such natural processes was central to Damien's faith, and dying at his appointed time would be his ultimate service to his God. Sure, it would be hard. Many things in this world were hard. That's what gave them power.

"Reverend Vryce?" It was the Patriarch's secretary, a young man Damien dimly remembered from two years back. "Please come in."

To his surprise the man did not lead him into the audience chamber, but opened the heavy mahogova doors for him and stepped aside for him to enter alone.

It was a large room, formal like the antechamber but more impressive in size and proportion. It reminded him somewhat of Gerald Tarrant's own audience chamber in his keep in the Forest. He stiffened as the memory of that tense meeting (so long ago that it might have been in another world, so real that it seemed hardly yesterday) came back to him. Back then one friend had been dying, another kidnapped, and the Hunter was his enemy. Now . . . he felt something tighten inside his gut as he walked toward the arbiter of his faith. Now he was . . . what? The Hunter's ally?

The Patriarch's expression was stonelike, unreadable, but a cold rage burned in his eyes. Such was the chill of it that Damien could feel his skin tighten in physical response. In two years' time he had managed to forget the power the Holy Father wielded: not simply the force of a unique personality, but the faeborn aggression of a man who molded the currents to his will without even knowing it. Now, standing against the force of that rage was like trying to keep his footing in a riptide.

If only you could learn to wield that power consciously, Damien thought, *no man could stand against you.* But the Patriarch never would. Sorcery was anathema to him, and so he had blocked all knowledge of his own natural skills, and lived an illusion of flesh-bound helplessness. *God alone knows what would happen to you if you ever learned the truth.*

"I've received your reports," the Patriarch said acidly. He gestured briefly to a table by his side, and the manuscripts that lay upon it. Damien saw the coarse sheets of his first report, shipped home from Faraday, and the thinner package of notes and drawings he had delivered himself to the Cathedral two days ago. At the time it had seemed like a good idea, letting the Patriarch see the nature of the war they were fighting in the hope he would be more forgiving about how the battle had been waged. But the ribbon which sealed the second package was still unbroken. He began to protest, then stopped himself. The Holy Father had deliberately chosen not to read his work in advance of their meeting as a gesture of his condemnation. To protest such a move would only bring that rage crashing down upon his head.

You knew this would be bad, he told himself. *Defiance will only make it worse. Swallow your pride for once in your goddamn life and wait this out. It'll pass.* But it was hard, so very hard. It went against every instinct of self-preservation that he had.

"I'm sure I don't need to comment upon your breach of protocol in leaving this continent without permission." The Patriarch's tone was like ice. "Your own report made it clear that you knew exactly what you were doing—and, I suspect, exactly what the eventual cost of such disobedience would be. To show such a level of disrespect for proper authority is a grave offense in a Church whose very foundation is hierarchical stability." He shook his head stiffly. "But you're not a stupid man, Reverend Vryce, though sometimes you play at it. You've read the Prophet's writings often enough to know your sin for what it was."

"I thought the situation merited it," he dared. Where was the safe ground in this scene? He wished he dared work a Knowing for guidance, but that was, of course, out of the question. "Under the circumstances—"

"*Please.* Don't insult us both. You knew exactly what you were doing, and what my reaction would be. And you also knew that your blatant defiance would give me the authority to discipline you in whatever manner I thought best, without interference from anyone."

There it was, the threat at last. *How bad will it be?* he thought desperately. He remembered the nightmare Tarrant had once crafted for him, in which the Patriarch had cast him out of the Church. Would he really go that far? Without even reading his report, which justified so many of his actions? He began to protest, then bit back on it in anguish. The Patriarch was radiating rage in waves that warped the fae all around them; he *wanted* the priest to react to him in anger, to justify the very harshest sentence. If Damien gave in to that influence and lost his temper, even for a moment, he might indeed lose everything.

"I am the Church's loyal servant," he muttered.

Yes," he said icily. "You are still that. For now."

He stared at Damien in silence for several long seconds. Studying him? Measuring his response? He forced himself to say nothing, knowing that any words he chose would be wrong.

"You traveled with the Hunter," the Patriarch said at last. His voice was cold, his manner utterly condemning. "A man so evil that many consider him to be a true demon. There's enough wrongdoing in that one act alone to condemn a dozen priests like you . . . and yet the matter doesn't end there, does it?" The cold eyes narrowed. "Does it!"

"We needed him," Damien said tightly. "We needed the kind of power he controlled to—"

"Listen to yourself! Listen to your own words! You needed his *power.* You needed his *sorcery.*" He shook his head sharply. "Do you think it makes a difference whether you fashion a Working yourself, or hire another to do it? Either way, *you* are responsible for the proliferation of sorcery. And in this case, for the proliferation of evil."

He waved his hand suddenly, as if dismissing all that. For an instant something flashed in his eyes that was not rage. Exhaustion? Then it was gone, and only steel resolve remained. "But you know that argument as well as I do, Reverend Vryce. And I have no doubt that you've gone over it yourself time and time again, trying to find some theological loophole to save yourself with. An intelligent man can justify anything in his own mind, if he's determined enough."

He paused for a moment then, and Damien could almost feel the waves of condemnation lapping about his feet. The man's power was vast, if unconscious; by now all the fae in the room would be surely echoing his words, undermining the foundations of Damien's confidence. How did you fight such a thing without Working openly? "My only intention—" he began.

The Patriarch cut him short. "You fed him your blood." It wasn't a question, but a statement of utter revulsion. "More than once."

He was so stunned by the accusation that he could manage no coherent response, could only whisper "What?" The Patriarch couldn't possibly have knowledge of that incident. Could he? What was going on here?

"Let's ignore for the moment the symbolic power of such an act. Let's ignore the vast power you added to his arsenal, by making a voluntary sacrifice of your own flesh. Let's ignore even the channel it established between you, which by definition cuts through the heart of your defenses and makes you vulnerable to all his sorcery. Thus making the Church vulnerable, through you."

Was this another nightmare that Tarrant was feeding him, in order to make him afraid? If so, it was working. How the hell did the Patriarch know such details of his travels, when his reports had made no hint of them? He found that he was trembling, and hoped that the Holy Father couldn't see it.

"Yes or no," the Patriarch said icily.

Did he really know, or was he only guessing? Why would one guess a thing like that? Feverishly he tried to work out how to minimize the damage. If the Patriarch's source of information was unreliable—

"Yes or no!" he demanded.

Nightmare. It was a scene out of nightmare. How many times had Damien dreamed this scene, or its equivalent? And yet those dreams had no emotive power at all compared to this, the real thing.

Where the hell had the Patriarch gotten his information?

"Yes or no."

He looked up into the Patriarch's ice-cold eyes, and suddenly knew the futility of denial. If the Patriarch had such detailed information as this, then there was no point in dissembling; the man had damned Vryce long ago, and long ago decided his punishment. Lying to him now would only make things worse.

He said it quietly, trying not to sound either guilty or defiant. "Yes."

A strange shiver seemed to pass through the Holy Father's frame. Had he expected some other answer? Damien felt as if he were being tested somehow, but not in any manner he could understand.

"You conversed with demons." There was no hesitation in the Patriarch's manner now; whatever confirmation he had required from

Damien, he was clearly satisfied that he had it. "You countenanced the slaughter of numerous innocents, in order that the Hunter might be fed."

It took all his strength not to snap back a sharp response; the fae was beating at his will, battering his self-control. "It was necessary," he forced out between gritted teeth. "If you would read my report—"

"*You gave in to corruption.*" The very air seemed to shiver with the power of the Patriarch's condemnation. "You fell into the Prophet's own trap, justifying your sins by the very scriptures that damned you." He paused, then demanded, "Must I deal with each transgression individually?" he demanded. "Or will you simply accept that I know them all? That I pass judgment on you not only for one sin, or several, but for nearly two years of continual defiance?"

He drew in a deep breath. "Your Holiness, if you would only let me explain—"

"In good time, Reverend Vryce. I'll read your report. I may even listen to what you have to say. *After* I've made my position perfectly clear."

He paced a few steps toward the far wall and back again. "If you were one of my own I wouldn't hesitate to demote you, maybe even cast you out of the priesthood entirely. Because allowing you to serve the Church is one thing, but allowing you to *represent* it is another matter entirely. If I had ordained you—if any of my people had—I might free you here and now of all your Church obligations, so that you could spend your years warring with demons and gambling for human souls without any concern for my interference. I suspect you would be happier that way.

"But you aren't mine. You're a guest from a foreign autarchy, with different traditions. Different beliefs regarding our faith. For all that we venerate unity, it would be unjust of me not to recognize that fact. Or to allow for it in my judgment."

Shaking, he struggled to voice some neutral respose. "I thank you, Holiness."

"Don't. Not yet." The sharp gaze was venomous. "I wrote to your Matriarch, and outlined the situation. A month ago I received her response." He pulled a letter out from his robe, cream-colored parchment folded in thirds; the gold seal of the Church hung from the bottom. "It gives me permission to wield authority in both our names." The cold eyes narrowed. "Do you understand me, Vryce? If I decided that you aren't fit to be a priest, there'll be no running home for redress. Judgment is here and now."

Damien said it very quietly, his heart pounding so loudly he could barely hear his own words. "Is that what you've decided?"

For a moment the Patriarch said nothing, only studied him. "No," he said at last. "Not yet. But the future's in your hands. I want you to understand that. Comport yourself like a priest and you'll remain one. Otherwise . . ." The words trailed off into silence, a threat too terrible to be voiced. *Otherwise you will have nothing*, the silent words continued. *Because without the priesthood, what are you?*

"I understand." He tried to sound calmer than he felt. If only the Patriarch had read his report before meeting with him! Surely knowledge of the situation would mitigate his rage at Damien, and direct his energies elsewhere!

What good will your holy protocol do if Calesta has his way? What good can the Church do in a world where sadism rules supreme? It's humanity's soul we're fighting for now, can't you see that? Can't you see how petty your rules seem by contrast, when the future of the whole world is at stake?

"Our most holy war is against corruption," the Patriarch reminded him. "In this world, and in ourselves. The first battle is easy compared to the second. So the Prophet taught. I suggest you reflect upon that, and seek guidance from his writings. It may help put things in perspective for you."

He nearly lost control then, nearly snapped at the Patriarch that yes, he damned well knew about the Prophet's writings, he had traveled with the bastard for two years now and probably had a better handle on his philosophy than any man alive. But—

The Prophet is dead in this man's eyes, he realized. *And maybe that's right. Maybe I sense a ghost of that identity in Tarrant because I want it to be there, not because it really is. Maybe I fear my own corruption too much to look at him objectively.*

He met the Patriarch's gaze head-on; in coldness and power it reminded him of the Hunter's own.

You would have no power over me if I weren't already plagued by guilt, he thought to the man. *You would have no power to make me obey if I didn't believe, in the core of my soul, that you were right.*

"I am the Church's servant," he said quietly. Trying his best to sound humble. "Now and always."

The Patriarch nodded; his expression was grim.

"Then let's see it stays that way, Reverend Vryce." His voice was quiet, but the threat behind his words was clear. "Shall we?"

Seven

Narilka remembered:

Kneeling on the ground, the cold ground, the Forest earth. Fingers raw and bleeding. Legs cramped from endless running. Exhaustion like a vise around her chest, and every breath gained a fleeting triumph against its constriction.

Wait, he had said, when the Hunt was over and he had decided to spare her life. *Just wait. My people will come for you.*

She tried not to be afraid. This was the Hunter's land, wasn't it? The people here were his. The beasts obeyed his will. Even the tentacles of thorny vines which had torn at her ankles while she fled, the black-barked trees which had blocked her path, the tangled branches overhead which filtered the moonlight so that practically none of it reached the ground . . . they were all his creatures, weren't they? And he wouldn't hurt her. He had promised her that. The Hunter would never, ever hurt her.

"Please come soon," she whispered, clutching the amulet he had given her. Blood from her roughened hands filled in the delicate etched channels, smeared across the golden surface. She could feel the Forest closing in around her like some vast living thing with a will of its own, its cold heartbeat throbbing beneath her knees. Every creature in its confines was a part of that system, every branch and insect and microbe. One living anatomy, all of it, united as the cells of a single body were united. And the Hunter was its brain. If he chose to kill her, then his Forest would rise up, every living and unliving thing within its borders, and crush her as surely as the swat of a human hand might kill an insect. All with no more thought than that, she knew. The Forest was his reflex, no more.

He had promised not to hurt her.

She clung to that thought as the cold breeze stirred branches too near her face, as their sharp tips scratched her skin ever so lightly. She jerked back, startled. There was rustling in the bushes all around her, and it took all her willpower not to struggle to her feet and start running again. Not that she would last long. She hadn't slept for nearly three days now, and her only food had been hard black berries that had made her stomach cramp and had bloodied her stool. Fortunately she had found water on her second day, or she might not have made it this long—

Fortunately! She laughed bitterly. There was no fortune in this place, nor any random hope to cling to. The Hunter had meant to chase her for three nights, therefore she had found enough water to keep going; his Forest had herded her properly. What kind of mind did it take to create such a place, what magnitude of power did it demand to keep it going! She couldn't begin to understand it, but she had heard its music. Black music, whirlpooled in his eyes. She shivered, remembering it. She shivered for wanting it so badly, and for fearing that desire.

The rustling had stopped, she realized suddenly. It seemed to her that it ended abruptly, or perhaps she was only suddenly aware of it. Trembling, she rose to her feet. Her legs shook and her feet burned in pain, but she managed to straighten up, her hand clenching the amulet so tightly that its edge cut hard into her palm. What new danger was this, that drove the normal denizens of the Forest to silence!

It was a man.

He stepped from the darkness suddenly, into a thin beam of moonlight that allowed her to see him. A ghost of a man, with ghastly pale skin and eyes that blazed blood-red in the darkness. His hands were long and thin and his fingernails had been sharpened like claws; his teeth, when he grinned, were long and sharp likewise, as though Nature had stripped them from some predatory beast and set them in his mouth. There was no color about him, not anywhere on his person, and his flesh had a nacreous glow that spoke of a chill, unwholesome power.

There was sudden movement behind her, about her, and she whipped about to see its source. Wolves, lean and hungry . . . but not any creatures that Nature had made. These were warped, obscene entities, whose thin legs ended in handlike extremities, whose eyes glowed redly like the eyes of their master, whose fur was as pale as the fur that he wore on his vest, as the hide that made up his boots. It took effort to turn away from them, to face the man again; but he was their master, that she sensed clearly. Growl they might, paw the ground with their mishapen limbs, but they wouldn't attack her without his approval.

"Well." His thin lips twisted into a smile, or at least a close fascimile. "What have we here? A damsel in distress, perhaps?"

His presence was like a chill wind that froze her skin as he approached. It took everything she had not to quail in terror before him, not to sink to her knees and beg wildly for mercy, though she sensed there was no mercy in him. He belongs to the Hunter, she told herself. The Hunter won't hurt me. He promised.

He came very close, so close that she could feel his breath upon her hair. The red eyes studied her—all of her—and as he glanced down at her chest with a smile, she realized that the Hunter's assault had left her half-bare, one breast and a shoulder exposed to the night. Did the white man stare at her in that way because he thought it would frighten her? Maybe in another time and place it would have. But she could still feel the Hunter's grip upon her arm; she could still taste the terror of that moment. She could still feel his power, death-born, demanding, and a desire inside herself so terrible, so all-consuming, that it was all she could do not to offer herself up in sacrifice to his hunger. What was the mere gaze of one ghostly creature, compared to that? Fleshborn or fae-spawned, he was a servant of the Hunter. And the Hunter had promised that none of his people would hurt her.

"I need to know the way out," she whispered. Her voice was weak, and hoarse from thirst. "Please."

The ghost-man laughed; it was a cruel sound. "Do I look like a tour guide to you?" He reached out a hand toward her face, and she forced herself not to back away. Fear hammered in her chest, but fear was what he wanted; she refused to give him the pleasure of seeing her give in to it.

"Such a pretty toy," he mused. The white hand cupped the side of her head, caressing her roughly; where his thumb pressed against her temple there was a searing pain, so sharp that it nearly made her cry out. "Such a shame, to discard it now."

Terror welled up inside her with numbing force, but with it came fury. Had she run for three nights from the Forest's demonic master, feeding him with her blood and her suffering, only to yield up her hard-earned survival for this ghostly creature's amusement? "No," she whispered. She pushed his hand away from her; her temple burned like fire. "No!" She thrust the amulet into his face, held the bloodied disk inches in front of those cruel red eyes. "He promised me safety. He gave me his word." There was no fear left in her now, nor room for any to take root. Fury had filled her to overflowing, and brought with it its own dark strength. "Take me out of here," she commanded. The pain in her temple was intense, nearly blinding, but she wouldn't give him the pleasure of seeing her react to it. "Or leave me alone until someone comes along who can."

The wolves behind her growled, and she heard one of them pad closer. She did not turn around. It was impossible to read the ghost-man's expression, or to guess at his intentions. She felt something hot trickle down from her temple, where he had touched her skin. Was it blood? Did he thirst for that, too, like his master did? If so, the bloodied amulet was doubly challenging. She held it higher, demanding that he acknowledge it. She was not afraid now, not at all. The Hunter had claimed all the depths of her fear, and no other man—or beast—might inspire such emotion again.

Then she sensed, rather than heard, the nearest wolves withdraw. She saw something in the white man's expression change. And then he, too, stepped back, and caught up the amulet from out of her hand. He was careful not to touch her again, she noticed. Wary of doing any more damage to the Hunter's prize?

"Come," he said shortly. He turned from her, and she dared to draw in a long, deep breath. Behind her the wolves fell into line; she could hear them sniffing at her bloody footprints as she began to walk. "Move quickly. It's almost dawn."

Only a little while longer, she promised her bruised and battered feet. Her muscles burned, but she forced them to move. Only a few miles more. A few hours. Then sleep.

Staggering along as best she could, she let the ghost-man lead her out of the Forest.

Eight

Damien walked the streets until long after midnight. Through the Street of Gods, where countless deities vied for man's worship. (How many of them were Iezu? he wondered. Did any of them know or care about Calesta's plans?) Past the Inn of the New Sun, where he and Ciani had shared their first dinner, so long ago. Down through the mercantile district, to where the Fae Shoppe had once stood—

It was gone now. More than gone. Its rubble had been carted away, its foundation reinforced with new concrete, and a three-story building had been erected in its place. That was high for a city plagued by constant small earthquakes; most architects preferred to keep their ambition under tight rein on such risky ground. But he could see the lines where resilient hask-fibers had been used to reinforce the walls, and a host of quake-wards marked every door, window, and potential weak point. God help Jaggonath if its wards ever failed, he thought. God help them if they were ever as helpless as Earth had been, in the face of an earthquake.

Domina was overhead when he began the long walk back to his hotel. The Patriarch had offered him a room in the Annex—more out of custom than genuine courtesy, he suspected—but under the circumstances he thought it best that his lodgings be separate. Not that it would keep the Patriarch from knowing what he did, he thought bitterly. Hard as he racked his brain, he could not come up with any explanation for the Holy Father's detailed knowledge of his sins. Sure, Calesta would like him to know, but how could the demon present such knowledge to a man like the Patriarch without him rejecting it utterly just for its source? Thus far Damien had not dared a Knowing, or any other form of Working, to try to uncover the truth. Because if he did *that* and the Patriarch found out there'd be no staunching his rage. Maybe Tarrant, with his more subtle skills, could manage it secretly enough. Maybe.

It was nearly one when he climbed the steps to his rooms. The lodging house was deserted, and only a faint chill clinging to the banister gave any hint that an unhuman presence had passed that way. But he knew that chill by now, and its owner, and therefore it was no surprise to him when he unlocked the door to his small apartment and found the Hunter waiting.

"I'd have thought you'd be keeping an earlier schedule by now," Tarrant challenged.

"Yeah. Well." He pulled the door shut behind him and locked it, then made his way wearily to a well-worn chair. Dust gusted up from the cushion as he sat. "I had a bad day."

He could feel the force of the earth-fae sucking at him as the Hunter's Knowing reached into his brain for surface details. Let him. It was easier to endure the invasion than try to capture the day's humiliation in words.

"I'm sorry," the Hunter said at last. Regret, not apology.

Damien managed to shrug. "I guess it could have been worse." He looked up at Tarrant, noted that as usual he looked neither tired, distressed, disheveled . . . nor human. "How's the Forest?"

It seemed to him that the Hunter hesitated. "Safe enough," he said at last. "But our enemy's workings can be subtle, and I wouldn't bet my life on such an assessment."

"Yeah. Same here."

"You believe that Calesta has made contact with the Patriarch?"

He gazed into Tarrant's eyes. Cold, so cold. Pits of anti-life. How could he have imagined that the Patriarch resembled him? Or any living man, for that matter?

"He knew," he said bitterly. "*Everything.* Details he couldn't possibly have learned from any other source." He met that inhuman gaze head-on, drawing strength from its cold inner fire. *This is my ally. My support.* He wished the thought felt more uncomfortable than it did. Had he changed so much in the last two years? "He knows I fed you my blood," he said quietly. "He knows about the channel between us. Do you realize how that damns me, in the Church's eyes? There's nothing I can say now to save myself. Nothing I can do, except avoid the source of corruption from now on."

"Is that what you want?" Tarrant demanded. "If it truly is, then I'll leave you. If you value your precious peace of mind more than our mission. Maybe Calesta will even forgive you in time, learn to leave you alone, once you've ceased to be—"

"Don't be a fool, Gerald." He reached for a bottle of ale he had left on the table earlier in the day; it was warm now, but what the hell. "Neither one of us is safe until Calesta's dead and gone. Hell, the whole vulking *world* isn't safe anymore." He drank deeply of the warm ale, wincing as its spices bit into his tongue. "Look what happened in the east. Look at how many lives would have been sacrificed to one demon's hunger, if you hadn't—"

The Hunter's expression darkened. Damien let the words trail off into silence.

"Sorry," he said at last. "I shouldn't remind you."

Tarrant turned away, toward the window.

"At any rate, we don't stand a chance singly and you know it. Like it or not, we're stuck with each other." *We may not even stand a chance together,* he thought grimly as he took another swig of the warm ale. The alcohol was slowly loosening a knot in his belly the size of Jaggonath. Well worth the lousy taste. "So how did your research go?"

Tarrant shook his head sharply in frustration. "Volumes of notes, centuries of study, and not one useful bit of information. Oh, I can recite you the names of over a hundred Iezu, complete with their aspects, preferred forms, and habitats, but according to Karril none of his family will get involved in this, not even to the extent of pointing us toward more useful information. Their progenitor's code is apparently enforced with vigor. Thank God for that, anyway."

"Thank God for it?" He raised an eyebrow. "That code seems to be our greatest impediment right now."

"Their progenitor also forbids the Iezu from killing humans, at least directly. Which is the only reason you and I are still alive."

"You said they have no power but illusion. Surely that—"

"How little work would it take to make me stay out past dawn, believing that the sun hadn't yet begun to rise? How little work to arrange an accident for you, how small an illusion to make you misjudge the edge of a pier or a cliff, or mistake the flow of traffic in the streets? No man can stay on his guard against such tricks forever, Reverend Vryce. No, if Calesta meant to kill us, then we would both have died long ago. As it is, I'm sure he's planned something far more . . . unpleasant."

He turned away again, and gazed out the window. Perhaps he was studying the flow of fae in the streets below, analyzing it for data. Perhaps he was only thinking.

"He's attacking the Church," Damien said quietly.

"I thought he might," he said, without turning back. "Tell me the details."

"Outbursts of violence all over town. Bands of the faithful desecrating pagan shrines, beating priests, destroying property. One group was just about to lynch a priestess for crimes against the One God when the police arrived, just in time. And such outbursts are more and more frequent. The Patriarch himself had to step in the last time, and even so there was a lot of damage done." He put the empty bottle down on the table again and wiped his mouth with a shirt sleeve. "The Temple of Bakshi is suing the Church for half a million in damages to person and property. If they win. . . ."

"Then there'll be more to follow."

He snorted. "That goes without saying, doesn't it?"

The Hunter nodded slowly. "He's subtle, our enemy, and all too clever. Multiple lawsuits could bring the Church to its knees faster than any direct Working. And the public humiliation involved would certainly affect the fae, weakening the Church's effect on local currents. Negating the very power which the Church was designed to wield. And after Jaggonath, others will follow. Until such momentum is gained that it no longer requires his direct interference."

He turned back to face Damien again; his silver eyes were blazing. "He means to destroy my greatest work. Morally, socially, financially . . . if that lawsuit goes through, then he's already won the first battle. How many more campaigns has he set in motion, which will remain secret until their culmination? Nine hundred years, Vryce! You perceive that I abandoned it years ago, but I tell you the Church is still my passion. My *child.* Nine hundred years of carefully crafted development, and this demonic filth will send it all spiraling down into Hell in a single generation!"

"There has to be a way to stop it. There has to be a way to nullify the effect—"

"We must kill him," Tarrant interrupted. "There is no other way."

"How?"

"I don't know." His voice was tight with frustration. "But there has to be a way." He thought for a moment, then added, "Their progenitor can kill them. So obviously the means exists. And I got the distinct impression that whatever technique he or she uses, the Iezu would be helpless to fight back."

"You think he could be convinced to help us?"

"To kill his own creations? Not likely. But there might be others who are privy to his secrets."

"Such as?"

"Maybe demons. Some other class, whom we can still coerce by simple means. Or maybe even adepts. Someone close to the Iezu, who might invite their confidence." He paused. "Maybe Ciani."

Ciani. Even after two years the memory was sharp and painful. Ciani of the quick wit and ready laughter, whom he had loved. Ciani the adept, whom a Iezu had saved. Ciani the loremaster, who valued knowledge more than any mere love affair and had gone to live among the rakh in order to study them more closely. Ciani, whom he had left behind.

"Ciani's gone," he said quietly.

"But not dead, Reverend Vryce. And not unreachable."

She would be in the rakhlands now, protected by unscalable mountains on one side and an ocean on the other. The Canopy would be there, too, a wall of living fae that no human Working could cross. If not for that they might Send for her, using the fae to communicate across the miles that separated them. With it . . .

"I don't relish going back there," he muttered.

"Nor I. If nothing else, it would mean our extended absence from Jaggonath, leaving Calesta free to do his worst here unopposed. I'm not sure we can afford that."

Ciani. Even now, years later, the memory of her made Damien ache with regret. But it had been a doomed match from the start, he accepted that now. Or at least he tried to.

"She's a loremaster," he said at last. "They take a vow of neutrality, don't they? Would she be willing to help us?"

"I don't know. She certainly has no vested interest in the Church's survival. She'd probably be more interested in chronicling its fall than in providing for its salvation. And then there are, as you say, the vows of her profession, which forbid her from taking sides in any fae-related conflict. The irony is, if it were anyone else, I could force her to serve us. But the lady Ciani . . . to harm her in any way would be to give myself over to the ones I serve, in soul as well as aspect." He laughed shortly, a forced sound. "And I suspect that they're not in a forgiving mood these days."

An unfamiliar emotion flickered in the back of those cold, clear eyes. Fear? "They haven't done anything to you yet."

"Not yet," he agreed. "But for how long?" To Damien's surprise he sighed heavily; the action was disturbingly human.

He walked the length of the room, then stopped; Damien thought he saw his shoulders tense. "Do you know, sometimes I pray to them? Not as a worshiper to a god, but as servant to an angry master. I try to make them understand that in seeking Calesta's destruction

I'm only ensuring my own survival, the better to serve them. If such an act happened to benefit the Church I founded, or humankind in general . . . that would be an unfortunate side effect, nothing more." He shook his head. "I wish I believed that myself."

Damien chose his words carefully. "You think it isn't true?"

The Hunter hesitated. "I was so sure of myself, once. I lived in a world without doubt, without any need for introspection. My soul was as pure in its darkness as the night-fae itself, which is banished by the merest hint of sunlight. Then you came into my life. You! With your questions and your warped logic and your bonds of mutual dependency and purpose . . . and I changed. Slowly, but I did change. No human soul could fail to do so, under the circumstances—and the core of my soul *is* human, Vryce, despite what Karril would call its "hellish trappings." That was both the source of my strength and my greatest weakness. In the end, thanks to you, it will be my destruction." The sharp eyes narrowed. "But that was what you hoped for, wasn't it? After all this is over, I could do you no better service than to die and be damned."

"Gerald, please—"

He waved a hand, cutting short his protest. "I don't blame you, Vryce. I blame myself for letting it happen. You did no more or less than your nature demanded. I only wonder what the price will be, when I'm finally called to answer for my actions."

"Surely a few months of weakness won't outweigh the record of nine hundred years."

"The Unnamed has no compassion, and nothing to lose by injustice. Its judgment is as much the result of momentary structure as of logic. Divided into parts, it can be petty and fickle and unpredictable; unified, it's the most ruthless evil this world has ever known. Thank God the latter state rarely endures for long."

"What do you mean, *divided?* I don't understand."

The cold eyes fixed on him: black now, and empty as the true night. "Better that you don't," he warned. "That force has a habit of devouring anything which touches it; better men than you have fallen to it in the past, for no greater sin than seeking to understand its nature. And I wasn't the first to court it for its power, you know. But I may be the only one to come through such negotiations with my soul intact. It delights in corrupting humanity, and will toy with its victims like a cat tortures prey. Also its servitors," he added grimly. "Anyone who gives it an opening."

"Maybe it despises Calesta as much as you do," Damien suggested. "Maybe it regards your current attempts as a kind of service."

"Doubtful." His brow furrowed as he considered the thought. "One would think Calesta's habits would be to its liking."

"Rivalry, perhaps?"

"The Iezu are petty demons. The Unnamed is . . . beyond that."

"Petty demons who can't be Banished, or otherwise controlled. Independent spirits who mean to remake the Unnamed One's domain."

"Perhaps," he said dubiously. "At least that might explain—"

He stopped then. And did not proceed.

"What?" When the Hunter didn't respond, he pressed, "Tell me, Gerald. What is it?"

"I Divined our conflict," he said softly. Eyes shut, recalling the Working to his inner vision. "It's an imprecise art at best, as you know, and in this case all it conjured was chaos. I watched the corruption of the Church proceed from a thousand beginnings, and in none of them could I see any hope of change. I witnessed both our deaths a dozen times—yes, yours and mine—in a dozen different forums. I saw worlds in which Calesta triumphed, and such change was wrought that our human ancestors wouldn't have recognized Erna's children as their kin. All tangled together, Reverend Vryce: a skein of futures so enmeshed that even my skill couldn't pull the threads loose. But there were patterns even in that chaos, things which recurred time and time again." He looked at Damien. "The interference of the Unnamed was one. I had assumed it would strike at me directly, in vengeance for my many transgressions, but who can know what passes for vengeance in a mind that knows no permanence? And more than once I saw a sorcerer at the head of the Church, a man whose power was equal to my own, who might lead that body down the one safe path among millions. But what sense does that make? Even if such a man existed, the Church would cast him out." He shook his head tightly, frustrated. "Too many futures, Vryce, and nearly all of them lead to failure. I can't make out anything useful."

He managed to keep his voice steady, though suddenly his heart was pounding. "There is a sorcerer in the Church, Gerald."

"What? Where?" Then he waved a hand, dismissing the thought. "This was a man in *control* of things, Vryce. They would never give a sorcerer such authority."

"They would if he were the Patriarch."

The look on Gerald Tarrant's face was one he never thought he would see: pure, unadulterated astonishment. "The Patriarch? But how—?"

"He doesn't know it. And I'm sure no one else has guessed. But I worked a Knowing in his presence once. . . ."

And he told him about his conversations with the Holy Father. About the way the fae responded to the man, even though he couldn't See it. About how it served his unconscious will even while his words denied its power.

"He's a natural," he concluded. "I'm sure of it."

Tarrant reached for the nearest chair and dropped himself heavily into it. It was clear that he hadn't been braced for this kind of news. And how could he be? His own damnation had been assured by the Church's rejection of any such power. How could he accept that suddenly the rules might change, without questioning his own existence? "An adept?" he breathed. "Could he be that also?"

"Is it possible?"

"You mean, could a man be born with Sight and deny it? Block it so utterly that he never even knew it existed?" He hesitated. "It might be. So many infants die or go insane each year, that we think might have been fledgling adepts. Is it unreasonable to think that a newborn might learn to deny its fae-visions, when no other family member acknowledges their reality? God of Earth and Erna," he whispered. There was a new note in his voice. Awe? "If so . . . that would explain more than one Divination."

"You think he would help us?" He tried to keep the doubt out of his voice, but it was hard. "Is that what you saw?"

"What I saw," he said slowly, "was Calesta subverting a powerful man. I saw great vision and great stubbornness, that might be harnessed for a thousand different purposes. I saw a man destroying himself, unable to face his own potential . . . and that would make sense, if it is who you suggest. But I also saw this: in any future where the Church stood the least chance of survival, this man's actions were pivotal." He looked up sharply at Damien. "*Pivotal*, Vryce. In its literal sense. The man I saw could save the Church, but he could also destroy it."

"Can you tell where those paths diverge?" he demanded. "What's the catalyst? We can go after that."

Tarrant's eyes were unfocused as he tried to remember what he'd Seen. At last he shook his head, clearly frustrated. "It was all too tangled to make out clearly. He's not even aware of his own power yet; how can I read a future that depends upon such awareness?"

"What if he were?" he pressed. "What if he accepted it?"

The Hunter's gaze fixed on him: diamondine, piercing. "You mean, what if he became a sorcerer in truth? Then he must face the condemnation of the Church as few men have known it . . . perhaps even the condemnation of his own soul. Would you wish that kind of torment on any man?"

Knowing the question for what it was, he met the Hunter's gaze head-on. "No," he said quietly. "I wouldn't wish that on any man."

The Hunter turned away from him. Sensing that he needed the moment of privacy, Damien upended his bottle of ale once more. There was still nothing in it.

"He must know the truth, then," Tarrant said at last. "Or all our efforts are doomed to failure."

"Yeah. Only who the hell is going to tell him?"

"Perhaps I—"

"*No,*" he said sharply. "You're right up there with the Unnamed as far as he's concerned. If not worse. What good can you possibly do? Stay out of this one. I'll think of . . . something."

Only, dear God . . . what?

"Very well, then," Tarrant muttered. It was clear he had misgivings about Damien's judgment, but for now he was acquiescing. Thank God. "See what you can come up with. If not . . . it need not be direct contact, you understand. Or anything he would connect with me."

Realizing what he meant, Damien rose up from his seat as he warned, "Don't you Work him! You understand me? We're talking about something that could cost this man his soul; leave him his free will to face it with!" When Tarrant didn't answer, he pressed, "You understand me, Gerald?"

The Hunter glared. "I understand."

"Promise me."

"Don't be a fool! I said I understood. I respect your opinion, although I don't agree with it. That's more than most men have had of me. Leave it at that."

"You'll leave him alone?"

The Hunter's tone was venomous. "I won't compromise his free will, I'll promise you that much. As for the rest . . . find a safe way to enlighten him, or I'll do what I must. The odds against us increase dramatically if he remains ignorant, and I won't risk that just to coddle your overblown sense of morality." Before Damien could protest again, he ordered, "You go see if the Church Archives have anything useful on the Iezu. I'll Locate the local adepts, see if they have any notes of their own." He shook his head angrily. "Damn Senzei Reese, for what he destroyed! If the man weren't already dead, I'd kill him myself."

For a moment there was silence between them, but it was a purely vocal phenomenon; the channel that linked them was alive with such hostile energy that Damien could hear the Hunter's next words as clearly as if they had been spoken. *Don't press me for assurances I won't give. All that you'll accomplish by that is to strain the tenuous foundation of our alliance, and that would put us both at risk.*

Tarrant started toward the door. Damien stepped forward quickly and put out a hand to stop him. With his other hand he reached into his pocket for the object he had stored there, drew it out, and offered it to the man.

The Hunter's eyes narrowed suspiciously. "What is it?"

"A key. Basement apartment in this building. It's paid for."

"For what? My lodging?" He stared at Damien as if the priest had suddenly gone mad. "Don't be ridiculous. I'll find myself a safe place—"

"This isn't the rakhlands," he snapped, "with miles between us and the enemy. He's here, all around us. Can't you feel it?" He held out the key toward him, urging him to take it. "There's a bolt on the front door that can't be opened from the outside. I boarded up all the windows. The landlady was paid well to leave you alone—she thinks you're a rich eccentric—and I even checked the quake-wards on the building, to make sure they were sound." When Tarrant made no move to take the key, he pressed, "Remember how he dealt with us? *Divide and conquer.* First Senzei, then you. Then Hesseth and me in the Terata's realm. He'll try it again, you can bet your undead soul on that. Let's make it as hard as possible for him, okay?"

He glared at the key, but finally took it from Damien's hand. "I'll assess the danger myself," he growled. "If the place seems safe . . . I'll consider it."

"Good enough." He stood back, giving Tarrant room to exit. At least one thing had gone right tonight; he had feared Tarrant wouldn't take the key at all. God damn him for his stubborn, pigheaded independence.

When the Hunter was gone, he went to the icebox, pulled out a fresh bottle of ale, and opened it with a sigh. Iezu and Unnamed demons, sadism and vengeance . . . each separate thing was terrifying in its own right, and he had to deal with them all at once. Yet those threats paled to insignificance in the face of an even more daunting challenge, and he grimaced as he swallowed the cold ale, dreading it with all his heart and soul.

How the *hell* were they going to deal with the Patriarch?

Nine

The lobby of the Hotel Paradisio was a study in conspicuous consumption, and an effective one at that. While Narilka was critical of its aesthetic approach—too gilded for her taste, too discordant, the artificially aged paint of the ceiling murals at odds with the gleaming fresh quake-wards that guarded the entrance—there was no denying that its message came through loud and clear. *Enter here, all ye who can afford it. And as for the rest of you, back to the streets.* She was glad that she had once delivered a commissioned necklace to one of the luxury suites here, and thus could find her way about without having to ask for assistance; the check-in staff was cold to mere tradesmen.

She traversed two halls and a short flight of stairs, all carpeted in velvet. After that came what she sought: a door, and a number. Suite 5-A. She stared at the letters—neatly engraved on a flamboyant golden plaque—and suddenly wondered what the hell she was doing here. What did she think was going to happen? What did she *want* to happen? She nearly turned around and started home then and there, but the anticipation of Gresham's certain scorn kept her from doing so. *What's the matter?* he would demand. *Lose your nerve?* And after he had tried so hard to talk her out of coming here in the first place!

But Andrys Tarrant's haunted face could not be banished from memory so easily, nor his eerie likeness to the Hunter dismissed so casually. At last she forced herself to raise up a hand and knock on the suite door, her heart pounding. *You have a legitimate errand*, she reminded herself. *He'll respect that, if nothing else.* Again she tried, but there was no response. What if he wasn't in? That was a real possibility, but not one she had prepared herself to face. Would she have to come back later and do this all over again?

"You're gonna have to hit harder than that, honey." The voice came from a uniformed maid several doors down the hallway. A heavyset woman, middle-aged, she grinned broadly as she told her, "They were up till all hours, that lot." When she saw Narilka hesitate, she urged, "Go ahead, hit it like you mean it."

She drew in a deep breath and did as the woman suggested. The sharp blows resounded in the hallway, and she half-expected some other lodger to appear to investigate. But long seconds passed and there was still no response. She knocked again, even harder. This time there was a shuffling sound from within the suite and murmurs of what might have been a human voice. She stepped back, wishing she could still the wild beating of her heart. Why couldn't she face this man calmly?

After a moment the ornate handle turned and the heavy door swung open. "I thought I ordered—" Andrys Tarrant began. And then he saw her—saw who she was—and all speech left him. For a moment he just stared at her, his green eyes wide with astonishment. It was clear that she was the last person in the world he had ever expected to find on his doorstep.

At last he whispered hoarsely, "Mes Lessing."

He was dressed in a loose white shirt and crumpled pants, and had obviously just rolled out of bed. His golden-brown hair was tangled about his head, his eyes faintly bloodshot. He blinked heavily and drew in a deep breath; he was clearly struggling to compose himself. "I didn't . . . I'm sorry . . . I thought it was breakfast."

She glanced toward the hall window with a smile, acknowledging the fading sunlight. "Little late for that, isn't it?"

He brushed the hair back from his face with a hand that seemed to tremble slightly; a lock of hair fell back across his eyes as soon as he released it. "I had a late night," he managed. Then a smile flitted across his face: awkward, self-conscious, but sparked with genuine humor. "Or maybe I should say, a late morning. I didn't expect company today, that's for sure." *Least of all you,* his expression seemed to say. For a moment she wondered if she shouldn't make some apology for disturbing him and just give him the item he had left in the shop, so that she could beat a hasty retreat. It seemed a more merciful course for both of them. But then he stepped back, giving her room to enter. "Come in. Please."

She did so, acutely aware of his closeness as she passed by him. "If this is a bad time—"

"Not at all. Really." He closed the door gently behind her; she barely heard the latch snap shut. "We played late, that's all. I should have been up hours ago." He dared to meet her eyes then, and it seemed to her he hesitated. "Forgive my poor manners. If I'd thought it was you at the door . . ."

The words faded into silence. He brushed awkwardly at his crumpled attire, ran his hand again through his mussed hair; he was clearly not accustomed to receiving women in such a disordered state. "I'm hardly dressed for company," he dared.

Despite herself she smiled. "It's my fault. I should have let you know I was coming. If you'd like to change . . ." Why did his awkward vanity attract rather than repel her? So many other men with similar qualities had done just the opposite. "I can wait."

He brightened visibly at the suggestion. "If you're sure you don't mind."

"I'm sure," she assured him.

She was offering him more than a minute in which to change his clothing, she knew that. She was giving him time to adjust to her presence, a few precious moments of privacy in which to compose himself. And she'd be giving herself the same thing, too. She wondered which of them needed it more.

"I'll just be a minute," he told her. "I promise."

His bedroom was apparently at the far side of the parlor; he made his way there hurriedly, awkwardly, clearly conscious of her gaze upon him. Not until he was safely inside, with the door shut behind him, did she dare to draw in a deep breath and try to relax. Infinitely grateful that circumstances had gifted her with a minute in which to do so.

She looked about at the apartment he had chosen, a master suite in one of the city's most expensive hotels. The parlor was as lavish as the lobby had been, but infinitely more tasteful. It was decorated in the Revivalist style: high vaulted ceiling, polished stone floor with finely patterned rugs, slender windows with stained-glass caps. The furniture had been chosen to match that style, all except for half a dozen gilt chairs that were gathered around a table at one end of the room. Those were lighter and more graceful in form than the rest of the decor, and were clearly inspired by a later period; the stylistic mismatch seemed jarring to her, but she doubted that the hotel's guests would be sensitive enough to notice it. There were cards strewn across the table and two dozen bottles of various sizes on and about it. Drawing closer, she saw piles of wooden chips set before two places, others scattered across the silken tablecloth. There were several bottles on the floor as well, and one bright red thing that winked at her from underneath a chair. She leaned down to see what it was, then picked it up. A woman's shoe: high-heeled, velvet covered, smelling faintly of wine. Holding it in her hand, imagining its owner, she felt suddenly faint. *What am I doing here? What do I know about this man?* She tried to put the shoe down, but her hand wouldn't release it. *This isn't my world.*

"I bought that for two hundred, so she could stay in the game."

It was Andrys, dressed now. He walked toward her with an easy grace, as if his confidence had been restored along with his attire. Gently he took the shoe from her and placed it on the table, his fingers brushing hers as he did so; the touch left fire in its wake. "I'd have gotten the other one, too, if her luck hadn't changed for the better."

He had put on a sleeveless jacket, black velveteen with narrow bands of dull gold trim; it fit him tightly, a deliberate contrast to the flowing white sleeves which accentuated his shoulders. In such attire, with his golden-brown hair gleaming, his green eyes alive with flirtatious energy . . . no woman could resist him, Narilka thought. Least of all she, who had so little practice in such things.

"How was your luck?" she managed.

He grinned. "Pretty good, until about three a.m. After that . . . it's all kind of hazy." He ran a hand through his hair again, as if trying to force it back into place; it fell back in his eyes as soon as he released it. "So what brings you here, to this den of iniquity? I can hardly believe I made such a good impression the last time we met."

She managed to look away from him long enough to find the object she had brought for him; drawing it forth from her shoulder bag she explained, "You left this at the shop." Rolled canvas, nearly two feet in length: she held it out to him, an offering. "Gresham was going to mail it, but parcel service is pretty slow around here; I thought you might need it sooner than that."

He didn't take it. He didn't respond. For a moment he just stared at the rolled-up canvas with an odd look on his face, as though it were the last thing in the world he wanted to see. At last he said, in a voice that was strangely distant, "Did you look at it?"

She shook her head.

With a sigh he shut his eyes. "I thought I might have lost it on the street. I made myself go back and search, but there was no sign of it. I think I was . . . relieved." He put his hand on the roll of canvas but didn't take it from her; his hand was so close to hers that she could feel its heat. "I guess I owe you an explanation" he said quietly. The words were clearly hard for him. "That other day, in your shop—"

Someone knocked on the door then, hard; the sharp noise made Narilka jump.

"Room service," he muttered. He went to answer it. She followed more slowly, the canvas roll still in her hand. What was inside it, that upset him so greatly? It had taken all her self-control not to look at it there in the shop, when she had found it, but she'd wanted to respect his privacy. Now a part of her regretted that choice.

Andrys opened the door, and a uniformed hotel employee wheeled a small cart into the room. When he was done Andrys reached into his jacket pocket for a suitable tip, then spilled coins into the man's hand without even checking their value. What was such small change to him? His manner made it clear that he expected the servant to withdraw immediately, and the man was quick to obey. The tray he had brought in was neatly laid out with breakfast, Narilka observed, each item in its place, each accessory expensive: toast and pancakes on a silver tray, coffee in an engraved carafe, slices of pale fruit and some nondescript cereal in bowls of translucent china. All of it balanced on a fussy little cart that suited the hotel's lobby better than it did this sleek Revivalist chamber.

Avoiding her eyes, Andrys studied the hotel's offering. At last he shrugged. "It seemed a lot more appetizing when I ordered it yesterday." He lifted the coffee cup and studied it intently, as though its rim harbored some great secret. Refusing to look at her. Finally he put it down, and after a long and awkward silence dared, "Have you eaten?"

The question startled her. "I'm sorry?"

He looked at her then, and the intensity of his gaze made her heart skip a beat. "Have you eaten yet?" he asked again.

Despite herself she smiled. "Most people have, this time of day."

"Recently?" he amended.

"I had lunch. That was a while ago."

"Then come to dinner with me. Please. I hate to discuss serious matters on an empty stomach. And this . . ." he faltered for a moment, then continued with forced humor. "This place is hardly conducive to confession."

Though she knew she should leave the question unasked, she couldn't help but voice it. "Is that what this is about? Confession?"

Something sharp and hot flashed in the depths of his eyes. Pain? Fear? Maybe both. He turned away. "Yeah. I'm afraid so."

"What about this?" She held out the canvas toward him, offering him its secrets.

He reached out and closed his hand over hers. Warm, strong fingers: the touch was electric. This close to him she could smell his cologne, subtle but sensual. A delicate musky scent, precisely calculated to appeal.

Men that attractive are dangerous, Gresham had warned her. *Especially when they know their own power.*

Sweet, sweet danger. She could drown in it, gladly.

He whispered: "Bring it."

He led them to a restaurant. It didn't surprise her that he knew such a place, a shadowed hideaway where lovers might whisper sweet endearments in the privacy of high-walled booths. Doubtless he had brought women here before, for more blatantly amorous purposes. The hostess gave them a table near the rear of the restaurant, in a section that was all but deserted. In such a place one might comfortably court a lover, she thought. Or share terrible secrets. Or both.

They ordered drinks, a house wine, and braised fillets of a local fish. They made small talk over sauteed dumplings, frothy mousse, steamed coffee. He asked about her work, and seemed to be genuinely interested in the details of her art. Was that real enthusiasm, or a prelude to seduction, rehearsed so many times with so many women that it now seemed natural to him? How could one hope to tell them apart? In return, she asked him about his journey to Jaggonath. She discovered that he had never traveled out of his region before this, but she could not get him to tell her why he had done so now. And through it all she waited, watching as he tried to build up his courage, drawing strength from rituals of courtship so familiar to him that he probably could have played them with his eyes closed. Sensing the darkness that was within him, not knowing how to address it.

At last he pushed his coffee away with a sigh and shut his eyes. It seemed to her that he was in pain—or remembering pain, perhaps. Finally he dared, "The other day . . ." It was clearly meant as a beginning, but the words seemed to catch in his throat. After a minute, hoping to help him, she urged, "At the shop?"

He nodded stiffly, then looked away. "God, this is so awkward. I just want to explain. . . ."

When he faltered once more she prompted softly, "Go on." Her hand rested upon his, a gentle reassurance. "I'm listening."

At last, with great effort, he managed, "What do you know about Merentha?"

"Not much," she admitted. "A few basics from history class, and from seismics. Very little, really."

"My family's lived there for nearly ten centuries. They . . . you might say we founded the place. Thrived there. It was a well established family, highly respected, active in civil service through most of its generations. Its founder . . ." He faltered then, and shook his head as if rejecting that line of disclosure. "I was the youngest of the main line, but there were others. So many others . . ." She could feel his hand trembling now beneath her own. "Five years ago . . . I was out all night. . . ." He lowered his head, his shoulders trembling, and raised up his other hand as if to shield his face; clearly he was remembering that time, reliving some secret pain. "Just like any other night," he whispered. "Or so it seemed. I came home . . . I had no idea anything was wrong, you see, no reason to expect it. . . . I came home." He looked up at her, but his eyes were focused upon another time, another plane. "They were dead," he whispered. His voice shaking as he relived the past. "Murdered. All of them. The floor was covered with their blood. . . ."

He lowered his head once more, overwhelmed by the memory. She longed to comfort him, to seek out some gentle words which would bring him back to the present, but the shock of his revelation had left her momentarily speechless. Because she *knew* about this tragedy. She remembered it. And the family name which had seemed vaguely familiar to her now sharpened into clear and horrible focus.

"That was you," she breathed. Remembering the headlines. Bloody details splayed across local newspaper headings for months, exploitive articles that dwelled on every horrific aspect of the crime. And on every perceived weakness of the one survivor. *"You."*

He managed to look up at her. "I was wondering how long it would take you," he said bitterly. *"The murder of the century,* they called it. It must have made all the papers."

Stunned, she whispered, "They thought you did it."

He nodded tightly. "They wanted to punish someone, and I was the obvious candidate. The youngest son of the Tarrant line, selfish, undisciplined, the black sheep of the clan . . . it was no great secret that the family and I fought a lot, usually about money. And it was likewise no secret that the slaughter of every other Tarrant had guaranteed me an inheritance that many men would kill for. As you can see," he said bitterly, indicating his person: the rich clothes, the fine jewelry, the air of easy wealth. "Only I would never have killed for that. Not my own family! I could never. . . ."

She tightened her hand about his, and it seemed to her that his pain flowed through the contact. Maybe it did. Maybe the fae was so stirred by his emotion that it allowed her to glimpse the very core of his despair, unmasked by social repartee, unfettered by the bonds of language. The sheer intensity of it left her breathless. She could only hope that the same faeborn link would allow her to give something of herself in return, if only a shadow of emotional support. Even that little, she sensed, was more than he'd had in years.

"Of course not," she whispered.

He took a deep drink of wine; it seemed to lend him strength. "The trial lasted over a year," he told her. "It seemed like forever. A year of having to relive that dreadful night over and over again, so that strangers could pick it apart for incriminating details. I thought I'd go crazy. I nearly did. There are whole segments of time I don't remember now, parts of the trial I've blocked. I was so close to the edge back then. Once I even tried to give up all the money, to sign away my inheritance in the hope that they would take that for proof of my innocence. I guess it seemed the only way, at the time. My lawyers stopped me. Thank God." He laughed bitterly; his hand tightened into a fist beneath her grasp. "What did I know about earning a living? What did I understand of poverty? *They* knew. They gave me meaningless forms to sign, and didn't tell me the truth until the fit had passed. Thank God for them. Thank God."

She made her voice as gentle as it could become. "So what happened?"

"The state let me go, in the end. Not because it judged me innocent, but because it considered me incompetent. I was a wastrel, a freeloader, a waste of human life . . . but I wasn't a murderer. Wasn't *capable* of murder." He drew in a deep breath. "They had that right, at least. Maybe all of it. I don't know."

"Don't," she whispered. "Don't think that."

He lowered his head again, trembling. "I didn't want to tell you. God knows, I didn't want to tell anyone. But when I tried on the armor at your shop . . . it all came back to me, then. All of it at once, all the blood and the fear and the hopelessness. . . ."

"Why?" she asked him. Trying to understand the connection. When he didn't answer for several long seconds, she pressed him gently. "What does the armor have to do with all this?

In answer he disentangled his hand from hers—reluctantly, she thought—and reached across the table. The canvas roll had been tied shut with a slender cord; unknotting it, he set the string aside. He made room to spread the canvas out on the table, then did so. Handling it gently but firmly, hands trembling as he unrolled it. It was an old piece which had been torn and repaired more than once; stripes of tape had yellowed across its back, eating into the linen canvas. As he unrolled it, she saw aged paint, a webwork of fine cracks, the edges of a piece that had been hastily and carelessly hacked from a larger painting—

And then it was laid out before her, and she saw.

"Oh, my gods," she whispered. Stunned.

The painting was part of a formal portrait, and it was marked with several parallel slashes where a knife had scored the canvas. The object of the portrait was a young man, and even this tattered remnant of a larger painting conveyed the power of his presence, the beauty of his person. Tall, slender, he wore a breastplate emblazoned with a golden sun and a coronet decorated with mythological figures. *That* breastplate. *That* coronet. Fine golden-brown hair flowed down about his shoulders, tousled by an unseen wind. Gray eyes, cool and dominant, met the viewer's own as if there were some living will behind them. Sardonic, seductive. Seeing him rendered thus, Narilka felt herself tremble. Because there there was no mistaking the portrait's subject. And no denying that she knew him all too intimately.

The Hunter.

"Who is it?" she managed. Finding her voice at last.

"Gerald Tarrant. Founder of my family line, first Neocount of Merentha." He hesitated; when he spoke again she sensed him picking his way through his words carefully, perhaps choosing which facets of the story to reveal to her. "In his day . . . he slaughtered all his kin. All but one. His son returned home to find . . . what I found . . . it was he who did this." He indicated the slash marks in the canvas, their edges cracked and yellowing. *"That's* what I saw when I looked in the mirror. Do you understand? Not my face, but *his.* A man who could murder his entire family. . . ."

"Shh. It's over now." She took his hands in hers, warming them gently. "The armor's just a piece of metal. And the coronet. No more." It hurt her inside, to know what the next words had to be— her artist's soul rebelled at the thought—but she knew they had to be said. "If they cause you pain, then destroy them. Unmake them. Commission something else, which has a better meaning for you."

The green eyes were fixed on her, their surface glistening; were those tears gathering in the corners? "I could never destroy your work," he whispered.

"It's only metal," she assured him. Trying to make the words come easily, so that he wouldn't sense how much this was costing her. "We can melt it down and make something worthwhile out of it. Something equally beautiful, that doesn't have memories attached."

He managed a wry smile. "Your boss would hardly approve of that."

"Some things are more important than Gresham's approval," she assured him.

And for a moment, in his eyes, it seemed that she could see into the core of him. Sensing a frightened young man who had thought that the world would always indulge his pleasures, now forced into a hellish maturity of fear and isolation. All that, masked to perfection by this practiced persona: gambler, seducer, carefree aristocrat. Where was the real Andrys Tarrant, balanced between those extremes? How did one begin to seek him out?

"I could never destroy your work," he repeated. His hand turned over beneath hers, catching her fingers in a warm embrace. "And having these pieces restored . . . it's part of my healing. Supposed to be, anyway." He shook his head. "I don't really understand it. But someone I . . ." He hesitated, as if seeking the proper word. "Someone I *trust* advised me to have these things made, and I believe in him. Enough to try it." He laughed sadly. "Even if I can't for the life of me see how it's supposed to help."

His hand folded tightly over hers: warm contact, hungry touch. She could sense the need in him, not just for communion of the spirit but a far more substantive interaction. Passion and intimacy were allied within him; it was hard for him to seek out one without the other.

"Thank you," he said at last. "Thank you for listening. For giving me a chance."

"I wish I could do more," she said quietly. Knowing the words for the opening they were. Not even sure of how she meant them. "To help."

The bright eyes glittered, viridescent in the darkness. "You've done more than any woman has for years. Or any man, for that matter."

"Even your lawyers?" she chided gently. Aware that her heart was pounding anew, in response to words not even being said.

"In a way," he said softly. He drew up her hand to his lips, and kissed it gently. Soft touch, gently erotic; she felt fire spreading up her arm, fanning out from the contact.

"Come," he whispered. "It's getting late. I'll walk you home."

He made no move to call for the check, but laid a handful of coins on the table that would have paid for such a meal three times over.

Then he helped her out of the booth, his touch warm upon her arm, his manner at once protective and possessive. The waiters did not question his leaving before a bill had been rendered, which meant that he had done this many, many times before. With how many women? she wondered. Had they all trembled like she did at his touch, or were they veterans of the same game, who knew what words and special gestures might be employed to maintain control of each move?

It was a long walk to her apartment, for which she was grateful. She needed the long dark streets, half-abandoned, quiet. She needed time to pull herself together. He walked by her side companionably enough, but she could sense the tension in him. Pain. Uncertainty. Desire. She could feel his warmth near her arm as their steps brought them close to each other, as his hand almost—*almost*—reached out and took hers. So very close. Her skin tingled with the nearness of him, but she was afraid to initiate any contact. What would such an act signify in his world, in that endless round of courtship and flirtation which was his normal venue? How did one approach a man like this, without giving him license to claim one's soul?

And then: Her building. Her stairs. Two flights of them, wide and well-lit. A landing, with four doors. He let her lead the way, to the third door in line. Keys. They were somewhere. She fumbled for them, fearing to look at him. Afraid she would get lost in his eyes forever if she did. Afraid she might wake up in the morning to find him beside her and never know how he had gotten there, or if he would ever leave. Or if she ever *wanted* him to leave.

Then he took her face gently in one hand—ever so gently, a butterfly's touch could not have been lighter—and tipped her head back until she was looking right at him. Warm eyes, living eyes, not like the Hunter's at all. And yet the two men were linked, not just in appearance but in essence. The Hunter's passion had sired this man; the Hunter's blood ran in his veins. How could she look at Andrys Tarrant and not feel the power of his forebear's presence?

"Thank you," he said softly. "For listening." His fingers stroked her cheek gently as he spoke, sending shivers down her spine. "It's been a long time since anyone did that."

She tried to respond, but the words caught in her throat. His fingers moved into her hair, twining amidst the dark strands. Sweet, possessive caress. "I . . ." she whispered, but the rest of the words were all gone. Lost, as all of language was lost to her now.

He studied her for a moment and then leaned down to kiss her slowly—oh, gods, so slowly—so that she might pull away if she wanted to, drawing her close to him, one arm about her waist now and one hand entangled in her hair, his lips warm and so very sweet against her own. With a soft moan she shut her eyes, and her keys fell to the floor with a clatter as she clung to him, her heart pounding wildly against his chest. So close that she could feel the ridges of gold braid pressing against her breasts, the caress of fine silk against her cheek. She trembled as she held him, frightened by the hunger she sensed in him, even more frightened by that which she sensed in herself. Never in her life had she felt such an utter lack of control—

And then the moment was over. He drew back from her slightly but did not release her. Studying her, she thought. Assessing her response. And what if he decided to press on with this evening's sport? She had no strength to resist this man, she realized that now. Even more: she had no *desire* to resist him.

But he stepped back, gently, his fingers releasing her hair with obvious reluctance, stroking her cheek as they withdrew. His fingertips left lines of fire on her skin, that spread heat throughout her body. It took everything she had not to move into his arms again, to invite a more lasting intimacy. Then, suddenly, his feet brushed the keys on the floor; the unexpected noise shattered the fragile moment like glass. With a smile he stooped down and scooped them up, then placed them in her hand. Gently he folded her fingers over them, each motion a tiny caress.

"I'd like to see you again," he said quietly.

"I would like that," she whispered. Somehow managing to get the words out.

She thought that he would kiss her again—it seemed that he almost did—but instead he drew back from her. He was going to leave, she realized. Now. Before . . . Without . . . She didn't know if she was more relieved or disappointed.

"I'll call on you," he promised. And then he stepped away from her, and he bowed ever so slightly—an outdated gesture, so ridiculous for others, so graceful for him—and with a parting smile he strode casually down the stairs. Owning her soul, as perfectly as if he had stayed the night to claim it in passion.

Head pounding, knees weak, she leaned against the door to her apartment and tried to catch her breath.

Dear gods, she prayed. Even her inner voice was shaking. *What have I gotten myself into?*

He could have done it, he thought. Could have had her tonight. Could have lost himself in the heat of her body, drowned out his sorrow in a few desperate hours of pleasure.

But he hadn't. And that wasn't like him.

What had happened?

Walking down the night-shrouded streets, he struggled to comprehend his own feelings. What made this woman so unnerving? What made him so uncertain about how to handle her? Surely it wasn't a fear of impotence this time; his body had signaled its willingness to cooperate hours ago. So what was the problem? Fate had provided him with a cool, clear night and a beautiful woman, and hours of leisure to have his way with both. . . .

Only I don't want to hurt her, he thought.

It was a strange sensation. Usually he didn't care what happened to women once they left his arms; the stronger ones came back for more, the weaker ones would learn to be more careful in the future. But this girl . . . she awakened wholly new feelings within him, emotions he didn't even know how to name, much less respond to. The thought that he might cause her pain for an instant, even by so harmless a vehicle as seduction, was unbearable to him. And he had seen the fear in her eyes. Pleasure also, and a hunger to match his own, but the fear was there. And he couldn't bear to make that worse. Not for any price.

He remembered her touch on his hand, in the restaurant. So tender. So caring. When was the last time a woman had really cared about him? Or anyone, for that matter? When was the last time he'd kissed a woman and sensed nothing but pleasure in her—not some cold calculation of how much he was worth, how much he might be enticed to spend on her, how much she might manage to get from him in the long run if she played her cards right? It had been bad in the days before his family's death, but a thousand times worse afterward, when the whole Tarrant fortune was his. It was all part of the game, he'd told himself. He'd come to expect it, and learned not to be bitter.

But this woman was different. This woman, when she kissed him—

He had to stop in the street for a moment, as the memory of that experience overwhelmed him. How long had it been since he had felt such acute desire for a woman? His hands shook as he remembered the silken smoothness of her hair between his fingers, the velvet softness of her cheek. Her scent was alive in his nostrils, sweet natural perfume more perfect than any man-made imitation. The desire he felt was more intense than any sensation which drugs might have spawned, and for the first time in months it occurred to him that he might make it through a night without some artificial aid to support him. Just memories. Just sweet, tantalizing memories, melding into erotic dreams before the dawn.

With quickened step he hastened toward the hotel. The gambling rooms would be open by now, spreading their heavy doors wide to greet the night; perhaps he should take to the card table and see what fortune this mood could win him. Who could say what wagers he might not win tonight, with energy like this pouring through his veins?

But gambling no longer meant to him what it once did, and even the prospect of such a triumph was not enough to tempt him into the company of strangers tonight. Inheriting the Tarrant fortune had accomplished what all the stern disapproval of his family never could, and soured the taste of such games forever. Oh, he still played, but it was more for sport than fortune now; his only real delight was in breaking those whose skill or audacity made them seemed charmed, in pitting his fae-luck against their own. And finding such men required prowling the casinos like a hunter, alert for the smell of rich and arrogant prey ... no, he was not in the mood for such games tonight.

Maybe a whore, he thought, as he climbed the gleaming numarble stairs at the Paradisio's entrance. Nodding to the very doorman who had so recently challenged his right to enter the lavish hotel. With the right money and some connections he could probably find himself a pale, slender girl; if not one with jet-black hair, then one who would be willing to dye it for a price. It certainly wouldn't be the first time he had used his wealth to purchase a fantasy. What would that be like, he wondered, to douse the night's fire in a woman so like *her*. . . .

Only there was no one like her, he knew that. The complex essence of womanhood that so affected him with Narilka Lessing could not be found in a whore. And if he thought that imagination alone could bridge such a gap, that it would be enough to have any pale, black-haired woman spread out beneath him ... then he was asking for failure yet again. And he had tasted enough of *that* experience in the last few years to last him a lifetime.

No, he thought, as he headed toward his suite, the memory would be enough for tonight. A memory that would meld into sweet dreams when he retired, for once unobscured by a haze of drugs or the bitter distortion of alcohol. Because tonight he felt no need for drugs or liquor, or even a passing desire for them. He was drunk on this girl, (so slender, so fragile, not even his type!) and it was a heady intoxication. Far more intense than mere drugs could supply.

Optimism stirred within him, an unfamiliar emotion. If he could make it through one night without artificial aids, could he do it again at some future date? Could he perhaps, in time, learn to take control of his life again? The concept was elating. Maybe when this nightmare was over, maybe if Gerald Tarrant died and he survived, he could start his life all over and do it right—

"Welcome home," Calesta greeted him.

His fragile hopes expired in an instant, smothered by the power of the demon's presence; a cold and hungry hate took its place. The transition was so swift that it was physically stunning, and it was a long moment before Andrys could pull himself together enough to close the suite's door, so that none might hear them. And an even longer moment before he could find his voice.

"What do you want?"

The demon chuckled coldly. "Hardly a suitable welcome for your ally."

He drew in a deep breath, struggling for control. Trying to recover his image of the girl, his fragile hopes, anything of the last half hour . . . but his effort was in vain. Such gentle emotions had no place in Calesta's presence.

At last he stammered, "Why are you here?"

"You wanted instructions. I came to supply them."

He dared to look up at the demon, to meet those inhuman eyes head-on. "Why now?" he challenged him. "I've called to you often enough. I've begged for instruction! Why come to me now, the one night I don't need you?"

The demon hissed softly; the sound reminded Andrys of a snake about to strike. "You don't need me?"

The threat behind Calesta's words chilled him to the core. *I could leave you alone forever. Then what would you have?* Hurriedly he struggled to explain himself. "I didn't mean . . . it's just . . . tonight. . . ."

The demon laughed; the harsh, grating sound made Andrys quail. "You poor fool! Is it the girl who inspires such courage? You found yourself a single night's comfort and now the battle is over?" His voice was a jagged thing, that scraped Andrys' skin like shards of glass. "And what do you think the Hunter will do when he finds out that his mortal enemy has fallen for a woman? Do you think really think he'll allow you that comfort, once our battle is fully joined? Or any other? You're a walking death sentence, Andrys Tarrant, and anyone you touch—anyone who touches *you*—will be felled by it. Or did you think that you could make war on the Hunter without him striking back?"

The room seemed to swirl about him. He reached for a chair and somehow managed to fall into it, heavily. His hands seemed numb; his heart was ice.

"Perhaps you've forgotten what manner of creature you've sworn to fight." The demon paused. "Perhaps I should remind you."

"No—"

Memories swirled about him, horrific images all too familiar. A hundred times more intense than what he had recalled in the restaurant, a thousand times more horrible. The dismembered head of Samiel Tarrant gazed down at him from its grisly throne, a sardonic smile twisting its lips. *Dared to dream of love, did you?* The bloodsoaked eyes narrowed in amusement. *What makes think you're worthy of loving anyone?*

"Make it stop," he begged. Shutting his eyes, trying to shut out the visions. Samiel staring at him. Betrise. All of them. "Please. Make it stop!"

The visions faded. His hands, white-knuckled, gripped the chair with painful pressure.

"I think we understand each other," the demon assessed.

Shaken, he whispered hoarsely, "What do you want me to do?"

"You will go to the cathedral in the great square of Jaggonath. You will attend the services of your God. Pray with your fellows as Gerald Tarrant instructed, as if you intended to fulfill his misplaced vision."

It seemed to Andrys that there must surely be more instructions, but the demon said no more. After a long moment of silence Andrys dared, "And then what?"

"That's all. For now."

"I don't understand," he protested weakly. "How will that hurt him?"

The demon hissed sharply. "Do you question me now? Or doubt my plans? A thousand elements must all be orchestrated to perfection in order to bring the Hunter down, and you're just one of them! Go where I tell you. Do what I say. Your own hand will bring about Gerald Tarrant's downfall, I promise you." He paused. "Or isn't that enough for you?"

He lowered his head, lacking the strength—or was it the courage?—to argue. "It's enough," he whispered. "I'll go."

"Every sabbath. You understand? I want you to be seen there. One of the faithful."

"I understand."

The gift came then, inserted into his brain with sure demonic skill, the ultimate reward for obedience: visions of vengeance that flooded his soul, catching him up in a whirlwind of anticipated triumph. He fought it for a moment, clinging to the gentleness of his former mood like a lifeline—and then it swept him away and he was lost in it, lost in a hatred and a blood lust and a hunger for revenge so desperate that he shook as it swept through him. It lasted forever and yet it could not last long enough, and when it was over he collapsed back into the chair, shaking from the sudden withdrawal.

"Someday those dreams will become reality," the demon promised. "Think of the pleasure of that moment! Worth more than a little sacrifice now, I should think."

He said nothing. He had no words. The memory of the girl was hazy now, unclear, its outlines obscured by clouds of blood. Had he imagined that he might love? Where was there room for love in this life of his, lived in the Hunter's shadow?

"There is something else," the demon warned him.

"What?" he choked out. *What more than this?*

"He'll never kill you because you're the last living Tarrant. That's what makes you capable of striking back at him; under any other circumstances such a move would be suicidal." He paused meaningfully. "But what would happen if another Tarrant were born? Maybe not one to whom you gave the name, but one who might, in time, lay claim to it."

"But I never—" he began.

And then what the demon was saying hit him. It hit him hard.

"I think that you should be careful where you spill your seed, Andrys Tarrant. Because the moment you impregnate a woman—*any* woman—the Hunter will have no more reason to spare you." In a chilling tone he added, "And I doubt very much that he would be merciful in killing you, after you so flagrantly defied him."

Andrys shut his eyes tightly; fear churned coldly in his gut. Dear God in Heaven! how many chances had he already taken, never thinking, never realizing. . . . Oh, he had always been careful, but sex was a gambler's game and he knew it; sooner or later even the best contraceptive might betray you. And if so . . . if so . . .

"I see that my meaning is clear," the demon approved.

Something landed in his lap, startling him; it was a moment before he could muster the physical control to take it up, and even then his fingers seemed numb. A small object, that rattled when it moved. Cool glass, with a rubber stopper.

Pills.

"I thought you might need them," Calesta said dryly. "After all, we have a long battle ahead of us. I would hate to see you lose your nerve."

The coldness in the room faded; the demon was gone. Andrys gripped the bottle in his hand, feeling hot tears squeeze from his eyes. What color were the pills, what essence was their magic? It didn't matter. They all brought forgetfulness, one way or another. They were all ways of escaping this world, with its inescapable nightmares. The only escape there was, other than death.

His hand clenched tightly around the bottle, Andrys Tarrant wept.

Ten

The Patriarch dreamed of war.

. . . hundreds on the mountainside, maybe thousands, men and women, priests and layfolk, and the energy that arises from them ripples in the air overhead, like heat . . .

. . . armor in bits and pieces, mismatched . . .

. . . and banners: the circle, the Earth-in-circle, and some that are simply red. Red for blood, red for triumph, red for cleansing. . . .

. . . These are my people, he thinks, and he gazes out upon them in wonder. These are my people, who only yesterday brought down a pagan temple and terrorized its faithful. These are my people, who were willing to risk imprisonment and worse to vent their intolerance, and now are channeling all that negative energy into this blessed enterprise. These are my people, who may die on the morrow or live to go home again, but who will never forget this moment, or its transforming power.

He walks among the troops, his children, looking for familiar faces among the scores of strangers. There are people here from all across the continent, come to test their faith in this special arena. He loves them. He loves them as one loves children. He loves them as the birds must love, when they push their babies out of the nest to force their wings to open. It is a special and terrible love, and he thanks God for letting him taste it.

Over the mountains, beyond vision but not beyond march, lies the Forest. Heart of evil by man's own decree, it is a symbol more powerful than any the Church could devise. Men are drawn to it, obsessed by it, and many will die fighting it in the battle yet to come. But it will not be as it was before, five hundred years ago in the age of their defeat. This time they will use the tools that Erna has pro-

vided, and focus their energies on one single point within that cor-rupted realm. Night's keep—Hell's watch—the Hunter's lair. Destroy it and the Forest will shake. Destroy its owner and the Forest will crumble, its power soured to chaos, its very earth made malleable by that action.

Five hundred years ago the Church tried to conquer a universe, and reaped its own devastation. This time they make war against a symbol, and all the power of God will back them. He feels the thrill of that utter certainty as he looks out over his troops, as his eyes fix upon the one special weapon which will make their invasion possible—

He awoke. His heart was beating loudly, and he lay still while it slowly quieted. His fists were clenched by his sides; he forced them to open. Was this the third time he'd had that dream, or the fourth? It clearly wasn't a clairvoyancy, as so many other dreams were, but the scent of prophecy clung to it nonetheless. Should he take it seriously or dismiss it, as he had done before? Surely persistence should translate to something.

With a groan he got out of his bed and drew on a robe that lay waiting for him. The heavy silk overlapped tightly about a body that was losing weight from its battle with stress, and tonight it seemed that even his slippers were loose. He was wasting away along with his people, he thought. Some day he would be gone entirely, and only a shadow would remain to guide them.

Leaving his bedroom, he walked down the narrow corridor that led to his private chapel. The servant who was posted outside it against his midnight need jumped to his feet as he came by, startled into sudden waking by his footsteps on the hardwood floor, but he waved him back to his slumber. His was a need that could only be met in solitude.

At the end of the corridor was the door to the chapel. He opened it and stepped inside, shutting the door behind him. There were candles burning beside the altar—it was the servant's job to keep them alight at night—but their illumination was minimal, and most of the chamber was shrouded in shadow. He came to the altar and knelt before it, and all the fear and the doubt which he had been cloistering within his heart came pouring out, an undertide to prayer.

Most holy God, whose Eye is upon us always, whose Word is our salvation. Grant me the grace of Your Insight, that I may serve Your Will more perfectly.

It wasn't the first night he'd come here since the dreams started, and if he stayed until dawn to pray, it wouldn't be the first time that happened either. And now *this* dream was back, and he was no less tormented by it than he had been the last time, or the time before. Because it promised him an answer to his problems, and at the same time posed an even greater question. If it was a true prophecy—if this battle was the course that God intended for him—what would the cost of it be? Not to him, or to the men who fought beside him, but to the generations that would come after?

How tempting it is to live in that dream, where all my people's hatred and destructive energy can be redirected against a more suitable enemy. How tempting, to imagine that the catharsis of battle can wipe our souls clean of this violence. But that's not how the human mind works. If we indulge our darker instincts, if we tell ourselves that yes, they are acceptable if properly channeled—even admirable, under the right circumstances—what do we do when this battle is over! How do we make these soldiers into plain men and women again, and cleanse them of their taste for blood so that they might retire to normal lives! How do we teach them to savor the peace their efforts have won them, rather than seek a new forum for violence!

He had been tormented by those questions since his first dream of battle. It was a torment which only grew worse as the riots continued, as night after night he was called from his bed or his study chamber to witness some new act of violence. All in the name of God, the rioters claimed. Couldn't they see that by worshiping violence they had created a new god, who was slowly consuming them? That worried him far more than the lawsuits. which might drain his Church of economic vigor but could never quell its spirit. This violence threatened the very heart of who and what they were.

And then there was Vryce's report. He felt himself tense up at the mere thought of the man, at the name which now automatically inspired his rage. But whatever he might think of Vryce himself, the report could not be ignored. How did the Iezu demon Calesta connect to all of this? Was he the unseen instigator in this wave of violence? If so, then it would do little good to address human issues in the matter. Any solution which the Church pursued would succeed only up until the point when Calesta was willing to strike again. How did you fight a creature who could read the darkness in men's hearts and stoke it to such new strength, as naturally as a man drew breath?

He lowered his head to pray again, but a faint sound from behind him alerted him to the presence of someone or something else in the room. He turned about slowly, expecting no more than a young acolyte with a message to bear, or perhaps his chamber-servant coming to see if there was anything he needed. What he saw was something else again, and he rose to his feet quickly, wondering how a stranger had gotten in past his private guard.

The stranger stepped forward as he watched, just far enough that the candlelight could pick out highlights along his pale, aristocratic features. He was tall and slender, and dressed in a manner that was at once modern and reminiscent of the Revival period. Flame-born highlights played upon shoulder length hair, and sparked along the gold headband that held it in place. His features were so unmarked by worldly trouble that his face might have seemed that of an angel, had the eyes not been so dark, so hungry, so . . . empty.

"Do you know who I am?" The man's voice was clear and fine and his words, though no louder than a whisper, seemed to echo in the small chamber like some strange music. The Patriarch studied him, and then nodded. Yes, he knew. Vryce's sketches had been good enough for that. The knowledge both elated and terrified him, but he was statesman enough not to let those emotions show, or to let them sound in his voice.

In a voice that was tightly controlled, he asked, "Why are you here?"

The dark eyes flickered toward the altar, then back again. "A fate that neither you nor I would court has made us allies, it seems. I came to offer my services."

"No." His heart was racing; it took everything he had to sound calm and collected when he was anything but. Was he really standing here talking to the man who founded and then betrayed his Church? Up until a year ago he would have considered that patently impossible. Even now, knowing otherwise, it was hard to absorb the truth. "Not allies, Neocount. Enemies."

The man's expression darkened ever so slightly, and he stepped forward as if to approach the Patriarch; with a flutter of fear in his heart, the Holy Father moved back. Then he realized that his visitor wasn't moving toward him, but toward the altar. The Patriarch's soul cried out for him to protect his holy symbols from the touch—or even the scrutiny—of this damned creature, but a distant, more reasonable part of him knew that it would be suicide to even attempt it. And it didn't really matter, did it? The gold on the altar was simple metal, no more. The symbols themselves could be melted down to slag without injuring his faith. If the Prophet had taught them nothing else, it was that God didn't reside in such things.

The Prophet. A cold thrill shivered through his flesh as he realized just what it was that stood before him. Not the Prophet any longer, but a damned and degenerate creature who wore the Prophet's identity like a ragged bit of cast-off clothing. Was this the chill that Vryce had felt, when he first stood in his presence? Did he grow numb to it after a time, or simply learn to ignore its warning?

When the man reached the altar he reached out to its central figure, a double circle sculpted in gold. He traced the interlocked shapes with a death-pale finger, and his nostrils flared as if taking in the scent of this place. Was he testing the Patriarch, seeing if he would respond? Despite his powerful instinct to protect the altar, the Patriarch forced himself to hold back. God alone knew what this creature would do if he moved against him.

After a moment the Hunter turned to face the Holy Father once more. His eyes were no longer black but a pale, glistening gray. There was a coldness in them that reminded the Holy Father of glacial ice, and of death. They were the eyes of the damned, that had gazed upon the glories of the One God and then turned away forever. Gazing at them, the Patriarch couldn't help but shudder.

"Believe as you will," the visitor said. "It's taken me years to come to this point; why should you accept it in a single night? We have the same enemy, therefore we fight the same war. Let that be enough."

Calesta. He felt the name take shape within his brain, etched in ice. For one brief moment he envisioned what power the Church could wield, with this man's knowledge and skill harnessed to its purpose—and then that image shattered like glass, as the real threat of the situation hit home. *This is how Vryce started,* he thought, chilled. *And this is how the Prophet fell.*

"It isn't enough," he said quietly. The strength in his own voice surprised him. "Not for that kind of alliance."

For a moment the Hunter said nothing. It was impossible to read his expression, or otherwise guess at the tenor of his emotions. The death-pale face was a mask, that permitted no insight.

"I've come to make you an offer," he said at last. "For the sake of our common cause. Nothing more."

He shook his head slowly. "I want nothing of yours."

"Even if my gift would enable your Church to survive?"

"It would be at the cost of my soul, and the souls of all my faithful. What kind of triumph is that?"

The pale eyes narrowed, and he sensed a cold anger rising in the man. He neither moved back nor looked away, but met the unspoken assault with a shield of utter calm. His faith would preserve him. Even if this man killed him now, his God would protect his soul.

At last his visitor said, in a razor-edged voice, "You already have what you need to safeguard your Church. What you lack is an understanding of how to use it. I came to bring you that, no more."

"And I reject that offer," he said coolly. Watching a flicker of anger spark in those pale, dead eyes. "I'm not Damien Vryce, or any of the other souls you've corrupted over the years. Some of those must have started out just this way, yes? Wanting your power enough to compromise their faith. *Trusting* you, long enough to forget who and what they were." Strength was coming into his voice now, and the full oratory power of a Patriarch. "I won't make Vryce's mistake," he said firmly. "I won't take that first step. We'll wage our battles alone, and win them or lose them according to God's will."

He shook his head. "You don't understand what losing means in this case. The threat to all you stand for—"

"*I understand* that what stands before me now is a man who's lived apart from the Church for nearly ten centuries. Should I favor his interpretation of the Law over my own? Should I abandon all my learning, and the centuries of struggle that came before me, for an alliance that would make mockery of my faith? I think not."

"Then you'll go down," he said sharply, "and the Church will go down with you."

"If that's God's will, then so be it. At least our souls will be clean."

"Who knows your God's will better than I? As your Prophet—"

"The Prophet is dead!" the Patriarch snapped. "He died the day that he murdered his wife and children, and no man's will can resurrect him. Something else took his place that night, that wears his body and uses his voice, but that *thing* isn't a man, and it certainly isn't an ally of the Church. However well it pretends to be."

An icy fire burned in the depths of those pale eyes, reflections of a rage so venemous that if Tarrant should let it loose, even for a moment, the Patriarch knew it would consume him utterly. It was hard not to tremble in the face of such a thing, but he sensed that fear— any kind of fear—would allow this creature to take possession of his soul. That he must never permit.

"I could have killed your guard on the way in," Tarrant told him. "In another time and place I would surely have done so, and gained strength from his death. I didn't. Let that be a sign of my sincerity. A token—if you will—of my true intentions."

"The day I judge a man by such standards," he retorted, "is the day I turn in my robes."

"We're fighting the same war!" There was anger in his voice now, frigid and dangerous. "Can't you see that? How do I get through to you?"

"You know the way," he said quietly. Inside his heart was pounding wildly, but he managed to keep his voice calm. In the face of the Hunter's rage there was power in tranquility. "You've known the way for nine centuries now."

The Hunter's eyes narrowed, and he took a step backward. He reached one hand into a pocket as though seeking some kind of weapon, and the Patriarch stiffened. But the object he drew forth was no weapon, at least not of any kind the Patriarch had ever seen. It was a large crystal, finely faceted, of a deep blue color so resonant that it seemed to give off light of its own. Such a color couldn't exist naturally in this chamber, the Patriarch realized, not with the golden light of the candleflames compromising its hue. Its very clarity sang of sorcery.

The Hunter turned the object so that the Patriarch might see all sides of it; there was no denying the sense of power that resonated from its polished planes. "Do you know what a ward is?" he asked. Watching him, watching the stone, the Patriarch did not reply. "It's a Working designed to be independent of its maker, so that the two are no longer connected. It has a trigger—in this case your own will— and the ability to tap the currents for power, in order to fuel itself. In short," he said, indicating the object in his hand, "this is no longer connected to me, or to any other living creature. It will fulfill its one purpose and then expire. Do you understand that?"

"I want nothing of yours," he said quietly.

"Then you're a fool!" he snapped. "And you'll drag your Church down with you!" He held up the deep blue ward to catch the light; cobalt shimmers ran across its facets like ripples on a dark lake. "All I offer you is knowledge. The chance to see your own arsenal for what it is, without delusion masking it. That knowledge could save your people!" His pale eyes fixed on the Patriarch again, with fierce intensity. "It will also, most probably, destroy you." He held the crystal aloft as if in illustration, then slowly laid it down upon the altar cloth. "Are you willing to make such a sacrifice for your Church? I wonder."

"Don't pretend to test me," the Patriarch warned. "You of all people have lost that right."

The Hunter tensed, and for a minute the Patriarch thought that he had finally pushed him too far, that he would give in to his rage and strike out at him. He braced himself, praying for courage, trying to master his fear so that this damned creature couldn't benefit from it.

But a minute passed, and then two, and then he sensed that the crisis was over. In a voice that was as chill as death itself, the Hunter said, "Take it up if you want to use it. Fold it in your hand, and it'll do the rest." He bowed, stiffly and formally. "It's your choice."

He turned then, and left the chamber quickly. Too quickly for the Patriarch to voice a protest. Far too quickly for him to do what he wanted, which was to take up the crystalline ward and force it upon him, to make him take it back to whatever hellish domain had forged it. Silk faded into shadow and without any sound to mark his passage, be it footstep or a whisper of flesh-upon-flesh or the soft creak of a door hinge, Gerald Tarrant was gone.

The deep blue crystal lay where he had left it, between two candles on the altar. There it shimmered with a life of its own, sparkling with reflected flames. What was this thing that the Hunter had left? Knowledge? Perhaps. Sorcery? Without question. A chance for victory? Maybe.

Temptation.

Slowly he lowered himself to his knees before the altar. *Oh, my God,* he prayed, *fill me with Your strength. Guide me with Your certainty. Keep my eyes fixed on Your path, so that I may never waver.*

Blue facets, glinting in the candlelight. Power, in carefully measured dose. Was this thing salvation? Destruction? Or both? *The world isn't made up of black and white, but shades of gray.* Who had said that once? Vryce? He shivered as the words struck home. *Too easy an answer,* he told himself. *Too tempting a refuge. Indecision is cowardice. Uncertainty is weakness. And we can afford neither, in the face of this enemy.*

Trembling, he prayed.

Eleven

The Jaggonath cathedral was a far more impressive building than Andrys had expected, and for some time he just stood in the square opposite it, savoring the strange mix of emotions it aroused. It wasn't merely a question of how grand the building looked, but of what that grandeur implied. Here in the east, where moderate quakes shook the city several times each month, it was rare to see a building more than two stories in height, and even the simplest hovel was studded with quake-wards designed to keep it intact. Yet here was an edifice that rose into the heavens in seeming defiance of earthquakes, its gleaming arches bright against the sky, its polished facade brazenly naked of any protective Working. Could faith alone manifest enough power to keep such a building standing, or were there internal secrets of construction wedded to the polished stone that lent it a more earthy strength? Andrys knew that the walls of his own keep back in Merentha had been built in such a manner, with resiliant inner layers designed to keep the building standing should its stones and mortar ever give way. Even so, it, too, was reinforced by wardings, and he had little doubt that without them the keep would have been shaken to pieces long ago. Could prayers alone maintain such a building as this, when sorcery was forbidden within its bounds? It was a wondrous and intimidating concept.

And more.

Gazing up at the stained glass windows so similar to those in the Tarrant keep, drinking in the familiar line of arches and buttresses, pierced-work and finials, he felt an upwelling of homesickness in his soul so powerful that for a moment he had to fight back tears. What he wouldn't give to go home now! No, he corrected himself bitterly: what he wouldn't give to *have* a home to go to, rather than that skeleton of a keep filled with ghosts and memories and the scent of Tarrant blood. There was no home for him now: not there, not anywhere.

With a shiver he forced himself to start toward the cathedral, though the thought of going inside it filled him with dread. There was something unclean about entering this building at the bidding of a demon, and he half expected to be struck down for it before he crossed the portal. When he finally managed to bring himself to enter, his heart was pounding so wildly that he was sure the other people there could hear it. But they passed him by in utter ignorance of his state, leaving him alone to face his fears.

Always alone.

He drew in a deep breath for courage and made his way hesitantly into the sanctuary. No one and nothing stopped him. Surely this was just a temporary reprieve, he thought. Surely the One God would sense his purpose in being here, and would rage at his use of the Church for a private vendetta. Could Calesta save him then? Could any demon even enter this place, which the God of Earth had sanctified?

The sanctuary was large, and not yet half full. He chose a seat in the very last row, in the shadow of the balcony. From there he could watch the proceedings without being seen clearly by anyone. It wasn't exactly what Calesta wanted—the demon had ordered him to "be seen"—but for this first visit it would have to be good enough; he felt too vulnerable to do otherwise. He watched as the priest approached the dais, as his ritual words began the afternoon service. Andrys knew the rites of the Church vaguely, distantly, as one recalled something from one's childhood. Family rituals had been repeated often enough to carve out a place in his memory without his being aware of the details. Little good it had done his family to dedicate their lives to the One God, he thought bitterly. Perhaps a pagan deity would have done more to protect its worshipers. Perhaps it would have given them some power to stand up against the horror that stalked them, the death that was waiting—

Stop it, he ordered himself. He folded his shaking hands in his lap, and tried to breathe evenly. A cold sweat had broken out on his forehead, but it was long minutes before he felt steady enough to raise up a hand and wipe it away. What was the point of this visit? he wondered. Why was Calesta making him endure this? Was there something the demon expected him to *do* here? And if so, why wouldn't he just tell him what it was and get it over with?

It was then that his eyes, seeking something to focus on other than the priest, looked beyond the podium at the head of the aisle and fixed on a mural that adorned one section of the upper wall. It caught his attention because of its human subject matter—the Church forbade all but a few symbolic representations of human-kind—but then it held his attention, it *gripped* his attention, because of who and what that human was.

Despite himself he rose to his feet, drawn to the brilliant mural even as he was repelled by it. He was all but deaf to the service going on as he stared at the painting in horrified fascination. It was the Prophet, there was no doubt of that. The figure had no face as such— that was Church tradition—but it glowed with a light that made the absence seem a deliberate artistic choice, rather than philosophical censure. At its feet a creature writhed whose outline was unclear, but it hinted at a form that was at once serpentine and spiderlike: black and sinuous, with a large fanged head like that of a snake at one end, and a hint of several dozen smaller heads at the other. The Prophet-figure had a foot on the neck of the greater head and was running it through with a spear that glowed hot white, sun-pure in its energy. Symbolism, Andrys thought, his heart pounding wildly. It was only symbolism. The faith of the Prophet had bound the Evil One to darkness, and rendered it unable to maintain earthly form. The faith of the One God was more powerful than all the evils which this planet had conjured. It was a familiar image, and one that he had seen rendered before in the books of his faith. It was familiar. It was traditional. It should have passed without notice, just like all the other symbolic murals that adorned the inner walls of the sanctuary.

But this one was different.

The figure wore the breastplate. *His* breastplate! Embossed with the Earth-sun in that unlikely golden color, rays spreading out in just the way that he had drawn them, copying Gerald Tarrant's own ren-derings. Andrys felt sick as he looked up at the mural, as the power of its image hit home. Was this what Calesta wanted him to see— that his fear and his shame were emblazoned on the cathedral wall for all to witness? The vast sanctuary suddenly seemed very close, and its air was hard to breathe. He had to get out of here. He had to get away from that thing, far away, before its presence strangled him utterly. Weak-legged, he struggled to work his way down the row of seats to where the exit was. It seemed to him that there were eyes in that painted face, pale gray eyes that watched him from across the sanctuary. Thank God he was far enough from the other congregants that few seemed to notice his departure; as for the priest, he probably saw him from his standpoint up at the dais, but he wouldn't interrupt the traditional service to comment upon the departure of one way-ward parishioner. Dear God, if he only knew. . . .

He managed to get outside—somehow—and made his way from the great double doors to a place some few yards away where trees provided a modicum of shade. Several strangers noticed his shaky passage and began to approach as if they meant to offer help, but he warned them off with a look and leaned heavily against a tree trunk, trying to catch his breath.

I failed you, Calesta. Despair was a knot in his heart, a knife in his soul. *You told me what to do and I couldn't. I couldn't!* But if he'd hoped for any kind of response from his patron, he wasn't going to get it here. No demon could manifest on the One God's doorstep. He had to face this moment alone.

God, why couldn't he have brought his pills with him? Even a few grains of slowtime, just to act as a tranquilizer. He saw a few passers-by staring at him, and he tried to look stronger than he felt so that they wouldn't come over to help him. After a moment they looked away and continued walking, and he breathed a sigh that was half re-lief and half dread.

He knew what he had to do. He knew, but he couldn't face it. How could he go back in there, back in where *that* was, and endure a whole service beneath that living image of his enemy? *I'm not that strong,* he despaired, and sickness welled up so strongly inside him that for a moment he could hardly breathe. *I can't do it.*

Then you will never have your revenge, a cool voice warned.

Startled, he stiffened. Was that Calesta? Here? For some reason that possibility scared him more than all the rest combined, that his demon-patron could speak to him so close to God's holy altar. Wasn't the very point of the Church worship supposed to be control of such creatures?

Did you think it would be easy, Andrys Tarrant? Did you think you could conquer the Hunter without pain?

The words didn't comfort him, but rather made him feel horribly isolated. In that church were hundreds of worshipers sharing a com-munion he could never taste, a faith he had no right to counterfeit; here was he with his demon guide, utterly alone even in the midst of a crowd. How long could he go on like this, pretending that he was coping? Pretending that he was truly alive? He needed more than a demon's voice in his head to keep going; he needed human warmth, human contact, human touch . . . a vision of the black-haired girl took shape before him, and he cried out softly in pain for wanting her. Not that. Never that. To court her now was to condemn her to death—or worse—and he could never, ever be the cause of that. Not even though it made his soul bleed to have her so close, so very close, and not reach out to her.

If you prefer to continue without me, the cold voice warned, *that can be arranged.*

That fear was worse than all the others combined. "No!" he whispered. "Don't leave me!" What would he be without Calesta? He no longer had a life of his own, but was defined by the demon's will, the demon's plans. How would he survive alone, facing his memories with no hope of redress?

Then go, the voice commanded, and its tone was like acid. *Obey.*

Slowly, reluctantly, he turned back toward the cathedral. The outer doors were still open; the inner doors, leading to the sanctuary, beckoned. Slowly he walked up the polished stone stairs once more, and then hesitated. Could he sit through the rest of the ritual without staring at the portrait of his ancestor, without reliving his one bloody memory of the man? Why should his quest for vengeance demand such a trial?

"Calesta—" he whispered.

Obey, the voice hissed, and its tone made his skin crawl. *Or our compact ends here and now.*

Terrified of the memories that the mural would awaken, but far more afraid of being abandoned by the only living creature who could give him back his soul, Andrys Tarrant forced himself to cross the foyer and enter the sanctuary once again. May God forgive him for his presence here, for his use of the Church to further a demon's plans. May God understand that in the end he would be serving His cause, ridding this world of one of the greatest evils it had ever produced. May God forgive . . . everything.

Behind him, out of hearing, Calesta laughed.

Twelve

In the depths of the Forest

In the Hunter's citadel

The albino moved silently, secretly, grateful for the Hunter's absence.

Through fae-sealed doors he went, well-warded portals protecting the Hunter's domain. He knew the signs to open them. Down curving stairs, well-guarded by demonlings. He knew how to turn them aside. Into the workshop, and through it. To the secret room beyond, and its torture table: the heart and soul of Gerald Tarrant's dominion.

Wisps of blackness trailed behind him, like smoke from a candle flame. *There there there,* voices whispered as it passed. *It must be in that place. That place only.*

If one's eyes were sensitive enough, one could see the memories that clung to this place. Almea Tarrant, dying a slow and painful death by her husband's hand. Gerald Tarrant's two youngest children, crying out as their father betrayed them. Three elements in a compact established centuries ago, with power enough to sustain a man past death. Three deaths. Nine centuries. Not a bad deal, when all was considered.

The blackness followed him into the chamber and paused there, where it coalesced into a single dark flame. *It should be done in Merentha,* a voice whispered hungrily. *It should be done where the pact was first made.*

"If I go to Merentha he'll find me out," the albino said sharply. "This place is a perfect copy of the original; it'll be good enough."

The blackness parted into a hundred tiny flames, a thousand; its voices fluttered like insects about the room. *Then do it do it do it now now NOW!*

He put a hand to the cold stone table, feeling the power that was lodged within it. The whole room was filled with power, centuries of it building and feeding and growing here in the subterranean darkness, seeded by memories of bloodshed and cruelty. Power such as few men ever knew. Power such as no man but the Hunter had ever controlled.

"State the terms of our compact," the albino demanded. It was his first command to the unnamed power that had approached him so very long ago. For one who had never commanded demons in his own right, it was a heady tonic. "Clearly and simply. I want no room for confusion."

We will sustain you as we once sustained him, beyond natural death. We will give you the Forest which was his, and show you how to control it. We will take him from the face of the planet, so that all his domain may be yours to claim.

"And in return?" he asked hungrily.

The lightless presence coalesced into a single flame, a limitless shadow; it hurt his eyes to look at it directly. *We must have him,* a single voice demanded. It was deeper than those which had sounded before, and power echoed in its wake. *Because his soul is independent of Us, We must have a channel in order to claim his flesh. You will give that to Us.*

"And Hell?"

It seemed to him there was laughter in that blackness; the tenor of it made his skin crawl. *He betrayed Us, and must be made to answer for it. Hell may have what is left when We are done.*

And then it asked: *Agreed?* A thousand voices once more, all echoing the same demand.

For a moment the albino hesitated. Only a moment, and not because he was afraid. This was an act to be savored: the moment in time at which his path and the Hunter's would separate forever. Centuries from now he would look back on this night and celebrate the birth of his soul, as mortals celebrated the birth of their flesh. And were not the two acts congruent in spirit as well as form? A baby's flesh existed for months before its arrival in the world; all that its "birth" signified was passage from one state of being to the next. So it was with him. So it was exactly. The Hunter was a fool, if he didn't see it coming.

"Agreed," he said.

He pulled a knife from his belt, white steel blade with a handle of human bone; the seal of the Hunter was etched into the blade. "When I first came to him, when I swore to serve him, he fed me a portion of his blood to bind us. He said that it would be with me always, part of my own blood for as long as I lived. A channel between us far stronger than mere fae could ever conjure." He drew the blade across his palm, sharply; blue blood welled up in the wound. "If so, then here it is." He made a fist and squeezed; the viscous fluid dripped to the tabletop and pooled there. "Flesh of his flesh: the blood of the Hunter. Take it from mine and use it to bind him. I give it to you freely."

A thousand sparks of black flame spurted to life on the tabletop. The hunger they exuded was so sharp that the albino stepped back quickly, lest he be drawn into the flames himself. How many men throughout history had summoned these demons with the intention of bargaining, only to be devoured themselves in the midst of their offering? Even the Hunter didn't trust the Unnamed Ones, and he had served them for over nine hundred years.

And just see where it got you, he thought triumphantly.

At last the flame drew back from his offering. The pool of blood seemed undiminished, but how little flesh did that awesome Power need for its work? A single cell would do it, or even a fragment of a cell, if it came from the Hunter himself. Freely sacrificed, it gained in power tenfold.

The skin of his palm twitched suddenly where he had gashed it; he looked down, to find the wound already closed.

It is done.

"The Forest is mine?" he asked hungrily.

When he has left the world of the living, then the Forest will be yours. Until then—

Hunger welled up inside him with such force that it left him reeling, a hunger that filled every cell of his body with such frigid fire that he shook to contain it. Not hunger for cruelty, or even for power; this was a need more simple, more primitive, more driving. The need to devour blood. Life. Hope. The hunger to destroy those things which the living cherished most, and consume them into his own dark soul. Into that boundless pit of cold, dark hunger which would never, ever be filled. . . .

With a cry he fell to his knees, his flesh convulsing as the black need filled him. More hunger than any human body could contain; more raw *need* than any human soul could ever satisfy. It remade him from the inside out, pulping his body and his soul until both were a raw, bleeding mass, and then it sculpted him anew. Making him into a more perfect container for its crimson frenzy.

No! he screamed. Pain folded about him like a fist and squeezed.

Dendrites tore loose in the confines of his skull and reattached in new, unhuman patterns. A section of the forebrain, pulped to liquid, oozed forth into his bloodstream to be processed as waste matter.

As it should have been for the Hunter, the voices proclaimed. *As it almost was, nine centuries ago.*

Shivering in hunger, the creature that was once called Amoril twitched in pain as the final ripples of transformation coursed through its flesh. It still looked human, to a degree. It could still act human, if it had to. Beyond that point all similarity ended.

What a pity that you lacked your master's understanding of Us, a thousand voices mused aloud. *And his strength. But then, that will make this relationship so much easier.*

Then the voices were gone, and there was only hunger.

Thirteen

Her children were restless.

She wasn't sure yet if that were good or bad. She had no way to communicate with them, to test them to see if their natures were right, if they were indeed what she had created them to be. Only a few of them could speak to her at all and those were, by that definition, her greatest failures. As for the rest, sometimes she was aware of them. Most often she was not. Sometimes the few who could speak to her brought her news of their distant siblings, but they themselves understood so little that their reports were hardly better than a dream.

She wondered if she should try again. In theory she could. In theory she had the strength and the knowledge, so why not make another attempt? But she lacked the emotional stamina she had once had, she was drained from an eternity of wasted efforts. She had cast out her hopes into the world countless times before and so few of her children had come back to her, so few of them tried to communicate, so very few understood their own nature, or why she had created them in the first place. So what was the point? Her first children were long gone now, and she could no longer remember what it was like to bond with them. These new children, the seeds of her desperation, would never know such intimacy. Why go on creating them as if that formula would change? As if somehow, magically, the same forces which killed her first family could be made to nurture these, the offspring of her despair?

These new children were restless. She knew that. She sensed it. They were testing the boundaries she had set for them, and soon she would have to decide their fate. Should she endure their rebellion, or wipe the slate clean and start over? With her first children—her *proper* children—the question would never have arisen. But with these strange creatures, in whom the bonds of family were so weak as to be virtually nonexistent, how was she to judge?

She would give them time, she decided. She would see where their restlessness led them. If it proved that their transgressions were serious, then their lives might be put to better use as fodder for a new generation. For there must be children. There must *always* be children. Living and learning, dreaming and needing, playing their parts without knowing they did so, in the hope that one of them might some day glimpse the greater game that controlled them all.

And then, she thought, then at last—

Dreams of the first family. Union. Hope.

She waited.

The Dark Within

Fourteen

The main temple of Saris was at the edge of town, just beyond one of Jaggonath's better neighborhoods. Though the goddess had other temples elsewhere in the city—one on the Street of Gods, even one in the slums of the south side—this was by far her most prosperous, and the best attended. Little wonder. The worship of Beauty is a luxury for most, and is ill attended to in areas where such basic needs as food, shelter, and safety are still at issue.

Narilka walked to the temple. It was a good five-mile hike from where she lived, but she thought of the walk as part of her worship. It gave her time to relax her mind, to focus it on the issue she wished to address. Normally that was some artistic project for which she hoped to gain special inspiration, Saris' most precious gift. Sometimes it was an offering, the joy of a project completed or a moment of aesthetic inspiration realized. But today . . .

I shouldn't be going here. This isn't right.

Today she was far from calm, and far from certain that she was doing the right thing. She had discovered Saris in her youth, when she was still working on her parents' farm; it was the goddess who had made her acknowledge the spark of an artist in her soul, and who had helped her to see that her restlessness was the result of stifling that inner fire. It was Saris who had granted her the courage to confront her parents, and to demand a situation that would give outlet to her innate talent. Thus, after much teary-eyed debate, her apprenticeship with Gresham had been arranged. And she had learned the joy of molding liquid silver into forms so beautiful that they might have graced this very temple.

But today it was not art that drove her here, but need; need for the kind of reassurance that only a god could offer. Would Saris respond?

She was a minor goddess, as such beings were measured, and her domain was a limited one. Was it right to bring these problems to her, when there were at least a dozen other gods dedicated to that kind of turmoil?

You are the patron of my soul, she thought, gazing upon the gleaming temple. Even now, tormented by doubts, she felt a sense of serenity at the sight of the familiar building. It was simple, clean-lined, conspicuously undecorated; only Saris' faithful would understand how its plain columns and carefully sculpted empty spaces were like a blank canvas to the mind, supporting a greater beauty than any human architect could achieve.

Slowly she walked up the broad stairs and entered the temple proper. Like the facade the sanctuary was plain, but infinitely beautiful. Sunlight fell in shafts from the pierced-work roof, that wove amongst themselves to sculpt shifting patterns on the floor. Open spaces in the walls allowed the breeze to play through, carrying with it all the scents of spring. Water flowed within, a natural fountain over which the temple had been built, and she paused to scoop up a mouthful in her palm and taste it. Would that it could calm her. Would that it could convince her that she'd been right to come here, to place her inner torments before a goddess of beauty and peace.

She looked up for a priest or priestess, and found one waiting in the shadows. As soon as Narilka began to move toward him (her?), the figure glided forward, silken robes in delicate mottled hues fluttering in the sunlight. The mask the figure wore was of silver, finely polished, and gave no hint of gender or identity. Anonymity and grace, in perfect combination.

"I've come for communion," she said quickly; could the priest hear how hard her heart was pounding? "If that's possible."

Wordlessly the wraithlike figure turned to lead her to a communion chamber; she fell into step behind him. They left the main sanctuary and entered the part of the temple reserved for private offerings. She tried not to think of Andrys Tarrant or the Hunter as she walked, but struggled instead to focus on images that the goddess would find pleasing. It was no use. Images of her finest work faded into images of the coronet, and Andrys' hand testing its substance; abstract images re-formed themselves, becoming images of the young nobleman. By the time they reached an empty communion chamber she was trembling, wondering if she could manage the self-control that prayer required. How would Saris respond to such images?

Goddess, help me. I don't know where else to turn.

The priest left her alone in the communion chamber. Grateful for privacy, she shut the door behind him and locked it. There was a robe laid out in the antechamber, of soft white linen, and a basin of water beside it. She took off her clothes and laid them aside, her hands shaking as she undressed. The white robe was soft against her skin, the water cool and bracing as she rinsed her face and hands. Dressed thus, cleansed thus, she left all the cares of the real world behind her, and entered into the goddess' presence a blank slate, an open soul. At least that was the theory. But her memories and her need were too powerful today, and the ritual failed to calm her.

Saris, I'm sorry. I tried.

Slowly, hesitantly, she moved into the communion chamber. There a low brazier filled with charcoal awaited her, with a circle of cushions about it. She chose one of the cushions and settled herself onto it, heart pounding. Beside the brazier were small bowls of dried herbs, and she chose a few handfuls of the ones that pleased her. Rosewort. Briarwood. Nuviola. Opening her hand slowly, she let the leaves and bark bits fall onto the glowing charcoal. Scented smoke began to rise, twining in tendrils as it worked its way up to the ceiling vent. Stare at the smoke, she thought. Let the visions come.

She prayed. Not in words but in images, because words could never capture all that she felt. The Hunter in all his dark and terrible glory, with the music of the night surging up about him and a secret world so rich in beauty it was painful to behold. And Andrys Tarrant in his need. So wounded, so irresistible, so like the Hunter in outer aspect and utterly unlike him in spirit. She saw them take form in the smoke, and suddenly was unsure of herself. Why had she come here? What did she expect the goddess to do? She shivered and wrapped her arms about herself; the faces in the smoke faded and were gone.

If I let myself love him, I'll lose myself forever. It was a thrilling, terrifying thought. *Guide me,* she begged. Not knowing who else or what else to turn to, not even sure that her goddess would listen. *Help me!*

Slowly an image began to form within the smoke, that was not of her own making. The heady scent of nuviola filled her lungs as she watched it, trembling. Wisps of silver danced in the smoke, twining about each other like serpents. Slowly, sensuously they knotted, melded, re-formed, redefined themselves . . . with a start she realized that the vision had begun to take on human form, neither male nor female but a wispy, slender figure that might be either. Or both. The image looked so solid that she felt as if she could reach out and touch it, and yet it seemed utterly weightless as it floated there before her.

Silver eyes. Silver face. Silver hair like fine-spun silk, that wafted weightless in an unseen breeze. The smoke became a silken veil that rippled across the figure's surface, adorning rather than concealing its form. It was so detailed, so lustrous, so *real.* . . . With a start she realized that she couldn't see the far wall through it, as she should have been able to do with a normal vision. Nor did the walls at her sides frame the vision with clean white plaster, as they should have done. The entire room seemed to have faded—walls and pillows, brazier and herbs and yes, even the smoke—leaving her alone in a sweet-scented darkness with a figure that gleamed like moonlight.

"Saris?" She whispered. She barely got the name out past the tightness in her throat. "Is it. . . ?"

Tell me your need.

She opened her mouth to speak—and emotion poured out, raw and primitive, unfettered by the bonds of language. All the hope and fear and lust and need and love (was that love?) in a flood tide of memory that she could neither control nor comprehend. Pouring out of her blindly, into the surrounding darkness. When it was over, she fell back shaking, and her eyes squeezed forth hot tears. "Saris?"

For a moment the figure just stared at her. Digesting her response? At last it said, in an even voice, *Andrys Tarrant is doomed.*

It took the words a moment to sink in, and then it was a few seconds more before she found her voice. "What?"

He's fighting a war he does not understand, for stakes he cannot begin to comprehend. He has given himself to one who will use him and then discard him, taking pleasure from the destruction of so tender a soul. He is a pawn, Narilka Lessing, nothing more. A blind, unwitting soldier in a war of gods and demons. The figure paused. *A sacrifice.*

"No," she whispered.

I speak the truth, it assured her. Its tone was cool, emotionless. *I have no vested interest in this matter to cause me to lie.*

"No!"

If you bind yourself to him, you will make yourself part of his war.

"What war?" she demanded. "Who's he fighting? Tell me that."

The figure seemed to hesitate. A cloud of silk twisted about its thighs.

He means to kill the Hunter, it said at last.

The words were a cold thrill in her flesh. "He can't," she whispered. "No man can."

A single man, no. But a man with a demonic ally and an army behind him . . . perhaps.

"An army? What army?"

The figure hesitated again, then shook its head. *I can't tell you that.*

"What demon?"

I can't tell you that.

"Why? Because I know the Hunter?"

The figure didn't answer.

Wrapping her arms even tighter about herself, Narilka shivered. Andrys or the Hunter. If the two of them pitted all their strength against each other, one would surely die. Maybe both. The thought of that loss was an ache within her. The thought that the loser would probably be Andrys—desolate, wounded Andrys—was almost more than she could bear.

"What can I do?" she whispered. "Anything?"

In terms of affecting the outcome of the conflict? The figure hesitated. *I can't counsel you on that issue. Such interference with another . . . it's forbidden. As for Andrys Tarrant, I will tell you this: he would be fortunate to lose his life in this endeavor, for his ally intends to destroy him in soul as surely as he means to destroy the Hunter in body.*

Even more softly: "What can I do?"

You know the options. Now you know the risk. Make your choices accordingly.

"What would you do?"

The figure drew back; if it had been more human in countenance, Narilka might have thought it was startled. *I lack the emotions that would make such a question meaningful. The Hunter has created great beauty in his time, though of a cold and inhuman sort; part of me would regret his passing. As for his enemy . . . we do not share priorities, he and I. And I think that in a world where he ruled, I would have no comfortable place. But the concept of taking sides is meaningless, when I am forbidden to interfere. Only to protect my own may I act.*

Her heart was pounding so loudly she could barely hear the whispering voice above its beat; her hands twisted nervously, one about the other. "You can protect me?"

From his ally. From the illusions that are his power. No more than that.

"How?"

It seemed to her the figure smiled. *The same rules bind us all,* it said. Silken veils swirled about its thighs. *For as long as you are mine, he cannot touch you.*

She shut her eyes; the figure was still bright in her vision. "I've always been yours. I always will be."

For now. Until this war is over.

"Always!"

You may choose differently when this is finished.

"I won't."

We shall see, the figure said quietly. *Until then, however you choose, know that I am watching you. Always.*

The figure began to fade slowly, becoming translucent first so that the walls (there were walls again!) showed through it. Then the veils misted into smoke, and were scattered by the air; the gleaming flesh dissolved into random glitter, then dissipated before her eyes. Nothing was left of the image of the goddess, save the memory which even now made her tremble.

"Thank you, Saris." She could barely find enough voice to shape the words. "Thank you."

She managed to get to her feet somehow. Managed to get to where her clothing lay and put it back on, piece by piece. How few mortals ever saw a god incarnate, much less were counseled by one? Her hands were shaking as she put the communion robe aside. Saris was watching, she told herself. She would always be watching. For whatever reason, the goddess seemed to care about the outcome of this . . . what had she called it? A war.

Fully dressed now, she shivered. *Oh, Narilka. What are you getting yourself into?*

Had she looked behind her as she left the temple, she would have seen nothing unusual, for Saris no longer maintained the illusion of a solid form. Had she listened closely, she would have heard nothing unusual, for Saris no longer couched her words in cadences the fleshborn might hear. But there was a presence behind her, and there were words, and both were echoed by the fae as it flowed about her feet.

Careful, my brother, the Iezu/goddess whispered. *We are all watching now.*

Fifteen

The snake is black, and its eyes are drops of blood. At one end its many necks twine like tentacles, promising to enmesh the unwary in a living web of cold flesh and sharp teeth. At the other end is a face out of Hell, whose hot breath stinks of sulfur and carrion as it lunges for him, jaws snapping shut mere inches from his throat as he throws himself backward—

Damien awoke suddenly, heart pounding. He was lying on the couch of his rented apartment, and his body was drenched with sweat. What a nightmare! He tried to sit up, but his muscles were like knots and he had to work them loose before they would obey him. What the hell had brought that on?

He would have suspected Tarrant, but the dream wasn't his style at all; the Hunter generally preferred a more complex scenario, a sophisticated blend of fear and despair that was light-years beyond the primitive biochemical terror of this experience. What *was* that thing anyway? It reminded him of representations of the Evil One that the Church favored, only far more real and terrifying than those formalized portraits. And why would he suddenly start dreaming about the Evil One now, after all he'd been through in the last two years? Certainly there were more concrete fears to occupy his mind.

He froze suddenly as a particularly nasty thought hit him. For a moment he couldn't move, but sat rigid on the worn couch as his sweat chilled to ice on his skin. *No,* he whispered silently. Willing it not to be. What words had Tarrant used when he referred to his patron? *Divided into parts, it can be petty and unpredictable. Unified, it is a ruthless evil.*

Divided and unified, both at once. He thought of the creature in

125

his dream, and cold certainty filled him. What other image would his mind choose to represent such a Power?

Where the hell was Tarrant now? He'd been supposed to come up as soon as the sun set, so that they could compare notes and discuss future strategy. But it was well past sunset now and the Hunter hadn't shown his face. Damien could think of only two reasons why he wouldn't show up on time, and the simpler one—forgetfulness—just wasn't like him.

Someone—or *something*—must have interfered.

With a sinking feeling in the pit of his stomach Damien caught up his keys and exited the small apartment. By the time the door slammed shut behind him he was already running down the narrow stairs to the first floor, his hand skimming along the demon-wards that had been inscribed into the banister. His feet hammered on the worn stairs in a rhythm only slightly louder than his heartbeat. A voice inside him warned, *Even if it is what you think, what can you possibly do?* but he forced himself to ignore it as he darted to the next staircase, the one that led down beneath ground level.

Tarrant's door was shut, and looked just as it would if nothing were wrong. He banged on it with a heavy fist, calling out the Hunter's name. Again. His blows were hard enough to make the door vibrate, but still there was no response.

"Who's down there?" The voice came from behind him, a woman's. He heard her steps descending the narrow stairs as he banged on the door again, with force enough that even the frame shivered. No response. Damn Tarrant to Hell, what was going on?

"Is something wrong?" It was the landlady, an older woman whom Damien had met but once. Her tone was more suspicious than concerned, and her tone made it clear that he looked more like a raving madman than a reliable tenant. He spared her a quick glance, trying for one moment to look calm enough to reassure her. He doubted it worked.

"I think my friend's in trouble." He banged on the door again, hard enough to shake the frame. "Gerald! Are you in there?" There was cold sweat beading on his brow now, and his hands had started shaking. He tried to remember what the windows of the apartment were like, which he had boarded up only two days ago. Too narrow for him to slide through, he decided at last, even if he could kick the boards free. Worse and worse. He was about to start banging again when the landlady pushed him aside. Her expression was harsh and frankly suspicious, but she had a large ring of keys in her hand and was reaching toward the lock with it. He let her. The brass key entered the lock and turned, and he heard the metallic snap of a bolt being withdrawn. With one last glance at him she turned the door handle and pulled. Nothing. He pushed her aside and pulled himself, but the door wouldn't budge. Clearly it was bolted from the inside.

Damn!

"What did you expect?" she demanded.

He tried to work a Knowing aimed at the apartment within, despite the fact that fear and frustration combined made it hard to concentrate. The Working he conjured was a weak thing, that barely made it past the wood of the door. Images took shape before his eyes: dark shapes, bloodstained and evil, whose chill power constricted his lungs until it was hard to breathe. Great. That could be Tarrant himself, for all he knew. How did you distinguish the Hunter from true demons, when the two were so very similar?

"Look," he told her, "I'm going to have to break in—"

"Oh, no, you don't!" She forced herself between Damien and the door. "Your friend wanted a secure apartment, and that's what he got. Already I've put up with gods know how many nails and such being hammered in the windows, and now—"

"I'll pay for it," he said quickly. "I'll pay for any damages in cash, right now." He dug hurriedly into his pocket, praying that he had enough money on him. There were coins in the bottom, large ones by the feel of them; he pulled them out quickly and offered them to her. "Here." They'd pay for the door three times over, he estimated; even so she was reluctant to accept them. "Take them!"

"I never had such trouble like this before," she muttered. But she got out of the way. He stepped forward and ran his hands over the door, trying to Know its substance. After a few seconds he cursed in frustration, stepped back, and tried to think clearly.

The bolt was a solid one, affixed in a steel chamber that was firmly attached to the wood. It wasn't going to come loose easily, not by virtue of any Working he knew how to do. Damn the Church, which had limited his training to the sorceries it approved of, making him helpless in the face of such a simple mechanism! He drew in a deep breath and tried to think calmly, tried to reason his way through the problem the way Tarrant would have done. The lock was steel through and through. Steel was hard to Work. The slot that received it was also steel, and well fortified against a forced assault. But where the steel parts were affixed to the wood, and within the wood itself . . .

He Knew the door and the wall beside it, and chose the wall as the more vulnerable of the two. Then he reached inside it with carefully focused fae, in the same way that he had done to a tree in the Black Lands so long ago. Insinuating himself into its cells, smelling out the microbes that crouched between the woody fibers, analyzing their hunger. At last he found what he wanted, and he Healed. The microbes grew and multiplied, their life cycles accelerated by his Working. As they grew, they digested the wood that surrounded them, breaking down the hard cell walls, rotting the powerful fibers. Two generations of microbes, then three. He guided them through their newly paced life cycles, making sure their hunger was focused on the one part of the wall he meant to weaken; there was no point in causing more damage than he had to.

At last he sensed that the process had done as much good as it was likely to. Despite his rush, he took care to stabilize the hungry microbes at a normal level before he withdrew his senses from the wall; otherwise the rest of the house could be undermined in a fortnight. Then he stepped back, drew in a deep breath, and pulled on the door as though his life depended on it. At first it didn't move. He persisted. At last, slowly, the wood of the door frame began to give way. Softly at first, then with a splintering crack that made the landlady step back with a gasp. He gave the door a good jerk, as hard as he could muster, and the wood gave way utterly: the steel housing of the deadbolt tore through the wall and the door was open at last, the mechanism of its closure dangling from its edge like a broken limb.

"Gods'v Earth," the woman muttered, but Damien had no time to coddle her. As soon as the door was open, he moved into the dark apartment—

—and malevolence swirled up about his legs with such force that he nearly crashed to his knees, cold fae invading his flesh with a power that made bile rise up in his gut, his stomach spasming as if it could vomit up this repulsive evil. Loathsome, unspeakably loathsome; it took all his self-control not to abandon his search and desperately try to find a Working that would scrub his flesh clean of the sickening power. *Go ahead,* the power seemed to urge, in a voice that stabbed like knives into his flesh. *Try it.* He could feel it sucking him down that path, toward that insane, doomed effort, and he knew in that moment that more than one living man had scrubbed his body raw in response to its presence, until skin and muscles both were abraded like cheap rope and even the hot blood which flowed freely was not enough to guarantee a cleansing.

With a sinking heart he staggered toward the bedroom, and somehow gathered enough strength to call the Hunter's name. He no longer questioned what had happened here; the fae itself made it clear what type of creature had visited, and there was only one thing a creature like that would want. "Gerald?" He searched the bedroom quickly, desperately, but he knew even as he did so that the Hunter wasn't here. Cold fae stabbed into his flesh like knives as he searched the living room and the small kitchen; he felt as if his limbs were rotting away beneath him, infected by every wound. *It's illusion*, he thought desperately. *It has to be. Ignore it.* As he verified that the last room was empty, and gazed upon the basement window he had boarded up himself, he felt a black despair rise up inside him. It was still sealed from the inside, just as he had left it. Just like the other two had been. That and the bolted door guaranteed that the Hunter had been caught inside, and had been taken . . . where? What kind of creature had the power to kidnap him out of this place against his will, despite such solid barriers?

With effort he managed to stagger out of the apartment, past where the malignant force now lapped hungrily at the doorsill, to the tiled floor beyond where cool, clean air flowed. He fell to his knees there, and the vomit surged up in him, his stomach spasming as if somehow such activity might exorcise the terrible unclean presence from his flesh. For a few gut-wrenching minutes he was not aware of the landlady standing beside him, or of any other normal feature of the building. Then her voice brought him back to reality.

"It'll take more than a few coins to clean up this mess," she said acidly.

Shuddering, he looked up at her; his eyes would hardly focus. "Shut the door," he gasped. When she didn't move, he squeezed his eyes shut in the hopes that forcing tears would clear them. "Shut the door!"

She took one step toward the small apartment, and then he heard her gasp. Even without a Knowing she could sense what was in there, and despite the urgency in his voice she clearly wasn't willing to risk contact with it. At last, half-blinded by the tears he had forced, he lunged forward toward the door. Malevolence stabbed into him as he braced himself with one hand on the floor, grabbing at the door with the other. He narrowly missing smashing his fingers in the door frame as he slammed it shut. For a moment he feared that the presence inside the room would flow under and around that simple barrier, but whatever wards Tarrant had put on the apartment were clearly enough to keep it enclosed now that the door was shut. Thank God for that.

Shuddering, he struggled to his feet. There was fluid on his shirt, and a hot bitterness in his throat. Numbly he wiped a shirtsleeve across his mouth, drying it. His whole body was shaking, and for a moment he could barely catch his breath, much less speak.

At last he looked up at the landlady. If she was afraid of the presence she had sensed in the room, that emotion was swamped by a far greater one: rage.

"I want you out of here," she growled. "You and your friend both, right away. I'll keep your deposit to pay for damages, and for cleaning. You get out of here tonight, and don't come back! I don't ever want to see you here again, not you or that—"

"You'll have to break open the windows," he interrupted. "From the outside. Let the sunlight in. That'll do most of the work, and then you can bring in mirrors—"

"I know how to do an exposing," she snapped. "Damn you to hells for making it necessary!" She looked down at the pool of vomit, then at him, in disgust. "Now get your things and get out of here. And gods help you if you ever cross this threshold again."

Legs shaking, he forced himself up the stairs. *Got to find Tarrant,* he thought. *Got to.* But even if he did, then what? Could he help him? Did he have the kind of power it took to stand up to a demon who left such malignance as its calling card?

Have to try, he thought grimly. Not questioning his own motives, for once. Not asking himself whether it wouldn't be better to let the Hunter stew in Hell at last while the world went on in innocence, a better place for his absence. Because Damien needed him. The Church needed him. And therefore—though most didn't know it, and would probably deny it if asked—the very world that he had haunted so ruthlessly needed him.

We're fighting for man's survival, he thought. Remembering Calesta's work in the east, and its loathsome harvest. *We're fighting for humankind's soul.*

Pulling on a clean shirt as hurriedly as he could, sweeping up what little cash he had left and forcing it into his pockets, he hurried out into the night in search of his dark companion.

It was a warm night, a sticky night, and half the walls in the Temple of Pleasure had been rolled up in hopes of admitting a cooling breeze. On the broad steps which surrounded the temple some singles and couples sprawled languidly, and it was impossible to tell if the sweat which glistened on their skin resulted from their "worship"—which ranged from half-naked petting to the delights contained in wine bottles and water pipes—or from the night itself.

There was a circle delineated by the temple light, and Damien stood just beyond it. He could feel its presence before him almost as a physical barrier, and for a moment he lacked the courage to cross it. If the Patriarch knew of his search, if somehow he knew that a priest had come *here* . . . well, his reaction wouldn't be a pretty one, that was sure. And it damned well might prove the last straw between them, one transgression too many for the Holy Father to tolerate.

He was trying not to think about that. He was trying not to think about what he would do with himself if the Patriarch really did cast him out of the Church. Such considerations belonged to the future, and right now the future itself was in jeopardy. Would he want to remain a priest if he knew that the cost was the sacrifice of everything he believed in? Could he value the robes he wore and the ritual sword he carried if he knew that the price of maintaining them was the submission of this world to Calesta's hunger? And yet . . . stepping into that circle of light was a commitment such as he had never made before, to a mode of operation he had hitherto rejected. Only sorcerers bargained with demons. Only the damned. Never the Church, whose very existence was dedicated to making such bargains impossible. Never, never one of the Church's priests.

Trembling, he shut his eyes. *So the Patriarch does find out,* he told himself. *So what? Which do you value more, this avocation you've grown so accustomed to, or the chance to do something to help save your world? Is one man's comfort such a great sacrifice for God to require, in order that His people might be defended?*

But despite all his internal arguments he felt sick as he stepped into the light, and as he approached the temple he could feel his heart pounding in his chest with such power that it seemed to make his whole body shake.

He hadn't been inside a pagan temple since his childhood, since the day when his mother had taken him to Yoshti's house of worship in the hope that it would appeal to him. Even then he had found it uncomfortable, though it would be many years before he could articulate the reasons. Now all that discomfort was back again, and more. He looked at the intertwined couples, at the sweaty groups who sprawled on rugs and couches and wherever the inclination struck them, and thought, *This is not worship.* He watched an old man blissfully accepting a wad of gummy substance from a priest and stuffing it into his water pipe, and he thought, *There is no god in this place.* He walked stiffly through what seemed like chaos, dozens of men and women who had nothing in common but a hunger for immediate gratification, and he reminded himself, *This is a Iezu they worship. They feed him with their lusts, and he gives them illusions of ecstasy. A simple contract, easily comprehended, readily fulfilled. It's really a wonder that men follow the One God at all, with such relationships available.*

There were priests in the temple, male and female both, but they wore no special costume to identify themselves, merely a silver neckpiece with Karril's blatantly phallic symbol engraved upon it. He began to approach one, but suddenly hesitated. What was he supposed to say? *Excuse me, I really need to talk to your god in private, could you arrange an interview?* How did you make contact with a godling, other than through prayer? He flushed as he considered what manner of worship Karril might require, and for the first time since coming gave serious consideration to turning back. He even glanced back the way he had come, as if to assure himself that his way out was unimpeded—

—and the worshipers were gone. All of them. The walls had been replaced by tapestried hangings, and a cool breeze flowed between them. Even the priests were gone, and the buffet table that had been set up by the back wall banished as if by sorcery. Only the central fountain remained, and the wine that poured from its ornate spigots was no longer red but crystal gold, and smelled like champagne.

"Well, well." The voice came from behind him. "Look who's come to be a guest at our festivities."

He turned around to face the source of the voice, a woman of thirty or so clad in a few meager bits of silk. A lot of woman, and all in the right places. Shaggy blonde hair half-obscured the priest's necklace she wore, but—like her clothing—obscured little else. He found his eyes wandering of their own accord to vistas that were better left unstudied, and at last managed to focus on an ornate piece of jewelry hanging precariously from her shoulder. "I need to find Karril," he muttered. Bright jewelry glittered on a bed of tanned flesh at her waist, on her breast, down her arm. "I need to talk to him." Did he sound as awkward as he felt? Her perfume came to him on the breeze and he felt an involuntary stiffening in his groin; given the gravity of his mission here, the response was doubly embarrassing. What kind of power did this woman have, that so easily overbore his self-control, his fears for Tarrant, his revulsion for the very temple that surrounded them?

And then it all came together. The jewelry. The illusion. His response to this woman . . . and the woman herself. He forced himself to look upward, to meet her eyes. It was no easy task, given the alternatives.

"Karril?"

With a soft chuckle the woman bowed; it was a precarious angle for certain parts of her clothing. "At your service, Reverend. Whatever that service might be."

"I didn't . . . that is . . . I thought you were male."

"Neither male nor female, as humans know gender. And either one, as the need of the moment dictates." Her eyes sparkled flirtatiously. "Given the Hunter's attitude toward women, I usually avoid the feminine in his presence. Too distracting. As for you . . ." She glanced down at Damien's crotch, imperfectly curtained by the hem of his shirt, and smiled. "Perhaps as a good host I should make things more comfortable. . . ."

He never saw the change happen, though he watched it from start to finish. There was no surging of the earth-fae, as with Tarrant, and no melding of flesh from one form to another. One instant the woman was standing before him, and the next instant a man stood in her place. That simple. He was shorter than Damien, stouter, and slightly older. The tasteless brooches fastening his full velvet robe at the waist were the same ones the woman had worn, and jeweled rings flashed on his fingers as he gestured broadly to a couch some few yards away. "Will you be seated, Reverend? I can offer you refreshment, at least."

He breathed in deeply and exhaled, trying to clear his head of the cloying perfume the woman had worn. "What about the others?"

"Who?" He saw Damien look around the temple—now empty— and he chuckled. "What, my faithful? They're still there. Surrounded by curtains of illusion so fine that each one imagines himself truly alone, in an environment that caters to . . ." He grinned. "Shall we say, to individual taste? I try to be an obliging god."

"I saw them all."

"You *wanted* to see them all, my dear Reverend. You needed to despise them—and me—in order to set yourself at ease here." He shrugged. "As I say, I try to be a good host."

He walked to the fountain and dipped a hand beneath its surface; when he withdrew, there was a chalice of finely engraved silver in his hand. "I would love to think you came here for a simple diversion, but, alas, I'm not so naive. Though the illusion is tempting." He sipped from the chalice as if assessing its contents, and nodded his approval. "So what brings a Knight of the Church to this den of unholy indulgence? Surely not an attempt at proselytizing." Again he chuckled. "My worshipers are too loyal for that game."

He forced the words out somehow, past the knot in his throat. "Gerald Tarrant's gone."

The demon's expression darkened. Damien thought he saw him stiffen.

"So?" His voice was low now, and quiet, and all humor was gone from his tone. "What does that have to do with me?"

"I need help finding him."

Karril snorted, then drained the chalice of its contents and cast it into the fountain; it disappeared before it hit the surface. "I'm not a Locater, you know that. There are some in the town. Go to them."

"I know what you are," he said sharply. "And I know how close you were to him. Close enough that I'd think you'd want to help if—" He couldn't finish the sentence. Dared not give the threat a name, for fear of making it real. "I've tried every Working I know, consulted everyone I dared. You would think with the channel between us, a Locating would be easy, but . . ." He shook his head. "Nothing, Karril. Nothing! What do I do? How do I find him? You're my only hope."

"Then I'm sorry." He turned away. "I can't help you."

"He called you a friend."

It seemed to him the demon winced. "Did he?" he whispered. "Shame on him. He was usually more careful with his choice of words." His robes were black now, and the bright jewels were muted as if by smoke. "I'm not a friend to him, or to anyone else. Not as humans know the word. Friendship implies a full range of emotions, a wide assortment of bonding criteria. Humans can do that. Iezu can't." He looked at Damien; his expression was strained. "All I am, my dear Reverend, is the hunger for pleasure that resides in your own soul, given a face and a voice and enough knowledge of etiquette to mimic human interaction. That's all. No love, no loyalty, only a ghost of self-interest in human guise. So you see," he said, turning away again, "you came to the wrong place."

"He didn't believe that," Damien challenged. "And I'm not sure I do."

"Oh?" The demon's voice was strained. "Is the Church claiming a monopoly on demon lore, now?"

"You came to warn us about Calesta," he reminded him. "Was that self-interest? You said that you liked humankind, that its foibles . . ." he struggled for the proper word, ". . . *amused* you. Was that just hunger speaking? I don't think so." He walked to where the demon stood and grabbed him by the shoulders, as he might any man; Karril's "flesh" was comfortably solid, utterly human in temperature. *"You saved Ciani's life."* He forced the demon to turn toward him, forced him to meet his eyes. "I don't remember all the details of that incident, but I seem to remember you saying it wasn't easy. You could barely stand the pain of it, I recall. Was that hunger that drove you then? Or was it something else? Maybe a more human emotion."

For a long moment Karril was silent. At last he pulled himself loose from Damien's grasp, and turned away; the priest let him go.

"He knew the risk all those years ago." Was that pain in his voice, or some demonic emotion? "Knew it and accepted it. Let him go, Reverend Vryce. He made his own fate. You make yours."

"Where is he?"

For a long time Karril was silent. Damien waited him out, though his hands were shaking from impatience. At last the demon said, in a voice that was little more than a whisper, "Where Gerald Tarrant has gone, no living man can follow."

Damien breathed in sharply. "Where?"

"To be judged." As the demon turned back to him, Damien saw that now even his jewelry was black. "By those whom he feared the most."

"The Unnamed?"

He hesitated only a moment, then nodded. "There's nothing you can do, Reverend Vryce. You have to believe that. His own word gives them the power to judge him, his own blood makes him vulnerable. . . ."

"How do I get there?" he demanded. His heart was like ice as he heard his own words, as he felt the power of his own commitment. "Tell me!"

The demon shut his eyes as if in pain. "Through the nightmare of his own fears. That's the only path left, now that he's in their hands. But no fleshborn being can travel that road safely. Even my kind—"

He stopped, but not soon enough.

"You can go there."

He hesitated.

"Karril. *Please.*"

"I can go there," he admitted. "I can also die there. I'm not willing to risk that."

"Gerald told me that no Iezu has ever died."

"Because we don't take chances! Because we're selfish spirits, who trade illusions for food in our neat little houses and mind our own business when meaner demons come calling!"

"Is that what Calesta's doing?" he demanded. "Minding his own business?"

The demon winced. "I don't . . . leave him out of this."

"He can't be out of it! He's part and parcel of this whole mess, and you know it!" He took a step closer to the demon, into what would have been his personal territory had he been truly human. "Or don't you care if he has his way? Don't you care if the whole human species is remade to suit his taste, bred and winnowed like animals until all they can do is eat and sleep and *suffer*. Is that what you want, Karril? Is that what *any* of the Iezu want? Where will you find your worshipers then?"

"I'll survive," he muttered. "But some of the others . . ." He shook his head and whispered hoarsely, "I can't get involved. It's simply not allowed. The penalty—"

"Is worse than what I just described?" he demanded. "All right, so I was wrong. Maybe you and Calesta aren't so different after all." He made his tone as venomous as he could, hoping scorn might stir the demon where loyalty and compassion had failed. "Sorry to have bothered you."

A shudder seemed to pass through the demon's body. "That way is pain, and worse," he whispered. His voice was strained, barely audible. "Don't you understand? I couldn't endure it. Even if I wanted to, even if I were willing to risk *her* displeasure . . . I'm not human. I can't absorb emotions which run counter to my aspect. No Iezu could survive such an assault."

"So I'll masturbate for you," he said harshly. "Is that good enough? In the midst of Tarrant's nightmares I'll dream acts of pleasure, so you can stay on your feet. Hell, it worked for him, it should damn well work for you."

The demon turned away. "I'm not human," he whispered. The hanging tapestries had all turned black; even the wine in the fountain was dark. "The rules for us are . . . different."

"Yeah. I guess so." Rage and despair churned in his gut at the thought of this, too, being a dead end. Where else was there to turn? He forced himself to turn away, while adding bitterly, "Sorry to bother you."

He began to walk away from the demon, assuming the illusion surrounding him would fade when he tried to leave. It didn't.

"Even if you survived the journey," Karril pressed, "what would you do once you got there? Do battle with the Unnamed? Try to reason with it? It's too powerful for the former, and far too unstable for the latter. And it might make things even worse for Gerald Tarrant, that a man of your stature cared enough to try to save him. Have you thought about that?"

"I've thought about everything," he said sharply. "Most of all about what this world will be like if Calesta goes unopposed, and how little chance I have of stopping him without Tarrant's help. As for the rest . . ." He shrugged stiffly; despair was a cold knot within him. "I guess it doesn't matter much, does it?" And he snapped, "Hope the new order works out for you."

He turned to leave then, and the tapestries did fade. The amorous couples were visible once more, but thinly, like ghosts. The half-clad priests and priestesses fluttered like wraiths about the borders of his vision.

"Reverend Vryce."

He didn't turn back, but he did stop walking. The entire room seemed frozen in time, as if the very walls were waiting.

"True night falls for an hour tomorrow." The demon's voice was low and even; there was only the faintest tremor of fear in it. "Eat well and drink well before that, and rest with a pitcher of water by your side. In a secure room," he added quickly, "so that no one disturbs your flesh." He whispered, "It can't make the journey."

And then the tapestries were gone and the demon also, and the warm smell of the temple filled his nostrils and his head. "Can I help you?" a priestess asked, approaching him. He shook his head and waved her away. His legs felt weak beneath him. What had just happened? Did Karril mean to help him, or merely point him on his way and say good-bye? Either way—

Either way I have to go, he thought grimly. *Because there is no other option. May God have mercy on my soul.*

Then he thought of the risk that Karril had already taken, of the rules the Iezu had broken just to talk to him—of the pain that he might yet endure, in order to betray his own brother—and he added, *May God have mercy on us both.*

Sixteen

The Patriarch dreamed:

Armies on a plain, arrayed in Church regalia. Beyond them lies the Forbidden Forest, whose trees even now cast blackened shadows before the setting sun. He lifts his hand to bless them and the armies start forward, into that haunted darkness. . . .

. . . and the Forest is alive, it tears them apart, it strews their blood upon the ground to nurture its foul growth. . . .

Armies on a plain. He lifts his hand to bless them and a chosen few start forward, armored with sigils of fire. . . .

. . . and the Forest swallows them whole, so that not even the light of their Worked weapons shines forth, so that not even their fellow soldier can find them. . . .

Armies on a plain. He lifts his hand to bless their purpose and a few men move forward with firebrands, setting them against the nearest trees. . . .

. . . and rain lashes down from the heavens in fury, sun-bright lightning striking in the midst of their encampment with thunderous fury while the downpour douses their flames. . . .

Armies on a plain. He lifts his hand to bless them and one man rides forward, accoutred in the Prophet's glory. . . .

. . . and the Forest parts before him. Tall he rides in the saddle, and proud, and his armor glints in the dying light like molten gold. He is an image out of mural splendor, this brave soldier, with the coronet of Merentha holding back his golden hair, and the armor of

that doomed neocounty glittering upon his chest and limbs. He is the living image of the Prophet himself, and as he approaches the twisted trees of the Forest, they give way before him, thinking him their master. Safely he rides into its depths, making a path where none have been able to before.

The Patriarch lifts his hand in blessing and the troops begin to follow. Riding in the wake of the false Neocount, they encounter no opposition, but make their way toward the heart of the Forest with a prayer upon their lips and the song of the One God loud within their hearts. The Forest thinks that they belong to him, its master, and it makes no move against them. Wave after wave moves into the preternatural darkness, as the spear of the Church is leveled against the Hunter's throne. . . .

He awoke in a cold sweat, his heart pounding. The last moments of his dream were as fresh in his brain as if he had really lived them, and the implications of it were so stunning that as he rose to a sitting position, he noticed that his hands were shaking.

Was this what all his war-dreams had been leading up to? He reached over to his lamp and cracked open the hood slightly, letting a faint light into the room. God in Heaven. Was there really a man like that, whose mere presence could disarm the Forest's defenses? If so . . . He breathed in deeply, trying to accept the implications. The Church had lost its Great War when its armies turned against the Forest; that cursed land was more powerful than mere human troops could ever hope to be. But if there were a key to that realm, a way of entering and traveling through it without setting off its defensive sorceries . . . then they might indeed make it to the heart of the Hunter's domain, and make war with him outright. They might then destroy the tyrant who had dominated that land for centuries, and thus free the human lands of his predations forever.

As spokesman for the One God's Church, the Patriarch knew the power of symbols all too well, and this one reverberated in his soul with stunning force. A symbolic victory over the Forest's prince would affect the fae in a way that generations of sorcerers could never manage, winning a far greater battle in the long run. It wouldn't be necessary for men to make war against the Forest itself, or even try to contain it; that was the mistake the Patriarch's predecessors had made, which had resulted in the Church's greatest defeat. No, if they made war against the *symbol* of the Forest, by attacking its demonic monarch, and if they won, the planet itself would be their ally.

It could be done, he thought. Numbed by the concept. *It could really be done.*

For a moment he shut his eyes and prayed, opening himself up to the wisdom of his God. *If this is foolishness,* he begged, *then tell me now.* Could there possibly be a man like the one he saw in his dream, who so resembled the Hunter in outer aspect that he might pretend to be him, and lead Church troops to victory? It would take more than mere physical resemblance, the Patriarch suspected. What kind of man would be able to take on the Hunter's persona—become him, in essence—and still serve the Church's purpose in attacking his stronghold?

He'd have to be crazy, he thought. *And if he wasn't crazy to start with, he sure as hell would be by the time it was over.*

With a sigh, he forced himself to lay back down. What were the odds that someone like that could be found, even if he existed? A million to one, if that. It was a dream, nothing more. Not a vision this time. Just a dream, like other men had. Just that.

But the image wouldn't leave him. And even when he forced himself to shut his eyes—even as sleep shuttered his restless brain once more—he couldn't help but imagine what it might mean to his Church if this dream, like so many others, proved true.

Seventeen

He ate a big meal at the end of the day, just as Karril had advised. It was hard for him. His appetite had faded long ago, and it went against all his best instincts to load himself up just at the moment when danger was beckoning most strongly. But if he couldn't trust Karril then he figured the whole game was lost anyway, so what the hell.

He rented a small room in one of the poorer neighborhoods, using Church credit for the deposit. Having given the better part of his remaining cash to his previous landlady, he had no other option. He winced at the thought of the Patriarch hearing about it, but then, if the Holy Father heard about this incident at all, Damien would be in such deep shit anyway that a little bit of cash more or less would hardly matter. If the Patriarch found out that he was traveling with demons now, and knew what he planned to do . . . he didn't like to think about that possibility.

In the small, dingy room, by the light of a single lamp, he lay back on the worn coverlet of the bed and tried to relax. Beside him lay his sword, its leather-wrapped grip reassuringly familiar in the gloom. Outside the window Casca was setting, and the Core had yet to rise. True night would come soon, whether he was ready or not. He dreaded what kind of power Karril might be conjuring, that required such a forum. Or was it Tarrant's own nature that gave the true night special power over his affairs?

He lay still for a few minutes, and then it occurred to him that the lamplight, dim though it was, might hinder whatever process Karril meant to initiate. He turned the wick down nearly all the way and closed the hood tightly, leaving the room in nearly perfect darkness. *Good time for demonlings to strike,* he thought grimly, resting one hand upon the grip of his sword. God, what he wouldn't give to be back in the days when the worst of his worries was that some hungry brainless thing would try to snatch a bite of his flesh while he slept! That seemed like heaven, compared to the dangers he was courting now. He could hear little things scrabbling under the bed and for a moment he tensed, but then he realized they were probably no worse than bugs and rodents, arguing over some choice bit of refuse a previous occupant had left behind.

Damn it all, I hate waiting. He trained his vision on where the ceiling must be, darkness within darkness within darkness. There was no longer moonlight coming into the room, or any other light that could help him. His hand closed reflexively about the hilt of his sword as the thick, surreal blackness of the true night closed in around him. Now what? Was he supposed to change, or the room, or . . . what? He listened to the scrabbling for another few minutes, until he thought he would go insane from doing nothing. Maybe Karril had chickened out, he thought; given the demon's state of mind, that was a real possibility. If so, what was his next step? He tried to work out some kind of plan in his mind, but the close-lying darkness made organized thought difficult and, besides, he had already exhausted every plan he could think of. If Karril failed him now, then Tarrant was gone for good. In which case Calesta might as well chow down on the whole western continent, because there was nothing Damien could do to stop him.

He sensed several hungry things flitting outside the window, no doubt spawned by the brief bout of true darkness. Fortunately for them, none mistook him for prey and tried to enter. He almost regretted it. It would feel good to cut something to pieces—anything— for the sheer physical relief of such action.

Then, slowly, it dawned on him that he could see again. A rectangle of dull light where the window had been. A shadow in place of the back of a chair. With a muttered curse he rose up to a sitting position, and

Stopped moving. Stopped breathing. Stared.

The walls were gone now, and in their place was something far less substantial, through which he could see the lights of the town beyond. The floor of his room was still dark, but beneath it—*through it*—he could see currents of fae-light coursing like water over the ground, sparkling here and there with silver and silver-blue highlights. The rest of his room was gone, simply gone—all the furniture, the rug, even the sad little picture that hung crookedly on the far wall—and only shadows of those things remained, some clear to his eye, others barely discernible.

"Ready to go?"

He started to hear Karril's voice from right beside him, and grabbed reflexively for his sword as he turned to acknowledge him. The demon had exchanged his velvet robes for a tight-fitting jacket and breeches not unlike Damien's own; a short cloak was clasped to his shoulders by jeweled brooches the size of a man's fist. He seemed unarmed, but who was Damien to judge the nature of a demon's arsenal? He also seemed tense, which was so uncharacteristic that it heightened Damien's own sense of impending danger.

"Where?"

"Following the path Gerald Tarrant left for us. Or for you, more specifically. It's the channel between you two that gives us any hope of finding him." A dark smile crossed his face, a bleak attempt at humor. "Not exactly a road your Church would approve of, but it's the one you ordered."

Damien stood. The action was surprisingly difficult, as though something were being wrenched from his flesh as he moved. He swayed a bit afterward, made vertigous by the sight of the earth-fae less than a yard beneath his feet. Was that dim shadow the floor? He tried to focus on it, to gain a sense of solidity.

"Don't look down," the demon instructed. "Follow me, and trust your footing. It's solid enough."

"Where are we?"

"Exactly where we were. But you're seeing it like I do now . . . and like your enemy does. Don't stare at the floor," he said sharply, as Damien stumbled over some shadowy obstacle "Look at me. Only me."

He did as he was told and fixed his eyes on the demon. Even by this light he could see how nervous Karril was, how agitated. If he took time to think about the implications of that, it would probably scare the hell out of him. Drawing in a deep breath, he forced himself to place one foot ahead of the other without looking down. It seemed to him that some kind of power was prying at the edges of his brain, trying to get in. In answer to his unspoken question the demon nodded slightly, and Damien tried to relax and let it happen. He had committed himself to this alliance back in the temple; there was no point in holding back now. God alone knew what kind of power the demon had to apply to bring a living man into this surreal place.

God help me if the Patriarch ever finds out about this.

Walking as if in a dream, he followed Karril out onto the street.

Only this wasn't the real street, the one he had seen on his way to
the lodging house. This was a place of dreamlike images, where silver
earth-fae lapped up against walls of misty shadow in forms that implied houses, wagons, storefronts. Bright power swirled up about his
legs and he could feel the current pulling him forward as he walked,
stunned, past buildings with walls of smoke and crystal, through
which ghostly interiors might be glimpsed. There was light in some
places, lamps and hearthfires glowing with a brightness that shone
through the nearer walls. The view made for an eerie sense of dizzi-
ness, and he had to shut his eyes for a moment to regain his sense of
balance.

"What is this?" he whispered. A wave of earth-fae crested near his
knee, sending a cascade of shimmering sparks up his thigh. He
looked down at his body, expecting to find it also changed, but to his
surprise his flesh was wholly normal; except for the droplets of power
that clung to his legs, he looked as if he had just come in from a
mundane walk in the park. "What's going on?"

"This is the world the Iezu inhabit." The demon's voice was surprisingly real, a lifeline of sound in a domain of dreams. "Defined not
by boundaries of matter but by human perception." He brushed his
hand against a nearby wall as he walked; the ghostly substance gave
way like water to his flesh, and ripples coursed outward to the edges
of the structure. "This is how the Iezu see."

Despite his tension, Damien was fascinated. "Is that why you take
on human form? So you can see the world as we do?"

"We never see as you do. At best we glimpse reflections of the material universe, filtered through your minds. Some of us learn to interpret these forms and can then interact with your kind. Some never
gain that skill, and your world remains a mystery to them."

He looked from the misty walls to the demon's rather solid form.
"Your body seems real enough," he challenged.

"Merely illusion, produced for your benefit. Like your own body.
Figments I plucked from your imagination, to clothe you in comfort
while you brave the nether regions. Humans," he said dryly, "require
such things."

His mind raced as he considered the implications of that. "Then if
this body is hurt—"

"The wounds won't translate, no. Your real flesh is still in that
bed," he nodded back the way they had come, toward the boarding
house, "with just enough spirit remaining to keep it alive. But that
doesn't make the danger any less real," he warned.

"Why? If I can't be hurt in any permanent sense, what's the risk? No more than in a dream, I'd think."

"Don't kid yourself." The glowing fae whirlpooled around the demon's feet, then settled back into its natural current. "First of all, any pain you experience in this form will be real enough as far as your brain is concerned. And if your spirit expires in this place, your body will never reanimate. Death is death, Reverend Vryce. Here and everywhere else." They passed what must have been a tree, a shadowy shape which glowed with a soft light where lover's initials had been carved into it: human perception, leaving its trace upon the Iezu's reality. All about them the world was a fairy landscape, with objects and buildings and even living creatures more or less visible as humans accorded them focus. And through it all flowed the fae, more clearly visible than Damien had ever seen it before. Far more powerful. Was this what Tarrant saw, when he viewed the world through an adept's eyes? It was wonderful, but also terrifying.

"And," the demon added, "there is one other very real danger."

He made the mistake of looking down, and stumbled. *The ground is solid only when I perceive it to be.* He forced himself to look ahead, to take his footing for granted. It took enough effort that for long minutes he could not respond to the demon's warning, could only concentrate on his immediate physical need. When at last he felt sure of his balance once more, he asked him, "What?"

"Time is your enemy," the demon warned him. "In the shadow of the real world its passage is easy enough to define; we still have the sun and the fae-tides to go by, as well as the actions of living creatures surrounding us. But what happens when we leave those things behind?" Even as he spoke, the walls about them seemed to grow mistier, less substantial, as if responding to his words. "Your perception will be our only timepiece, my friend. And human perception is notoriously subjective."

"So what? Say my time-sense gets stretched out for a while, or whatever. What difference does that—"

And then he knew. He realized what the demon meant. The knowledge was a cold knot inside him, that clenched even tighter as he contemplated how easy it would be to fail in this arena, and what the cost would be.

His body still lay on the bed, helpless now that he had abandoned it. It would require certain things to maintain its viability, so that he might return to it. Air and energy, food and water . . . how long could a body survive without some kind of liquid? It seemed to him that three days was the maximum, but perhaps that was only when it exerted itself. Was there a wider margin when flesh was thus suspended, requiring little maintenance to keep its minimal processes working?

Three days. Not measured by a clock, but by his own internal sense. Three days in the real world might seem to be minutes here, or an eternity. And once that time had passed, his body would wither and die, and the soul that it anchored would follow.

"I see you understand," Karril said quietly.

"Yeah." He grimaced. "I'm afraid so." They were moving through a different kind of neighborhood now; the shadow houses were farther apart, the sinewy tree shapes more common. "So what should I do?"

"Only be careful. That's all I know how to tell you. No other human has willingly gone where I'm about to take you. And those who went unwillingly . . ." he shrugged stiffly. "They had other problems."

He looked at Karril. "Tarrant never came here?"

For a moment the demon said nothing. "Not willingly," he answered at last. Refusing to meet Damien's eyes.

The demon turned toward an arching form, and motioned for Damien to follow. Sparks glittered overhead as they passed beneath what must have been a door frame, and over a smoky threshold. If being in the street had been disorienting, being inside this building was a thousand times more so. Damien had to stop for a moment to get his bearings, sorting out the path ahead from the lights and objects that bled in from adjoining rooms. There were people here, and their images seemed almost as solid as Damien's own. "Self-perceptions," Karril muttered, in answer to his unspoken question. They passed beneath a glowing disk incised with glittering lines—a quake-ward, it looked like—and then another, with a sign in the lower left quarter that he knew to be Ciani's own sigil. Suddenly the two seemed familiar, and their height above his head. . . . He turned to Karril and asked, in a whisper, "His apartment?"

"Of course," the demon confirmed. "What did you expect?"

From out of the shadows a human figure emerged, headed straight toward them. Damien moved to step aside, but Karril grabbed his arm and shook his head. In amazement he watched as the figure approached, its heeled shoes striking the floor silently, silver power lapping about its ankles. It was a woman, heavily made up and just a little past her prime. Her body was a parody of sexual attractiveness, from her aggressively protruding breasts to her incredibly padded buttocks, to the tight cinch belt which threatened to separate those two parts from each other. It was a surreal image, too grotesque in proportion to be human, too solid to be otherwise. When she had passed by, Damien looked at Karril in amazement. The demon was smiling faintly.

"Your former landlady, I believe."

"What?"

"As she sees herself." The brief smile faded. "Come on."

They went down the stairs into the basement, a trial all its own; Damien tried not to think about where the stairs were, or what they were made of, just trusted his feet to the surging waterfall of earth-fae where he knew that stairs should be. He stumbled once, but otherwise it worked. At the base of the stairs was a place filled with memories so sickening that Damien felt the bile rise in his throat again just to approach it. (Could he vomit here, he wondered? Would it do any good if he did?) Through the smoky film that was a door he could see a glistening blackness, like an oil slick, that covered most of the floor. As the earth-fae flowed into it, it, too, turned black, and its passage sent ripples flowing thickly through the black stuff's substance. Hungry, it seemed. Terribly hungry. Despite the door's seeming barrier, a cold wind flowed from that place toward Damien, the first he had felt since true night fell. It tasted of blood and bile, and worse.

"Your perception," the demon said quietly. "I only make it easier to see."

He could feel the dark power sucking him forward like a rip tide, and it took all his strength to fight its drag. Though he would have guessed it to be inanimate, it seemed to be aware of his presence, and bulged at the end that was nearest to him. Slowly the oily blackness seeped forward over unseen floorboards, making its way toward them. Toward *him*.

"They didn't expose it to the sun," he whispered.

"I'm afraid they did."

He stared in horror at the thing. His skin crawled at the thought of touching it again.

"They banished the Presence that had come for Gerald Tarrant," Karril explained, "But they couldn't erase its footsteps. That's all this is, Reverend—a faint echo of what came here before." He looked at the priest. "You're still sure you want to follow it?"

He whispered: "Is that what we have to do?"

The demon nodded. "Gerald Tarrant probably took a more direct route, but his struggle left a path marked in his soul's blood. That, and the residue you see here, are the only ways I know of to find him." He paused. "Are you still sure you want to go? Because if you're not, I would be all too happy to abandon this little pleasure trip, I assure you."

For a moment Damien faltered. For a moment it seemed so impossible that he could survive this crazy mission that he almost stepped back, almost said the words, almost ended their doomed venture then and there. Had he really thought that he could stand up to a Power that even Tarrant feared, and emerge unscathed? The mere thought of touching this thing before him, no more than its residue, made him sick; how would it feel to plunge into it body and soul, without knowing if he ever would rise up again?

But then he thought of Calesta, and of the holocaust that demon had deliberately provoked in the east. He thought of Calesta's plans for his world, and of what would happen to his species if the demon should ever triumph. And he knew in that moment that it wasn't death which frightened him most, or even the thought of facing the Unnamed. It was the prospect of failure.

God, when I first took my vows, I said that I would be willing to give my life to serve You. I meant it. He breathed in deeply, shaking. *But don't let that sacrifice be in vain. I beg of you. Use me however You will, take my life if it pleases You to do so, but help me free this planet from Calesta's grasp. I beg you, God.*

"I have to try," he whispered.

For a long moment the demon just looked at him. Could he read into his heart, see all the doubts that were there? Tarrant had said the Iezu had that kind of power. "The path we have to take," he warned Damien, "lies through the substance of the Hunter's own fear. Are you ready for that?"

It seemed to him that the blackness was closer now. A foul odor rose up from its surface, a stink of blood and carrion . . . and worse. "He feared sunlight. Heat. Healing. All the things that life is made of."

"Don't be naive, Reverend Vryce."

The blackness was extending an oily finger now, that oozed slowly toward him. If he stayed where he was it would soon make contact. "Death," he said sharply. "He feared that more than anything." How could he face death without dying himself? Karril must know some special trick, or he wouldn't have brought him here.

"Not death," the demon said.

Startled, he looked at Karril. The Iezu's eyes were dark, unreadable.

"Death isn't a thing or a place," Karril told him. "It's a transition.

A doorway, not a destination. Think," he urged. "You know the answer."

And he did, suddenly. He knew it, and grew weak at the thought. Was that what lay ahead of them? No wonder Karril didn't want to get involved.

"Hell," he whispered. "He feared Hell."

"His own perception of it." Could this Iezu experience gut-wrenching fear, or was that not part of his aspect? *Some people mix passion and terror*, he thought. *So the emotion should be in his repertoire.* "You still mean to follow him?"

"There's no other choice for me." Damien drew in a deep breath, exhaled it slowly. "You know that."

"Yeah." He sighed. "I know."

He shut his eyes for a moment, and tried to still the rising tide of terror in his soul. *Damn you, Tarrant! Damn you for making me go through this, just to save your murderous hide.* But in the face of such a journey his accustomed curse was rendered powerless, even ludicrous. Tarrant was in Hell already, or someplace beyond it. And he was going there to save him.

He drew in a deep breath, and didn't look down at his feet. He could feel how close the evil stuff was to him without needing to look, could feel its hunger sucking at his legs with growing force. Instead he looked to the demon, and tried to steady his voice long enough to manage two words without sounding as afraid as he felt.

"You coming?"

The demon hesitated. And sighed. And then, to his great relief, nodded. "Can't let you go in there alone, can I?"

He offered his hand. After a moment, Damien grasped it. And then, with only the briefest grimace, the priest stepped forward. Onto the path that Tarrant's soul-blood had marked. Into the blackness that waited there.

Damn you, *Calesta.*

Eighteen

MORDRETH: *Police have confirmed reports that forty-three men were killed last night by a pack of animals that came out of the region known as the Forbidden Forest. The men, who had established temporary residence just outside Jahanna's borders, were taken by surprise shortly after midnight when the Forest beasts stormed their camp without warning. Although a few men managed to arm themselves before being struck down, the sheer ferocity of the assault quickly overwhelmed their defenses. Less than an hour after the pack's arrival, every man inside the camp was dead.*

Lestar Vannik, who was returning to the area when the attack took place, managed to flee the camp before the animals caught his scent. According to a press release from Darvish Sanitorium, he described them as "white monsters, with hands instead of real paws, and eyes that glowed bright blood red." The beasts were apparently accompanied by a swarm of demonlings, who descended upon the camp's would-be protectors and blinded them so that they could not fight back effectively. Sanitorium officials will not confirm rumors that Vannik also saw a human figure running with the pack, whose coloration and ferocity matched those of the animals.

It is not yet known what prompted the attack, but communities throughout the region are concerned that the border truce between the Forest and its neighbors may no longer be protection enough. Several have begun collecting arms and training men, in order to defend themselves against similar assaults. The mayor of Sheva, a prosperous city which borders on Jahanna to the east, is negotiating for special troops to guard its periphery, and it is expected that neighboring cities will do likewise. A special meeting of mayors is

*expected to be convened within the month, to discuss the financing
of such operations.*

*The informal truce which has been observed in the region for
nearly five hundred years has permitted the commercial development of areas surrounding the Forest, notably in the fertile Raksha
Valley to its east. Tradition has it that the arrangement was origi-
nally established by the Hunter, a demon or sorcerer who came to
the region at approximately that time. Under the terms of the truce,
communities who offered no threat to the Forest would themselves
not be threatened, although individuals of either side were fair
game. The truce was broken only twice: in 1047, when an expedition
of twenty men breached the Forest borders with intent to find and
destroy its sorcerous ruler, and in 1182, when a radical faction from
Mordreth set fire to the Forest in the dry season, in hopes of burning
it to the ground. In both cases vengeance was swift. In the fall of
1047, twenty heads minus eyes and tongues were impaled on stakes
outside the gates of their city. In 1183 the Mordreth Massacre, now
infamous, turned a thriving port town into a ghost city overnight.
Historians are quick to note that both these incidents were in response to real provocation, and that neither was succeeded by any
further acts of violence.*

*It is not yet clear in what way, if any, the men of this camp pro-
voked their sorcerous neighbor to new atrocity. But amidst rumors
of the Hunter's disappearance, the border cities are doing what they
can to protect themselves. Authorities hope that as Vannick recovers
he can shed further light on the details of this conflict, but for now
all concerned must assume that the ancient truce is no longer being
honored by its Forest patron, and defend themselves accordingly.*

"He's here."

The priest who spoke was a short man, round in the belly, red-
faced, congenial. The words he spoke so sharply seemed ill-suited to
him, as if some other mouth had formed them. Or was that only the
Patriarch's perception, knowing as he did what those words implied?

"Are you sure?" the Holy Father asked.

The double chin bobbed as he nodded. "Elerin spotted him in the
foyer. I can have him come in if you want."

"Please do."

As the priest went to the door to summon his acolyte, the Patriarch reached into his desk to pull out the sketch he kept there. It was

a pencil drawing on low-quality paper, well worn from handling. He studied it once more as the priest fetched his acolyte, filled with wonder and more than a little misgiving. If he really had seen this man . . . He shook his head, banishing the thought. One thing at a time. Confirm the sighting first.

The acolyte Elerin was a freckled teenager with bright red hair and a line of pimples along his chin. The Patriarch couldn't remember having seen him before, but that was hardly a surprise; lesser priests handled the training of such boys until they took their vows in his presence.

The youth bowed clumsily, clearly anxious about this interview, and mumbled something that might have been, "Your Holiness."

The Patriarch handed him the drawing. "Have you seen this man?"

The boy glanced at the picture and then back toward the priest, who nodded his encouragement. "I think so, Your Holiness. The drawing I saw was a little different, though."

"That was a copy. This is the original."

He looked at it again and then nodded, somewhat stiffly. Clearly he wasn't comfortable in such august company. "He was at the afternoon service, I think. On Tuesday. Yesterday," he added helpfully. "I was watching in the foyer, like Father Renalds told me to. This guy came out of the sanctuary right after the service, almost the first one out. He was in a real hurry." He looked down at the picture again, then nodded. "I'm pretty sure it was him. His hair was a little shorter, and he wasn't quite this thin, but the face looked about the same."

"Did you find out who he was?"

He shook his head, scattering the red hair out of its embankments. "I tried to talk to him, but he wouldn't stop. I asked a few people who were there if they knew who he was, but no one did."

"Did you follow him?"

The boy looked stricken. "No, Holy Father, I . . . I'm sorry." His face had flushed so bright a red that it almost rivaled his hair. "I didn't think of it. I didn't realize. . . . Please, forgive me."

"It's all right." He took the drawing back from the boy. "There's no reason you should have thought to do that. We're not training you as a spy." He tried to keep his tone as beneficent as possible; the boy was so nervous he looked as if a light breeze would knock him over. "Thank you, Elerin. You may go now."

He did so anxiously, bowing repeatedly as he backed his way toward the door. Not until he was gone did the Patriarch let his smile fade, and a more businesslike expression take its place.

"I want to know who this man is," he told the priest, tapping the drawing. "If that means following him, then do it. If our people lack the skill to pull that off gracefully, then hire someone who can." He glanced at the picture again. "Get one of our priestesses to keep watch outside the sanctuary during services. Someone young and pretty, whom he might be willing to talk to. Unmarried," he added sharply.

Would that be bait enough? The face in the picture, though roughly sketched, was clearly a handsome one. Such a man might stop to talk to a pretty woman, while ignoring the man right beside her.

"Are you sure he'll come back, Your Holiness?"

He shut his eyes for a moment; visions rose unbidden before his inner eye. "A vision showed me that he would come here, and he did. It also showed me that he would return."

"Of course, Your Holiness." The priest's voice trembled with awe as he bowed deeply before his religious master; clearly he was of the faction that considered the Patriarch's visions to come directly from God. "We'll find out who he is, I promise you."

I am a prophet in their eyes, the Patriarch mused, as the priest made his way out of the chamber. *Would that I could be so sure of it myself.*

As he gazed down at the drawing in his hands, he could not help but shiver. And a chill wind of awe coursed up his back as it seemed to him, for one fleeting instant, that Reverend Vryce's sketch of Gerald Tarrant was looking back at him.

JAGGONATH: Violence shook the Street of Gods once more as vandals skirmished with police, following the fifth in a series of assaults upon houses of worship here.

Police estimate that the vandals gained entrance to the Maidens of Pelea Temple sometime between three and four a.m. through the servants' entrance in the rear of the building. As in the previous incidents, the only motivation appeared to be desecration of the temple and its relics. Banners, signs, books, and other flammable items were assembled in the worship chamber, doused with kerosene, and burned. As in the previous incidents, the nature of the articles destroyed, combined with lack of theft in the incident, suggests either a hostile secular organization, or rivalry between religious factions based within the city.

Neighborhood watches along the Street have been doubled, and a Street of Gods defense fund has been established to defray the cost of private guards and additional investigators. Several local leaders have demanded an inquiry into the Unity Church's possible interest in this matter. The Church, which has been the source of several anti-polytheism riots in recent months, has made no official statement regarding the matter, but sources within its hierarchy indicate that the leadership is deeply concerned over recent developments, and has retained several lawyers specializing in religious liability to advise them.

ANDRYS TARRANT.

The Patriarch looked at the letters written before him as though they were foreign shapes, sounding them out one by one, tasting their meaning. So few symbols. So potent a message.

ANDRYS *TARRANT.*

A shiver ran up his spine as he considered the implications of that name. The Prophet had killed his children, or so the Church taught. Was it possible that one had survived? Was this Andrys Tarrant not only a man who looked like the Hunter, but who bore the Hunter's blood within his veins as well? A man so like him in the substance of his being that the very patterns of his DNA were echoes of the Prophet's own?

If so—Dear God!

Help me, Lord, he begged. *Guide me, so that I may serve You more perfectly.*

Tarrant. There was a wealth of power in that name, a power that might save or destroy. He remembered the man who had led his dream-army into the Forest—so bright a symbol, the focus of all their hopes—and for the first time since his war dreams began, he felt the stirring of hope. This was the key they needed, this stranger with history running in his veins. That he had suddenly appeared in Jaggonath's cathedral now, when their need was greatest, only served to confirm his purpose in the Patriarch's mind. With him, they could fight this war and win it. They could break the Forest's hold upon this region and send its ruler up in smoke. The centuries would resound with their triumph.

But did they dare?

Help me, Lord. Give me the wisdom to deal with this.
By night, he dreamed of holy war.
By day, he dreamed of Gerald Tarrant's offering.

MORDRETH: The murder of two brothers that took place in the city last night has all inhabitants of this northern city bolting their doors and cleaning their weapons. Benjin and Sorrie Heldt were found by their housekeeper at eight a.m. this morning, having been murdered in their beds less than three hours before. The bodies had been savaged by one or more large animals who apparently gained entrance through a window, but no flesh was eaten.

While police will not confirm a link between this incident and last week's slaughter in Jahanna, many locals are convinced that the Forest's inhabitants are moving to expand their territory. Sales of small arms are already up 400% in the region, and a continued increase is expected.

The blue stone lay within its box, deep cobalt light reflecting from the polished alteroak.
Help me, Lord. Guide me.
The Patriarch bowed his head before the altar, and his body trembled like a branch in a high wind. Was it sin to take up this gift, if all it offered him was knowledge? Was it wrong to use the Hunter's power, if in the end that power was to be turned against him?

For a long time he remained as he was, bowed before the hateful object. Since the moment when it had been placed here he had been continually aware of it, as if it had already established some kind of link to his mind. He felt its presence while eating, while reading, even while conducting services in the sanctified hall of the cathedral. But most acutely of all, he felt it when reports of escalating violence were brought to him. Violence within his church, that must be cleansed. Violence surrounding the Forest, that must be answered.

The dreams were so tempting, with their dramatic solution: a war against the Forest, in which the growing violence in his people could be channeled toward a positive end. A second Great War, in which the Church would at last be triumphant. The spirit of his people was ready for it. The means existed. The funds could be assigned.

The consequences were terrifying.

He had prayed for nights on end for some new insight, but none had come to him. It was so tempting, those dreams of triumph. But if he obeyed his visions and started a war, how would he end it? *Violence begets violence,* he despaired. How could he encourage it among his people, and then expect it to disperse at the campaign's end? What kind of act or symbol would be powerful enough to disrupt such a cycle?

Through it all, silent witness to his torment, was the Hunter's gift. The ultimate temptation. Not power, but something far more subtle. Not sorcery, but something even richer.

Knowledge.

He took the blue crystal up in his hand, and held it out toward the candlelight. It was so cool in his palm, and so very still. He had half-expected that it would show its power by radiating heat, or vibrating, or in some other way indicating that the fae contained within it waited only for the proper sign before it could break out. But there was nothing. Except for its eerie light, the crystal could have been no more than glass, a finely faceted paperweight.

There was no other way, he told himself. No other way. God would understand that, wouldn't He? And if He didn't (he told himself), then He would damn only the Patriarch, and spare those innocents who followed him. Wouldn't He?

Slowly, hesitantly, his fingers closed around the stone. His hand was shaking so badly that the cobalt light shimmered across the altar like waves. Then, with a sudden spasm of determination, he clenched his fist shut about the crystal, trapping its light.

In Your Name, God of Earth. For the sake of Your people.

A roaring filled the chapel, and light flooded the small room. The sudden brilliance was stunning, blinding; he fell back with a cry and threw an arm up across his eyes, as if that could protect them. But the vision stayed with him even when his eyes were closed, as if it were burned into his eyelids. Light on the floor, like liquid fire; light on the altar, sizzling as it spread out from the blessed candle flames; light that seeped in from under the door frame, light from the distant windows, light from his very flesh. The blue crystal fell from his hand and was lost in the swirling tide as bright as the sun itself, that lapped at his legs and left shimmering rivulets to run down his robe.

Power. It was power. The raw power of the planet itself, made visible by the Hunter's ward. *Fae.* He fell back from it in horror and saw the currents stir as if in response to his fear, saw the patterns of light draw back from him as though in obedience to some unspoken command. *No!* The light was taking shape, gaining color and substance and solidity, and

mother lies on the floor, and the earth-fae gathers up about her, forming itself into dark little creatures that reach with sharpened claws toward her skull

No!

cathedral and he stands there praying, and the fae takes his words and gives them life and makes the people breathe them in, so that his faith becomes part of their flesh

No!

anger like a fist about Vryce, earth-fae squeezing hard to provoke the desired reaction

He screamed. Not to be heard, not to be saved, but to empty himself of the terror which was choking him. Still the visions pounded at his brain; memories, hopes, and fears rushing through his head in one vast chaotic onslaught, and beyond that the knowledge that the power had always been there, that he had always controlled it, that the price of denial had been to lose a part of his soul. Until now . . .

Something slammed behind him. A door, struck open? It seemed a universe away to him. So did the footsteps that ran toward him from behind, and the hot hands that lifted him up from the floor, struggling to make him stand. Another world, another time. He couldn't go back to it now.

He saw the future. The *futures.* He saw his war won, and the Church triumphant. He saw it lost, and watched the Church wither away in the shadow of that failure. He watched the Church triumph again and again, and he watched it fail also, and each time it was different: future after future unveiled before him in one blinding flood of raw potential. The war was won, but the violence continued; the war was won, but his people's faith was poisoned; the war was lost and all, all was lost with it. . . .

He was aware of a hand pressed against his throat to catch his pulse, and the fevered concern of the men at his side fluttered about his head like batlings. They were saying something to him, but their words couldn't make it through the roar of the fae in his ears. Where was the future with hope in it? he despaired. Where was the path to salvation? Symbols and human figures and fears that had wings swirled wildly about him as he struggled to find some focus. *Father?* they chittered. *Holy Father, are you all right?* He saw a demon with the eyes of an insect cut open his head and place dreams inside. *Holy Father?* Faster and faster now, visions of the past and future tumbling over one other, pouring into his soul faster than he could sort them out. *What's wrong?* He needed the right future. *Someone call a doctor, fast!* The war was over and the Patriarch called his soldiers together, and the fae gathered at his feet in response to him just as it always had, obeying this man who had been a sorcerer since the day of his birth—

There was terror in that image, but also exultation, for it was a new pattern, a new path. This was the one way he could save his people; this was their only hope. He saw it acted out, he watched it replayed a thousand times within each second as his heart pounded, shaking his body, sending ripples out through the fae

Hold him still!

and there was a stabbing in his arm, not fire now but cold, icy cold. He could feel his heart struggling against it, and the visions began to shatter like glass about him. Pain spread through his veins and the fae turned to ice and cracked from his skin, and a darkness descended from the ceiling and a weight came crashing up from the floor—

Fine. He's fine.

What happened?

I don't know.

What did you give him?

Hard to hear. Hard to see. Impossible to move.

Is the ambulance—

Coming.

Pulse is strong.

What the hell happened?

Cling to the vision. Don't forget!

Hold on.

Help's coming.

Darkness.

Nineteen

The color of pain was red. A raw, ugly red, that stank like rotting meat and oozed inward through his pores until he was filled with it. A red that flayed his nerves alive and then scraped along their surfaces, arousing pain beyond that which any living body could endure. A pain so total that it stripped him of his humanity, it bled him of all intelligence, it left him no more than a core of terror and agony in a universe gone mad, in which waves of pain were the only marker of time.

And then, in that madness: a human hand, grasping his. The touch was like fire, but Damien gripped it desperately, allowing the contact to define him. Fingers. Palm. Soul. It became the focus of his universe, the single point about which worlds revolved, the core of his private galaxy. Fire blazed along his arm as his muscles split from the strain, bloody strips curling back upon themselves, laying the moist bones beneath bare and vulnerable. Skin, he needed skin, nature's own armor: he fixed his mind upon that one need until it seemed to him that his muscles were no longer bare, clothing them with the power of his imagination. It was instinct that drove him rather than knowledge, but the instinct seemed true and he clung to it desperately, unwilling to sink back into formless agony again.

Arm: define it, feel it, *believe* in it. Shoulder. Chest. Fire lanced across his torso like whip strokes, and in those seconds when his concentration wavered he could feel his newly imagined skin peeling from his body in heat-blackened strips, edges charred to a glowing ash . . . the hand that held his gripped him tighter as he fought to regain consciousness of self, and another clasped his shoulder. Good. That made for two points of contact in a universe of burning blood.

Two points defined a line. Three points defined a plane. Four points defined a solid. . . .

And then the redness was gone and he was on his knees, choking on air that reeked of sulfur and burning meat. The hands that held him helped him to his feet, and he accepted their aid with gratitude. The ground was so hot that already his breeches had begun to smoke, and the stink of burning wool added new strength to the noxious melange surrounding him.

"What was that?" he whispered. He didn't expect an answer, so much as he needed to test his voice. To his surprise the words indeed sounded, though he distinctly remembered his vocal cords having burned to bloody ribbons at least twice.

"Did you think the transition would be easy?" a voice from behind him asked. The hands that were gripping him released him, and a wave of panic nearly overcame him at the sudden loss of contact. There was no doubt in his mind that without Karril's touch he would have been lost in that pain forever. A numbing fear grew in him, that perhaps he had indeed taken on more than he could handle this time. If that was just the gateway to Hell, what lay beyond?

And then he grew aware of the voice that had spoken. Not Karril's, nor anything like it. A more musical voice, higher-pitched, that was painfully but indefinably familiar. He turned around suddenly, so focused on the source of that voice that he hardly saw the surreal landscape surrounding it.

It was Rasya. No, not Rasya exactly. It was a woman of Rasya's height and coloring and general form: sun-baked bronze skin, short-cropped platinum hair, long, lean limbs with capable muscles playing visibly beneath. But the face was different, and the clothing also, and this woman's eyes were so like Karril's that he shivered to see them set in a body so like that of his lost lover.

"Why?" he gasped. The stink of sulfur was stronger now, and it was getting difficult to breathe. It was hard to say whether anger or mourning played louder in his voice as he demanded, "Why, Karril?"

"My life is on the line here, too," he said. *She* said. "And I can't change form in this place, any more than you can. I needed a body that would be strong, enduring, and versatile. Given your orientation, it had to be female. Given your memories. . . ." The woman shrugged stiffly. "I'm sorry. I didn't catch the mourning until it was too late. I meant no disrespect."

He shut his eyes for a moment, painfully aware of the heat that was baking through his boot soles. "Do you expect some kind of response from me?" he whispered hoarsely. "Is that what this is about?"

"If I required that to survive, would you be so quick to deny me?" She reached forward and took Damien's hand again, in a grip more reassuring than affectionate. "Like you, I try to keep all options open." She pulled his hand, gently but firmly, forcing him to move. "Come on. Time matters."

He forced himself to look away from her, toward the bizarre landscape that surrounded them. The land all about was black and glassy, and it smoked with a heat that made the very air shimmer. Overhead a sun blazed, not the wholesome white star of Erna but a bloated yellow shape that sent streamers of flame down almost to the landscape, sparking explosions which in turn sent gouts of lava spouting into the air. The sky surrounding it was as dark as night, as were the shadows its harsh light etched upon the landscape. Beneath his feet the ground seemed to tremble, and as he watched, it cracked not ten feet to the right of him, revealing a glowing red subsurface.

"Damn," he breathed.

"What?"

"Too vulking realistic for my taste." He glanced toward the demon, then quickly away. "Which way's out?"

"*Out's* the way we came. Which route I will gladly point out to you, whenever you've had enough. As for what we came here to do . . ." She looked out over the landscape, and at last indicated a direction. Thank God, it was away from the crack. "That way, I think."

"You *think?*"

"This isn't my realm," Karril said testily. "I wonder if it would even exist without your Church doing constant publicity for it. Come on."

He needed no urging to move, and he moved quickly. He had been in a place like this once and had almost gotten killed, and that was just on its border. How much of the black rock beneath them was solid, and how much was a paper-thin shell hiding rivers of molten lava beneath? Any one footstep might prove the difference. And if the similarity between this place and the real world was unnerving, the discrepancy was downright terrifying. In the real world, if the shell lava cracked beneath your feet, you fell and you cooked and you died. But here, in this unearthly place, where death was a threshold more distant with every step . . . could one burn forever? Choking on molten rock, *drowning* in it, as the flesh was seared from one's bones over and over again? It wasn't a theory he was anxious to test.

"What about Tarrant?"

"You mean, is he still here?" The Rasya-thing glanced at him. "If he were, there'd be no trail."

He looked out over the landscape ahead of them, squinting against the sickening yellow light. "I don't see a damned thing."

"Then it's lucky I came along, isn't it?" She nodded ahead and toward the right, to an area pockmarked by pools of glowing lava. "That way."

He followed her more by touch than by sight, across a landscape where any step might be his last. The ground split as they passed, but though his heart lurched with every new fissure it was only to vent clouds of burning ash and noxious gas, to fill the air with poison. It clogged his lungs as he breathed it in and set off a spasm of coughing so violent that he feared the vibrations of his body might do more damage to the ground beneath them than the weight of his footsteps. He tried not to remember the time in the westlands when he had almost gotten killed, traversing a lava field all too much like this one.

... *ground giving way beneath his feet with a sudden crack and he throws himself sideways as the rock beneath his feet shatters, fragments raining down into a heat so terrible that the hairs on his head sizzle and curl as he grasps at a nearby protrusion ... rock so hot that he can feel the palms of his skin burning, but if he lets go more than that will burn, and he pulls himself across rock no more solid than that which just failed him, praying that the vagaries of Luck will protect him one moment longer. ...*

"Don't," Karril whispered hoarsely. "Stop."

Her hand had released his. Her face was white.

He stared at her in amazement, as it hit home just what he had done. *Her life is dependent on my state of mind,* he thought. Awed— and also frightened—by the concept. Must he not only endure the rigors of Tarrant's Hell, but do so without undue suffering? He didn't know if he could manage that. Suddenly it hit home just what Karril had risked by coming here. And what depth of friendship there must be between Tarrant and the Iezu—however well-disguised—to inspire such a journey.

A geyser of flame spurted suddenly behind them. They sprinted forward across the black rock, but not fast enough to escape its downpour. Molten drops rained across the landscape, and where they struck Damien, a blinding pain stabbed into him; it took all his strength to keep running even as his flesh burned, the stink of woolen ash mixed with smoking meat as he choked on the fumes of his own destruction. Then one foot came down too hard, or else the ground was especially weak; he felt the rock giving way beneath him and threw himself forward in utter desperation, praying for solid rock ahead of him. In that instant of utter panic he thought he had lost Karril forever, but the demon had chosen his form well; the light, lithe body that so mimicked Rasya's was still by his side as the rock gave way behind him, freeing a blast of heat so violent that it almost knocked him down.

"This way," she said. Urging him onward.

Gasping, he struggled to follow her. The soles of his feet felt as if they were on fire; the leather which hardly protected them had begun to smoke, promising even greater pain in the future. *I was a fool to come here!* he despaired. What had he hoped to accomplish? *Tarrant, you'd better be worth this!* Then a fit of coughing overcame him and he staggered forward blindly, guided only by her hand.

"A little late now," she said dryly. As if he had spoken aloud.

The ground was giving way all around them now, and more and more often they were forced to break into a run despite the risk, to keep themselves from falling with it. *This is Tarrant's true Hell.* Damien thought, *unbridled fear.* What more fitting torment could there be for such a man, who had made fear into an elixir of immortality, and turned the whole world into his hunting ground? Then another sulfurous cloud enveloped him and he fell to the ground, choking; his hands and back were seared by the hot rock like meat on a grill.

"Come on." Strong arms were gripping him, fighting to raise him up. "There's a cool spot ahead, I think."

Yeah, he thought dully, *an oasis in Hell. I believe that.* But even that weak fantasy was enough to give him focus, and he struggled to his feet again. The clouds of ash were so thick about them that he could hardly see, but the sound of rock splitting just behind them was warning enough to keep him moving. He followed Karril blindly, clasping her hand in a grip that was sticky with blood, and prayed that the demon's sight was better than his own.

And then, incredibly, the heat did abate somewhat. The ground felt more solid beneath his feet. (That could have been because the nerves in his feet had been seared to numbness, he told himself, but then again, it could be real.) He took the opportunity to stop and bend over, gasping for breath in the sulfurous air. Since Karril didn't urge him to keep moving, he assumed that they were safe. For the moment.

When at last burning tears had cleared his eyes of dust, and his shaking muscles had loosened enough to let him stand upright, he looked back at the way they had just come and shuddered. Bright streamers of lava had broken through the ground in so many places that he could hardly trace their path; red fountains of molten rock spewed up like geysers where they had only recently been running. He had been near volcanoes in his life—too near, on occasion—but he had never gone through any realm like this. No living man could, he realized. Only in a place where *life* and *death* were meaningless could man traverse such a hell.

"Please," he gasped. "Tell me we don't have to go back that way."

"No need to worry," the demon assured him. "Personally, I think the odds are very slim of us going back at all."

He glared at the demon and opened his mouth to voice a nasty response to his wisecrack, but when he saw what the Rasya-body looked like the words died in his throat. Karril was paler than the real Rasya had ever been, and his (her?) skin was an ashen gray. There was fear in the demon's eyes now, and exhaustion so human that for a moment Damien thought that it, too, was just part of the masquerade.

My pain is draining him, he realized. Sickened by the thought. *Can I kill him, just by suffering?*

There was a sudden crack beside them; instinctively he grabbed Karril by the arm and jerked her away from it, breaking into a run as soon as he was sure that the demon wouldn't lose her balance. The seemingly solid rock they had been standing on collapsed into a swirling orange river beneath; a gust of heat slammed into them with hurricane force, flames licking at their backs.

Another island of cool rock beckoned, and they stopped there just long enough for Damien to catch his breath. His muscles ached as though he had been running for days, and his parched throat struggled to draw in enough air to support him. He raised a hand to his forehead to wipe away the sweat that was streaming into his eyes, and to his surprise found that it was whole, unbloodied. Uncooked. Was he healing even as he ran? For a moment it seemed impossible . . . and then, with a chill, he recognize the pattern. Yes, his flesh would heal itself, just fast enough to allow it to suffer more. Like the Hunter's own flesh had done when the enemy trapped him in fire, forcing him to regenerate just fast enough to burn anew. To burn *eternally*.

Had those eight days in the rakhlands been so traumatic that they had etched their way into Tarrant's soul, carving out a niche in his private Hell in which the fire would always burn him? Or did the nightmare already exist within him, and Calesta merely tapped into it when he bound Tarrant within the flames? Either way, it was a terrifying concept. How could a man experience such a thing, and not lose his sanity altogether?

Whoever said he was sane?

"Look." Karril pointed into the distance. "Something's changing."

Despite the harsh light—or perhaps because of it—he found it hard to make out anything in that direction. Nevertheless, it seemed to him that there *was* a difference. After a moment he realized what it was. No lava spurted from the region ahead of them. No clouds of choking ash arose from the landscape. Try as he might, he could see no bright red rivers coursing across the terrain where Karril pointed.

For some reason, that scared him more than everything which had come before. He started to speak, to try to voice his misgiving, but then a gust of noxious gas filled his throat and his nose, setting off a new round of coughing; his stomach heaved as if somehow that could cleanse the delicate membranes. Behind them the rock was giving way again in long, thin sections, bright lava eating away at the shelf they stood upon, inch by inch, whittling down their haven. Soon nothing would be left to stand upon. There was no alternative but to run, and nowhere to run but to that still region up ahead . . . and it scared him.

"Vryce?"

"Is that the right way?" he gasped. To his relief Karril nodded. What would he have done if it weren't? Dived into the lava stream, and swum through the boiling currents to their destination? It didn't bear thinking about.

They sprinted forward, just in time. With a roar like thunder, the very ground they were standing on shattered like glass and collapsed into the current beneath; fire lapped at their heels as they ran for the refuge which seemed to beckon, just ahead. The whole land was in flux now, and Damien could feel the ground trembling beneath his feet as it buckled in waves, sending red fountains spouting into the air on all sides of them. Molten droplets gouged his flesh as he struggled to keep on his feet. It seemed impossible that he could keep moving, but he did. Somehow.

Falter now, priest, and you'll be stuck here forever.

Finally they came to a place where the ground was still steady, and Damien paused for a brief instant to catch his breath. Ahead of them the black rock had crumbled and fallen, providing a sloping path down to the region beyond. Despite his misgivings, Damien began to scramble down the precarious slope, scoring his flesh on the razor-sharp rocks that lined it. Was there pain ahead? More fear? Anything was better than the glowing rivers and burning rain that were closing in behind them. Wasn't it?

At the bottom of the slope he paused, and lay back upon the harsh gravel, trying to catch his breath. But his lungs, constricted by cloud-borne poisons, would not relax enough to draw in air. For a moment he debated the relative risk of trying to Heal himself, and at last decided he had nothing to lose by trying. He took hold of the current with his mind and began to weave it, drawing together the wild power into a Workable whole—

Or he tried to. But there was no fae here, or perhaps just no way to Work it. *Earth,* he thought, looking up at the swollen yellow star that shone down on them, recognizing it at last. *Earth was his passion, and also his nightmare.* He remembered the Hunter sharing his dreams of Earth with Damien to make him afraid, and there was no denying their power. Had the Prophet feared the very world he idolized, and mourned the concept of a world without sorcery even as he worked to bring it into being?

"Look," Karril whispered.

He got to his feet quickly, prepared for some new assault. But the rock beneath his wounded feet was steady, and the air down on this plain was almost breathable. He looked in the distance, following Karril's own gaze, and saw what looked like the ground moving up ahead. No, not the ground, but something on top of it that shifted and writhed like a living blanket. It was lighter than the ground itself, a sickly yellowish color that might, in a gentler light, have looked like flesh. Human flesh, discolored by the unrelenting sun.

Filled with misgivings, he nonetheless started forward toward it. *If the path leads that way, we have no alternative.* He disciplined his mind by recounting all the various ways he would make Tarrant pay for forcing him to come here, and thus managed to keep his fear under tight rein. But as he drew closer, as he saw the strange realm for what it was, that strategy failed him utterly.

It was bodies. Human bodies, stretching ahead to the horizon and beyond. *Women's* bodies, strewn across the landscape like discarded refuse, gathered together in such numbers that in places they were stacked in mounds, like heaps of living garbage. As he watched, they twitched and shivered, and their combined motion gave the illusion of waves passing across the surface. He saw thin limbs, pale skin, fingers that clutched at air and then withdrew again, burrowing deep down into the flesh-blanket that seemed to cover the whole planet like crabs seeking shelter.

"What *is* it?" he whispered.

Karril breathed in sharply, for once without a pat rejoinder. "Damned if I know."

With a wrenching sensation in his gut he realized that the living blanket was parting, ever so slowly. Limbs contracted to draw the nearer bodies out of their path; their motion was crablike and horrible, not at all human. *What is this place!* he thought desperately. A narrow path was forming, flanked by twitching limbs. It was just wide enough for them to walk single file, if they watched where they were going. Just narrow enough to make him feel sick at the thought of such a passage.

But . . .

That was the path, without question; he didn't need Karril to tell him that. Tarrant's own fear had marked it for them. How many miles did this horror stretch onward, glazed eyes staring out of undead faces as spider-fingers struggled to clear the way? His stomach churned at the thought that one wrong step might put him in contact with those gruesomely contorted bodies, but a hissing behind him, like steam off approaching lava, warned him that to stay where he was might prove an even worse alternative.

There's no other choice, he told himself grimly. *Not unless we want to go back the way we came.* And that was out of the question.

"All right," he muttered. "Let's do it."

He went first, moving toward the narrow path the bodies had made for them. On both sides the mounds of flesh still twitched and writhed, and periodically a leg or a hand would be flung across their path, a gruesome reminder that their new-made road might disappear as quickly as it had begun. The thought made hot bile rise in his throat, but still he forced himself forward. *There's no other way,* he told himself, repeating the words over and over again, a mantra of endurance. Behind him he could hear the hiss of lava as it flowed down the rocky slope and enveloped the nearest bodies, and the stink of burnt flesh filled the air like a choking perfume. He could see details of the bodies now, faces and breasts and buttocks made waxen and distorted by death, undead eyes gazing out of hollowed sockets as if facing some unseen horror. The movements of their limbs were not random, he could see now, but each body twitched as if running, or striving to run, while the weight of all its neighbors trapped it in place and turned the motion into a mockery of flight.

His foot landed close to the head of one, then by the clutching hand of another. It took almost balletic skill to avoid coming in contact with them, a trial his burned and aching body was no longer up to. It seemed to him that every step must surely be his last, and only

the sheer horror of the bodies surrounding him gave him the strength
to keep going. Karril followed silently behind him, wrapped in her
own Iezu thoughts. Were these unalive creatures human enough to
disturb her? Did they give off waves of pain of their own, or some
other, more virulent suffering? He glanced back now and then to
check on the demon, but though Karril's expression was grim her
short nod told Damien that all was well with her. For the moment.

And then he stopped and stared, as one human fragment among
many caught his eye. A dark arm atop the paler ones. Thick hair, as
black as night. Eyes that he knew, staring into the sky like eyes of
the dead even as the dark limbs twitched in a mockery of life.

"Sisa," he whispered.

He heard the Iezu curse softly as she, too, realized who this body
belonged to. Tarrant's latest victim, strewn atop this lake of human
remains like so much garbage. How many others here were his victims, or at least vivid simulacra of the same? He looked out upon the
acres and acres of twitching flesh and shuddered. They were all
women, and from what he could see they were all within a narrow
age range. Mostly pale, as befit the Hunter's taste in victims. Doubtless attractive during their lives, although now that quality made
them seem doubly gruesome.

Then: "Move!" the demon hissed from behind him, and he did so
without thought, trusting Karril's warning. Fingers scratched his ankle as he moved just beyond the reach of *something*, and for a moment a wave of fear surged through his blood with such force that his
limbs bound up like a frozen motor. Frightened, he struggled to keep
moving. From behind him the demon hissed sharply as if in pain, but
when he stopped to turn around, a hand shoved him from behind as
if to say, *I'm fine! Keep going!* Glancing down at the ground before
his feet, trying to locate the safest ground, he saw with horror that
human limbs were closing in on the path from both sides. Arms
grasped at him as he lurched past, some closing on air behind him,
some coming close enough to scrape his boots. For some reason that
sight made him more afraid than all of Tarrant's lava hell combined,
and he broke into a run. Forcing his way past the grasping arms,
whose fingers sent waves of terror coursing through his soul whenever they made contact. Where was the end of this path? he thought
desperately. How many bodies were there? He found it impossible to
believe that so many women could have fallen victim to one man's
hunger, but what did he really know about the Hunter? How many
numberless atrocities had the man indulged in, in the years before his
semi-retirement in the Forest?

And then one of the arms grabbed his ankle and held it. His own weight sent him plunging forward and down, into the hands and the arms and the legs that were waiting for him, and—

—*running. Tree branches spreading across the path like spider silk, dark webs catching her as she runs, she struggles, she convulses madly, desperately, as the black thing that has chased her for three days and nights closes in—*

—*running while the ground comes alive, crawly things oozing out of the very pores of the earth to trip at her ankles, sending her facedown into a bed of hungry worms—*

—*running from the thing that has chased her for days, manlike but demon-strong, whose hunger licks at her flesh as she stumbles, as she feels sharp talons piercing her skin, setting hot blood to flow free—*

Strong hands took hold of his hair and his collar and yanked upward; it was the pain more than anything which made the visions scatter, allowing him one precious instant in which he could gasp for breath. The hands about his ankles shifted grip, and the visions began to close in once more—but the demon dragged him forward, hard enough and fast enough for them to be thrown lose. Left behind.

Shuddering, he gasped, "Tarrant's victims—"

"I know," Karril said grimly. "Keep moving!"

He knew in that moment, as he struggled to his feet once more, that the demon had experienced those awful visions through him. And he knew with dread certainty that if he should fall again, if those bodies should overwhelm him, the demon would be trapped alongside him in an endless hell of suffering, reliving the last moments of each of the Hunter's victims over and over and over again. . . .

He ran. Fast enough that the hands couldn't take hold of him, or so he prayed. Hard enough that any which did would be shaken loose by his momentum, before the memories they stored within their flesh could take hold. One arm lashed out across the path and he landed on it, crushing its dead flesh into the rock ground beneath; a spear of memory burned up through his leg and he felt cold teeth bite into his throat, the hot wound of despair as his lifeblood gushed out. It took everything he had not to stumble, but terror lent him a strength that cold logic could never have inspired, and he managed to stay on his feet. There were moans all about him now, and while some were echoes of pain and fear, others seemed to be sounds of hunger. Were the bodies aware of him? Did they think he was Tarrant? Ahead of him the path was closing up now, and he realized

in horror that to get beyond this region he was going to have to wade
through a sea of bodies, each of which had the power to send him spiraling down into unending nightmare. Panic assailed him, and he
glanced back over his shoulder—stumbling as he did so—to assess
the odds of retreat. There were none. The path in the distance was already gone, and as they ran forward, a wave of flesh came at them
from behind, threatening to submerge them utterly.

And then he reached the wall of limbs and he surged into it,
knowing even as he did so that no human velocity could possibly
overwhelm such an obstacle, that a realm which had been designed
to overwhelm the great Gerald Tarrant could easily overcome a mere
human like himself—

—*running/falling/fearing into darkness darkness, running DE-
SPAIR! and the great bird closes in, talons red, feathers white—and
the man with eyes of blue flame—and the wolves/spiders/snakes/
shadows/HUNTER!—*

A hand grasped hold of his shoulder; he felt it distantly, like a
thing from another world, as the terror of the Hunter's victims reverberated through his flesh, drawing strength and solidity in each new
second.

—*face like a ghost and hunger a palpable force that licks at her
with an icy tongue—*

He struggled to surface and failed. Struggled to define himself, to
divide himself from the tsunami of pain and fear that surged through
his brain, but the memories were too strong, too compelling . . . too
many. He was drowning in terror.

—*face of a monster—*

Another hand grasped him, held him tightly.

—*face of a god, too dark and terrible to behold. She lies trans-
fixed as he bends down over her, her heart pounding like a frightened animal's . . . and then, suddenly, there is something besides
fear in her. A rising heat, sharp and shameful, that makes her stretch
back her throat as his shadow embraces her, baring it for the kill—*

—*secret, shameful thrill—*

—*power all around her, throbbing like a living thing, HIS power—*

—*raw and terrible and magnificent—*

—*ecstasy as flesh is torn from her bone, one last glorious moment
in which she shares his pleasure and is willing to die for this terrible
embrace—*

With a gasp he surfaced long enough to see Rasya's face just above
his own, expression drawn and strained as if by some private agony.
"Can you move?" it whispered. A dead hand grasped at his thigh as

he nodded, and it sent him plummeting down into nightmare once more. But they were no longer cold dreams of horror and despair; this was a hot sea he sank into, fear transmuted into desire, horror made into beauty, resistance giving way to a blissful acquiescence. He could sense the real terror behind it, masked by Karril's hedonistic illusions, but its edge had been blunted. Just enough, he thought, to give him a fighting chance.

Panting, he struggled to his feet. His groin was painfully swollen, and when an undead hand brushed against it from beneath he cried out, waves of pain and pleasure radiating out from that point in stunning, shameful confusion. He held onto Karril's arm and let the demon guide him, accepting the transformed memories as they washed over him like a wave. Once, for a brief instant, his sight of the real world grew clear enough that he could study the land ahead of them, searching for some end to this trial. But the ground was covered in flesh as far as he could see, bodies piling upon bodies in all the directions he might choose to turn. There was no end to this, he realized. Already it seemed like he had been here forever. Each memory that took hold of him seemed to last forever, and the journey yet to come—

With a strangled cry he acknowledged an even greater danger facing him, and as the next memory dragged him down into the past he fought the time-numbing power of its imagery, and struggled to regain some kind of temporal framework. At last he was reduced to counting seconds in his brain even as he ran, on remembered legs, through the Hunter's Forest. Time and time again, in the dreams of the Hunter's victims, he ran and suffered and desired and died—and all the while the counting ticked in his skull like some vast springwound clock, marking the parameters of his body's survival. One minute. Two. Ten. An hour . . .

It'll never end, he thought grimly, *unless I make it end.* He struggled to win free of the nightmares that assaulted him long enough to get a good, hard look at his situation. If he had managed to gain any forward ground thus far, it wasn't visible. There was still no end in sight. And Karril, whose bizarre ministrations had allowed him to cling to sanity, was clearly weakening from the strain of such sustained effort.

With the kind of courage that only sheer desperation could muster, he drew himself upright and raised up his fist against the black sky. "Damn you!" he screamed, in a voice so hoarse it hardly sounded human. "You know we're here! You know *why* we're here! Why play these games?" A cold hand closed around his ankle and he began to sink into memories once more; he struggled to cling to consciousness long enough to voice the challenge that his heart was screaming. "Are you afraid?" he demanded. "Afraid of one man and a Iezu? Afraid that if we get through this nightmare, we'll lay waste to all your plans?"

"Don't," Karril whispered fiercely. "You don't know what they'll do—"

But I know what'll happen if they don't do anything, he thought grimly, as the horrific images began to flood his brain anew. Already the black sky was fading, and his image of the swollen sun, and the bodies on the ground were giving way to night-black, Forest-spawned underbrush—

And then there was a rumbling beneath his feet, so like that of a volcano's flank that he nearly turned back to see if some new eruption had followed them here. But Karril was clutching him too tightly for him to turn. Another quake shook the ground, and it seemed to him that the bodies before him were beginning to withdraw, clearing the way ahead. The one that grasped his leg let loose, and he felt an almost unbearable relief when, for the first time in hours, his mind was wholly his own.

"Karril—" he began.

"You're suicidal, you know that?" Amazed and exasperated, the demon shook her head. "How on Erna did you manage to survive this long?"

The ground split before them with a roar, and a vast, black chasm opened just before their feet. The bodies on its edges spilled down into the guts of the earth, still twitching their death-dance as they fell. It seemed to Damien that the bodies moaned as they fell, or perhaps some hellish wind that scoured the chasm's depths merely mimicked the sound. Instinctively he stepped back, but the demon would not permit him to retreat.

"You summoned it," she growled. "You deal with it."

Something in the chasm's blackness made his stomach clench in terror, but he knew in his heart that Karril was right. Tarrant's captors were clearly aware of their journey here—as he had guessed—and they had answered his challenge. It was too late to undo that. All he could accomplish now, by refusing their invitation, was to anger them enough that they closed the way out of here forever.

He walked slowly to the edge of the chasm and gazed down into it. Though his human eyes could make out no details in the blackness, other senses picked out motion within the lightless depths, of things that slithered and flew and . . . waited. A sickening reek rose up to his nostrils, all too like the one that had been in Tarrant's apartment. He had barely been able to tolerate that assault; how well would he handle this, its hellish source? As he stared down into the abyss, he suddenly wasn't sure.

Well, you should have thought of that before you came here, priest. It's too late now.

The lip of the chasm near his feet wasn't a sheer drop, as elsewhere, but an angled and rocky slope. Clearly it was the only way down, short of jumping. With a last glance at Karril and a pounding in his heart, Damien slipped free of the demon's grasp and began the precarious descent. Into the black, rent earth. Into a darkness so total that despite the light from above, sharp yellow shafts making the lips of the chasm glow as if they were burning, he couldn't make out the shape of his own hand in front of his face, much less any detail of his surroundings.

Then the darkness closed in overhead, and all sight of the world above was gone. He breathed in deeply, trying not to give way to the claustrophobia that suddenly gripped his heart. At last, when he felt capable of moving again, he began to work his way down the slope by feel alone. When the path seemed to dissolve beneath his hands, he fought hard not to panic, and waited it out. The blackness surrounding him was close and thick and evil-smelling, but his sense of impending danger had become so great that those things took a back seat in his consciousness. As did the pain of his many wounds, now burning anew as the darkness rubbed against them.

"Karril?" he whispered. "You with me?"

"Unfortunately." He felt the demon brush against him and reached out to take her hand; from the strength of her returning grip he judged that she wasn't any happier about this place than he was. He was suddenly glad that she had come here in a female form. It didn't matter worth a damn in reality—a demon was a demon—but he would have felt like an idiot squeezing hands with a man in this darkness, even knowing the truth. Thank God for Karril's insight.

Something brushed against his leg—and a wave of loathing rose up in his gut, clogged his throat, made his brain fill with images of hatred and destruction. An instant later it was gone. *What—!* Then another thing slithered against his back, and for an instant he was consumed by such jealous rage that all conscious thought gave way before it. That, too, passed quickly, fading into the darkness that surrounded as soon as its messenger lost contact with them.

"Hate-wraiths," Karril whispered. "Rage-wraiths. And more. Every species of evil that man has ever produced is here, given independent life by the force of the planet. Congregating in this one place, like drawn to like, until their sheer mass gave them a kind of consciousness no lone demon could ever enjoy." Damien could sense her eyes fixed on him; could her Iezu senses function in this darkness? "That's your Unnamed, priest. Erna's great devil. Like everything else, a creation of your own species." Damien could feel her twisting, as if to look about them. "And a damn lousy host, besides."

He was about to respond when a voice whispered, *See.* Others echoed it, fragments of speech that entered his skull not through his ears, as human speech might, but through his very skin. Whispers that etched their way into his brain matter without ever making a real sound.

See
Intruders!
No place
Go
Go
See
Invasion!
Strike out
Destroy

And then a deeper voice, more resonant, that seemed to contain a thousand others: *See what it is you came to see, priest. Know your own helplessness.*

A figure some ten yards distant from Damien was made visible, but not by any natural light. Eerie phosphorescence illuminated the form of a man hanging as if bound to some frame, but gave no view of his supporting device. It gleamed off the polished surfaces of belt buckles, buttons, and embroidery, but was swallowed by the darkness surrounding those things before it could illuminate any details of the chamber surrounding. It etched in harsh relief the visage of a man so wracked by pain that his features were almost unrecognizable, and the shreds of his clothing where they hung from his lean frame were little more than wisps of dying color, bleached by the unnatural light.

"Gerald," he whispered.

He was bound as he had been in the fire of the earth so long ago: cruciform, his arms stretched out tautly to his sides, his legs separated just far enough to make room for the bonds at his ankles. But where the Master of Lema had used plain iron to bind the Hunter, the Unnamed had more gruesome tools. The ropes that were wrapped about him glowed with an unwholesome light all their own, and they shifted and twitched as Damien watched, like living creatures. Horrified, he saw one raise its head as if noting his approach; when it decided at last that Damien was no threat to it, it returned to the work at hand, burrowing down between the tendons of the Hunter's forearm like some hungry animal, leaving a band of sizzling flesh wherever it passed. Now that he knew what to look for, Damien could see that the other "ropes" were much the same, serpentine creatures that twined inside and out of the Hunter's body, their flesh burning into the man's own like acid every time they moved.

He wasn't surprised that Karril let go of his hand and refused to approach with him. Gazing at Tarrant's tortured visage, sensing a man so lost in pain that he wasn't even aware of their presence, he wondered that the Iezu had managed to come even this close.

You see? a slithering voice pressed, and another whispered, *Your Church would approve.*

He tried to focus on why he had come here, on the arguments he had been running through his mind since his discovery of Tarrant's disappearance. It was hard, with that horrific display hanging just overhead. He flinched inside each time he heard one of the serpent-things move, guessing at the pain they caused.

"Is this some kind of punishment?" he demanded.

This is his judgment, many-voices-in-one answered him.

"For what crime?"

He could sense agitation in the darkness around him; one or two of the damned creatures flitted near him, but none made contact. *For the act of forgetting who he is, and what power sustains him. For the crime of pretending to be human.*

"It must have been a terrible thing he did, that overweighs nine centuries of service. Tell me what it was."

You were there, priest.

Was that anger in its voice? He tried to keep the fear out of his own as he urged it, "Tell me how you see it."

He saved a civilization from ruin, one voice whispered into his brain.

He circumvented a holocaust that would have fed us all, another proclaimed.

He gave your Patriarch a weapon no man of the Church should ever have.

"What—?" He looked up at Tarrant, eyes narrowing in anger as he realized what the voices must be referring to. *You son of a bitch. You did it!* It was hard to say if he was more amazed or angry, now that he knew. What kind of desperation must the man have felt, to have risked such a thing?

He forced himself to turn away from the Hunter's body, to face the unseen creatures once more. He had an answer for that argument, and for any other they might come up with. "Each thing you name, he did for his own purposes. Each thing he did, he did to stay alive so that he could serve you."

Doesn't matter

Doesn't matter

Doesn't matter

Traitor!

His mind racing, Damien struggled to regain control of their interview. "And so what? You'll keep him here forever? Is that your intention?"

Until judgment is rendered

Until the compact is broken

Traitor!

"A death sentence," he mused. "Is that what nine centuries of service are worth to you?"

He could feel something swelling in the darkness, like a wave gathering overhead, preparing to crash down on him. The next voice was deeper and infinitely more resonant, and played against a background of utter silence; the whispering voices had been sucked into a greater whole.

We reclaim a gift he no longer deserves, it told Damien. *What he does after that is his own concern.*

"You're sentencing him to death."

Again there was the dizzying sensation of something gathering just beyond his sight, drawing back like an incipient bore wave. Panic shot through his flesh like hot spears, but he sensed that it was some kind of assault from that presence, and he struggled to stand his ground.

Whether he lives or dies is not Our concern.

"Your sentence means his death," he persisted. Sensing that there was an intelligence behind the voice now, and a malevolence, far greater than anything it had contained before. "You know that. *He* knows it." And he dared, "Taste the knowledge inside him, if you doubt me."

Something dark and unwholesome moved close by his cheek, almost touching him as it passed; it took everything he had not to collapse in a heap of gibbering panic at the near-contact. God in Heaven! What would happen if it had actually touched him, like the others had? Then he heard a sharp cry behind him, and the straining of flesh against living bonds. Whatever method of Knowing the owner of that voice was using, it was clearly painful.

I'm sorry, he thought to Tarrant. Wishing the man could hear him. *There was no other way.*

At last the struggling behind him subsided, and he was aware of the dark thing withdrawing to its place. *What you say is true,* it rumbled. *It's still no concern of Ours.*

"He served you for nine centuries," Damien challenged. "He tortured and killed and maimed and corrupted whole generations, all in your name. He warped an entire region so that it would serve his hunger—*your* hunger—and made himself into a legend that'll feed you with fear long after he's dead." He paused dramatically; his heart was pounding. "For all that service he should deserve some kind of chance for survival, don't you think?"

Perhaps, a lighter voice whispered, and others echoed the thought. The sense of overwhelming malevolence had faded ever so slightly, for which Damien was grateful. Would that greater being have accepted his argument? For the first time he sensed what Tarrant must have gone through, putting his soul in the hands of a creature who changed its very definition with each passing second. *Or perhaps instead We should judge him by the company he keeps. You defend him as if he were one of your own, priest. If he were truly as evil as you claim, no living man would stand up for him like that.*

"I need him!" he snarled. Making his voice as callous as it could become, smothering every last bit of sentiment his human heart might nurture. "I need him as a tool, and when that's done I couldn't give a damn what happens to him. Let Hell have him if it wants. God knows, he's earned it."

Silence. Damien glanced over desperately to where Karril must be, but saw no sign of her in the darkness. Would his argument work? Clearly the Unnamed's response to such things had as much to do with the form it was in at the moment, as any inherent merit his argument might have. Was it in Damien's favor that the voices had stayed joined together through most of their interview, or would the fragmented whispers that flitted about like insects have been easier to convince?

At last, after long minutes of silence, the voices whispered, *Judgment is rendered.*

He looked back at Tarrant, then into the heart of the darkness once more. "What is it?" he demanded.

Death may take him, another voice whispered. *But not by Our hands.* There was a pause; Damien could feel the blood pounding hot in his head, and it felt near to bursting. *One longmonth from today, the compact that sustains him will be dissolved. If he can find an alternate means of survival before that, so be it. If not, then Hell may have him.*

You will see that he understands Our terms.

"Yes," he whispered. Numbed by the seeming victory. "Of course."

A stench of foulness spilled into the space surrounding Tarrant, a smell so unclean that it made Damien's stomach heave in protest. A hot, bitter fluid filled his mouth; he forced himself to swallow it down as the living ropes unwound themselves from about The Hunter's limbs, withdrawing themselves from his flesh. One by one they slithered off into the stink and the darkness, and became invisible. One and one only remained, coiling about Tarrant's neck like a restless serpent.

We leave him with this, the voices whispered, *as a reminder of Our power.*

The snakelike creature lashed out at Tarrant's face suddenly, and such was its speed and its force that it cracked like a whip as it struck his flesh. The Hunter cried out sharply, and his body bent back in agony. Then that creature also slithered away, leaving Tarrant's body to fall from its unseen frame to a lifeless heap on the floor. A shapeless sack of bones, no more, so tortured and starved and exhausted by fear that it lacked even the strength to cry out as it struck.

The light was beginning to fade, but it seemed to Damien that the source of the whispers was also gone. "Karril?" he dared. "Can you do something?"

He heard something move toward him, and then the demon was by his side. "Here." She handed him a candle—or the illusion of a candle, more likely—whose feeble light was just enough to illuminate Tarrant's face. Damien rolled the Hunter gently onto his back. Where the serpentine creature had struck him there was now a scar, that glistened wetly as it coursed from his jawline to the corner of his eye. The flesh was puckered about it as if it were a wound badly healed, enhancing its disfiguring power tenfold. *He'll love that*, he thought grimly. Tarrant's eyes were open but glazed, unseeing, their pupils so distended by pain that no hint of the iris was visible. *Just as well*, Damien thought. *Not much worth looking at around here.*

He readied himself to lift the man's limp form up onto his shoulders—and then shuddered, at the thought of where he had to carry it. "Tell me the way back is easier," he begged Karril.

"It's easier," the demon assured him.

He looked up at her.

"It really is. I swear it." She reached out to the Hunter's face as if to touch it gently, but then drew back before contact was made. Afraid to share his pain? "You have him now. I can lead you home directly."

"Thank God for that," he muttered. For a moment longer he crouched by Tarrant's side, his body aching from its many wounds. Then, with a practiced grip, he heaved the unprotesting body up onto his left shoulder, and rose with it. The weight hurt like hell—so to speak—but that pain was ameliorated by the knowledge of his victory.

Well—he cautioned himself—partial victory, anyway.

As he turned to follow Karril, the weight of Tarrant's limp form heavy on his shoulder, he thought, *Pray God it will be enough.*

Twenty

"**Well, well.** Look who's here."

Narilka looked up from the window display she was working on and blanched as she saw who was approaching the shop. Gresham must have seen her stiffen, for he asked, "What is it, Nari? Something wrong?"

"No." She whispered the word, wishing she could make it sound convincing. "I was just . . . surprised."

She hadn't seen Andrys since that day outside her apartment. She hadn't heard from him at all, other than to process his payments for the work in progress. She was frightened by the lack of contact, frustrated, mystified. Hadn't he felt something for her that night, that should surely draw him back to her? Could a man expose his soul like that and then just close it up again, as if nothing had ever happened? Or was the whole thing just an act, part of the game his kind played so well—and if so, why had he never come to take advantage of his gains?

It frightened her how upset she was, and how out of control she felt. If any other man had acted like this she would have written him off, or taken matters into her own hands and initiated some new contact. With this man she couldn't do either. At night she lay awake, hopelessly sleepless, aching with a need that was as much pure sexual hunger as any more civilized drive. She had sensed a like need in him when he had kissed her. So why hadn't he returned? And if it was just a fleeting moment's pleasure for him, a brief sidetrack in his sport, why couldn't she call it that and forget it?

He was coming across the street now, and there was no denying where he was headed. Her heart pounding wildly, she pushed the last few cake knives into place and stood up straight again. Her hands smoothed her clothing with a desperate need to have everything in place, even as she chided herself for such foolishness. Did she really think a few wrinkles would make a difference?

Then the door swung open, its silver bells jingling, and he stepped inside. He met her eyes for an instant, then quickly looked away. Was that shame in his expression, or fear, or simply disinterest? Suddenly panicked, she realized she had lost all ability to read him.

"Mer Tarrant. A pleasure." Gresham came around the end of the counter and offered his hand. He glanced at Narilka with some concern as he did so, and she could read his expression clearly enough. *Is something wrong? Did he hurt you?* She shook her head ever so slightly, her heart aching. No, he hadn't hurt her. She'd hurt herself.

"I got your note." He nodded a token greeting to Narilka (and how distant he was! Like a stranger again, as if their last meeting had never taken place) and then he clasped Gresham's hand, accepting his welcome. "Is it really finished?"

"I think you'll be very pleased." Again Gresham glanced at Narilka, but she turned away. Andrys Tarrant's presence in the room made her feel strangely naked, painfully vulnerable. Blessed Saris! How had he done so much to her, by doing so little? "Come into the back. I've got it all laid out for you."

They went through the door at the rear of the shop, letting it swing shut behind them. After a moment of hesitation, Narilka followed. She snapped the inner lock shut on the front door out of habit, so that no one might enter the shop while it was unattended. Did it really matter? she wondered. Did anything matter, when he treated her like a stranger?

She caught up with them just as they reached the polishing bench; Gresham was explaining to Andrys all the fine points of the work they had done, as if expecting that his appreciation of the coronet and armor would somehow fall short if he were uninformed. Even from behind him, she could see him stiffen as he saw the finished product. She ached to reach out to him, to tell him with a touch on his shoulder, his hand, that no, he wasn't alone, she knew his pain and she would help him bear it. But that gesture belonged to another world, a place of dreams where their fragile connection had flourished. Not here.

"It is . . ." He breathed in deeply, as if struggling for courage. "Magnificent."

It was indeed. Gresham had put the breastplate on a body form, with its matching bracers and greaves arranged in their proper positions. A golden sun blazed on the breastplate with a brilliance that rivaled the Core itself, and the delicate inlaid forms that spiraled around it were without doubt the finest work Gresham Alder had ever produced. The curve of the breastplate did not mimic the shape of a human torso, but improved upon it; picturing Andrys' strong shoulders encased in that steel, his full flowing sleeves caught up in polished bracers at the wrist. Narilka felt tears come to her eyes.

Gresham had fixed a wire to the form to support the coronet in its proper position, and as Andrys' attention turned to it, she felt herself flush with pride. It was, without question, the best work she had ever done. Its delicate form embodied not only a talent that had been finely developed through the years, but a sensuality that paid homage to the feelings he had stirred within her. Now, watching as he studied her work, imagining him as cold as a stranger to her, she hurt more than ever to have her feelings so exposed.

"Just magnificent," he breathed. "Far beyond the original." She saw Gresham draw himself up with pride, and wished she had the heart to do the same. Why couldn't she hear only his words, and not sense the pain behind them? Why couldn't she stop caring?

"Would you like to try it on?" Gresham asked. She saw Andrys stiffen, and could guess at the turmoil within him, but there was no way he could deny such an offer. He nodded, and moved as if to help Gresham remove the pieces from the body form. But no, the master indicated, he was the guest, the beloved patron, and such a man was meant to be served. He stood still while the pieces were removed from their places one by one, and Narilka came around to where she could see his profile. Hurting for him. Hating him. Wishing she could be anywhere other than where she was, or that the time could be made to move faster so that there was some hope of escape.

She saw him shiver as the breastplate was fitted to him, but only because she knew to look for such a response; Gresham would never notice. She watched as the bracers were fitted on his arms, their straps buckled tightly over his shirt sleeves. She knew that to him they felt like manacles, binding him to a past he would far rather forget. She bled for him as the greaves were fitted about his lower legs, and hated herself for doing so. This man had done everything but reject her to her face; why couldn't she force him out of her heart?

And then the coronet was lifted and offered, and Andrys took it up in his own hands and set it upon his head. She could see him quake as the band of finely worked sterling settled down about his forehead, and his eyes fell shut in a manner that made her fear he would faint—but Gresham was busy getting a mirror into place for him, and didn't notice. The glass was turned toward him, reflecting a figure so finely adorned that it might have stepped out of the pages of a fairy tale. Or a romance novel. *Or a horror tale,* she thought, sensing what he saw when he looked into that mirror. Knowing the courage he must have nurtured over these past few weeks, to be able to endure this moment in front of strangers.

"I have no words," he murmured, and Gresham glowed at the perceived compliment. Andrys' hand touched the golden sun at the center of his chest, fingers splayed along its rays. "This is beyond anything I could have expected." And then he turned to Narilka, and for an instant she saw, in his eyes, the torment that was in his soul. She could hear his silent screaming, as he forced his voice and body to obey the forms of gratitude without any hint of the pain that was inside. "More beautiful than the original," he whispered, and then he quickly looked away. As if he feared, looking longer, what he might see in her eyes.

She turned away herself as the two men divested him of his shell, unable to look at him any longer. She felt faint herself, and frightened by her own reactions. Why did she feel like every word was a knife in her flesh? When had he gained the power to hurt her like this? After a moment she realized that Gresham wanted her to do something, and she went and got his leather-bound notebook for him. Yes, he would be happy to have the pieces delivered. Of course, that date would be fine. And if there was anything else that Mer wanted, anything at all, Gresham would be happy to get it for him or make it for him, whichever he preferred.

She took his check without making eye contact and wrote a receipt with a trembling hand. *This is it,* she thought. *I'll never see him again.* It was better that way, wasn't it? Did she really want to get involved with a man like this? Let him play his games with the women who enjoyed them. There were enough of those in the world, weren't there?

But she ached inside to see him go, crumpling Gresham's copy of the receipt into a shapeless wad in her hand. And as he walked down the narrow street, out of her life forever, a thin voice began to scream inside her. *How can you let him go like this? Without a word of explanation, a hint of apology? Don't you deserve better than that? Isn't this just another kind of abuse, albeit more subtle than the rest? Why do you just stand there and take it?*

She looked up at her boss, shaken. "Gresham—"

"Go ahead," he told her. His expression was dark, his disapproval clear, but he nodded his permission. No more words were needed. She started toward the door, then remembered the receipt in her hand. Fingers trembling, she struggled to straighten it out. But he came to where she was and took it from her crumpled, and kissed her gently on the forehead. "Go," he whispered.

She went.

He had gone a block by the time she caught up to him; rather than touch him, she ran up beside him and willed him to notice her. He did, and his face grew suddenly pale. He stopped walking, but she had the impression it was more because his legs had failed him than because he really wanted to talk to her.

"Why?" she demanded. "Just tell me that, all right? No pretty lies, no petty excuses. *Just tell me.*"

He opened his mouth, then shut it again. She could see the tension in his jaw, in the tightening of his brow. At last he turned away and whispered, almost inaudibly, "I don't want to hurt you."

"And what the hell do you think you've been doing?" There were tears coming to her eyes now; she wished she knew how to stop them. "Did you think you weren't hurting me with your silence, back there? Did you think I wouldn't hurt all those days that you avoided me? Was that all for my sake?"

He flinched, but didn't turn back to her. "You don't know my life," he whispered hoarsely. "You don't understand the risk involved—"

"Then explain it to me!" She reached out and grabbed him by the nearer sleeve, pulling him back to face her; her strength in doing so seemed to surprise both of them. "Let me make my own decisions, damn it! I'm a grown woman, not some empty-headed doll that can't think for itself! Give me a little credit for intelligence, will you?"

A fruit vendor from down the street was watching them. She didn't care. The only thing in the world that mattered to her now was the man before her, and the tear she thought she saw forming in his eye. *Good,* she thought fiercely, *so you can hurt, too. Maybe when you've hurt as much as I have, then we can do something about it.*

"Look." His voice was tender as he took her by the shoulders, his fingers warm about her arms. "I've been . . . cursed. Do you understand? Everything that I touch falls to ruin. Everyone that I love dies. I don't want that to happen to you."

"Andrys—"

"I can't ask you to share in that kind of risk. I can't let you be involved—"

"I love you." The words came unbidden to her lips, but as soon as she spoke them she knew they were true. "Don't push me away. Please."

"Oh, God." He turned from her, and lowered his head into his hand. Where his sleeve pulled back from his wrist she could see a narrow scar, freshly healed, right above the vein. "Don't do this. You don't want me. You don't want my burdens."

She put a hand on his arm, ever so gently. "You don't have to face them alone," she told him. A passing woman with a dog stared at them for a moment, then walked quickly past. "Not if you don't want to."

He drew in a deep breath, shaking, and wiped his hand across his eyes, smearing their wetness across his cheek. "You don't know where I'm going," he whispered hoarsely. "You don't know what I'm doing, how dangerous it is—"

She hesitated for only a moment. "I know you want to kill the Hunter. I know he's your own flesh and blood, the man in the painting you showed me. I *know*. . . ." she thought of his pain in the shop, and his panic the first time he tried on the armor. "I know it's tearing you apart to even think about it."

His eyes widened in surprise, and she could sense the unvoiced question behind them; *How did you find that out?* But instead of voicing it, he said, "Then you know the risk. You can understand that when he finds out what I'm planning, he's sure to strike out at me, and anyone who gets in the way—"

"He can't hurt me," she told him. Feeling her heart pounding anew, as she sensed the power of those words.

"What? What do you mean?"

"He promised that he would never hurt me. And he keeps his word, Andrys. I know that for a fact." There were tears in her eyes now, too; with the back of a hand she quickly wiped them away. "So you see? I'm safe." *Safer than you, my love.*

"But how—?"

She told him all of it. The chance encounter on a lonely road so long ago. Her abduction from the city by men whose faces she never saw. The three nights in which she was hunted, only to find that the Hunter, once recognizing her, stood by his promise.

"He won't hurt me," she said quietly. "So don't push me away from you for my own protection. If you don't want me, that's something else . . . but don't do it because of that."

He brought up a hand to the side of her face; the touch brought back memories so powerful that she had to take a step back to the wall of a building behind her, for support. "I want you," he whispered, and he moved closer to her. Pressing her back against the coarse brick as he kissed her, his entire soul focused upon the act. It wasn't a gentle kiss, like last time, but something hard and desperate and hungry. It was fear and loneliness and desire all wrapped up together, and when he finally drew back from her she could feel herself shaking from the force of it, and from the heat of response in her own body.

"You're making a big mistake," he warned her. Running a finger down the line of her throat. She trembled as he touched her, and wondered just what she was getting herself into.

"Maybe," she whispered. She was dimly aware of a couple walking by them, muttering in low tones of their disapproval of such a public display. The fruit vendor was still watching. "I'll try to learn from it, all right? So I can do better the next time."

Then he kissed her again, and this time there were no passersby. No street vendors. No Hunter. No anything.

Only him.

Twenty-one

Tarrant lay on a velvet couch in the basement of Karril's temple, not breathing. His torn silk clothing had been replaced by a heavy robe, rich and plush and festooned with embroidery. Somehow it made him seem that much paler, that much more fragile, to be in such an overdecorated garment. His eyes were shut and his brow slightly drawn, as if in tension, but that was the only sign of life about him. That, and the fact that his hands grasped the sides of the couch as if fearing separation from it.

The scar still cut across his face, an ugly wound made uglier still by the aesthetic perfection which surrounded it. No other wound had remained on his body but that one. He had healed even as Damien had healed, the marks of imprisonment and torture fading from their flesh as they wended their way back to the world of the living. All except that one.

"I had blood brought for him," Karril told Damien. "and I think he drank enough to keep him going. If he needs more, I can get it. Don't offer him yours."

"Why? Is there some special danger in that?"

The demon looked sharply at him. "War's been declared, you know. Maybe not in words as such, but it's no less real for all that. Keep your strength up, and your guard. You'll need them both." He reached down to Tarrant's face and laid a hand against his forehead. "He'll wake up soon, I think. I'll leave you two alone to talk about . . . whatever."

"There's no need for that."

"Maybe not for you, Reverend. But for me?" He sighed. "I've broken so many rules it's a wonder I'm still here to talk about them.

Let's leave it at that, all right? From here on you're on your own. I've taken on enough risks these last few days to last me a lifetime."

With a nod of leavetaking he turned away, and started toward the stairs.

"Karril." He drew in a deep breath. "Thank you."

The demon stopped. He didn't turn back. It seemed from his posture that the words had shaken him.

"He was a friend," he said at last. "I wish I could do more."

His velvet robe brushing the stairs as he ascended, he exited the cellar and shut the heavy door behind him. The silence he left behind was thick and heavy, and Damien breathed in deeply, trying to ignore its ominous weight. On all sides of him, racks of bottles rose from floor to ceiling, punctuated by ironbound casks and small wooden crates. He hadn't asked what the latter were for. He didn't want to know. It was bad enough taking shelter in the cellar of a pagan temple, without also implying approval of its contents.

There was nowhere else to go, he explained silently. To Tarrant, to the Patriarch, to himself. *Nowhere else we could be safe, for the hours it would take him to recover.*

Hell. There was a time when even that argument couldn't have gotten him to stay down here, when he would have safeguarded the sanctity of his person as vehemently as he now protected the Hunter's flesh. When had the last vestiges of that righteous dedication faded? When had he come to regard such things so lightly, that it no longer bothered him where he was or who his allies were, as long as they served his purpose?

With a heavy sigh he reached for the pitcher Karril had left beside him, and poured himself yet another drink. Since the moment when he had first awakened in his hotel room his thirst had been insatiable, yet drink after drink failed to moisten the dryness in his throat. Was that thirst born of fear, perhaps, instead of bodily need? Had a clear view of Hell and the creatures who thrived there given him a new perspective on their conflict with Calesta, and made him realize just how unlikely it was that a war like this could be won?

Gerald Tarrant groaned, and shifted upon the plush couch as though in the grip of a nightmare. Seeing him, Damien couldn't help but remember the thousands of women who inhabited his private Hell, and his stomach tightened in loathing at the thought. What kind of man was this, that he had made his ally? What kind of man was *he*, to have accepted him?

With a sharp moan the Hunter stiffened, and his eyes shot open. For a moment it seemed that he wasn't focused on the room, but upon some internal vision; then, with a shudder, he looked at Damien, and the truth seemed to sink in.

"Where am I?" he whispered. His voice was barely audible.

"Karril's temple. Storage cellar."

"Karril?" His brow furrowed tightly as he struggled to make sense of that. "Karril's Iezu. Why would he. . . ?"

"You don't remember?"

"I don't . . . not him . . . I remember you. You came for me." His tone was one of amazement as he whispered, "Through . . ."

"Yeah," he said quickly. Not anxious to rehash it. "Through all that."

The Hunter shut his eyes and leaned back weakly. One hand moved up to his face, to where the newly-made scar cut across his skin; his slender fingers explored the damage, and Damien thought he saw him shiver. "We're back," he whispered. A question.

"You were given a month's reprieve. Don't you remember?"

"Not clearly. I wasn't . . . wholly cognizant." Again his hand raised up to his face, seemingly of its own accord, and traced the disfiguring scar. Then his eyes unlidded, and fixed on Damien. "Why, Vryce?" The words were a whisper, hardly loud enough for the priest to hear. "Not that I'm not grateful for the brief reprieve, mind you. But it is only that. Was that worth risking your status for?"

He stiffened at the reminder of his professional vulnerability; it wasn't a welcome thought. "I need you," he said curtly. "We're fighting a Iezu, remember? I can't do that alone."

Wearily he shut his eyes once more; his tired flesh seemed to sink back into the cushions, as though soon it would fade away entirely. "And I'm to give you all the answers? In one month? You should have just left me there."

"Maybe I should have," he snapped, suddenly angry. "Maybe the man I went through Hell to rescue didn't make it back. Oh, his flesh is alive enough—as much as it ever was—but where's the spark that drove it? I must have lost track of it, somewhere on the way back."

"He's a *Iezu*," Tarrant whispered hoarsely. "We don't even know what they are, much less how to fight them. If we had unlimited time to come up with new theories and test them, time to do research, then maybe, *maybe*, we'd have a chance. But one month? You're going to figure out how to destroy the indestructible in one month? Not to mention," he added hoarsely, "that if I don't find another means of sustaining my life by the end of that time . . ." He winced, and the shadow of remembered pain passed across his face. "Can't be done," he whispered. "Not like that."

With a snort Damien rose from his side and walked away, moving toward the door that Karril had used for his exit. Heavy planks banded with cast iron, now securely shut. He listened to see if any sound could make it through that barrier, and at last decided they were safe enough. Karril could hear them if he wanted to, he suspected, but he didn't think that demon was the eavesdropping kind.

"What would you think," he said quietly, "if I told you that I knew how to kill a Iezu?"

He heard the couch creak behind him, and guessed that Tarrant was struggling to a sitting position. Given the man's condition, it was little wonder that long seconds passed before he finally managed, "What?"

"You heard me."

"How could you have gained knowledge like that? After all my research failed, and yours as well?"

He glanced once more at the solid door, satisfying himself that it was fully shut, and then turned back to Tarrant. The Hunter looked ghastly even by comparison with his normal state.

He said it simply, knowing the power that was in such a statement. "Karril told me."

"When?" he demanded.

"Before we came after you. I went to his temple to ask for his help, and we argued. He told me then."

"Why?" he asked in amazement. "Oh, he might have rendered Calesta vulnerable, but also himself as well. He's too practiced a survivor for that."

"Oh, I don't think he was aware of doing it. Not in so many words."

The Hunter's eyes were fixed on him now, and there was a brightness in their depths that Damien had feared he'd lost forever. A hunger, but not for triumph. Not even for survival. For *knowledge*.

"Tell me," he whispered.

And he did. He told him what the Iezu had said to him, back when he'd first come to the temple. How he had expressed his own fear of what the journey might mean to him.

The way is pain, and worse. I can't endure it. Even if I wanted to, even if I were willing to risk her displeasure . . . I'm not human. I can't absorb emotions which run counter to my aspect. No Iezu could survive such an assault.

"Well?" he said at last. "Does that mean what I think it does, or not?"

The Hunter's eyes were focused elsewhere, beyond Damien, as he digested the thought. "Yes," he said at last. "You're right. I've heard Iezu express similar fears before, but voiced as a question of discomfort, rather than survival. This would seem to imply there's more to it."

"So there's hope, then."

"A long shot at best. What runs counter to Calesta's aspect? Perfectly counter, so that he can't adapt? Karril can deal with pain if he must, so the matter's not a simple one."

It came to him, then, from the fields of memory, so quickly and so clearly that he wondered if the fae weren't responsible. "Apathy."

"What?"

"Karril's negative factor is apathy. The absence of all pleasure. The absence of ability to *experience* pleasure."

"Where the hell did you come up with that?"

"He told us. Back at Senzei's place, when Ciani was first attacked." Good God! The memory seemed so distant now, half a lifetime away. He struggled to remember what the demon had said, at last had to resort to a Remembering. The fae took shape in response to his will, forming a misty simulacrum of Karril before them. *There are few kinds of pain I can tolerate*, it said, *fewer still that I can feed on. But apathy is my true nemesis. It is anathema to my being: my negation, my opposite, my destruction.* Then, its duty accomplished, the image faded. The room's cool air was heavy with silence.

"Apathy," the Hunter mused.

"There's got to be something like that for Calesta, right? Something similar, that we can use as a weapon."

The Hunter shook his head. "Karril was talking about trying to endure something, not having it forced upon him. How would you inundate a spirit with apathy? If it were deadly to him, he would surely flee from it, like any living creature. And apathy isn't something you can nock to a bow, or insert into the wood of a quarrel. It can't be made into a blade, to cut and pierce on its own."

"Not yet," Damien agreed. "But that doesn't mean there isn't some way to use it. You and I just have to figure out how."

Exhaustion seemed to cloud the Hunter's expression; he turned away and whispered, in a voice without emotion, "In a month?"

"If that's all we have."

Though the Remembering had faded from sight, some vestige of its power must still have remained in the room; Damien could see bits and pieces of the Hunter's recollections taking form about his head. Images of pain and horror and terror beyond bearing, still as alive in his memory as they were in that dark place inside his soul. Hell was waiting for him. So was the Unnamed. Thirty-one days.

"Not enough," he whispered. "Not enough."

Anger welled up inside Damien with unexpected force. He walked to where the Hunter sat and dropped down beside him, grabbing his shoulders, pulling him around to face him. "I went to Hell and beyond to bring you back, and so help me God you'll earn it. You understand? I don't care how little time it seems to you, or how vulking depressed you get, or even whether or not you're going to make it past that last day. What we're talking about is the future of all of humankind, and that's a hell of a lot more important than my fate, or even yours. *Even yours.*" He paused. "You understand me?"

The Hunter glared at him. "Easy enough words, from your perspective."

"Damn you, Gerald! Why are you doing this?" He rose up from the couch and stepped away, afraid he would hit the man if he remained too close. "Do I have to tell you what the answer is? You're a free agent for the first time in nine hundred years. Take advantage of that!"

"I am what they made me to be," he said bitterly. "None of that has been undone. Going against their will means going against my own nature—"

"Damn it, man, no one said redemption would be easy! But isn't it worth a try? Isn't that better than handing yourself over to them in a longmonth, without so much as a whimper of protest?"

"You don't know," he whispered. There was pain in his voice. "You can't possibly understand."

"Try me."

The pale eyes narrowed; his expression was strained. "Those sins you saw," he breathed. "Would you forgive them so quickly, if the matter were in your hands? Would you wipe clean a slate of nine hundred years, for one single month of good intentions? For a vow made in the shadow of such fear that its true motivation could never be judged?"

"I wouldn't," he said shortly. "God might. That's the difference between us."

"*Might* is a hell of a thing to bet one's eternity on."

"Yeah," he agreed. "About as shaky as trying to stay alive forever. Only in the latter case, you know it has to end someday." He paused. "You did know that, didn't you? That it had to end sometime. Today it's Calesta and tomorrow it might be something else, but you can't run forever."

The Hunter turned away from him. Though Damien waited, he said nothing.

"All right," the priest said at last. "You think about it. I'll be back in my room if you decide you want my help. Karril has the address."

He turned toward the stairs and was about to leave, but a single sound, voiced quiet as a breeze, stopped him.

"Damien."

He didn't turn back, but he did stop. Waiting.

"Thank you," the Hunter whispered.

For a moment longer he stood where he was. Then, without voicing a response, he climbed the short flight of stairs and pushed open the heavy door. The sounds and smells of Karril's temple greeted him, unwelcome reminders of the world that surrounded. Millions upon millions of men and women and helpless children, whose futures were all at risk.

I saved you, he thought bitterly to Tarrant. *Now you do your job, and help me save them.*

Twenty-two

Pleasure was to *apathy* as *sadism* was to . . .

What?

The analogy ran through Damien's head obsessively, forever uncompleted. And though he tried to satisfy the pattern with over a dozen words, none of them were quite right. The answer continued to elude him, and only the knowledge that it must surely exist gave him the strength to rise above his frustration and keep searching.

The key to it all was the insight that Karril had given them, regarding his own counter-aspect. *Pleasure* was the opposite of *pain*, and yet a man's soul could be filled with both things at once. *Apathy* was Karril's true nemesis, the absence of any strong feeling, a state in which pleasure could not even be experienced. Yet it wasn't an opposite exactly, or a compliment, or any other type of thing which Damien's language had a name for. That made dictionaries all but useless, and even more sophisticated linguistic tools confusing at best.

It didn't help to know that Tarrant had indeed confronted the Patriarch. Even after the Hunter had finally admitted that fact, even after the emotional storm that was inevitable had played itself out and subsided to a sullen resentment, Damien couldn't stop thinking about the incident long enough to focus clearly on anything else. What had the Hunter said to the Patriarch, and how had the Patriarch reacted? Tarrant would say only that he had offered the Holy Father knowledge, and that whether or not the man chose to use it was his own concern. Damien could only guess at the torment such an offer would cause. Worst of all was the guilt in the priest's own heart, the certain knowledge that if he had only come up with some better plan, if only he had initiated some milder contact on his own . . . then what? What could he have said or done that the Patriarch would accept? The man's heart was so set against Damien that maybe the Hunter, with his ages of experience, stood a better chance with him. Maybe this was, in its own painful way, a more merciful form of disclosure.

He struggled to believe that, as he applied himself to the challenge at hand. He had to believe it, if he was to think about anything else.

Thirty days left now. He had no doubt that the hours were counting down inside Tarrant's skull, in much the same way that he had counted seconds when traversing Tarrant's Hell. And for much the same reason, he thought. It was all too easy to let such small units of time slip by one after the other, until suddenly they were all gone.

Thirty days.

Help him, God, he begged. *If he is to die, help him to make the best of that. Now that the last barrier is being removed, help him rediscover his humanity.* But though he wished for the best for his dark companion, he knew Gerald Tarrant's stubbornness well enough to guess that such a prayer was futile. The habit of nine hundred years was not a thing to be discarded lightly. And the Unnamed had indeed remade him to suit its own special hunger; the Hunter still required blood and cruelty to live, every bit as much as Damien required food and water. How did you fight a thing like that? How did you win redemption against such odds?

I'll get you through this, he promised silently. *Somehow.*

He prayed there would be a way.

"He'll see you now, Reverend Vryce."

A servant in Church livery opened the door of the Patriarch's study as he approached; another stood at attention by the outer door, prepared to serve the Holy Father's every whim. In the distance Damien could hear the cathedral bells signaling the call to evening service. It all seemed normal, so utterly normal . . . but it wasn't. He knew that. The rules had changed, and while the men and women who served the Patriarch might not yet be aware of it, it made his own game doubly dangerous.

What did Tarrant do? he thought desperately. As he walked across the polished threshold, he felt his stomach tighten in dread, and as the door shut softly behind him, he was aware that his body had gone rigid as if expecting some physical punishment. That wasn't good at all. Even the old Patriarch would have noticed such a thing, and as for the new one.... He tried to relax, or at least mimic relaxation, and then dared to look up at the man. His superior. God's servant.

A sorcerer?

The Patriarch was dressed in his accustomed robes, but they hung about his lean form in deeper folds than before, accentuating his thinness. His face was ashen and drawn, and the circles under his eyes spoke eloquently of sleepless nights. Whatever change Tarrant had wrought, it had clearly not been an easy one for the Holy Father. But he had survived. In their bed of wrinkled flesh the man's clear blue eyes stood out like jewels, and they fixed on Damien with a strange, calm sort of power. It wasn't at all what the priest had expected, and therefore it was doubly unnerving.

"Reverend Vryce." The Patriarch bowed his head ever so slightly, a formal greeting. It was a far more mild reception than Damien had expected, and he tried not to look flustered as he returned the gesture. What was going on here? "Have a seat." The Patriarch indicated a tufted chair set opposite his desk. Damien hesitated, then moved forward and sat as directed. Was this some other creature that had taken over the Holy Father's body? In that moment it seemed that anything was possible.

Then the blue eyes fixed on him, and the fae stirred between them, and he saw what was truly behind that measured gaze: not calm, nor any other kind of human peace, but a pain so intense that it hovered near the brink of madness. And he knew in that moment that he had seen it because the Patriarch had *wanted* him to see it, that the man's natural power would have masked such a weakness from Damien's sight unless he willed it otherwise.

He began to shiver, deep inside, without quite knowing why. He had prepared himself for the Patriarch's rage, or worse; how was he supposed to deal with this stranger?

The Holy Father sat down opposite him, behind the broad mahagova desk, and for a moment said nothing. Damien was intensely aware of that stern gaze fixed on him, studying him, assessing him. At last the Patriarch said quietly, "I believe we have some things to discuss."

Damien nodded stiffly, but said nothing.

"Your recent activities." He paused, perhaps waiting for a response, but Damien didn't dare commit himself without first knowing how much the Patriarch had discovered. "Your journey of a night ago," he prompted. Damien felt his throat tighten in dread but he said nothing. At last the Patriarch leaned forward and accused, "A trip through Hell, Reverend Vryce, to rescue its darkest prince."

"How do you know that?" The words were out of him before he could stop them. That would never have happened with the old Patriarch, but this man unnerved him in ways his former self never had. "Where do you get such information?"

The Patriarch leaned back in his chair. There was an infinite weariness about the movement that made him seem suddenly fragile, as though a strong word might cause him to shatter into a thousand fragments. "I have dreams," he said quietly. "Visions of the truth, that take place in real time. I thought once that they were clairvoyancies. I thought that God had blessed me with a gift—or perhaps cursed me—so that I might serve my people better. Now . . ." He paused; a muscle tensed along the line of his jaw. "Now I know them for what they are. Visions crafted by a demon, to herd me along his chosen path. He thought me blinded by my faith, and thus never tried to hide his marks. Only now . . . I see them. Now I know."

"And you trust these dreams?"

He had expected anger in response—at least a hint of it—but the hollowed face was maddeningly calm, perfectly controlled. Whatever terror raged inside the Patriarch as a result of the changes Tarrant had wrought, he kept it well hidden. "Thus far all his visions have been true, at least as far as I can test them. But that could change at any moment. Perhaps it has now." He leaned forward and placed his arms upon the desk. "I saw you call a demon for a guide and then walk through Hell, all to save the soul of a man that God himself reviles. Was that a true vision, Reverend Vryce, or a demon's lie? You tell me."

For a brief instant he considered lying. Then, an instant later, his face flushed hot with shame. A year ago he would never have considered lying to the Patriarch, not for any reason. That he had done so now, for no better cause than to evade just punishment, was a jarring reminder of how much the last year had changed him. He had been ready to cast aside his vows of obedience for no more than a moment's comfort; how much else might he be willing to sacrifice, if the moment's temptation were right? For the first time he saw himself through the Patriarch's eyes, and realized just how far he had fallen. He couldn't meet his gaze, but looked away. "It's true," he whispered. "All true."

For a moment the Patriarch just stared at him; Damien could feel the scrutiny as if it were a physical assault. "Such an incredible dream," he mused aloud. "I didn't want to believe it. I told myself, this time the demon has gone too far. This is beyond the scope of

Vryce's transgressions." A pause. "I prayed, Reverend Vryce. I asked to be shown that the vision was a lie. For your sake."

Shamed, he lowered his head.

"But it isn't." His long fingers steepled on the desk before him; Damien focused on his heavy ring as a way of avoiding his eyes. "What I should do now is ask you to tell me what kind of judgment is suitable for such a crime. What should be done to a priest whose every action defies the vows he made to God? But we both know where that kind of question leads, don't we? We both know what the end result would be. And the fact is . . ." Was that a tremor in his voice? "The fact is, these dreams were given to me for a reason. It was Calesta's intention that I should react in anger and cast you out from the Church, thus breaking your spirit and rendering you vulnerable to his assaults. And for that reason—that reason alone—I won't do it."

Damien looked up at last, and met the Holy Father's gaze. There was pain in the man's eyes, and a moral exhaustion so immense that it seemed impossible any human soul could contain it. How long had he tormented himself over this decision? How many hours had he gone sleepless, while Calesta tried to push him to the breaking point? "I won't give him that victory, Vryce. I won't serve a demon's will in any way. Even when he's right."

Shame flushed his face. "I've tried to serve the Church."

"Yes. As have thousands of unordained worshipers, each in his own way. Loyalty isn't an issue here. Or even judgment. I thought once that it was, but now . . ." He hesitated. "I have a somewhat broader perspective." He shut his eyes for a second, and Damien thought he saw him shiver. "The issue isn't loyalty, or the quality of your service. The issue isn't even whether or not a man must do terrible things to serve his God. Obviously, there are times he must. The only issue is whether or not a man who has defied Church tradition should represent that Church, and so cast doubt upon its teachings in the public mind. That's an issue I can't judge, Vryce. Not when condemning you means that I strengthen our enemy's hand."

He said nothing. It seemed amazing to him that the thing he had feared most, his expulsion from the Church, now was overwhelmed by a horror more subtle, but infinitely more terrifying. The Holy Father of the Eastern Autarchy, the living representative of the One God, must now hesitate in performing his duty for fear of pleasing a demon! Is that what the Church had come to? Is that what Calesta had done to them? He despaired to see this sign of it, and to feel it echo in his own soul.

"I see you understand," the Patriarch said, after some time of silence had passed. He slid open a drawer by his side and drew out an envelope from it. "As of today, you have no more duties in this autarchy. You'll still be granted full access to all Church facilities; the campaign which you're fighting deserves no less. Other than that, I think it best for all concerned that you act as an independent."

He could feel the weight of that icy gaze upon him, and he nodded. "Yes, Your Holiness." The words barely made it past the knot in his throat. "I understand."

The Patriarch studied him for a moment longer—was he using the fae in some way, Knowing him as well?—and then handed him the envelope. "This will provide you with some revenue for room and board, and other basic necessities. Whatever remains may be addressed to your cause as you see fit. You needn't bring me an accounting of it, unless you intend to ask for more."

Surprised, Damien looked up from the envelope, searching for some hint of purpose in the Patriarch's expression. *He can't officially approve of me,* he realized, *but he doesn't dare drive me away. Not only because it would please Calesta, but because I'm one of the few people who really understand what's at stake here.* Had the Patriarch looked into the future and decided that Damien's role was vital to the Church's survival, or was the inspiration less focused than that? Damien folded the envelope in his hand; the pulse in his palm made the paper tremble. "Thank you, Your Holiness."

"It leaves open the question of what your role should be in larger issues, of course. But you can address that in your own conscience far better than I can. You were trained as a priest, Damien Vryce, and ordained in a centuries-old tradition of sanctity and obedience. I pray that you will reflect upon that tradition during the trials yet to come, and consider how your actions reflect upon us all." He paused, as if to ascertain that his point had hit home, and then said quietly, "That's all. You are dismissed."

Stunned, Damien managed to get to his feet. He wanted to say something, to protest, *anything*—but the Patriarch's attention had already turned elsewhere, cutting that option short. And what was he going to say to him anyway? How would his petty trials of conscience measure up to this man's, whose shoulders had taken on a burden so terrible that God's own Church might topple if he stumbled? What were one priest's paltry misgivings, compared to that?

Shaken, he pushed the folded envelope into his pants pocket without looking at it. The Patriarch's words had given him freedom to act as he saw fit, yet he felt more bound than ever. The man had acknowledged that conscience must sometimes give way to expediency, and yet Damien's conscience burned even hotter as a result. Had he done right, he wondered suddenly, to cling to the priesthood with such desperation? Was that true service to God, in the face of all he had done, or service to himself?

Swallowing hard, he forced himself to bow. Deeply: a motion not only of ritual obeisance, but of heartfelt respect. *You had the right to judge me,* he thought somberly. *Only you, of all men. I would have respected it. I would have obeyed.* Now, instead, the Patriarch had left that judgment in Damien's hands. It wasn't a burden as heavy as his own, but it was heavy enough. The priest flinched as he accepted it.

"May God be with you," he whispered, bowing again. Meeting the Patriarch's eyes for one fleeting second as he rose, sensing the torment behind them.

And may the fae be merciful.

Twenty-three

YAMAS: *The violence surrounding the Forest took a dark turn last night as residents of Yamas sacrificed two of their own people, in what appears to be an effort to placate that hungry power.*

Nile Ashforth and Maklesia Sert were hanged shortly before dawn at the western gate of Yamas, barely ten miles from the Forest's edge. Both men had apparently been rousted from their beds by an angry mob of some two dozen townspeople and dragged to the site, where they were stripped, hanged, and mutilated. Police say that the symbols carved into their chests correspond to those used by the Hunter's servants for identification, and that the bodies may have been meant as a kind of offering, intended to propitiate the Hunter and protect the town. If so, it marks the first time that living men have turned against their own kind in this region, and officials in Yamas consider it a dangerous precedent.

A joint funeral for the two men will be held at the Leonia Funeral Home at six p.m. on Sunday. Offerings in memory of Mers Ashforth and Sert can be made to the gods Keruna and Tlaos at that time, in accordance with their respective traditions.

Twenty-four

The waiting room outside the Patriarch's study was exactly ten paces by six. Long paces, hurriedly measured, with a pounding heart for accompaniment. As he completed his tenth circuit—or was it his twelfth?—Andrys wondered if he might not be better off fleeing right now, rather than waiting for the Father of the Church to frighten him into doing so.

What did he want with him anyway? In another time and place he might have imagined it had something to do with the perceived importance of his family (he had told that priestess his name, after all) or some other matter connected with the fact that the Tarrants had been avid Church supporters for longer than most families had even been in existence. But to take refuge in such a story now, no matter how tempting, was to be hopelessly naive. Calesta had brought him to Jaggonath, and had ordered him to attend services here. Now, less than two weeks after he had begun to establish a pattern of regular attendance, the single most important man in the Eastern Autarchy had asked him to come here for a private interview. Obviously it had something to do with Calesta's plan. What he couldn't figure out was why the demon hadn't given him some kind of guidance—what he should say, how he should act—or even some warning that this might happen.

The door at the far end of the chamber opened suddenly; startled, he quickly brushed his hair back in place and turned to face it. The servant who had brought him here smiled pleasantly and told him, "He'll see you now." She held the door wide for him as he passed through it, and then shut it quietly behind him. She was a pretty thing, and ordinarily he might have regretted that he had no chance to make her acquaintance. Now, however, his focus was elsewhere.

The Patriarch had been sick, it was said, struck down for a day and a night with a malady so serious that they had thought he might die. The harsh notes of illness still echoed in his flesh, clearly enough that even Andrys, a stranger, could see it. Yet beneath that the man was undeniably powerful, with a physical presence that belied his years and an aura of dignity that no sickness could compromise. He looked like what a Patriarch should look like, Andrys thought: a leader of men, a spokesman of God. Never before had he been in a presence that so totally defined itself.

With a faint smile of greeting the Holy Father moved toward him, and suddenly Andrys realized that he had no idea how one was supposed to greet such a personage. Did you bow, or maybe kneel, or just nod and mutter something suitably acquiescent? Samiel would have known what to do, or Betrise, but he had no idea. He was acutely aware of his own lack of religious background as the Patriarch studied him, nodded, and then deliberately offered a hand. Thank God. He shook it, and the man's firm grip lent him newfound strength. Maybe this wasn't going to be so bad after all.

"Mer Tarrant. I'm glad you could come."

"The honor is mine, Your Holiness." Now that the first awful moment was over with, some bit of his accustomed ease was coming back to him. "Although it was a bit unexpected, I must admit."

The Patriarch's eyes—a startling blue, as bright and clear as sapphires—fixed on him with unnerving intensity. For a brief moment he had the impression that not only his physical person was being judged, but his very soul. At last, after what seemed like an eternity, the man turned away and gestured toward a pair of chairs arranged beside a window. "Please," he said. "Will you join me?"

He nodded, and hoped the motion looked natural. He felt like a bug pinned to a dissection board when the Patriarch looked at him, and he hoped those piercing eyes would find other things to focus on while they spoke. The chairs, heavily upholstered, flanked a small table outfitted with a plate of confections, crystal glasses, and a chilled pitcher. What on Erna did this man want with him, that he had taken such obvious trouble to set up an environment conducive to casual conversation?

The pitcher apparently contained a light wine, and he accepted a glass of it gratefully, glad to have an object to hold in his hands, another focus for his attention. The wine was cold and sweet and delicate in flavor; not a vintage that he recognized, but clearly an expensive one. As Andrys looked around the chamber, taking in its paintings and its rugs and its gold-embossed books, he realized that for the first time he was seeing the Church as his ancestors had known it—rich, proud, and timeless.

"It's rare we have guests from so far away," the Patriarch said. An obvious lie, Andrys thought; the center of the Eastern Autarchy must surely draw tourists from all the human cities, some that would make Merentha seem like a close neighbor. "And rarer still, from so illustrious a family. Our cathedral is honored."

It was obviously the time for him to say something complimentary, and he did. The words of social concourse flowed like honey across his tongue, while all the while he wondered, with increasing alarm, *Why did he bring me here? What's this all about?* He didn't believe for a minute that the mere presence of a Merenthan noble had prompted this interview. He hoped the Patriarch didn't expect him to believe it. But the forms must be observed, and so Andrys gave over control of his speech to the part of his brain so well versed in social repartee that he could hold a conversation like this in his sleep. While all the while another part fluttered in panic like a caged bird, waiting for the blow to fall.

Was the Church thriving in Merentha? Was that city still populous? Had it made successful conversion from a port city to something less ambitious, when the Stekkis River shifted its course five centuries ago and left it high and dry? These were all questions that any history book could answer, and Andrys had no doubt that the Patriarch had read them all. Was his family still a patron of the Church, as it had been in the early days? He hesitated over that one; the words *my family is dead* almost came to his lips, but instead he said simply, *the Tarrants have always been devout.* He didn't add, as honestly prompted, *except for me*, but the Patriarch's piercing gaze and slow, knowing nod suggested that he knew that as well.

Two glasses of cool wine lubricated his tongue, and by the end of the second, against his will, he could feel himself starting to relax. The Patriarch seemed to sense it, for he leaned back into his chair with seeming casualness and said, in a voice that was artfully calm, "There are some issues I would like to discuss with you, Mer Tarrant, that I think are of mutual interest."

Heart pounding anew, he poured himself another glass. If he could have exchanged it for a hypodermic full of tranquilizer right now, he would have done so. "Oh?" He tried to make his voice sound equally casual, but instead it had the forced ingenuousness of bad melodrama.

The Patriarch said nothing for a moment; Andrys had the distinct impression that he was waiting for him to compose himself, so he drew in a deep breath and tried to do so. When his heartbeat had slowed enough that he could make out its individual strokes again, the Holy Father said, "You've heard, no doubt, of our troubles in the north."

Feeling that he was expected to say something, he offered, "I've read the papers."

"The Forest has always been a thorn in our side. I'm sure you know that the Church once tried an all-out effort to cleanse the place, once and for all. It failed, of course. You can't do battle with the planet itself, and that's what the Forest is: a whirlpool of fae that no act of man can unmake. They didn't understand that then, or perhaps they simply chose not to believe it. It cost them dearly."

He nodded, and muttered something meant to indicate that yes, he knew Church history, he remembered the salient details of the Great War and its devastating finale.

"For years now the Forest has been a reasonable neighbor: evil, but civilized. Its neighbors enjoyed a tense and wary peace, and it in return has been permitted to flourish unopposed for more than five centuries." He laid his own glass down on the table and seemed to be studying its rim thoughtfully as he said, "Obviously, that truce no longer exists."

"Are you sure about that?" he dared. He wished he had read the newspapers more closely, so that he had a better understanding of the matter to draw upon. "After all, there have only been a few incidents."

The blue eyes were a cold fire that sucked in his soul. "I'm sure," he said quietly. "What we've seen is only the beginning. The Forest will devour its neighbors—body by body, acre by acre—until in time it has the strength to do battle with us upon our own holy ground. That is," he added, "if it goes unopposed."

Fear was a sharp thrill inside him. "You're going to make war against the Forest?"

"I'm going to make war against the Hunter," he answered coolly. "Once the prince of that domain has been humbled, his unholy construction will topple from the center outward. His most fearsome creations will become no more than nature meant them to be: simple demons, subject to the sword or to prayer or to any of a thousand other simple tools. With our triumphant song resonating from mountaintop to river shore, with our victory echoing in a million human souls, we will do the Forest more damage than all the armies of our greatest age could manage in their time." He paused then, perhaps waiting to see what Andrys' reaction would be. Could he sense the hunger in him, Andrys wondered, the fear, the sense of standing balanced on the edge of a pit, so precariously that a light breeze might cause him to topple forward into the darkness? "I was told," he said at last, "that you might have an interest in serving this cause."

Heart pounding, he struggled to keep his face and voice calm as he answered, "I might."

"You have a special connection to all of this, Mer Tarrant." He stressed the last name ever so slightly, as if testing its veracity. "One that you and I must explore a bit, before I can offer you your place in our enterprise." *With your permission,* his eyes seemed to say. As though they were discussing some mundane bit of business over afternoon tea.

"Of course," he murmured, and he nodded.

He picked up his glass and sipped from it again, studying Andrys over its rim. When at last he was done, he placed it carefully before him, sculpting the moment of silence so that it lent double weight to the words which followed. "How much do you know about your ancestor, the first Neocount of Merentha?"

The only Neocount of Merentha. The words echoed in his memory with stunning power, voiced in the inhuman tones of his family's murderer. For a moment it was hard not to lose touch with the present moment and return to that time; the scent of fresh blood was thick in his nostrils as he tried to force out some kind of coherent response. "I don't . . . what is it you want to know?"

"Do you know that he lives today?"

He hesitated, knowing that the crux of his future lay in this one moment. If he meant to feign ignorance in order to back out of this enterprise, this was his last chance to do so.

He thought of his family lying dead upon the ancient stone floor. The fire dying in the hearth while he wept, unmanned and unfutured, in a heap in the corner. He thought of all the months that he had suffered after that, the accusations leading to a nightmarish trial, hallucinations driving him to the brink of madness . . . and the girl. *She* knew what was going on. What would she say, if he had his chance and backed away? How could he face her again?

"I know," he whispered.

Something in the Patriarch's posture seemed to relax ever so slightly, as if he, too, knew what that acknowledgment signified. "The man once called Gerald Tarrant became transformed at the end of his mortal life, into the creature we now know as the Hunter. He moved into the Forest soon after our last assault against that realm failed, and remade it to suit his own needs. To reflect back upon him his own damned nature."

He nodded slowly, trying to see where this all was leading. What was it they wanted him to do?

"The Forest in Jahanna is now so perfectly ordered that it functions like a living body, with all its parts in harmony. Like a construct of natural flesh it depends upon its center, its brain, for purpose and for balance. And like a body of flesh it defends its brain with utmost vigor. Anything of foreign origin which breaches its borders would be subject to immediate attack, much as a microbe which invades human flesh would be set upon by antibodies. Only in this case, the antibodies are the stuff of our own nightmares, turned against us by a man who can sculpt our very fears."

He nodded ever so slightly—afraid of what was coming next, but unwilling to cut the narrative short. *Calesta,* he begged silently, *give me strength. Give me courage.*

"The Hunter can come and go as he pleases. So can his minions, who are but an extension of his own will, and his beasts, and all his infernal creations. But any creature which has its origin in the world outside—or any army composed of such—would no sooner step into his realm than the earth itself would move against them, and every living thing from microbe to man would become their enemy." He paused, then added quietly, "Unless the Forest believed that such creatures were also a part of him. Then and only then could they proceed."

The Patriarch's plan hit him so suddenly that it drove the breath from his body; his numbed hand dropped the glass as he pushed himself up and away from the man, overturning the chair in his panic. "No!"

The Patriarch did not respond. If he had—if he had said anything at all—Andrys would surely have bolted from the room at a dead run and never looked back. His nerves were trigger-taut, and any word— even one of intended comfort—would set them off. But the Holy Father said nothing. Time passed. After a small eternity had come and gone, Andrys found that he could breathe again. Several millennia later, the urge to flee subsided somewhat. Terror maintained its painful edge, but it no longer mastered his flesh.

"I see you understand the situation," the Patriarch said quietly.

"I . . . I think so," he managed. His voice was hoarse and strained, and seemed to him like the voice of a stranger. "You want me to . . . lead . . . some kind of group? Is that it?"

"More than that, I'm afraid." His eyes were coolly sympathetic, and their message was clear: *We understand the pain we cause but cannot turn aside. This mission is greater than both of us.* "I need you to stand in for the Hunter. I need you to *be* him. Not in truth— not in your heart or in your soul—but in those aspects which his creatures will recognize." He paused, as if waiting to see if his guest would flee at this new revelation. Though he was afraid to hear more, Andrys nodded. "The resemblance between you is uncanny. With the proper accoutrements—"

"I have his armor," Andrys said quickly. "And I have his crown. Like the things he wore into war. In the mural," he stammered, and he nodded stiffly in the direction of the sanctuary, toward where that hateful painting hung. He had thought that the Patriarch would be startled by such a revelation, but the man only nodded, as if he had expected to hear it. The local Church was rife with rumors of his visionary power, and some murmured that God's own prophecies came to him in the night and showed him what was to be. Had he foreseen Andrys' coming, and the role he was to play? Was he weighing every moment now against a host of futures revealed to him, trying to choose the one that would not send his guest running away in a fit of panic, never to return? He remembered the Patriarch's long silence, so perfectly measured against his own fear, and began to tremble deep inside. What kind of power did this man wield, that gave him such terrible control?

"Then you're with us?" the Holy Father asked.

He shut his eyes, and felt his very soul quake. "Yes," he whispered. The sound was barely loud enough for a man to hear, so he said it louder. "Yes. I'm with you."

Was this the fate you meant for me, Calesta? Was this why you wouldn't tell me what the crown and the armor were for? For fear that sheer terror would drive me back to Merentha before your arrangements could be completed? He lowered his head and thought dully, *How well you anticipated everything. How well you controlled it all.*

"I'm very grateful for that, Mer Tarrant. With your assistance we may yet triumph over Erna's most vicious demon. Praised be God, who in His wisdom brought us both to this point."

"Praised be God," he muttered weakly. Suddenly needing to escape this place, and all the plans within it. Suddenly needing clear air and room to move . . . and the healing arms of a woman. Narilka was waiting for him back at the hotel, he knew that. More loyal a woman than he deserved by far, but now as necessary to him as the very air he breathed. Could he make it through all this without her quiet strength supporting him? He hoped he never had to find that out.

He muttered a leavetaking, hoping it was polite. Evidently the Patriarch sensed his need—or had he foreseen it?—for he made no attempt to convince him to stay longer. And why should he anyway? The deed was done. The contract was all but signed. Andrys Tarrant belonged to the Church now, proud soldier in its maddest enterprise.

But at the door he stopped, unable to leave the room, There was still something unspoken here, something the Patriarch should know. Something he *needed* to know, if Andrys was to play his role effectively.

He turned partway back, not far enough that he had to meet the Patriarch's eyes but enough that his words would be clearly audible. "Gerald Tarrant killed my family," he whispered hoarsely. Choking on the words, and on the painful memories they conjured. "I want him to pay for that. I . . . I would do anything to hurt him."

It seemed to him that the Patriarch sighed. Then, with a soft whisper of silk on silk, the Holy Father rose from his seat and came over to where Andrys stood. He put a hand upon the young man's shoulder, and it seemed to Andrys in that instant that the man's own strength and certainty flowed through the contact, bolstering his own fragile hopes.

"He'll pay for that sin in Hell," the Holy Father assured him. "And so many others. We'll see to it."

Twenty-five

"Tell me about Senzei Reese."

Startled, Damien looked up from the volume he was studying. "What? Why?"

"Tell me about him."

He stared at the Hunter for a moment as if that action might net him some information, but as usual Tarrant's expression was unreadable. At last, with a sigh, he closed the book. "What do you want to know?"

"The man. His habits, his beliefs. Tell me."

"May I ask why?"

"Later. Just tell me."

So he did. It wasn't the easiest task in the world, but after half a night's frustrating dedication to dusty tomes and wan hopes, it was as good an assignment as any. He tried to remember Ciani's assistant, and to describe him for Tarrant. Thin. Pale. Studious. Utterly devoted to Ciani, and to their work. What was it that Tarrant wanted? he wondered. Why did a man who'd been dead for nearly two years suddenly matter so much? Not knowing what his focus of interest was, Damien floundered through a description. *Meticulous. Focused. Frustrated.* He went through the easy adjectives first, and then he came to the painful part. *He was obsessed by the desire to become an adept. He was convinced that somehow it could be managed. He believed . . .* He struggled to remember, to find the right words. *He thought that the potential was there inside him, waiting to be let out. That somehow, if he could only "set it free," he'd be the equal of Ciani.*

He remembered what that obsession had cost Senzei, and pain welled up inside him as fresh as the day it had happened. He saw

Senzei's body, twisted and tortured, lying on the mountain grass where it had been struck down. And beside him the flask of holy Fire, which he had tried to take into his body to burn through his inner barriers. Though they hadn't recognized it at the time, that was Calesta's first victory over their small party. The first death in a war that had now claimed thousands in the east, and threatened to do the same here.

"Earthquakes," Tarrant prompted. "Did he talk about them?"

Puzzled by the request, he tried to remember. They had discussed so much on that journey, desperate to pass the time in something other than silence. "He was so fascinated by the fae-surge," he said at last. Struggling to remember. "I think he wanted to harness it, but didn't dare try."

Tarrant hissed softly. There was an alertness about him that reminded Damien of a hunting animal. "He thought it might make him an adept?"

"He thought a lot of things," Damien said warily. "The last one got him killed. What's on your mind?"

The Hunter looked at him. His eyes were black and hungry. "Did he take notes?"

"I think so. Why?"

"Might they still exist?"

He considered. "He lived with a woman before we left. I sent back word to her of what happened, when we got out of the rakhlands. Your guess is as good as mine what she did with his things, after that. Why?" he asked suddenly. "What are you thinking?"

"A possible plan," he said softly. "But I need more data before I can assess its practicality. I think Mer Reese would have collected that data. I think that some of it may be in his notes."

"You won't tell me what it is?"

He shook his head. "Not now. It's too great a long shot. Let me confirm what I suspect, and then . . ." He drew in a deep breath. "I'll tell you as soon as I know for certain. I promise."

"Yeah. Thanks. I live for secondhand research."

If the sarcasm in his tone bothered Tarrant, the Hunter gave no sign of it. "Come," he said, rising. "Let's see if his notes are still around."

Out of habit, Damien glanced at the clock. "Isn't it a little late to go visiting?"

The Hunter's gaze was venomous. "I have twenty-nine days left." he said icily. "In the face of that, do you think I care if I inconvenience someone?"

"No," he muttered, embarrassed. "No reason you should. I'm sorry."

"Do you remember where this woman lives?"

"Not exactly. But that's what the fae's for, isn't it?" Then he hesitated. "Are you sure she'll be willing to help us this late?"

"No." The Hunter smiled coldly. "Not at all. But that's what the fae's for, isn't it?"

The house was just as he remembered it: small and warm and utterly domestic. There were more quake-wards on the front porch now, as well as several new sigils etched into the window; he felt a pang of mourning at the irony of that. When Senzei Reese had lived here, his fiancée had been wary of such devices. Now that he was gone, and the house was free of his obsession, Worked items became acceptable again. It surprised him how bitter he felt about that.

"All right." He sighed, and started toward the stairs. "Let's do it."

"One moment." Tarrant's eyes were focused on the ground before the house; Damien sensed him grow tense as he took hold of the currents with his will and began to mold them. As always, he found it eerie that a human being could Work without any sign or incantation to focus concentration.

When it seemed to him that Tarrant was done, he asked, "What are you doing?"

"Merely compensating for the late hour. I understand that anything more would be offensive to you. You see?" The pale eyes fixed on him, a spark of sardonic humor in their depths. "I do learn, Reverend Vryce."

"About time," he muttered, as they climbed up the porch stairs together.

It was Tarrant who rapped on the door, and Damien could sense his power woven into the sound, making it reverberate inside any human brain within hearing range. He waited a moment and then knocked again, and suddenly a light came on near the back of the house. She had been sleeping, no doubt. Damien wondered how effective Tarrant's Working would be if she were barely awake.

After a minute they could see a figure padding through the house, a lamp in its hand. It came to the door and fumbled with the latch, then opened it. A short chain stretched taut as the door was pulled open a few inches.

"Yes?" It was a man. "What do you want?"

Damien couldn't find his voice; it was Tarrant who filled in. "We're looking for Allesha Huyding."

"What's it about?" he demanded. "And why can't it wait until morning?"

Damien was about to risk an answer when a female voice sounded from the back of the house. "What is it, Rick?"

"Two men," he answered curtly. "I don't know either of them."

There was movement in the room behind him now, as someone else approached. "Let me see," she said softly. She peered over his arm and studied Tarrant, then turned to look at Damien. And gasped.

"Sorry to bother you—" the priest began.

"No bother," she answered quickly. She nodded to the man. "Let them in."

"But, Lesh—"

"It's okay. Let them come in."

He clearly thought otherwise, but he pushed the door closed for a moment, undid the chain, and then opened it wide. Whatever Tarrant had done to keep her calm and cooperative, it had clearly not worked on him. "Hell of an hour," he muttered, as they stepped into the small, neat living room. He radiated hostility.

Memories. They rose up about Damien as the lamplight flickered, picking out details of a room that was painfully familiar. Here, on that chair, he had waited to see Ciani. There, in the room beyond, she had lain in a state near death. There, in that place, the demon Karril had started them on a journey more terrible than any could predict. . . .

He forced his awareness back to the present time, and to the matter at hand. Allesha's new boyfriend was regarding them with the kind of hostility a wolf would exhibit upon finding that another wolf had pissed in its den. He was a thick-set man, heavy with muscle, and Damien suspected that he harbored a violent temper. A dark man, bearded, who was the opposite of Senzei Reese in every way. Again the priest felt a sense of acute mourning for the loss of his friend, and the manner in which this house had been so thoroughly cleansed of his presence.

"My name is Gerald Tarrant," the Hunter said, focusing his attention on Allesha. "I was a companion of Senzei Reese during his recent travels, as was Reverend Vryce."

She nodded slightly to Damien. "Yes. I remember you."

"I'm sorry to bring up what must be painful memories, Mes Huyding, but we have great need of some notes that were in your fiancé's possession. I was wondering if you could tell us what became of his things."

"What the hell is this?" her new boyfriend sputtered. "Can't it wait until morning? Who the hell are you, to show up on our doorstep at this hour and—"

"It's all right," she told him. To Damien's surprise, the words seemed to quiet him. "I don't mind. You go back to sleep if you want. I'll be there as soon as we're finished."

"I'll be damned if I'm going to bed while you—"

Tarrant caught his eyes then. And held them. Something passed between them that Damien could sense, an invisible power that soothed, smothered, silenced.

"Yes," he said quietly. His eyes were half-lidded, as if sleep were already reclaiming him. "I'll do that."

They were silent as he turned and left, walking as slowly as if he had never awakened. At last, when he was safely behind the bedroom door and well out of hearing, Allesha said softly, "I'm sorry. He's protective, that's all."

"We understand," Damien assured him.

"The truth is, I didn't really know what to do with Zen's things when he died. He didn't have any family that I knew of, and as for friends . . . he was close to Ciani. You know that. But there weren't many other people in his life." She picked up a lamp from a nearby table and lit it with her own; the flickering light picked out warm shadows amidst the furniture. "I kept the things that looked important, notes and such, and a few valuables. They're upstairs." She handed the second lamp to Damien and gestured toward the staircase. "This way."

The two men followed her up into the attic, into a room that brought back painful memories to Damien. There was the rug Senzei had knelt on while they planned their trip to the rakhlands; there was a box of Ciani's papers he had rescued from the Fae Shoppe fire. The rest was stacked in boxes in a corner of the room, books and notebooks and papers and charms that filled their wooden crates to overflowing. "There's no order to it, really." She sounded apologetic. "I didn't know what to do with it all—"

"You did fine," Damien assured her.

"I wouldn't know where to look for anything. I—"

"It's fine," Tarrant said. The power behind his words was musical, compelling. "Everything's fine. Leave us here, and go back to sleep. We'll lock the house behind us when we go."

For a moment it seemed as if she might make some protest, but then the fae that Tarrant had conjured took hold at last and she nodded. Wraithlike, silent, she made her way downstairs again.

When she was out of hearing Damien said softly, "That would have bothered me once."

"And you would have been a pain in the ass about it. Fortunately for us both, you changed." He knelt down by the nearest pile of crates, running a hand along the rough surfaces. "Can you Locate what we need, or do I have to do this alone?"

"If you tell me what I'm looking for."

"Any notes he might have made regarding the use of earthquake surges. Or volcanic hotspots, for that matter. Any fae-current too intense for human skill to Work."

"And you want notes on Working it."

"Exactly."

Apparently he didn't see the contradiction in that statement, and Damien wasn't in the mood to argue with him. Drawing in a deep breath, he focussed his own attention on the fae, and envisioned the mental patterns that would allow him to control it. When he had impressed it with his need, he went over to the nearest pile of crates and began to search through them, using the fae to stroke each page, each book, searching for a connection.

It took nearly an hour. They had to rearrange the room twice, to gain access to the crates that were buried in the rear. But at last Tarrant stiffened and breathed, "This is it." And together they managed to unearth the crate in question and free its contents.

"Why don't we just take it all?" Damien whispered. He felt like an intruder, acutely conscious of the innocent people sleeping just downstairs from them. "We can carry it."

"I want to make sure we have what we're looking for." He was rummaging through a stack of clothbound books—ledgers, from the look of them—and at last he pulled out one that seemed to please him. It was a large volume, leatherbound, that had seen much handling in its life. An inkstain marked its spine and spread across one cover, from some accident long in the past. Tarrant put it down on the floor and set the lamp beside it. As Damien crouched nearby, he began to turn the pages.

God in heaven. . . .

It was the scrapbook of a man obsessed, maintained for more than two decades. Newspaper articles were glued to the pages with meticulous care, chronicling every attempt that humankind had made to harness the wild power of the earth. Every sorcerer who had tried to Work the earthquake surge was in there, along with a description of

each gruesome demise. Damien would have guessed that few men
were stupid enough to attempt such a thing, but apparently there
were hundreds. As Tarrant turned page after page, as the volume of
human tragedy gained in weight and horror before them, Damien
could only wonder at the lunacy of such men, who would give their
lives to test themselves against a force that no human will had ever
harnessed.

Senzei would have done it, he thought grimly. *Given enough
time, enough frustration, he would have tried the same thing. And
he would have died the same way.*

"This is it," Tarrant said at last. "The rest can go back."

Damien lifted up the nearest crate and hauled it back to where it
belonged. "Is it time to tell me what all this is about?"

He could hear Tarrant hesitate. "Not yet. Let me go through this
in detail. I need one piece of information, and I'm more likely to find
it in here than in any other source. If it's here, if it says what I think
it does . . . there'll be time enough then to discuss things. If not, why
waste the effort?"

"I don't know what you have in mind," Damien said sharply, "but
remember: none of those people survived. *None of them,* Gerald."

"None of them survived," he agreed. "But that doesn't mean that
all of them failed, does it?"

"What does that mean?"

But the Hunter didn't answer. And at last, realizing that nothing
he could say was going to change that, Damien resigned himself to
putting the room back in order.

♛

It was nearly dawn. Domina's light shone down through the window of the rented room, illuminating well-worn pages. There was
weariness in Damien's body, and in his soul.

Then the Hunter closed the book and said, "It's here."

Sleep, which had been closing in about Damien, was banished in
an instant. He sat up in the chair and demanded, "What is?"

"The data I was looking for. He found it." He put his hand on the
leather cover and shut his eyes; Damien thought he saw him tremble
slightly. "All through human history men have tried to harness the
fae-surge that precedes earthquakes. It's common knowledge that it
can't be done, yet they keep trying. The thought of that much power
outweighs all natural caution, it seems, and not until the fae fries
their brains to ash does it become clear that there are some things

men were never meant to do." His hand spread out across the mottled leather of the scrapbook, as if drinking in its contents through that contact. "Likewise there are those who try to Work at the site of an active volcano, for the same reason. The results there are identical. Man can't channel that kind of power and live to talk about it."

"You needed Zen's notes to tell you that? Hell, I could have saved you the trouble."

Instead of being irritated, the Hunter smiled faintly. "But you see, there were other questions left to be asked. Questions no one thought of, except our obsessed friend Mer Reese."

"Such as?"

He indicated the volume before him. "These men and women all died Working. What happened to their Workings when they perished? Were they obliterated alongside their makers, dispersed in that one fatal instant? Or did they take hold of the wild current, impressing the fae with their purpose even as their owners burned?"

"Does it matter?"

"It might." Though his voice was calm, his posture was rigid, as if all his tension had been channeled into that one outlet. "It might matter very much."

"Why?"

In answer the Hunter pushed the heavy book away from him, and forced himself to lean back in his chair. For a moment he was still, his eyes fixed on a distant, imaginary horizon. At last, in a tense voice, he said, "The negative of *sadism* is *altruism*."

Damien inhaled sharply. "Are you sure about that?"

"Is it possible to be sure? I think it likely."

Altruism. Unselfish concern for the welfare of others. Damien tried to fit it into the Iezu pattern, to see if it would work. Could one want to spare others from pain, and at the same time take delight in hurting them? "It feels right," he said at last. "Better than anything else we've come up with, that's for sure."

The Hunter nodded.

"But how does that help us? I mean, we can hardly force Calesta to do charity work."

"With enough power," the Hunter said evenly, "we can force him to do anything."

It took a second for Tarrant's meaning to sink in; when it did so, he felt his gut tighten in dread. "Gerald, you can't. No man has ever survived that kind of Working—"

"And what is altruism, if not the sacrifice of one's self for the common good?"

"So you'll burn out like the others? For what? How does that help us?"

"Read this," he said, pushing the heavy book toward Damien. "Read the articles that Senzei Reese put in here, and the notes he made. These men who risked their lives to Work—"

"They all died, Gerald!"

"*But they didn't all fail.* Read it! In three separate cases he was able to demonstrate that their Workings survived them. Think of that, Vryce! Think of the power!"

"Three out of how many?" he demanded. "You're talking about odds so low I can't even do the math. Be real, Gerald."

The Hunter looked out the window; the morning sky was brilliant with starlight, and a faint band of gray marked the eastern horizon.

"Beyond my home in the Forest," he told Damien, "is a source of power so immense that if there weren't mountains bounding it, no human being could live on this continent. You've seen its power active in the Forest itself, and yet that's but its edge. Its shadow. Its focus is Mount Shaitan, an active volcano, and its fae is so wild that few men dare to even approach it."

Shaitan? It sounded strangely familiar to him, but he couldn't place it. "I've heard the name."

"I'm not surprised; it's legendary. Every now and then some sorcerer makes a pilgrimage to its slopes; a few live to talk about it. I've been to its valley myself, and seen that awesome power. Nothing on Erna can rival it, Vryce. No earthquake surge, no sorcerer's will . . . no demon."

"But the Iezu aren't normal demons." He was suddenly afraid of where this was heading. "Remember?"

"Karril's first memory is of Shaitan. I know of at least two other Iezu for whom that's also true. There's a link between them that goes deeper than a simple question of power. What better way to destroy a Iezu than at the place of his birth?"

"And what about the creature that gave birth to him?"

A muscle tensed along the line of his jaw. "There's no record of any such creature active in that realm."

"No one ever tried to kill its children before."

The Hunter turned toward him; a shadow sculpted the scar on his face in vivid relief. "So there's risk, Reverend Vryce. Did you think there wouldn't be? Did you think we'd find an easy answer? Some simple incantation that would allow us to unmake our Iezu enemy without effort, without loss?" He shook his head sadly. "I'd have thought you wiser than that."

"You're talking about almost certain death, and damned little chance of success. It seems like one hell of a long shot to me."

"Yes," he agreed. "But what if that's all we have?"

Damien started to protest, then swallowed the words. Because Tarrant was right, damn it. As usual.

The Hunter rose to his feet. Damien knew him well enough to see the underlying tension in his body, and to guess at the inner turmoil that inspired it. But the polished facade was perfectly emotionless, and Tarrant's voice likewise betrayed no human weakness as he recounted the details of his fate. "As of this dawn I have only twenty-nine days left. At the end of that time the Unnamed will dissolve our compact, and I will, in all probability, die. So you see, Reverend Vryce, I have nothing to lose by taking such a chance. Perhaps the earth-fae will claim me, as it has with so many others, but if I can impress it with one last Working . . . I would like to take that bastard with me," he said, his voice suddenly fierce. "I would like my death to mean that much. Can you understand that?"

"Yes," he said. "Yes, I understand."

"It'll be a long and dangerous journey, and not one I would ordinarily relish. Few living men have survived it. And if Calesta should guess at my purpose, and turn his full illusory skill against me . . ." He drew in a deep breath, and exhaled it slowly. Damien thought he saw him tremble. "You don't have to go. I'll understand."

"Of course—"

"You have a life here, and duties, and a future—"

"*Gerald.*" He waited until the Hunter was silent, then said sharply, "Don't be a fool. Of course I'm going."

Backlit by the light of early dawn, the Hunter stared at him. What was that emotion in his eyes, so hard to see against the light? Fear? Determination? Dread? Perhaps a mixture of all three, but something else besides. Something that was easier to identify. Something very human.

Gratitude.

With a glance toward the window, as if gauging the sun's progress, Tarrant nodded. "All right, then." His voice was little more than a whisper, as if the growing light had leached it of volume. "Purchase whatever provisions you need. There won't be food available in Shaitan's valley, so pack enough for several weeks. We'll have to change horses to make good time; don't invest too much in that area. Do you have money?"

In answer, he took out the draft that the Patriarch had given him, and handed it to him. Tarrant's eyes grew wide with astonishment as he read it. In all the time Damien had known him, he had never seen him so taken aback.

"Ten thousand? From the Church?"

"And more if I can justify it."

"So they . . . approve of you?"

He snorted. "Hardly."

"But this draft—"

"The Patriarch's a practical man. He knows there are things I can do as a free agent which he, because of his rank, can't even try. And he knows that if we don't stop Calesta now, the Church he loves may have no future. That's all." He laughed shortly, harshly. "Believe me, I wish there were more to it."

He said it quietly, with rare compassion: "They didn't turn you out?"

"Not yet," he muttered. Color rising in his cheeks. *They're leaving that to me.*

Leaving the draft on the table beside him, the Hunter came to where he stood, and put a hand on his shoulder. Just for a moment, and then it was gone. A faint chill remained in Damien's flesh where he had touched him, and he nodded ever so slightly in appreciation of the supportive gesture. Then, without a word, Tarrant walked to the door and let himself out. The sky outside the window was a paler gray than before; he had little time to take shelter.

Cutting it close, Damien thought, but it didn't surprise him. With Tarrant's remaining lifespan measurable in hours, it was little wonder that he squeezed out every minute he could.

Alone in the rented room, his hand clenched tightly about the Patriarch's draft, Damien tried hard not to think about the future.

Twenty-six

It was nearly dawn. The city's central square was all but deserted, its myriad muggers banished by the growing light, its hidden lovers long since gone to bed. At its far end the great cathedral glowed with soft brilliance, its smooth white surface as fluid and ethereal as a dream.

Damien stood for some time, just staring at it, not thinking or planning or even fearing . . . just being. Drinking in the human hopes that had polished the ancient stone, the soft music of faith that answered every whisper of breeze. Then, as Erna's white sun rose from the horizon, he climbed up the stairs and rapped softly upon the door, alerting those within to his presence. After a moment he heard footsteps approach and a bolt was withdrawn along one of the smaller doors; he stood before it as it was opened, presenting himself for inspection.

"Reverend Vryce." It was one of the Church's acolytes, working off his required service hours as night guard. A thin and gangly teenager, he seemed strangely familiar to Damien. "Do you have business here?" Ah, yes. A face out of memory. One of the dozen lads whom the Patriarch had assigned to him as a student, several eternities ago when he had first come to Jaggonath. His fledgling sorcerers.

He nodded in what he hoped was a reassuring manner. "I came to pray." The boy looked considerably relieved, and stood aside to let him enter. *What did you think, that I would ask you to rouse your Patriarch near dawn so I could discuss sorcery with him?* Then he looked at the boy's young face and thought soberly, *You did think exactly that, didn't you?*

"I won't be long," he promised.

The sanctuary was empty, as he had hoped. The night crew had finished its cleaning and retired long ago. His footsteps echoed eerily in the empty space as he approached the altar. A familiar path. A familiar focus.

The altar. There was nothing on it to worship, really, as there would be on a pagan altar. The Prophet had dreamed of a Church without such symbols, in which the center of worship would be something greater than a silk-clad table, something less solid and more inspiring than a block of earthly matter. But Gerald Tarrant had lost that battle, like so many others. The children of Earth expected an altar, and their descendants did likewise. The baggage of humanity's Terran inheritance was not to be discarded so lightly.

He knelt before the ancient symbol of faith, feeling the vast emptiness gathering around him as he shut his eyes, preparing his soul. He wished that any words could ease the tightness in his chest, or dull the sharp point of his despair. He wished mere prayer had that kind of power.

God, he prayed, *I have loved You and served You all my life. Your Law gave meaning to my existence. Your Dream gave me purpose. In Your service I grew to manhood, measuring myself against Your eternal ideals, striving to set standards for myself that would please You. I live and breathe and struggle and Work—and accept the inevitability of my own death—all in Your Name, Lord God of Earth and Erna. Only and always in Your Name.*

He sighed deeply. The weight of centuries was on his shoulders, past and present combined into a numbing burden. If he died here and now, with this prayer upon his lips, there would be a kind of justice in that, he thought. And an easement, that he had been spared one final test.

Unto my dying day I will serve Your Will, obey Your Law. No matter how much it hurts, my God. No matter how hard it is. That was the vow I made so many years ago, when I first came into the Church; that's the oath I serve today.

He knelt a moment longer, head bowed, soul aching. The pain of despair was sharp within him now, and when he rose up to leave, it stabbed into his flesh with brutal force as if trying to bring him to his knees again. Trying to put off that most terrible moment, which beckoned to him like a spectre. He bore the protest silently, without complaint, knowing that it was a kind of communion with his conscience, and therefore the most perfect prayer of all.

Slowly he walked back down the length of the aisle. At the end of the sanctuary he paused, and he fingered the opening to the offering receptacle, the protective flap which would allow departing worshipers to commit a coin or two to the Church's coffers, without giving them access to the offerings of others. *Human nature being what it is,* he thought grimly. For a moment he fingered the flap without thought, moving it back and forth along its hinges. Then he reached into his jacket and pulled out an envelope.

For His Holiness, it said. Only that. He held it in his hand for a minute, trembling slightly, and then slid it beneath the flap. He could hear it fall to the smooth metal bottom of the offering case, and then there was silence. It would wait until the next well-attended service, when an attendant would take it up and deliver it. By then, he hoped, he and Gerald Tarrant would be long gone.

In Your Name, my God. Only and always in Your Name.

His formal resignation in its place, Damien Vryce began the long and lonely walk back to his apartment.

Twenty-seven

Her children were coming.

She sensed their presence as she brooded within her sanctuary, and wondered at the sudden stirring of activity. Most of her children never bothered to look in upon her once they were set free in the world. They preferred to make their own fates, and she had no argument with that. It was what she had intended so very long ago, when she had brought the first of them into existence.

But now they were coming here. All of them. The ones who could speak to her, and the ones who could not. The few who could share her memories directly, and the hundreds who were all but unaware of her existence. They were coming because several of their number had defied her, coming to see if she would accept their transgressions, or punish them . . . or what?

What indeed, she thought.

She had made rules for them so that they might live and learn and grow, and ultimately serve her purpose. For a thousand solar cycles those rules had gone unquestioned. That was as it should be: a mother giving life had every right to define what paths her children would take, and to eradicate those few who failed to accept her guidance. But what about a child who did understand, but who consciously chose to defy her? The concept was so alien to her that she could scarcely comprehend it. It would never have happened in her homeland, that was certain.

You don't know what's driving them. You cannot judge.

She had given them orders. They had disobeyed. She had set forth the laws of their existence, which was her right as their creator. They had chosen to ignore her.

They should die.

It was her right, without question. Some might have argued that it was even her duty. Certainly her first family, who had accompanied her to this place, would have been quick to condemn any of their own number who defied her will so openly. But these new children of hers ... these wild, defiant infants ... might they not have something to teach her, before they died? Had she not sent them out into the world for precisely that purpose?

They are only half mine, she reminded herself. Remembering that act which was neither passion nor pain, but simple desperation. So many matings. So many failures. She had thought once that by choosing the right mate she could ensure a successful brood, but that plan had gone awry so often she despaired of ever making it succeed. In fact she had lost nearly all of her hope, nearly all of what little strength remained to her ... until now.

Her children were coming! So many, all at once. They had never gathered together like this before, not for any one purpose. Would it make a difference? she wondered. Would there be a power in the sheer mass of their gathering, a force born of their limitless variety, that might shed a ray of hope into the void of her despair? If she killed the disobedient ones now, she would never know. They would disperse again, the strong ones and the weak ones and the ones so distant that it seemed none could speak to them at all. What would it take to bring them together again after that? What kind of tragedy would she have to invoke? It was far easier to withhold her punishment now, she thought. Far easier to let them all come here first, and then cleanse the family as tradition required.

Hope. It was almost an alien concept to her now. She savored it, reflecting.

And waited.

Where Power Abides

Twenty-eight

They came by ones and twos, and then—as the day progressed and they gathered courage and friends—in small, fiercely bonded groups. The Patriarch met with them all. His advisers protested that by doing so he was only encouraging people who would feign great faith in order to stoke the fires of their own self-importance, and—to be fair—they were not entirely wrong. For every genuinely faithful man there were half a dozen whose only purpose in coming was to brag at a later time that they had been in the presence of the Holy Father. For every truly devout woman there were half a dozen whose friends fluttered around the doorway to his chamber like anxious birds, their only purpose being to serve as witnesses that this unique honor had really taken place. But though he heard the truth in his peoples' warnings, he chose to disregard them. There was no other servant of the Church who could see into these people's hearts as he did, and therefore no other one who could choose. It was that simple.

At times his visitors were exactly the type he would have predicted: coarse and simple men, whose faith was as rough-hewn as their manner, whose innate preference for a world divided into clear domains of black and white was uniquely well suited to this enterprise. He didn't doubt that among those faces were many that had been seen in the pagan quarter at night, and indeed several of them seemed familiar to him from his brief appearance at Davarti's Temple. Those were the men he had expected his proclamations to draw, and he welcomed them in a manner that was sure to secure their loyalty. Others were more surprising. There were more women than he would have expected, for one thing; given that gender's lesser propensity for organized violence, he had expected that few would sign on for such a venture. But he had underestimated the symbolic power of the Forest in the minds of his female congregants, and the depths of their hatred for the Hunter. Some claimed that they would give their lives in order to bring that demon to his knees, and he did not doubt for a minute that it was true.

There is the kernel of a warrior in all of us, he thought grimly, as he watched the futures that swirled madly about each applicant. *God give me the strength to control it, once I have encouraged it to dominance.*

He judged them each individually, one after another, with his eyes and his new Vision both. With some it was instantly clear what manner of support—or danger—they might provide. With others he was forced to unravel a tapestry of potential so tangled, so volatile, that it took all his self-control to maintain a human conversation while trying to make sense of it all. It wasn't under his control, this new power, but swept him along in a flood tide of prescience that threatened, at each moment, to drown him utterly. Did his advisers suspect the weakness in him? Did they sense how fragile his grip on sanity was now, how easily he could lose his purchase and be lost to them forever?

Calm. That was the answer. Perfect, unshakable calm. It was a front that he cultivated as he interviewed dozens—or was it hundreds?—of would-be warriors. Calm, that most precious illusion, that kept his inner torment from being expressed and so kept it from being reflected back at him one, ten, a thousand times, in the mirror of others' souls. A stillness so absolute that Nature had no equivalent . . . save at the heart of a storm.

The hurricane bore down on him. Housewives. Craftsmen. Stevedores. Journalists. They came from all walks of life, some for reasons of faith, some for reasons of pride, a few out of sheer boredom. He could See the strength of their courage, or their lack of it. He could See which of these fledgling crusaders would accept the yoke of his leadership and dedicate their energies to the common good, and which would threaten the ranks by continual disruption. And he assigned them each a role in the coming war by virtue of that assessment. There were roles enough that all could serve the cause, and he was diplomat enough to make each offering sound like a unique honor. Fund-raisers would be needed, purchasing agents, advance men sent ahead to Kale and Mordreth to prepare for the army's passage; there would be crew chiefs to organize labor at the fringe of the Forest, where a vast swath of landscape must be cleared in order to contain the cleansing fire which would be their final effort; there were medics needed, and veterinarians, and seamsters, and messengers, and even envelope stuffers . . . so many duties that there was always a niche to be offered, hopefully one suitable enough that it was received with a nod of gratitude, not a glare of resentment.

What amazed him was how fast it was all coming together. How tempting it was to thank God for that, and ignore the role Vryce's demon had played in making it happen! *But there's no shame in that,* he told himself, as he waited for yet another warrior-applicant to present himself before the throne of God. *Using evil to destroy evil is a blessed enterprise. Didn't the Prophet teach that?* Clearly the world was ready for such action. The Forest had been a threat for too long. And there was no other organization on the face of this planet, religious or otherwise, with the courage to attempt such an assault, and the skill to make it succeed.

Only the Church.

His Church.

God save us, he prayed between interviews. And he bowed his head in guilt at the power he now wielded, the visions he could not turn away. They were there even when he shut his eyes, burning his eyes, a constant reminder of his damnation. *God save us all,* he prayed. Wondering if his God could ever forgive him for what he had done . . . or if he could forgive himself.

Dusk, the days' interviews over, the clamor of angry souls giving way, at long last, to silence.

Time to decide.

Wordlessly, the Patriarch left his chamber and descended to the secret room that waited far below. By now his attendants were used to his strange silence, and in their eagerness to anticipate his needs they ran down the corridor ahead of him, calling for assistance. By the time he reached the double-locked door there was a priest waiting for him, key in hand. *Awe* flickered about his head in a wild halo, belying the cool texture of his greeting. Two keys turned in unison, unlocking the ancient door. The Patriarch descended the stairs alone, leaving the priest behind him. To his surprise the ceaseless clamor of the earth-fae grew muffled as he descended, granting him an unexpected respite. He leaned against the wall and breathed the silence in deeply, desperately, as a drowning man might gasp for air. If he descended deep enough, would the earth-fae abandon him altogether? Was there a depth at which he might find peace—true peace—at which the tumult of futures would cease their racket and allow him a few seconds in which to think? To pray? To *be?* What a rare and precious gift that would be!

But it was not yet time to rest, not for a long while yet. The earth-fae still coursed about his feet as he continued down the long staircase, weaker than aboveground but undeniably potent. No peace yet. At the base of the staircase was a heavy door, banded with iron, and he fitted his key into the ancient lock with a steady hand. It seemed to him there was another light besides that of the earth-fae, one that seeped out from under the door as he cracked it open. For a moment he hesitated, afraid of what his new vision would disclose in the room beyond. Then, with a prayer upon his lips, he quickly pulled the heavy door open.

Beyond it was a sea of light so blinding that he cried out involuntarily as it struck his eyes, burning them, and threw up a robed arm across his face to protect himself. Above him footsteps clattered on the stairs as his people responded to his cry, but he called out harshly for them to stay where they were. This was his trial, not theirs. By feel then, without sight, he worked his way slowly into the room. All he could see was a field of black spots against a blazing sun, undulating in time to his heartbeat. Was this what Vryce had seen when he had conjured his special vision? Or was it one more facet of his own special Hell, the price of accepting a demon's gift, that he could not look upon the Workings of his own Church?

But slowly, painfully, his vision adjusted. By that time his face was drenched in sweat, and much of his body also. His eyes felt raw and tender, so that the mere act of blinking was painful. But he could see now, and with wonder and not a little fear he gazed upon the relics of the Great War, which had been Worked by priests of his faith so long ago.

Shards of steel, long since gone to rust. Fragments of cloth. Scraps of gilded leather. They were all imbued with the solar fae, that nearly untamable power, so that even in their decay they made the very air resonate with sunfire. Blazing like a thousand captive suns, they bore witness to a power so far beyond anything the Patriarch might command that for a moment he reached out to the nearest case for support, overcome by the memories they conjured. It was lost now. All of it. Those warriors, their strength, their dreams . . . all gone now. Only these few relics remained, that might with care be forged into a weapon again. To serve the Church anew, this time in triumph.

But as he gazed upon those few precious fragments, imagining what they might become, he realized suddenly that there was more than sunpower visible in their auras. There was a taint also, a kind of slithering darkness, that was visible just at the edge of his new vision. After a moment he realized what it represented, and the knowledge made him tremble inside, and brought tears of frustration to his eyes. To him these relics might be symbols of man's ultimate faith, but to his people they were reminders of the Church's greatest failure. To bear them into battle against the Forest again would be to shackle his army to that great defeat, to awaken echoes of a loss so devastating that the fae would be forced to respond, damning their efforts. They might as well just feed their blood to the enemy, he thought, as try to use this power. The end result would be much the same.

Oh, my God, he despaired. *Will You send us naked against the enemy? Will You make us batter at the walls of Hell with no more than cold steel in our hands?*

Let faith be your shield, a cold voice whispered, and its tone was such that his skin crawled to hear it. Was that some inner voice of his own speaking, or the whisper of his God? Or was it a suggestion from some more demonic source, Gerald Tarrant's ward, perhaps, or the demon Calesta, using the Patriarch's human weakness as a path of invasion into this holy place?

Take this trial from me, Lord. I'm not strong enough to handle it. Give it to someone who won't fail you.

But the visions refused to fade. The relics continued to burn. And about him, above him—within his very soul—an endless stream of futures clamored for fulfillment.

She was slender and delicate, and beautiful in the way that a porcelain doll might be beautiful, a priceless antique. For a moment he just stared at her, unable to grasp why such a woman would choose to be part of his mission . . . and then the tumult of images that cascaded about her flesh came into focus, and with it an identity.

"Narilka Lessing."

She seemed startled by the fact that he knew her name, but quickly regained her composure. He sensed a tension within her so great that it might have broken a lesser soul; the fact that she could contain such a thing and not even show it bore witness to a strength far beyond anything her physical self even hinted at. Was this the woman that Andrys Tarrant had fallen in love with? If so, it wasn't hard to see why.

"Your Excellency," she said. Hesitantly, not knowing if the honorific would please or offend. A curious pagan, this one, uncomfortable with his identity as the voice of the One God, yet anxious to do him appropriate honor. He accepted the honorific with a gracious nod, his eyes fixed upon the storm of images that surrounded her. Bright, sharp, volatile images; in all his interviews he had rarely seen such a tumult of potential.

"I take it you told my people that you belong to the Church."

Her face flushed hotly, but her gaze didn't flinch. "There was no other way to get in to see you. I tried."

He nodded, and watched as an image of blood and flesh spattered into fragments by the side of her head. What was that white face beside hers, grinning? "I regret that we forced you to such subterfuge. It wasn't our intention." He struggled to focus on her face through the whirlwind of images. "Now that you're here, what is it I can do for you?"

She drew in a deep breath, and then said bluntly, "I want to go with you to the Forest."

So that was it. He should have guessed. "Mer Tarrant already asked me if that was possible. I told him no."

"I can't accept that."

In another time, another life, he might have gotten angry at her. Now, in this transformed self, he felt strangely distant, as though he were watching two strangers converse. "This campaign is a Church matter. All the people involved serve the One God. You, Mes Lessing, don't." He nodded slightly. "At least, that's my understanding of it. Correct me if I'm wrong."

"Are you afraid I'd try to convert your people?" She challenged him proudly. "Is that what you think? Is their faith in your God so weak? Do you really think I'd be a threat to them?"

"That isn't the point," he said quietly. He turned away from her slightly, as if to gaze out the window while he spoke; anything to look away from the faeborn chaos that surrounded her. "Faith has power, Mes Lessing, real power. Unified faith can reWork the very currents, changing reality so that it favors our cause. One discordant soul might not seem like much of a problem to you, but its effect upon our mission would be like that of a sour note in an otherwise perfect symphony." He paused, giving her a moment to muse upon that. "If you came with us, it would increase the risk to all of us— and to Andrys Tarrant—a thousandfold. Is that what you want? To place him in even greater danger?"

"You don't know what you're doing to him," she said fiercely. "It's eating him up inside, taking on this role. It's making him crazy. You want him to face that alone?"

"He has us," he said coolly. "And he has his God."

"That isn't enough!" she retorted. "Your God doesn't hold a man's hand when he's alone in the night. Your God won't show up to comfort him when he's scared. Your God doesn't care if he hurts, as long as—" The words caught in her throat then, and she coughed heavily. He glanced back at her, just in time to see a white mask with frightened eyes scream as its throat was slashed, then fade into a mist of blood about her hair.

"I won't get in your way," she promised. Pleading now, all anger leached from her tone in a desperate bid to placate, to persuade. "I won't say anything to offend anyone. I can even hold my own when we fight. . . ." She drew in a deep breath, and dark images fluttered about her head like bats. "And the Forest can't hurt me. It's a . . . a kind of gift. Nothing that belongs to the Hunter will hurt me. I'd be safe." She took a step closer to him; futures flickered in and out of existence with blinding speed as she moved. "Please," she begged. "Let me go with him. He needs somebody."

If you care so much, he wanted to say, *then embrace his God. Join him in faith, and you can truly share in his enterprise.* The words were forming, balanced on his lips—and then a new set of images took shape around her, a chaos of futures so vivid, so powerful, that the breath meant for words was expelled in a gasp, and it was all he could do to stand there and stare at them.

He saw this woman accompanying Andrys Tarrant into battle, and he saw her left behind. Those two futures divided once, twice, a hundred times each, until the whole room seemed filled with images, blood-filled and fearsome. It was far more intense than the kind of Divinings he had experienced before—save perhaps with Andrys Tarrant himself—and he struggled in vain to absorb it all without losing himself. A storm of images, a riot of raw potential, bits and pieces that flickered in and out of existence so quickly he could barely focus on them. Was this one decision really so important? Could it be that whole futures depended on whether or not this woman joined their effort? A chaos of answers assaulted his brain, and he struggled to sort them out. If she came with them, they might succeed, but the chances of that were slim. If, on the other hand, she stayed behind . . . then there were a thousand new futures to choose from, and so many more of those led to success. He saw images of a white face grinning, of her slender throat being slashed, of ribbons of blood flowing down a wall of black glass . . . he shivered to watch her die time and time again, to watch her not die, to watch the Forest triumph and wither and grow and burn. . . . *Enough!* He took a step back from her and shut his eyes, shielding them with a trembling hand. *Enough.* It was too much for him to interpret, he knew that; if he tried to understand it all, he might lay waste to that fragile shell which was all that remained of his sanity. The pattern was clear enough, though painful to acknowledge. All his planning, all his hopes, all his faith . . . without this woman it might all come to naught. Without her in her proper place, his chosen futures might fall to pieces, like the fabrics of the Great War which rotted far below him.

His head spinning, his mouth dry, he struggled to find his voice. Not to guide her now, or to comfort her, but to drive her away. Even as the words left his lips, he ached inside to be causing her pain, but he knew it was necessary. He had Seen.

"If that's God's will, so be it." He tried to put scorn into his voice—just a little bit—so that his words would seem doubly callous. He could see futures dissolving as he did so, and others taking their place. "We're all risking our lives here, and much more. Did you think it would be easy? Did you imagine that war could be waged without pain, without sacrifice?" *Be careful,* he warned himself, as some frightening new potentials began to take shape about her. In one of them he was callous enough that she devoted all her energy to convincing Andrys not to go to the Forest at all. "I'm sorry," he said, and he kept his voice carefully neutral. "Genuinely sorry. But the answer has to be no."

She seemed about to speak, but apparently words failed her. "You'll kill him," she whispered at last. Hoarsely pushing the words out one by one, wincing as they left her. "Maybe not in body, but in spirit. Don't you care about that at all?"

He looked away, so that he need not see the thousand faeborn images that reflected her suffering. "I'm sorry," he said. Quietly but firmly, finality in his voice. "I can't allow it."

For a moment there was silence. He dared not look back at her, for fear of what the fae would reveal. Finally he heard motion: footsteps on the rug, the click of a latch opening, the hard, cold sound of a door slamming shut. Gone. She was gone.

"Dear God," he whispered. Feeling her pain as though it had somehow charged the air in the room, so that he drew it into his lungs with every breath. His legs felt weak beneath him and he permitted them to fold, his hand against the wall for support as he fell slowly to his knees.

Forgive me, Lord, for being the cause of pain in others. Forgive me for manipulating so many lives in ways that go against Your teachings. Forgive me. . . .

And then the weight of his sorrow was too great even for prayer, and he wept.

Twenty-nine

They left the city right after sunset, as soon as Tarrant could tolerate the light. The Hunter had wrapped his cloak about his head and shoulders in a manner that made him seem more like a spectre than a man . . . which was wholly appropriate, Damien thought, given the nature of their business. Not until the Core had followed the sun into its westerly grave did he push back his improvised hood and breathe in deeply, testing the scents of the night.

"Nothing," he said quietly, which might mean any number of things. Seemingly satisfied, he urged his mount forward. Marginally confident, Damien followed.

There were two routes available to them, and they had argued for over an hour about which one to take. One followed the west bank of the Stekkis River to Kale, along a road that catered to the needs of travelers. It offered supplies, shelter, and various other amenities that Damien found appealing. But it was also the road that the Church would take in its newly declared war against the Forest, and those troops would be leaving any day now. True, the odds of meeting up with them were small—hopefully they would be several days ahead of them at least—but Tarrant was loath to risk even those odds. And since, truth be told, there was nothing Damien would enjoy less than running into the Patriarch with the Hunter by his side, he had finally agreed to the eastern route, on the far side of the river.

He tried not to think about Calesta as they rode, but it was damned hard not to. Did the demon know about their mission, and was he even now making plans of his own to counter theirs? Tarrant had said that the Iezu could read the secrets in the hearts of men. How did you work up a defense against someone like that? Maybe the demon would be so busy with the Church and its campaign that

Tarrant and he were safe for the moment. The Hunter had said that Calesta was involved in that enterprise, although he didn't know exactly how. Maybe it would use up all the demon's energies—

Yeah. Right.

Two hours' ride brought them to the western bank of the Stekkis, at a tiny settlement called Lasta. The town's few businesses were all closed for the night, its houses locked and shuttered securely against the darkness. Tarrant used a Locating to find the ferryman's house. Left to his own devices the Hunter might have coerced the man into his service, but Damien took over, and eventually they agreed upon a price which was half coinage and half sorcery. Glaring, Tarrant worked a Warding on a piece of crystal the man supplied, and not until he was content that it worked would the ferryman step forth out of his house to lead them to the river.

Demonlings fluttered overhead as they led their horses along a narrow paved path behind the house, to where a simple wooden ferry waited. It seemed to Damien that there were a lot of them here, given the size of the town. Either the inhabitants were unusually creative or something else was responsible. Maybe the city-born entities that foraged in this direction found the water to be a barrier, and piled up here like trash in a cul-de-sac, too stupid to know that if they just turned around and went home their odds of finding food would increase a hundredfold. Their presence was a solemn reminder of just how many nasty things were out there, that usually kept their distance when Tarrant was around. No wonder the ferryman had insisted upon the Warding as part of his price.

The river here was broad but shallow, nothing like it was where it roared over Naigra Falls a hundred miles to the north of them, nothing like the vast delta that was host to half a dozen ports beyond that. The ferry was small but adequate, and if the horses had any complaints, they were quickly banished by Tarrant's faeborn skills. Leaning against the rail, watching the inky black water rush by, Damien remembered his protests the first time he'd seen Tarrant use that trick. Now it was just one more choice bit of sorcery, more practical than some, less offensive than most.

Face it, man. You've gotten used to him.

On the far side of the river there was no town, no road, only a rough dirt path that led away from the river. There would be settlements arrayed between there and the coast, but they would be few and far between and their inhabitants would be wary of strangers. Since the road west of the river offered both comfort and safety, anyone choosing the eastern bank would be highly suspect.

As the ferryman poled his way back home, Damien came to where Tarrant stood, one hand resting against the black flank of his horse. It was clear from his expression that he was Working, and not until Damien saw him move and judged him finished did he speak to him.

"Anything useful?"

Tarrant's eyes narrowed ever so slightly. "The Patriarch intends to lead his people into the Forest itself, straight to my keep. They mean to confront me in my lair, confident that God will favor them in their mission and lead them to victory."

No more. After a moment of silence, Damien pressed, "And?"

He shook his head; clearly he was perplexed. "There are futures in which they succeed. Only a few . . . but how could they make it through my domain? Do they think I have no defenses? The very ground will rise up against them, the species I nurtured will—"

"Gerald." He put a hand on the other man's shoulder, for once not noticing the chill of his undead flesh. "It doesn't matter any more. Not the Forest, not any of it." He didn't say the words, but let them hang between them in the chill autumn air, unspoken: *You have twenty-nine days left. That's all. You can't afford to lose your focus now.* "As long as Calesta's alive and kicking, everything's at risk."

The Hunter hesitated; Damien could see something dark flash in those cold, cold eyes. Anger? Frustration? Tarrant glanced northward toward the Forest, as though he wanted to Know what was going on there, but the strong northerly flow of the current wouldn't allow it. With a muttered curse he forced his eyes away and took up the reins of his horse once more. "You're right, Reverend Vryce. Much as I hate to admit it."

He mounted his horse and swung it around so that it faced east. But Damien didn't mount up, and after a moment Tarrant looked back at him, to see what was wrong.

"I'm not," Damien said hoarsely. "Reverend, I mean." He swallowed hard, forcing the words out. "Not a priest anymore."

For a moment there was silence.

"They cast you out?"

"No." He shook his head stiffly. "I quit. I was . . ." God, he wished there were an easy way to end this conversation. But Tarrant had a right to know. "It was my choice. Really. I . . ." Whom was he trying to convince, Tarrant or himself? "It was right," he whispered hoarsely. "The right thing to do."

For a long time the Hunter said nothing. Then: "I'm sorry."

"Yeah." He shut his eyes, trying not to feel the pain of it all over again. How long would it be before the healing started, before he could think about his choice and not feel sick inside? "Let's just go on, okay?" He vaulted up onto his horse's back and grabbed up the reins. "We've got things to do." He kneed his horse into motion, hoping Tarrant would just follow. He didn't want to look at him again, for fear that he would see something all too human in those death-pale eyes. Something he couldn't deal with right now.

Pity.

They rode hard, pausing only to rest the horses when they had to in order to keep going. There were no stables midway along this route at which one could trade for fresher mounts, hence the animals would have to keep their strength up until they reached the coast. That meant three days at the very least, maybe more. Damien and Tarrant pushed them as hard as they dared on that first night, but both of them knew that speed would cost them dearly if one of their mounts became injured as a result.

You could make the trip faster without me, Damien wanted to say. *You could put on wings and make the coast in a day or two, and Shaitan in little more than that.* But he didn't voice that thought. The Hunter was aware of his own capacity, and he knew damned well that having Damien with him slowed him down. Yes, he could reach Shaitan in less than a week if he traveled alone, but clearly he preferred not to. *He doesn't want to face death alone,* Damien mused. And, darkly: *I don't blame him.*

It was Tarrant who determined their route, leading them away from the packed dirt of the narrow road into the grassy lands beside it. There weren't many caves in this area, he explained. They would have to swing farther east to where the mountains started to rise, to increase their odds of finding shelter when dawn came. What went unsaid was an eloquent reminder of what their relationship had become. Tarrant himself could find shelter alone along any stretch of earth, using his fae-sight to locate an underground passage and his sorcery to facilitate entrance. What would complicate this search was that he meant to keep Damien with him. And that was the first time in all their travels together that the Hunter had voluntarily chosen to share a shelter with anyone.

He's afraid, Damien mused, as a third moon rose to shed light on their journey. *Hell, I'd be, too, in his shoes. Any sane man would be.*

As for being in Damien Vryce's shoes . . . he tried not to think about that.

Near dawn they reined up at last, and Damien dismounted with a sigh that was half relief and half pain. Ten months at sea had weakened his leg muscles enough that he could feel every mile of this trip.

If the Hunter felt any similar discomfort, as usual he didn't show it. In silence they led the horses to the place where Tarrant had Located shelter, and after a brief bout with a shovel and a wrestling match with several heavy rocks, Damien managed to break into the underground space. It was dry at least, which was more than he could say for some of the other places Tarrant had led him to.

"I'll stay up here with the horses," he said, nodding toward the camping supplies in his saddlebag. "They should be able to graze, which'll help stretch our supplies. I'll keep them close to home."

And then came the question he didn't want to ask. The answer he didn't want to know. He drew in a deep breath and forced the words out one by one, trying to make them sound casual. "I guess you'll need to . . . tonight or in the morning. . . ."

"Feed myself?"

He muttered something unintelligable.

In answer Tarrant unbuckled one of his saddlebags and drew out a large canteen. "As you see, I came prepared." He uncapped the container and took a long drink from it; something about the weight or the way he handled it made Damien certain it wasn't water. "No more nightmares, Vryce. Not this time. You need your strength as much as I need mine, and in the face of Calesta's power . . . there should be enough nightmares to go around soon enough, for both of us." He took another short swallow, then capped the canteen once again. "I can make it on this until we reach the coast. After that . . ." He shrugged.

Don't think about it, Damien warned himself, as the Hunter shouldered his supplies and slipped down into the darkness of his subterranean shelter. *The misery that this world will suffer if Calesta succeeds in his plans is a thousand times worse than anything the Hunter could devise.*

He wished he could be sure of that. He wished he were sure of anything.

Twenty-eight days left.

What will happen to the Church's troops if they do make it through? Damien had asked Tarrant. *If your creations let them pass and they reach the keep. What then?*

Then their fate will be in Amoril's hands, he responded. *And as for what Amoril is capable of . . .* He shook his head grimly. *The For-*

est is still mine, and will be until my death. He may tap into its power, but he can never fully control it.

So they could win out, then.

For a long time the Hunter didn't answer. It was a long enough delay that Damien began to wonder if he had heard him at all, and was about to repeat the question when the Hunter said, very quietly, *The price for that kind of success would be high. I wonder if your Patriarch is willing to pay it.*

It took them three days to reach the northern coast. Each night as Tarrant arose, Damien could see him stop and gaze northward toward their distant goal, and he could almost hear him counting down the days that were left to him. Twenty-seven. Twenty-six. Twenty-five. It was enough time to do what they had to, Damien told himself. It had to be. Shaitan wasn't all that far away, so if the journey didn't kill them outright, they should make it with at least a week to spare. Right?

Calesta had still made no move against them. Rather than reassuring Damien, that fact made him doubly nervous. Despite Tarrant's insistence that the Iezu would make no direct attempt to kill them, Damien wasn't so sure. Tarrant had said that the laws of the Iezu forbid them from interfering in human development, and Calesta was doing that already, wasn't he? God only knew what the demon was planning for them, but it was damned likely not to be pleasant. Maybe he would wait until they got to Shaitan, Damien thought. Maybe this first part of the journey would be relatively easy, as they all prepared for a confrontation on the Iezu's home turf. Maybe—

He sighed, and shifted his position in the saddle so that his legs ached a little less.

Yeah. Right. Dream on, Vryce.

They came within sight of Seth shortly after midnight on the fourth night of travel. It was a small town by Jaggonath's standards but adequate for their purposes, with the kind of harbor that should host at least one vessel willing to carry them. Damien saw Tarrant fingering the neck of his tunic as they approached the southern gate, and wondered if he had replaced the Forest medallion Ciani had torn from his neck so very, very long ago. It had made negotiations easier once before, but he wondered if wielding it now would be such a good idea.

As if in answer to his thoughts, Tarrant dismounted and motioned for him to do the same. "Try not to Work here," he warned, as he wrapped the horses' reins about a nearby tree limb for security. "The currents this close to the Forest may well overwhelm you." Damien nodded that yes, he understood. Senzei Reese had almost been swallowed up by the fierce currents in Kale, and that city was just across the river from them. He wasn't anxious to test himself against a similar power.

For a moment Tarrant stood still, gathering himself for a Working. It must be of considerable complexity, Damien noted; the Hunter rarely required such mental preparation. Then Tarrant reached out toward him; Damien could almost feel a gust of power whip about him like a whirlwind. For a moment he couldn't see, and then vision returned to him, and the wind died down. His flesh tingled as if it had just been scraped with a rasp.

"What the hell—"

"An Obscuring," the Hunter said evenly. "Not for the flesh, but for identity."

"You think that's necessary?"

"I think it's wise. Calesta's known our path for several days now. Why make ourselves more vulnerable than we have to be?" He took up his horse's reins again and remounted. "The fact that our enemy can be subtle makes him doubly dangerous," he warned, and he urged his horse into motion once more.

"I know—I agree—it's just—damn!" He mounted his own horse and urged it to a trot, to catch up with Tarrant's own. "You could have warned me."

He couldn't see Tarrant's face, but he suspected he was smiling.

Another half mile brought them to the edge of town. There was a guard stationed on the road there, which was something of a surprise; Damien wouldn't have thought that this small town, off the beaten track from anywhere, would require such security. Two men in armor hailed them as they approached, and gestured for them to dismount. Who were they? the guards asked. Why were they here, and why were they entering the town so late? Damien let Tarrant speak for them both, improvising false names and enough details of their supposed travels that the guards would be satisfied. *He was right*, the ex-priest thought, as he listened to the exchange. *Calesta could well have arranged for a welcoming committee, and we would never have seen it coming.* If so, that would certainly explain why the demon hadn't made a move against them before. It explained it so well, in fact, that as Damien remounted to follow Tarrant into the town itself he felt a knot of dread form in the pit of his stomach.

Calesta wouldn't kill them himself, Tarrant had said. Those were the rules that his kind lived by.

Yeah, but he can manipulate others into doing it for him.

Tarrant led the way to the harbor, following directions that the guards had supplied. The narrow streets were all but silent and the hoofbeats of their horses echoed back at them emptily, as if they were riding in a cavern. It had rained recently, and a thin film of water over the cobblestones made them glimmer like glass in the moonlight. Black glass. Polished obsidian. Bricks like those of the Hunter's keep, toward which even now the Patriarch and his chosen few were riding. He tried not to think about where the Church's army was now, or whether or not he hoped they would succeed. Right now they had enough troubles of their own.

They turned down a side street, narrower than before, which curved to the north. They were close enough to the water now that they could smell the rank perfume of the Serpent, salt and seaweed and decay all blended together into a dank miasma. The harbor must be close by.

They came to another intersection and were about to ride through it, when suddenly the Hunter reined up to a stop.

"What is it?"

Tarrant looked down the three roads available, then back the way they had come. Damien followed his gaze. There was an open-air market to the left of them, its wooden tables now empty until the morning. Some kind of factory stood to the right, its windows dark, its doors securely locked against the night. Up and down the street and to both sides of them it was the same: no signs of human habitation, or of any business that might be active after dark.

He watched as Tarrant worked a Locating, and breathed in sharply as the image took focus. The road to the harbor was wide and paved with flagstone, and even at this hour it was not wholly deserted. Not like this road that they had been sent to, which might have been in the midst of a desert for all the human life it contained. They had been sent in the wrong direction . . . and that could only mean one thing.

With a sharp curse Tarrant wheeled his horse about, and the Locating shattered like glass as he passed through it. Listening carefully, Damien could hear a faint noise approaching from the way they had come. Voices? There was a similar sound to the west of them, and the clear echo of hurried footsteps. No safety there, either. Damien was willing to bet that the other two roads were similarly guarded, or had been closed off.

"You said they wouldn't know who we were," he whispered fiercely.

"I worked an Obscuring," Tarrant snapped. "Either they're hunting mere strangers . . ." He didn't finish the thought, but Damien could finish it for him. *Or Calesta gave them a vision of who we really were. An illusion of his own, to take the place of the one you conjured.* Shit. If that's what had happened, then they were in real trouble—and not only here, but anywhere that men could be gathered together for action.

"That way will be a dead end," Tarrant declared, indicating the direction they had been riding. "And that way, too, most likely." He gestured toward the silent street to the right of them. "With an ambush waiting, no doubt." He studied the road down which they had come; Damien saw his nostrils flare, as if sifting the scent of the road for more information. "Calesta will have known that our destination is the harbor. Therefore they will have turned us away from it."

"So we go back?"

"That, or drive the horses forward and go elsewhere ourselves. Maybe the sound of their flight would detract attention for just long enough . . . we could take to the rooftops." He nodded toward the wooden awning that had been erected over the market area, and the buildings that abutted it. "They wouldn't think to look up there, at least not until they learned that the horses were riderless."

The sounds were getting closer now, and were loud enough that Damien could guess at the size of the approaching mob. If it was a large enough crowd, then the horses would never be able to break through it. On the other hand, trying to make it to the harbor and beyond without swift mounts to carry them was not an appealing alternative. "What's your preference?" he demanded.

Tarrant stared back down the way they had come, studying the currents that flowed along the street. "Calesta can point people to the roof as easily as he can control their vision. And then what would we have? In this district, where there are no homes to put in jeopardy . . ." He didn't finish the sentence. He didn't have to. Damien could picture the district burning up all by himself, along with the refugees who clung to its rooftops.

"All right, then." Tarrant steadied his horse with one hand and drew his sword with the other. The coldfire blade blazed in the darkened street with an almost hungry brilliance. "Let's do it."

"Gerald."

The Hunter looked back at him. The silver eyes were black as jet, and it seemed to Damien that something red and hungry had sparked to life in their depths.

"You can shapeshift," the ex-priest reminded him. "Fly out of here and reach Shaitan that way."

"Yes," he said shortly. "But you can't."

And he kicked his horse into sudden motion, forcing Damien to follow suit.

It was an eerie ride, back down those deserted streets. Tarrant had wrapped some fae about the horses' hooves that kept their footfall from being heard, but there was no way to tell if Calesta was circumventing that Working as well. *If so*, Damien thought grimly, *they'll be ready for us.* He had his own sword out, flame-embossed grip settled firmly in his palm. The sword of his Order, the Golden Flame, of which Gerald Tarrant had once been Knight Premier. And he still claimed that title, Damien knew. Assuming Tarrant dead, the Church had never bothered to throw him out. For some reason, in this dark moment, the thought pleased him immensely.

They could hear distinct voices up ahead, and see the glittering of lanterns. Not far now. With a sinking heart Damien realized just how many men had come to seal the trap, and he knew that there would be no way through them save on a road paved with blood.

"Jump," Tarrant muttered fiercely. Damien glanced over at him and saw a strange double image flickering about the head of his horse, as though there were two animals sharing the same space. A quick glance at his own revealed a similar situation. Teeth gritted, sword raised high in preparation for combat, he forced himself to ignore Tarrant's Working—whatever the hell it was—as he signaled his mount to leap. His old horse would have done it—his old horse would have followed him to Hell and back and not complained—but who could tell what this new mount would do? Ten feet closer to the crowd, now twenty. He could make out individual faces, torches and lamps, swords and spears. There was a rage in those faces burning so hot that several were flushed red with the force of it, and as he and Tarrant came into range, curses were wielded along with sharp steel. What the hell had Calesta told these people—or showed them—to merit such hostility? There were spears being leveled in their direction, and Damien knew that if his horse failed to jump, they would be skewered within seconds.

Please, he prayed. *Do it.*

It did.

He could see the false image peel off as his horse rose up, powerful flanks driving them up over the heads of the nearest townspeople. Behind him the false horse-image plowed into the crowd, and the men there, believing what their eyes told them, fell down before it. Tarrant's own phantom worked similar damage, with such brutal efficiency that row upon row of their attackers seemed to be trampled by the ghostly hooves. The men behind them pressed forward, thrusting spears and swords into the illusory flesh, believing in it enough that it seemed to them the bodies resisted, then punctured, then bled.

—And then the real horse was coming down with Damien still in the saddle, only it hadn't cleared the mob yet, not by a long shot. The men beneath him never saw it coming. One minute they were focused on the ghost-horse before them, and the next minute half a ton of steel and flesh was bearing down on them. Damien heard bones crack as they landed on a sea of moving flesh, and he clung desperately to his saddle as his horse struggled for solid footing, wincing at every cry from the bodies crushed beneath him. For a few precious seconds it was all he could do to keep his seat, and hope that no weapon reached him. Then he saw a blade swinging down toward the horse's neck, and with strength born of utter desperation he leaned out as far as he could to strike it aside, then cut back toward its owner's chest. His blade bit deep into leather and flesh, and the man fell back with a cry.

They don't know what they're doing here, he thought, as he whipped around to see what threat might be coming from another direction. *They probably don't even know who it is they're fighting.* He could hear screams of fury and pain now on all sides. Out of the corner of his eye he saw Tarrant's coldfire blade sweeping like a scythe through the mob. Some of the attackers were starting to back off now, horrified, and the look in their eyes was like that of men awakening from a dream. Damn Calesta, for whatever he had done to them! Wasn't it enough that armies had to die, without making the innocent join them!

Finally he was free, the last broken body fallen behind him. He glanced about to see Tarrant break out of the crowd, and gestured for him to take the lead. The black horse broke into a fevered gallop down the dark street, and Damien followed. He could see blood streaming along his horse's neck and could only pray that the wounds weren't too deep. The black flesh of Tarrant's mount, glistening with sweat, made it impossible to assess its condition, but it seemed to be moving all right. God forbid either horse should lose its footing now.

Two blocks beyond the mob Tarrant slowed, and focused the fae before them into a picture. Now they could see clearly, as if on a map, where the harbor lay. And they could see just as clearly that they had been sent in the wrong direction, into a trap that had almost killed them.

"Come," Tarrant said, and he kicked his horse into a gallop. Down through the dark streets they rode with desperate speed, across a broad avenue, onto a smoothly cobblestoned road. The few townspeople who were abroad that late fell back from them as though they were demons. At least there were no angry mobs here, Damien thought. God willing Calesta was arrogant enough that he never considered they would escape him. Or desperate enough that he had focused all his manpower at that one four-pronged trap, leaving no backup to cover their escape.

And then they turned right instead of left. "Gerald—" Damien called, but the Hunter waved off his protest and continued in that direction. Then he led them through another turn, equally mistaken. Damien struggled to remember the map Tarrant had conjured, and saw it all too clearly in his mind's eye. "You're going the wrong way!" he yelled. Heads appeared in the nearest windows as townies grew curious about the racket outside, then quickly withdrew. "Your map—" he began.

"Follow me!" the Hunter commanded. With a muttered curse Damien followed his lead. If Tarrant wouldn't stop, then there was no other choice; he wasn't about to let them be separated. *Damn the man*, he swore, as he urged his horse to even greater speed. The mob would never catch up to them now, not unless he and Tarrant did something stupid that would slow them down. Like getting lost. Like forgetting the goddamn map. Like turning left when they should go right, and maybe it was all Calesta's fault, maybe Tarrant wasn't *seeing* the right turn, but knowing who and what their enemy was, he damned well should have been prepared for something like that.

And then the houses gave way to an open road paved with flagstone, beyond which the moonlight glinted on surf. Damien could hear waves, and human voices, and the soft growl of a distant turbine. The Hunter rode to the end of the street and paused there.

"How—" Damien began.

"Later." The road dropped away sharply at its end, down to the harbor some hundred feet below. A long flight of stairs and a switchback trail offered equally uncomfortable ways of getting down to the water. The Hunter studied the boats splayed out below them, assessing each one's potential for speed as well as its position in the small harbor. "That one," he said at last, pointing to a small boat at the end of the easternmost pier. Its two masts flanked the exhaust pipe of a steam turbine. "I can raise a wind that will move it quickly, hopefully before anyone thinks to follow."

"What if its owner—?"

"Its owner is irrelevant," Tarrant said sharply. "If you have a problem with that, stay here and argue with him." And he turned his horse toward the switchback path that led down to the water's edge.

It was a nightmare descent, even for one as experienced in riding as Damien was. The path was covered with loose rocks and gravel, and the racing horses slid into several turns. At one time Damien's horse actually missed the edge, and his heart nearly stopped as it half-staggered, half-slid, down to the turn below.

And then they were on flat ground, mud and gravel mixed, clumps of earth tearing up out of the ground as they galloped toward the pier. No secrecy now, nor any attempt at it. Calesta knew where they were headed and that meant the townspeople did as well. The only hope they had of making it out onto the water was to get there before the locals had a chance to stop them.

Out onto the wooden planks, their horses' hooves beating emptily over the rocky shore below. Two men jumped back out of their way, and another few ran as they saw them coming. Good enough. Fear of a maddened horse could be just as effective as a direct assault, and in this case it proved even better. No one tried to stop them as they turned their mounts down the pier Tarrant had chosen, although Damien could see a few men running for help. Within minutes, no doubt, the whole harbor would be swarming with armed men.

Tarrant didn't stop to lead his horse across the water, but urged it into a leap that carried it from the end of the pier onto the boat's narrow deck. Damien saw it slide as it landed, and by the time Tarrant managed to bring it to a stop, they were nearly in the water. He slowed his own mount down as he approached, less than certain that he could manage the same feat. Sliding off the saddle, he moved quickly toward the boat with reins in hand. His horse was less than happy about stepping onto the swaying deck, but a hard jerk on the reins convinced it not to argue, and it managed a half-leap that got it across the water safely.

Damien cut through the mooring lines, not taking time to unbind them. Behind him Tarrant's sword blazed with conjured coldfire, and in response a wind began to rise almost at once, blowing from the shore toward the Serpent. At the other end of the harbor Damien could see spots of light moving—lamps?—and he could hear the cries of would-be pursuers as they made their way down the slope. *Faster!* he urged the wind, as he drew up the sails singlehandedly to harness its power. The small boat shuddered and then drew away from the pier, its sails billowing out white and strong in the moonlight. One of the horses whinnied its discomfort, but Damien doubted that either of the animals would actually be stupid enough to go over the side in protest. Maybe stupid enough to trample their owners, but not that.

"The turbine's below." Tarrant pointed toward the stairs at the rear of the small boat. "Get it started."

"I don't know how—"

"Then make an educated guess."

With a brief glare for his companion he hurried down the stairs, into the cabin and its attendant cargo space. In the galley he located a candle and a pack of matches by moonlight. That lit, it was a bit easier to search. The turbine was similar to one he had seen before, the last time he had made this crossing, and he tried to remember how its owner had worked it. He looked about for fuel, located the furnace door, and started things going. It would be a short while before there was enough pressure to drive the boat, but until then the wind would have to do. He allowed himself the brief luxury of sitting down beside the small engine and of taking several deep breaths in succession. Tarrant would keep the wind going until the turbine kicked in, and then he would turn it around to slow their pursuers. If he could. Damien reflected on how hard it was to command the weather like that—even within such limited parameters—and the fact that Tarrant couldn't use the currents for power, but must rely upon the limited amount of fae that was stored in his sword, surely wouldn't help. Then he decided not to think about any of it. He closed his eyes for a moment and tried not to reflect upon what they had just done. But he couldn't help it. The blood was still red on his sword, and a gory spattering covered his right leg and boot. The feel of his weapon cutting into human flesh was still hot in his palm, and he rubbed his hand against the thigh of his breeches as if somehow that could cleanse it. In his ears he could hear the sounds of innocent men screaming as the horses bore down on them, unseen but all too keenly felt—

"Well?"

It was Tarrant, calling down to him. He opened the valve on the turbine the way he had seen a captain do it once before and was somewhat surprised to hear the small engine rumble to life. Its owner must have had it Worked for it to start that fast; had Tarrant Seen that when he chose this vessel? "It's on," he called back, and he made one last check of its dials and settings before he climbed back up to the deck.

Tarrant had sheathed his sword, which meant that whatever Working he had crafted to control the wind was over and done with. God willing, it would work. The horses were grazing on imagined grass, and one of them had left its last meal as a gift on the deck. Damien almost stepped in it.

"Do you think they'll try to follow?" he asked Tarrant.

"Unlikely." He turned the wheel slowly as he spoke, forcing the boat to head into the waves. "Hunting down a small craft on the Serpent at night would be a nearly impossible feat, even for one of Calesta's power. However," he added grimly, "we can certainly bet that all the northern ports will be watched, and that we can expect a similar welcome there if we try to land."

"In all the ports?"

"If he anticipated our journey, then he's had a good week to prepare. If not . . . then he still has a whole day left to warp the minds of those who might otherwise assist us." He said nothing further on that point, but no words were necessary. The Hunter couldn't leave the shelter of the boat while the sun was shining. Either they reached the northern shore and found safe harbor within hours—an unlikely task—or they would have to remain on the river until tomorrow's sunfall. "I'll take the wheel until dawn. You go below and see that there's secure shelter for me somewhere, then try to rest. Oh, and see to the horses." He glanced at the animals. "Secure them inside the cabin if you can. They won't like it, but if the sea grows rough, they'll be safer there."

"Gerald—" He hesitated. "I can't handle a boat. You know that, don't you? I don't know the least thing about sailing—"

"Then I suggest you see if there are any books on the art lying about." The pale eyes glittered. "And pray that we make landing before dawn. Weather-Working is a chancy art at best, and to rush it as I did . . . that might well draw a storm."

Damien looked out at the choppy waves—was there more froth riding on them than before, or was that just his imagination?—and he shivered. How large a storm might the adept have conjured, in his need for an obliging wind? It wasn't a welcome thought in any context, but with him and Tarrant alone on this boat and half the northern coast setting traps for them, and then when the sun came up he'd be handling the boat alone—

Hell, he thought. Taking a deep breath, fighting to calm his nerves. *You knew it wasn't going to be easy.*

He went below to search for a manual.

Thirty

Gresham came to Narilka's workbench and sat himself down, straddling a nearby chair. For a moment she just went on buffing as if he weren't there, but the pressure of his gaze slowed her rhythm, and at last forced her to stop. Slowly, reluctantly, she looked up at him.

"You want to talk about it?" he asked.

It took her a minute to find her voice. "I don't know what you mean." The words sounded weak even to her, and Gresham shook his head gently.

"Don't, Nari."

"What?"

"Keep it all pent up inside. It just eats at you worse that way."

She turned back to her work and started buffing again. But his large hand reached out and took hers, and kept her from moving.

"It was polished long ago," he said quietly. "See?" He turned the piece over; its surface was gleaming. Gently he took it from her and set it on the worktable. Then he took up her hand again, folding it carefully in his own. "Talk to me, Nari. Let me help."

With a sound that was half-sigh, half-sob, she turned away from him. "You can't help. Nobody can help."

"Let me try."

She shook her head stiffly. Tears were forming in her eyes.

"You miss him?"

"I'm afraid for him. Oh, Gresham . . ." And then the walls broke down and the tears came, hot tears that had been days in the making. "What they're doing to him . . . nobody understands. They don't even really care, as long as he does what they want. So what if there isn't a whole man left when they're finished? What does it matter to them if he goes crazy?" She lowered her head, and wiped her eyes with the back of her free hand. "I've been having nightmares," she whispered. "I think they're his. Is that possible?"

"If you care that much for him? Yes, of course it is. That's how the fae works."

"He's so afraid, Gresh."

He snorted. "Any sane man would be, going where he's going."

She shook her head. "It isn't that. Nothing that simple. It's because—" She stopped then, because the truth was too private a thing. She couldn't even share it with Gresham.

He fears that this masquerade will really transform him. He's afraid of losing his soul. He had held her all that last night, barricaded in his apartment as if the enemy were at his door, and she had tasted the substance of his fear as if it were her own. She had felt the terror inherent in his masquerade, his gut fear that once the essence of Gerald Tarrant was invoked into his flesh he would never be free of it. To invite the substance of your enemy to take you over, to dim the flame of your own soul so that his might burn even brighter . . . was there any greater terror than that? She had managed not to cry that night, but only because it would have made him more afraid. Now the tears flowed freely.

"He needs me," she whispered.

He squeezed her hand, said nothing.

"I could help him."

"You said they had their reasons for not letting you go with them," he reminded her. "You said you'd try to accept that."

Reasons. She shut her eyes and trembled as anger seeped into her veins, a rage that was days in the making. "Damn his faith!" she whispered fiercely. "They think they'll have more control over the fae if I'm not there. Who's to say if they're right? Or even if they are, if it's worth the price he'll have to pay? What kind of a god is that, who rewards his people for suffering?"

He snorted. "No one I know has ever claimed to understand the One God."

Oh, Andrys. She reached out with all the power of her soul, wanting so badly to feel his presence, to know that he was still safe. But she lacked the kind of power it would take to establish such a link. Was he reaching out for her, too, with the same sense of desperation? Or was he beyond all that by now, subsumed by the essence of his masquerade? Shivering, she opened her eyes, blinking tears away.

"Look," Gresham said gently. "You can't go through all this and pretend it isn't happening. I've seen what it's doing to you these past few days, trying to work as if everything's normal while your soul's all tied up in knots. Why don't you take a few days off? Go somewhere maybe, take a break. Try to relax. You need it, Nari. Trust me."

She turned and looked into his eyes. For a long, long time she was silent, as his words echoed softly in her brain. "Yes," she said at last. Her voice was a mere whisper. "You're right."

"You're not alone, you know. In every war there are women left behind . . . and men, of course, and children, friends and lovers and relatives who care . . . sometimes you can lose yourself in work, and sometimes you can't. It's never easy, honey." He touched the side of her face lightly, lovingly; his finger smeared a tear across her cheek. "I think maybe for you a change would be best. Go somewhere peaceful, cut out the stress. That way you won't have to put on a show all the time, pretend that nothing's wrong."

She stared at him for a long time, then whispered—almost soundlessly—"Yes." She nodded slowly, very slowly. "A change. Somewhere fresh."

She leaned forward and kissed him gently on the cheek, trembling as she did so, loving him as much in that moment as she ever had her father. What would he say if she told him what his few words had inspired? How would he react if she told him right now what she was thinking?

She didn't dare. He'd talk her out of it, surely.

"Thank you," she whispered softly. "I'll do that."

As she gathered up her things, she wondered if she would ever see him or his shop again.

The apartment was just as Andrys had left it, and she stood in the doorway for a minute just drinking it in, remembering their short time together. In his weeks in Jaggonath he had trained housekeeping to come when he called, and at no other time. Now, with the apartment permanently silenced, the scattered glasses and rumpled bedding stood as a monument to the man who had lived here, and the few days she had shared with him.

Her lover.

How strange that word seemed. How odd to apply it in this case, where their time together seemed like a brief bout of passion between one tragedy and the next. They had not even made love in the traditional sense, although he'd known enough close variations to make the time pass pleasurably enough. Now, though, she ached for that shortcoming, and wished she had held him inside her once, just once, in that embrace which was so intimate that echoes of it lasted forever in one's flesh. But he'd been terrified of making her pregnant, and though the intensity of that fear was incomprehensible to her— like so much else about him—she had indulged him, stifling all the arguments that she might otherwise have raised about the efficacy of birth control, the predictability of her fertility cycle, the availability of abortion should all other things fail . . . those were things you said to other men, not him. His soul was too tender, too bruised, too vulnerable. If intercourse would increase his anxiety, then it would have to be avoided. There'd be time enough for it later, when his soul had a chance to heal.

If that time ever came.

She walked to the bed and sat down upon it, breathing in deeply; their scents were mixed together on the sheets, along with the sweat of love and the sharp tang of fear. Here he had trembled as she held him, shaking like a child lost in a storm as bloody memories enveloped him, images so horrible that he couldn't even talk to her about them, could only whimper as they flooded his brain, overwhelming his fledgling defenses. He'd tried to pull away from her when it happened, to run away from her so that she wouldn't see him fall apart; she hadn't let him go. That was a bond even more intimate than their passion, now, that she had seen his fit of weakness and accepted him. She sensed that night, with poignant clarity, that no other woman had done that.

Closing her eyes now, breathing in the scent of his presence, she could almost see him as he rode northward, every beat of his horse's hooves carrying him closer and closer to what he feared the most. How powerfully he must hate the Hunter, to commit himself to such a venture! They had never discussed his ancestor at length, partly because of her own mixed feelings about him. Now he was alone, headed toward a confrontation that only one of them would survive. If even one.

Time to choose, Nari.

The Hunter wouldn't hurt her, she knew that. His Forest was no threat to her. She didn't know enough about Andrys' demonic ally to predict what he would do, but the goddess Saris had promised to protect her in that arena. So she wouldn't need an army to protect her if she went north. Hells, she wouldn't even need weapons—although of course she would bring them, just in case—and she could make better time riding alone than the Church troops would be able to, with their wagons of supplies and their overladen horses slowing them down. If she played it right and made good enough time, she could follow them in secret, to be there when he needed her. . . . Or maybe even enter their camp openly and demand her proper place in it. And if their god didn't like it, to hells with him. Let him protest the move in person if he cared so damned much, and explain to all concerned why the suffering of one man was so important to him that his precious war could not be waged without it.

Oh, Andri. She shut her eyes and trembled, but not from fear this time. It was exhilaration coursing through her veins now, the sure high of certainty. This was *right*. This was what she was meant to do. And soon—within days, if all went well—she would be where she belonged, joining the man she loved in battle. Waging war not only for his Church, but for his very soul.

"Hang in there, my love," she whispered. "I'm on my way."

Thirty-one

They couldn't make it to shore before daybreak. Tarrant said that was just as well. At best they would have been rushed through a dangerous landing, with barely enough time left to find suitable shelter before the sun rendered him helpless. At worst their enemy would find a way to mobilize neighboring towns against them before they had a chance to lose themselves in the lands to the north. No, despite the risk of remaining at sea, this was surely the safest course.

Which was all well and good, Damien thought, but Tarrant wasn't the one who had to sail the vulking boat alone for twelve hours, with enemies to the north and south and a damned ugly weather system taking shape on the horizon. By dawn's cold light, and then by the mixed light of sun and Core, he watched as ominously dark clouds gathered to the west of him, and wrapped his jacket tightly about his chest as winds gusted heavily across the bow. Tarrant had raised a storm, all right; the only question was how long it would take to reach them, and whether Damien could ride out the fringes of the squall long enough to drown them both in the heart of it.

He dared to leave the wheel long enough to feed the horses from their store of special grain, not because he thought they couldn't make it a day without food but because he was afraid that hunger might disrupt the Working that kept them calm. There was water in the galley, too, and he gave them some of that, although the motion of the ship on the waves turned that normally simple exercise into a test of both agility and nerves. He checked their wounds to see that they were clean and that the bleeding had stopped, but he could do no more to help them; the fae he would have used for Healing was hundreds of feet beneath the surface of the water, inaccessible. He stoked up the furnace anew and fed it as much fuel as it would hold,

259

not wanting to think about what would happen if it went out while he was trapped at the helm. By the time he regained his post there was land clearly visible to the north of him, and he steered away from it as best he could. He tried to bear in mind what Tarrant had said about steering into the waves so that they wouldn't capsize the boat, but exactly how that worked when the sea was going one way and you wanted to go the other was something the Hunter had failed to explain. It seemed to take forever to accomplish that minimal maneuver, and when the northern shore finally faded into a curtain of mist in the distance, his every muscle ached from doing battle in a world whose rules he didn't really understand, and whose aspect was growing less friendly by the minute.

By noon a pattering of rain had begun to fall, and the waves that beat against the hull more than once sent a spray of saltwater up over the prow. It occurred to Damien that he probably should have tied down the loose items on deck, or at least brought them down into the cabin for protection, and that there was probably some special way the sails were supposed to be tied up in a storm—but when you were one man alone and the sea had turned against you, such distractions were luxuries you couldn't afford. He did dare to leave the wheel once more, long enough to make sure that there was enough fuel burning to keep him in steam for a while, and by the time he came back, the sheer force of wind and current had brought the boat about into the trough of a wave. It took everything he had to keep it from going over, and when he had at last forced it back into position, his hands were shaking and a cold sweat had broken out across his brow. He felt a sudden sympathy for the captains of legend who tied themselves to their wheels when a storm closed in on them. No doubt (he mused) they had the intelligence to supply themselves with rope before the storm really got going; God knows you couldn't go back for it later.

He tried not to remember that those men had crews, as he struggled to maintain the bearing Tarrant had chosen. He tried not to think about the fact that if those men wound up in the water, all they had to worry about was drowning. If this boat went under with the Hunter inside it, unable to save himself while any hint of daylight remained—

Not much danger in that, he thought grimly, as the sky overhead went from pearl gray to ash gray to a steamy charcoal. A film of rain enveloped the horizon, and Damien could only pray that he was still where he belonged, in the middle of the Serpent, and not north or south where the rocky shores lay hidden in the mist. Soon it would be dark enough that even the Hunter could come out . . . and Damien wouldn't have complained if he did.

"Tell me again how this is less dangerous than being on land," he muttered, as he fought the wheel into a new and hopefully more promising position. Damn the man for going below without doing something to control this storm! It was little consolation that without it their enemies in Seth would surely have overtaken them by now. Damien would trade this cold, rainy Hell for a hand-to-hand conflict any day.

At last, after what seemed like an eternity, the wind began to abate. Numbly, Damien noted that they were still afloat. It seemed nothing short of a miracle, for which he gave thanks as he tried to unclench his hands from the wheel, to force life back into his strained and frozen flesh. There was a pain in his shoulder blades that felt like a spear had gouged into his flesh there, and his feet were soaked and aching from the cold . . . but he was alive. That was worth a few deep breaths, surely. He watched foam-topped waves break against the prow with considerably less fury than before, and muttered a quick prayer under his breath. *Please, God, let that be the worst of it.*

It was.

At sunset Tarrant rose up from his hiding place within the cargo hold, and came to where Damien stood, shivering and exhausted. Without a word he took hold of the wheel and nodded for the ex-priest to withdraw. It took Damien a minute to get his flesh to respond, so frozen was he in that attitude. At last, stiffly, he started back to where the turbine still churned, meaning to feed it more fuel. "I've already taken care of it," Tarrant informed him, as he swung the boat about on a new heading. For a moment Damien could neither move nor respond, then he walked a few steps to where a narrow bench was fixed to the deck and fell down onto it, heavily.

"It would have been nice if you'd done something to calm down that storm," he muttered.

"I did. As much as any man can, who conjures wind in such a hurry."

"I meant during the day." Hell, what was the point of this? But he couldn't stop the words from coming, not after all those hours. "It was dark enough—"

"I *did*," the Hunter snapped. "Forgive me for not coming up on deck to make a show of it. Or did you think that the storm died down just in time out of liking for us?" He glanced toward the shore as if judging their distance from it, then back at the water directly ahead of them. "Weather-Working is a risky art, Vryce, I told you that before. Under the circumstances, I did the best I could." He glanced back at Damien; the look of concern on his face was almost human. "Get some sleep," he urged. And then, dryly: "I'll wake you before the fun starts."

He started to respond, then didn't. His mouth framed a question, then lost it. With a groan he forced himself to his feet—no easy task, that, not once he had allowed himself the luxury of sitting down— and started back toward the cabin. There should be a comfortable place in there somewhere, if the horses didn't trample him while he looked for it. Definitely worth the search.

That decided, he sank down to the deck beside the bench, lowered his head to the rain-washed wood, and drifted off into a sound and untroubled sleep.

Waves against wood. Wind slapping canvas. For a moment he couldn't place where he was, and then it all came back to him. Along with the pain.

"God," he whispered. His neck, the only part of him that hadn't hurt earlier, was cramped from his awkward sleeping posture. He tried to massage out the knot that had formed in it while pushing himself up to a sitting position. "Where are we?"

Tarrant was still at the wheel. "Check the furnace," he said, without turning around. Damien muttered something incoherent and moved to obey.

There was still fuel, but not much. He stayed around for a minute to watch it burn, reveling in the feel of its heat upon his face, and then climbed back up to the captain's perch.

"Everything all right?"

"Yeah," he affirmed. "If you don't count that the horses nearly killed me.

The Hunter glanced at him. "My Working didn't hold?"

"They're scared and they're hungry; you've got a lot to Work against." Heavily he sat down on the bench once more, gazing out at the water ahead. It seemed to him that there was something dark along the horizon, that might or might not be land. "You bringing us in?"

"Unless you'd care to spend another day on the water."

"Please." He shivered melodramatically. "Don't even joke about it."

It seemed to him that Tarrant smiled ever so slightly. Damien studied his slender hands resting on the wheel, so elegant, so confident—so different from his own anxious grip—and asked, "So when the hell did you learn to sail?"

"When I accompanied Gannon and his troops to Westmark." The Hunter shifted the wheel slightly to the right, toward the land ahead. "Unlike you, I take every opportunity to expand my store of knowledge."

"You also had a crew to back you up."

"You did fine, Reverend—" Damien heard his quick intake of breath as he caught himself. "You did fine," he said softly. "We're still afloat, aren't we? That's what matters."

Damien stood again and studied the view; the thing that might be land was growing steadily larger ahead of them. "So where are we?"

"Halfway between Hade and Asmody, if I judge it correctly."

Farther east than they'd planned on. "How can you tell?"

"I have Vision, remember? To my eyes this whole region is alive with power, and the Forest—" he nodded toward the darkness ahead and to the left of them, "—is as bright as a beacon to my eyes."

Something occurred to him then, that never had before. "You're never really in darkness, are you?"

It seemed to him that the Hunter smiled slightly. "Not as you know the word. Although when we were out in the ocean there were nights that came close. And the Unnamed—"

He stopped then, unwilling or unable to say more, but Damien could see the muscles along his face and neck tense as he remembered. What had the Unnamed done to him, there in his custom-designed Hell? Damien didn't want to ask.

"So what now?" he said quietly.

Tarrant exhaled softly, accepting the reprieve. "Calesta will no doubt expect us to put into Hade or Asmody, and continue northward from there."

"Which means he's probably prepared a reception for us in both places."

"Undoubtedly."

"Damn." It was hard enough avoiding pursuit on open land, where you could go in nearly any direction. How did you do it pulling into a harbor, where one man with a farseer could spot you in time to raise a regiment? "Any idea how he's controlling these people?"

The Hunter shrugged stiffly. "Dreams, perhaps. Visions. Or perhaps even direct control, using those few men who have bonded with him. Does it matter? The result is deadly for us, no matter what the technique."

"So what do we do?" he demanded. "Sail east past Hade, and hope we can make the next port by morning? Hope that he hasn't fortified that one as well?"

For a moment Tarrant didn't answer. Then, without a word, he pointed toward the dark mass before them.

Damien drew in a sharp breath. "You're crazy."

"Prima's full overhead, and Domina's half should rise soon. That should give us good enough light."

"For what? To see ourselves get killed?"

"I hope something less dramatic than that." He glanced to the left slightly, as if measuring their direction against the Forest's chill glow. All Damien could see was water. "We can't just sail into port. Surely you realize that. Which leaves only one way to land—"

"They built a port on every hospitable mile of this coast," Damien reminded him. "Which means, by definition, that any place without a port is going to be nasty."

"So it is," he agreed. "How fortunate that we both know how to swim." The pale eyes fixed on Damien. "You do know how to swim, don't you?"

"I can swim," he growled.

"It'll take us about an hour to get into position. The horses should be brought out by then, in case I miscalculate. As for supplies—"

"What chance is there of that?"

"What?"

"That you'll *miscalculate.*"

It seemed to him that a fleeting smile flitted across the man's face. *God damn him if he finds this amusing.* "I can get some sense of the ground beneath us by the light of the earth-fae, but that won't come into clear focus until we're very close. And there is, as you say, no truly hospitable shore. Nevertheless . . ." He adjusted the wheel again, ever so slightly; it seemed to Damien that the shadow ahead was noticeably larger. "Even such risk is preferable to marching right into Calesta's hands, don't you think?"

"Yeah," he growled. "Only . . . oh, hell." He drew in a deep breath and counted to ten. Exhaled it slowly. "It doesn't matter, does it? Just tell me when to jump."

Now the Hunter's amusement was clear. Damn him to hell for it.

"I will," he promised.

Damien had been on a freighter once that had gotten caught up in a tsunami. It had been a simple flood wave that brought them in, not a bore, but that made it no less frightening. The wave had borne them into the harbor amidst a sea of wreckage and then withdrawn beneath them, dashing them down upon the very pier it had deluged mere moments ago. He still remembered the sound of the hull smashing as mooring piles stabbed into it from beneath, the screams of men and women as the deck canted wildly, spilling the less fortunate into the madly churning harbor. It was a scene that still haunted his dreams, that had driven him to choose land over sea whenever possible, that had developed in him an almost pathological hatred of the sea and all its arts.

Compared to such a landing, he had to admit, this one wasn't the worst he had experienced.

But it came damned close.

Tarrant brought them in as close as he dared, then paralleled the coast for some miles searching for a promising site. Lacking his adept's Vision, unable to Work his own equivalent with a fathom of water between him and the earth-fae, Damien could only watch and pray as mile after dark mile passed to the starboard. At last he saw Tarrant begin to bring about the wheel, a look of grim determination on his face. "Good spot?" he dared. "Best we'll get," the Hunter responded.

Great.

They drove the boat aground on a rocky slope, their speed carrying them forward for yards more even as the ground ripped wood from the hull beneath them. The sound awakened memories in Damien that were better off forgotten, and he tried to focus on the mechanisms of immediate survival as a way of escaping them. Get the horses into the water as safely as possible, and see that they were moving toward shore. Clear the boat himself and get far away, lest it slip from its precarious grounding and drag him out into the sea in its wake. Try to keep sight of the shore as the breaking waves frothed over his head, pointedly not reminding himself how much he hated to swim even at a civilized beach. . . .

But Tarrant had done it well, give him credit for that. Not yards beyond the place where they ran aground Damien felt solid earth beneath his feet. Within yards more he was walking, as securely as one could with surf pounding at one's chest, and he saw to his satisfaction—and relief—that the horses had likewise found solid footing. He didn't bother to look for Tarrant—if, God forbid, the current dragged the adept under, he could use the earth-fae beneath the water to save himself—but struggled toward land, sputtering and cursing the fate that seemed determined to drown him.

And then at last he was on shore. A prayer of thankfulness rose to his lips as he struggled along the rocky beach, to a boulder-strewn slope that even the horses didn't seem anxious to climb. There he collapsed, cursed briefly at the impact of sharp rocks against his flesh, and took a few deep breaths to celebrate his safety. From where he sat he could see Tarrant coming up on the beach, and rather than come up directly to where Damien was he loosed the slip knot at his belt and began to pull in the rope that led back to the boat. For a moment Damien held his breath, wondering if their last-minute plan would bear fruit, and then he saw a low shadow coming toward them, riding the waves. He forced himself back up to his feet and down to the water's edge, where he helped the Hunter pull. Their makeshift raft trembled as the waves broke over it, but made it to shore without real incident. Quickly they unloaded the supplies they had lashed upon it, and carried them up to where the horses, milling nervously, waited for them.

"Whoever owns that boat isn't going to be happy about this," Damien noted, as the last of the small ship's stores was brought out of reach of the water.

"Let's hope he has insurance." The Hunter was running his hands over the horses' legs, making sure they had sustained no injury in the landing. "This one's bleeding," he warned Damien, and the priest limped over to Heal the wound. Was there a category of insurance for having your boat stolen by an undead sorcerer while the owner was away attending a demon-inspired posse? If so, the rate schedule must be interesting.

The Hunter walked back to the edge of the water. Damien almost moved to follow him, then decided that if the man wanted help he would have asked for it. He watched while Tarrant fixed his eyes on the wounded boat. Working, no doubt, but toward what end? Then the boat, half-submerged in the water, tore loose from its rocky mooring with a crack of wood and screech of metal so loud that Damien stiffened despite himself. Slowly, inch by inch, it began to back its way out into the Serpent. He could see it shaking as if struggling to rise up, some trapped air pocket not yet willing to acquiesce to the watery embrace, but Tarrant's power and the underwater currents held it fast. The rail slipped beneath the water's surface, then the cabin roof, then the polished wooden wheel, spinning madly as though in protest. Soon only the masts remained, rising up like sea serpents out of the black water. Damien could see Tarrant tense, as an athlete might before lifting a great weight. And then the masts began to bend to one side, and the waves seemed to tremble, and it seemed to him that the earth itself grew warm as the wooden beams finally cracked at their base and plummeted down into the waves. There the power of the Hunter weighted them down, until they sank into a grave that no mere sea might unearth.

"Can't Calesta just create an illusion that it's still there?" he asked as the Hunter came back up the slope.

"We don't yet know the limits of his power." Damien could hear the exhaustion in his voice, from an exercise which, however impressive, shouldn't have drained that much. "Why make it easy on him?" How long had it been since Tarrant had fed properly? Four days at least. He'd planned to find fresh blood in Seth, or across the Serpent if that failed. What would he do now that the cities were off limits?

When the animals were Healed and calmed—the latter by Tarrant's skill, and against considerable resistance—they negotiated the rocky slope at the point where it seemed most navigable. Though their mounts slipped once or twice and Damien had to stop to pry a stone out from between the toes of his, they made it to the top without major mishap, and finally looked out upon the land where fate had deposited them.

It was a bleak and barren landscape, and the cold, lifeless moonlight did little to soften its edge. The rocky ground was softened only by lichens and an occasional island of coarse grass, and jagged black monuments broke upward through its surface like knife blades, eerily aligned all at the same angle. There would be little grazing here, nothing on which to fuel a fire, and no certain cover come daybreak. Thank God they had brought the ship's store of supplies along with them, now strapped to their saddlebags in makeshift oilcloth packs.

"North," the Hunter directed, and they proceeded with all due haste. Once or twice he called for a halt, dismounting momentarily so that he might make direct contact with the earth-currents. Damien saw him Working, and guessed that he was doing something to hide their trail. An Obscuring? No, that would be too easily countered by their enemy. More likely some Working that actually stirred the dirt and stones until their marks were truly invisible, so that it would take more than a mere illusion to uncover them. Nevertheless he could see a hard truth in the Hunter's eyes, backlit by a growing fear: if the demon Calesta knew where they were going, how great an effort would it take for him to lead men to them? "Let him at least work for it," the Hunter muttered as he remounted. And they started off again.

Some two hours north of the shore the land grew marginally gentler, and plants could be seen to sprout where time and wind had broken the stone down to a hospitable soil. Tarrant Knew some five or six species of grass before at last he pulled up where one clustered, announcing, "This will do." As soon as he released the horses from the Working that bound them, they lowered their heads to the fresh plants and began to eat as if there were no tomorrow. Which, Damien mused darkly, there might not be.

"Where now?" he asked, as Tarrant rescued his maps from an oil-cloth bundle. The well-wrapped papers had suffered little from their immersion, thank Tarrant's power for that. The Hunter was nothing if not thorough. As Damien rescued a meal's worth of food from his saddlebag—the horses were so intent on their own meal that they didn't notice him at all—Tarrant studied the currents to all sides of them as a mariner might study the stars. "We're here," he said at last. He spread out the map on a mound of rock and weighted its corners down with stones. Sitting down on the opposite side of it, Damien studied the familiar handwriting with its assortment of notes. They had indeed come to land midway between Hade and Asmody, as Tarrant had guessed; even now the men of those two cities might be searching the rocky shore for traces of their passage. The Hunter's slender finger marked a place some miles north of the water, then moved upward: over the first line of hills, through the Raksha Valley, up to a mountain range labeled *Black Ridge.* "We have to cross this," he told Damien. "And there are only three ways to do that, short of riding up over the top. This pass—" and he moved his finger west, to a place near the Forest's own border, "—is by far the easier crossing, and the one I would have preferred. But there's little doubt in my mind, given our experience in Seth, that Calesta will marshal local forces to make that pass inaccessible."

"No argument there," he muttered, thinking of all the violence that had been taking place at the Forest's edge. The men of Yamas and Sheva would be all too happy to ambush a pair of sorcerers, if they believed that by doing so they might render their families safer.

"So: here." The Hunter moved his finger eastward along the Ridge, until it came to rest at a place labeled *Gastine Pass,* some forty miles north and twenty miles east of them. "It's bound to be safer than the other right now."

"And pretty far out of our way."

"Do you see an alternative?"

"You're the one who cares about time."

Did it seem that the Hunter flinched? Certainly he hesitated before answering, "I would rather lose a day reaching my goal than lose my life getting there."

"You're that sure he'll be waiting for us?"

The silver eyes met his. "Aren't you?"

"Yeah," he muttered. "That's the rotten part about traveling with you, you know? Even your enemies are competent." He took a short swig from his canteen, and watched as Tarrant did the same, trying to assess the weight of the Hunter's canteen by the way he handled it. Half-empty at least, he judged. Did he have others like it, or was he reaching the end of his supply? "What about the Gastine? Won't he try to whip up some kind of ambush there, once he guesses where we're headed?"

"Without doubt. But the towns near there are farther from the Forest, and its people will be less ready to rally to his cause." He paused. "The trick is to beat them there."

He drew in a sharp breath and glanced back at the grazing horses. "Our mounts—"

"Will need attention," he agreed. "And as Healing is your department, not mine, I leave you to it." He rose to his feet in a fluid motion, not unlike a snake uncoiling. "The currents here are strong, but you should be able to Work them. One benefit of having been driven so far from our chosen course," he said dryly. And then he began to walk away from the camp.

"Where do you think you're going?"

"Far enough from the three of you that I can Know what's happening in the Forest. Or, at least, try to."

"I thought it was all but impossible to do that from here."

"Yes. Well." The Hunter's eyes glittered in the moonlight, half-lidded and thoughtful. "Doing the impossible seems to be our order of business, doesn't it?" He gazed out at the endless dark vista to the west of them, and Damien thought he saw him stiffen in anticipation. "You just see to the horses."

See to the horses. Easier said than done, when the problem was not one wound or a simple illness but general systemic exhaustion. The animals needed sound sleep and a few good meals, not another Working. But with fifty or more miles ahead of them before they reached the Ridge, Damien and Tarrant had little choice. Calesta would certainly make sure that no town let them come close enough to purchase—*or steal,* he added grimly—fresher mounts.

"Don't go far," he warned Tarrant. The man was too far away to hear him now, but what the hell. He felt better for saying it.

With a sigh, he braced himself for a Healing.

They pushed hard for the rest of the night, hard enough that Damien wondered if the horses wouldn't collapse before dawn. If so, he didn't know that he could do much to save them. It was one thing to spruce up an animal's biochemistry when it was still relatively healthy, another thing entirely to save it once systemic breakdown had begun. But to his surprise they kept up a hard pace through the remainder of the night, enough to get their riders across the sloping line of hills which bordered the Raksha Valley to the south, and partway across the valley itself.

By morning's light Damien could see their eventual destination, a solid black wall that stretched as far as the eye could see to the east and the west of them, cutting short not only routes of travel but the very winds themselves. Weather systems rarely crossed the Black Ridge, he knew that from Geography 101, and the currents likewise tended to flow around it instead of across it. Which was in the long run what made the valley habitable, since the fae beyond that barrier was hot enough and wild enough that even sorcerers feared it.

And that's where we're headed, he thought, gazing at the snow-clad peaks. Not a happy thought.

From where they made their camp, Damien could see the pass itself, a place where the great ridge had folded in its making, creating a deep cleft through which men might travel without braving its heights. His stomach tightened at the thought of what might be waiting for them there, but he knew in his heart that there was no alternate route. Unlike the varied ranges of the east, the Black Ridge was an all-or-nothing climb for most of its length. And while they could push their horses hard along open ground and hope to make good time, Damien knew that if they tried to ride up there, where heat and oxygen were both in short supply, they would soon find themselves walking.

Nevertheless . . . "No other way?" he asked Tarrant as the man dismounted. Hoping that there was some route he didn't know about, which they could turn to.

"I'm afraid not," the Hunter told him. And that was that. Because if there was any man Damien trusted to know the layout of this land, and to assess its hidden potential, it was the Hunter.

He watched as Tarrant drained the last of his canteen's contents, and waited for him to say something about his need for further nourishment. But the Hunter offered no information, and he didn't want to ask him about it. If he needed something more than he carried with him, surely he would tell Damien. The Hunter had never been shy about his needs.

I'll feed him if I have to, he thought. Wondering even as he did so how he could do battle with Calesta's troops with less blood in his own veins than he needed, or weakened by an endless assault of nightmares. Then he thought about the pass and what would be waiting for them there. *Can you make me more afraid than I already am?*

"Get some sleep," Tarrant urged him. "Tomorrow will be a hard day."

Sleep. Could you sleep in the shadow of such a threat, pretending that it was just another day? When the wind grew quiet, he imagined he could hear men's voices in the distance, as Calesta used the daylight hours to prepare for combat. How many local warriors had he gathered there, how had he prepared them for the battle to come? Did they think they were fighting demons, or some other faeborn threat? What manner of illusion served them in the place of courage, that would keep them fighting long after every human instinct cried, *Enough!*

Shivering, he laid his head down on his pack and tried to sleep. Wondering if somewhere in between the nightmares that awaited him he might not find five or ten minutes of genuine rest, so that he could be fresh and ready at sunset.

Twenty-three days left.

Thirty-two

It took the Church's faithful five days to reach Kale. They followed the path that regional planners had laid out centuries ago,
when they first came to understand that in order to travel freely
across the continent man would need protection from the night and
its demons at regular intervals. The daes—small fortress-inns, solidly
walled and carefully warded—punctuated the road at planned intervals, and their facilities, designed to accommodate massive trade car-
avans when necessary, were not hard pressed to provide room and
board for the small band of warriors and their horses.

Eighty-seven men and women. Not all of those would be going
into the Forest, of course; there were a handful who would be assigned liaison duties in Mordreth, and at least a dozen more who
would man a supporting camp just outside the Forest's borders, to
guarantee their supply line should the conflict become an extended
one. Several hundred more were already in place at the edge of that
damned realm, stripping the land of all that could burn against the
day when the Church's final weapon would be wielded, and the Forbidden Forest would pass into history. It was a small force even in its
total, a deliberate contrast to the vast armies which had assaulted
that realm in ages past. Those armies had failed, the Patriarch was
quick to remind them. Numbers alone could not guarantee safety in
a war where the very battlefield was alive and hostile. So this time
they would field not an army proper, but a finely honed strike force,
who would pierce the Forest quickly, strike its blow, and then—
hopefully—get out.

The Hunter's realm, going up in flames. Andrys dreamed of it
daily, savoring the vision as his mount carried him closer and closer
to its fulfillment. The image sustained him when all else seemed

about to fall apart, when the strength he feigned and the courage he pretended to possess seemed more of a lie than ever. The heat of that fire fed him with life, and with hope, and gave him the strength to go on.

His companions were strangers to him. He walked among them, he ate dinner in their company, but they might have been from another planet for all he understood them. It was the religious thing, of course. Like all the Tarrants, Andrys had been raised to serve the One God, in word and deed if not in spirit, and he had been to services often enough for weddings and the like to be able to mouth the common prayers along with his fellows. But it meant little to him. These people were different. They were marching north to fight, perhaps to die, all in the name of a God so divorced from human affairs that they never even dreamed He would help them. Why? Between their motives and his comprehension was a chasm so vast, so darkly infinite, that all the well-intended prayers in the world could not begin to bridge it.

Faith. It meant nothing to him. Faith was a fantasy, a delusion. Faith was like wine: you poured it inside you and for a brief time it blossomed, it eased the pain of living, it banished the guilt that tended to clog up a man's head. And then it was gone, like wine: digested, expelled, forgotten. What was the point?

Did anyone really believe the One God was out there? Did anyone believe that He cared the least bit whether this venture of theirs succeeded? Did they honestly believe that a caring God would let a creature like the Hunter exist in the first place, much less reward his lifestyle with virtual immortality?

Maybe the pagans have it right, he thought bitterly. Envying his polytheistic brethren for the comforting simplicity of their faith. Do good or evil, and the world responds in kind. Maybe not the way you would have liked, maybe not in a way you even understand, but at least the relationship is there. That, he could relate to. This . . . this was a total mystery to him.

Perhaps if he could just be alone for a short while he could come to terms with it all. But there was little privacy in this new world of his. His days were spent riding with the troops, the Patriarch of the Eastern Autarchy on his right and the Company Commander, a woman named Tabra Zefila, on his left. Sandwiched in by authority like that, he felt self-conscious even sneezing; God alone knew what would happen if a muttered curse should escape his lips when his horse stumbled. At night he ate with the common troops, while the two leaders withdrew to converse in private. An alien in their midst, he rarely joined in their conversation. When it came time to retire, he joined his fellow men in a room prepared for merchant guards, six bunks to a room with a common bath. Never alone. Sometimes he felt so desperate for privacy that he wanted to scream. It wasn't just because he needed a drink so badly, so often; after dinner there was enough ale and enough wine making the rounds that he could sate his thirst without being conspicuous. In the past he'd had to hide his drunkenness in front of Samiel and Betrise so often that the skill was now second nature to him; he could drink himself to the borders of oblivion and still walk steadily to his room, even climb up to his bunk as if nothing were wrong. No, that wasn't the problem. And it had nothing to do with the drugs he had brought with him, a last desperate gambit in case the journey proved too much for him. He hadn't needed them yet, and if he did, he could always swallow a pill quickly in the bathroom and get back to bed before it took effect. No, that wasn't it either.

It was the memories.

Not just memories of the past now, though chilling images of his family's slaughter—and his own cowardly inadequacy—still churned in his brain. Now there were memories of the girl, as well. Sweet memories, warm and seductive . . . and more painful than all the others combined. Because he wasn't going back to her. He knew that. He was going to pit himself against the Forest in the hope of avenging his family, but the odds of his coming back from that quest were minimal. And even if he did, how could he take that gentle girl into his arms again once his flesh had housed the Hunter's spirit? Even if he did survive this, even if he somehow—impossibly—managed to salvage his sanity, how could he pretend to just pick up where he had left off as if nothing had changed? Could a man become the Hunter in spirit and not be poisoned by the experience?

When he could, he lost himself in drink. When he couldn't, he vacillated between fighting the memories—all of them—and giving way to the sweetest ones, a last fleeting indulgence before the darkness of the Hunter's realm swallowed him whole.

They were received warmly in Kale, even passionately, as befit the first visit of this Patriarch to the thriving port city. To Andrys, who had never paid much attention to Church hierarchy—or any other power structure, for that matter—it was an eloquent reminder of the importance of the man who rode by his side, and the significance of his position to the men and women who worshiped the One God.

There were thousands of them lining the south road when they arrived, the faithful and the curious both, come to see this man who embodied God's Will. Many reached out to touch him, and once or twice the Patriarch reined up and indulged them, offering his hand to be shaken or kissed or whatever. Watching him, Andrys was awed by the aura of the righteous authority which he exuded, and by its power over the people here. Some of them even fell to their knees as he approached, a gesture which he accepted as naturally and as regally as he did all the others. It was hard to remember who and what this man was when you saw him only in small rooms and on dusty horseback, running small affairs, dealing with trivial day-to-day matters, surrounded by people who were accustomed to his presence. It was something else again, Andrys thought, to see this. He found that he was trembling despite himself, and when the Patriarch turned once to look back at him he felt genuinely shaken, as if those blue eyes had been a channel to something greater, something any mere human should be frightened of.

The mayor met them at the city gate—an impromptu structure which had been hastily erected in order for there to be somewhere to hold such a ceremony—and showered them with verbal honor. Saviors of the north, he called them. Saints of the One God. But despite his surface enthusiasm, Andrys had the distinct impression that the man kept looking back over his shoulder, as if expecting something to creep up behind him at any moment.

It's the ghost of Mordreth, Zefila whispered to him. It took him a minute to place the name, but when he did so he nodded solemnly that yes, he understood. Mordreth was a town just across the Serpent, on the very border of the Forest, which had once hosted a similarly organized effort to destroy the Hunter's realm. In retribution, the town had been destroyed in a single night: man, woman and child; their pets and their flocks; and even the buildings that housed them, reduced to dead meat and rubble in one night of vengeance. It was little wonder that the mayor seemed so nervous, with such a reminder of the Hunter's power only miles away. Given the circumstances, it was almost surprising that the troops had been welcomed at all.

They were given rooms, and food, and offered supplies; the Patriarch accepted it all. He was pressed into holding an impromptu service in the local church, which had to be moved to the city square to accommodate all the people who came. Andrys knew enough about Church theosophy to recognize that as the man stood there, the center of attention for thousands of worshipers, he was in fact shaping the fae through their faith, weaving additional power for use in this venture. *Why can't they just do it openly?* he wondered. *Call a stone a stone.* But by the end of the service even he could feel the force of what had been conjured, and for once that night he retired without doubt, without fear, drifting softly into a realm where even the nightmares were gentle.

Would that it had lasted!

In the morning they set sail for Mordreth. Across the choppy waters of the Serpent (was the Hunter sending a storm to harass them?), past the dark bulk of Morgot (what enemies might emerge from that secret port?) into the muddy waters of Mordreth's harbor. This time there were no warm welcomes awaiting them, no crowds to shower them with honor, not even a low-level official or two to make sure that they followed local port custom. Their own agent met them at the pier, along with the four Church-folk he had brought with him. Other than that, the harbor was practically deserted.

"They're afraid," he told the Patriarch, and Andrys thought, *Who can blame them?*

Through a nearly deserted town they rode, and the sky added its own silent comment by drizzling rain down on them. Many of Mordreth's inhabitants had left the town in fear for their lives, and those that remained dared not even look upon the passing troops, for fear that the Hunter would read his own meaning into such behavior and exact a terrible vengeance. Nevertheless, there were signs that life—and hope—had not been totally extinguished. A shutter creaking open as they passed, so that frightened eyes might gaze through the opening. A curtain pulled aside to reveal shadowed faces. It seemed to Andrys that once or twice he could hear muttered words— fragments of a prayer, it seemed—but he was at a loss to identify its source, or even explain how the sound had reached him.

"This is the face of our enemy," the Patriarch pronounced, when they had all gathered at the far edge of town to hear his words. His arm swept toward the south, encompassing the town they had just passed through. "This is what we've come to fight. Can any man see what we have seen and doubt the inevitability of such a battle? Can any of you bear to stand back and do nothing and watch this influence spread, household by household, city by city, until the entire eastern realm scurries like frightened animals at the mere mention of the Hunter's name? Until your husbands and your wives and your children cower in shadows at the slightest hint of his presence? We will cleanse this land forever," he pronounced. "Not only to destroy an unclean thing which God Himself abhors, but to restore the spirits of our fellow men. It is the souls of humankind that we do battle for," he told them, and the winds of the fae etched that message into their brains so powerfully that it seemed the fate of the entire world was at issue in this one campaign.

They rode northward for several hours, until at last, atop a low rise, Zefila called a halt. In the distance it was just possible to see the grasslands give way to a tightly wooded expanse, and Andrys felt his soul clench up at the sight of it. For a long time they stood there, gazing down at the enemy's domain, and no one spoke a word. The air seemed to be thicker coming from that direction, and colder, and it carried a scent that was markedly unpleasant, of blood and illness and flesh gone to rot. One man was sickened enough by it that he went off to the rear of the company to vomit; Andrys could hear his heaving off to the left somewhere as he struggled to gather his own courage, and he wished desperately that he could sneak away and steal a drink. But there'd be no more ale now and no more wine until this matter was finished, he knew that. In a realm where one's every fear would be given wings and teeth and the hunger to kill, drunkenness was too volatile a weakness.

They made camp there, within sight of their enemy's domain. Amidst the wreckage of former encampments, now abandoned by the hunters and foragers who had erected them, they unpacked tents and bedrolls so new that price tags still dangled from the ends of many, and advertising leaflets fluttered to the grass as packs of foodstuffs were wrenched open. They would spend the night here and then move with the sun, letting that ultimate enemy of night light their way into Hell's domain. Not that the light would actually help them much beneath that canopy, Zefila observed, studying it with a farseer, but the symbolism was important.

Symbolism.

It was in the name of symbolism that he unpacked his armor late that day. It was in the name of symbolism that he would be expected to wear it now, so that the troops might become accustomed to him in his new role. It was in the name of symbolism that he would be introduced to them anew, not as a visitor from a foreign realm, but as one who held the key to the Hunter's domain: flesh of the Hunter's flesh, blood of his blood.

One of the men had been sent in to help him, and at last it was he who took up the heavy breastplate and fitted it around Andrys' torso, over his shirt. The youngest Tarrant shut his eyes and trembled, not only for what the moment represented in a military sense, but for the memories that were suddenly awakened. Her hands, soft upon the steel, gentle against his flesh. Her eyes, so deep and dark that a man could drown in them. Lost forever now. He felt a wetness come to one eye and wiped it away quickly, hoping that the man who was adorning him didn't see it. He had to be strong now, that was part of his new image. Part of his new *persona*. Andrys Tarrant, a leader of men . . . he almost laughed aloud. Was there ever a greater contradiction than that one? How Samiel would have roared with outraged laughter to hear it!

And then hands were guiding him and the man was telling him that all was finished, and he found himself stepping out of the tent, being led by a stranger's touch toward the place where his fellow warriors awaited, where the Patriarch awaited. . . .

Where his fate awaited.

The Patriarch stood at the crown of the mount, with the men and women who served him ranged in a half-circle beneath. Andrys came to the Patriarch's side and bowed formally, acutely aware of how much each gesture mattered now. They had schooled him well on the journey here, and he went through each move like a seasoned dancer, sensing the power of his performance. Eighty-seven men and women—for they had left none in Mordreth—gazed upon the image that he projected, and their response shimmered in the unseen currents, creating a reality more powerful than any one man could manifest on his own. The fae here was so volatile, it was said, that a man's dreams took on reality before they were even completed; what power did that give to the joint dreams of a hundred, when their minds were all fixed on a single focus?

Him.

He looked like the Prophet now, as much as any living man could. His hair had been cut straight across the bottom, in the Prophet's chosen style, and though it wasn't quite long enough for the illusion to be perfect, it was damned close. His armor was the same as that in the mural which overhung the sanctuary in Jaggonath, down to the finest detail, and the clothing he wore beneath it was likewise identical. He was an image out of history, a creature of living legend, and as the waves of reaction rose up from the small crowd, he could feel it like a dull heat on his face. God, it was hard to breathe. He pulled at his collar to loosen it, but that didn't help much. The constriction was internal.

He stood there as the Patriarch explained to them all just what the link was between Andrys Tarrant and the Hunter. He tried not to flush with shame as several of his companion warriors nodded knowingly, as if to say *yes, we knew he wasn't one of us, this at least explains why he's here.* Had he proven himself so unworthy in the past few days that such an explanation was required? As the Patriarch detailed the role that he would play, as the sun set in golden splendor behind him, Andrys heard few of the words. He was alone again, alone among aliens, and the one person who might have brought him comfort was a hundred miles behind him now, in another world.

The Forest will recognize this man as its own, the Holy Father explained. *It will let him pass through unhindered, and every man that belongs to him will likewise be protected. Therefore every one of you must swear fealty to him, here and now, so that the relationship is clearly established.*

They came to him one by one, then, to kneel before him and clasp their hands between his own. The words of oathtaking left his lips automatically, and he hardly heard them. Because as each man and woman knelt before him, as they repeated the ritual oath that the Patriarch had designed, the fae that coursed about them began to take on a new texture. He could feel it as he spoke, and the hair along the nape of his neck began to rise as if something loathsome were stroking him. It took everything he had not to draw back from them, to stand his ground and force the ritual words to his lips as if nothing whatsoever were wrong. After five of the oaths had been taken, it seemed to him that the loathsome *something* had somehow gained entrance to his brain, so that its presence seemed more intense when he struggled to think clearly. Panic welled up inside him, all the more intense because no one surrounding him seemed to be aware that anything was wrong.

Then, as the tenth oath was completed, it suddenly became clear to him what was happening.

The vows which these people were reciting had been carefully crafted for the occasion in much the same way that other prayers—and the Law of the Church itself—had been crafted in the past. Emotive phrases had been designed to evoke specific images, so that the fae might be imprinted with the Church's will. And it was working, all too well. The volatile fae at the edge of the Forest was quick to acknowledge the Church's chosen imagery, and to set it upon the flesh which served as its focus. As soldier after soldier knelt before Andrys, acknowledging him as the Hunter's kin, he could feel that fae pounding at him, driving the image home. He could feel bits of his identity tearing loose, and like a drowning man whose strength is failing him, he sensed the vast emptiness beneath him, which wanted only a moment's acquiescence to swallow him whole.

He panicked then, and if the Patriarch hadn't been by his side, he might have turned and run. But either the Holy Father sensed the turmoil in him, or his visions had given him warning; he came up behind Andrys and put a hand firmly upon his shoulder. Just that. The simple touch reminded him of everything that had driven him here, of the horror that his life had become, of his commitment to the Church and to these people who served it. Trembling, he stood his ground. Another man knelt before him, and then a woman, and then two men. Each oath spawned a new tidal wave of power that slammed into him, leaving him so breathless it was all he could do to mouth the words of acceptance which had been assigned to him, not hearing them, just struggling to survive. He was seeing visions now, vile hallucinations that would no doubt have pleased the Hunter, images of blood and death and violence so extreme that it seemed impossible anyone could have witnessed them. Were these Gerald Tarrant's memories, or some nameless, less precise horror? He shivered as they poured into him, struggling to hold onto his sanity. Twenty oaths. Thirty. The line seemed endless, and as each new soldier knelt before him, he wanted to scream at them, he wanted to turn and run, he wanted to be anywhere but here, doing anything but this. . . .

And then there was a familiar touch in his mind, and the visions shifted. Only for a moment, but the moment was enough. Calesta's touch, sure and effective, rekindled the hatred that was his only remaining strength. Visions of blood gave way to visions of his family's slaughter; dreams of violence gave way to the hunger for vengeance. He clung to the moment's offering as a lifeline, and somehow forced the required words past his lips time and time again: *I accept the dedication of your life to mine, I acknowledge you as an extension of my will, I swear unto you protection against all harm. . . .* He gasped as the cold malignance of the Hunter's presence surged through his flesh, and felt the Patriarch's grip tighten on his shoulder. *Oh, God,* he prayed, *if you're really out there, if you give a damn, help me!* But the God of Earth wasn't known for interference in such affairs, and His holy representative, for all his good intentions, had no idea what manner of power he had conjured with this ritual.

And then it was over. The last man retreated a respectful distance from the mound, giving Andrys room to breathe at last. Shivering violently, the young man prayed that he would be allowed to withdraw soon. Surely it was in all their best interests that his terror not be made manifest before the troops! But then there was a stirring by his side, and the Patriarch himself stood before him. The clear blue eyes met his for a minute and he felt himself pierced through by their intensity. Then, with a nod, the Holy Father slowly lowered himself to one knee and offered up his own hands for oathtaking.

No! Andrys wanted to scream. *I'm unclean now! Can't you see that?* But the Patriarch's gaze was steady, and his hands didn't waver from their position. At last, trembling, Andrys took up the required pose. "For this one occasion," the Patriarch's oath began. "In this single set of circumstances." He had chosen his words carefully, but Andrys could barely hear them. The cold grip of the Forest was squeezing his heart, and terror surged within his veins. What if the creature who received this oath was no longer entirely Andrys Tarrant, but some half-made being that was even now being re-Worked by the Forest's currents? He understood why the Patriarch felt that even he must be fully a part of their deceit, but wasn't the risk just too high?

Don't do it! he wanted to yell. *Save yourself, your people need you!*

And then it was truly over, all of it. Finally. Dazed, he listened to the closing rites, watching as the golden Corelight took precedence over the clean white light of the sun. The latter was wholly gone now, and the first stage of night was descending. Soon the demons of the night would come out in force, and if they didn't acknowledge Andrys in his chosen role—

Don't think about that, he thought desperately. Knowing, in the core of his soul, that the unclean essence of the Hunter was inside him now, and that any hungry demonling with eyes could see it. *Oh, God.* He had thought that it might drive him mad to pretend to be the Hunter; what would it do to him if the Forest's fae transformed him utterly, making him into a copy of that damned soul in truth? What would his Church allies do then—struggle to save him, to salvage his soul, or condemn him to the same fate as his forebear?

He suddenly felt trapped, and was desperately glad that the tents had already been erected; as soon as this nightmare scene was over, he could take refuge in the limited privacy of his assigned canvas quarters. The thought of that privacy was all that sustained him as the last prayers were said, the last evocations recited. . . .

He walked. He wanted to run, but that would only alert the others, and then they would follow him. He walked to the tent that had been assigned to him—a private tent, in deference to his new position of authority—and carefully ducked in beneath the flap. His heart was pounding so loudly he was amazed they couldn't hear it, but maybe their minds were on other things. Maybe in the face of what was coming tomorrow they had little time to spare for worrying about the mental health of their chosen figurehead.

His pack was lying beside his bedroll; he dropped to his knees beside it and struggled to open it, his hands shaking as he attacked its ties and clasps. *Soon,* he promised himself. *Soon.* Thinking of what was inside and the peace that it would bring, he could barely manage the patience required to get the damn thing opened. Then the top flap was open at last and he spilled his possessions out onto the ground, all of them in a pile. With feverish hands he sorted through the pile, having no concern for any item other than the one he sought. Buried, it eluded his searching fingers for long, painful minutes. He drew in a deep breath and started again, this time moving each item to a new pile as he searched beneath it. Clothing, first aid, toiletries . . . It wasn't there. *No,* he thought. Not daring to believe it. He searched through the pile again, this time less neatly, and when he was done the interior of the tent was littered with his possessions. Still the small bottle eluded him. He began a desperate search through the pack itself, forcing shaking fingers down into its deepest pockets, squeezing the lining to see if anything had fallen down into it, madly searching even the straps—

"Looking for something?"

The voice stopped him cold. The straps of the pack fell from his numbed fingers as he looked up from the ground to his visitor's face, scanning robes that were all too familiar. *God, please,* he prayed, *spare me this humiliation.* But no simple prayer was going to make the Patriarch go away, no matter how heartfelt it was.

"I removed the drugs from your pack en route to Mordreth," the Holy Father said quietly, "and I gave them to the Serpent. I assume that's what you're looking for?" When Andrys didn't answer, he nodded slightly as if reading confirmation into his pained expression. "What you did with your life before this point is your own business, Mer Tarrant, but now you no longer live for yourself. You live for all of us. And I will not have my Church's dreams compromised by a handful of pills, or by your willingness to parade your addictions in front of my people."

Shame rose to his face in a hot flush; he tried to stammer some kind of protest, but couldn't get the words out. Had the Patriarch known all along what Andrys carried with him? Was it a vision that had betrayed him, or some more human source? "I wouldn't—" he began. Then shame caught in his throat, and even those words failed him. "You don't understand," he whispered.

"I understand enough to see what would happen to my people if they perceived such weakness in you. Before tonight it might have meant little, but now, after all their vows . . . you have a responsibility, Mer Tarrant, and it's my job to see that you live up to it. Painful though that might be."

He hung his head, and thus didn't see what the Patriarch was doing as the wool robes shifted. He didn't see what the Patriarch removed from his pocket, not until the man cast it down in front of him.

A bottle.

"It's from Jaggonath," With numb fingers Andrys picked it up; the velvet black pills of a blackout fix tumbled one over another as he turned it in his hand, incredulous. "The founding fathers of that city, in their wisdom, declared that no man should ever have the right to burden others with his intoxication. They ordered that all mind-altering drugs be combined with a paralytic, so that the user must suffer its effects in the privacy of his own soul." He gestured down toward the bottle. "If you perceive such a desperate need for comfort that you would be willing to risk a period of paralysis, then here it is. You may do whatever you like in private, so long as you remember that your public life is no longer your own."

Lowering his head in shame, he whispered, "You don't understand."

"As one who has lived in the public eye for almost fifty years, I *do* understand," His tone was bitter, unforgiving. "I understand more than you know." He paused for a moment; his condemnation was like a gust of hot wind, that made Andrys' face flush even redder. "I won't have this mission compromised by a moment of weakness, Mer Tarrant—not yours, not mine. Remember that."

He left the tent as silently as he had come, but something of his condemnation seemed to remain behind him: Andrys could feel it as he turned the bottle over and over in his hand, hungering desperately to open it and swallow its precious contents, but knowing in the tortured depths of his heart that there would be no place and no time safe enough to do so until this campaign was over. Then even that vestige of the Holy Father's presence faded, and he was alone at last. Just him and the bottle. Just him and the night.

Just him, and the Hunter in his soul.

Thirty-three

"We're WHAT?"

"Going west," the Hunter repeated, in a voice that was so maddeningly calm Damien wanted to choke the life out of him. "Toward the pass that lies near the Forest. You remember, we discussed it last night."

"I know, I just . . ." He shook his head, torn between anger and amazement. "Just like that? You woke up and decided that we'd wasted the last ten hours, time to pick a new direction?"

"Not at all," Tarrant said coolly. "The decision was made long before that."

"You mean you lied to me."

"I regret that it was necessary."

He almost hit him. Really. Even though it wouldn't do any good. Even though the Hunter could Work the earth-fae and stop him faster than he could carry through the blow. It would feel that good just to try it. Only the look in those pale, cold eyes kept him from moving. The utter calm in them, and the unshakable certainty. Before those things he quailed.

"Think about it," Tarrant urged. "Our enemy has the power to read what's in our hearts. Which means that we can have no secrets from him. Unless he doesn't bother to look for secrets. Unless he thinks he knows all there is to know."

"So, in other words, you set me up. You told me we were going east when you never intended to, so that Calesta would believe it." His hands had curled into fists of their own accord; he forced himself to open them. "And what made you so sure he would look into my heart, and not yours? Wasn't that a hell of a risk to take?"

The pale eyes, golden in the Corelight, glittered with disarming intensity. "We already know he's not watching us every minute. What else explains the Locatings I worked in Seth? The one I conjured while we were in flight was masked by an illusion meant to mislead us, but the one before that wasn't. Such trivial games were of no concern to him when he thought he had us cornered. He has a war to fight, remember." He nodded west, toward the distant Forest. "No doubt he's anxious to focus on it."

With a hot flush Damien remembered their flight through Seth, and his own angry cries. *Dammit, man, you're going the wrong way! Remember the map!* He hadn't noticed that the two images Tarrant had conjured didn't match up. He had trusted in the Hunter's power. . . .

"In the face of Iezu illusion," Tarrant said, answering his thoughts, "even my own Workings must be suspect."

"How do you know he's reading *my* mind?" he demanded. "What if you're his source?"

"Unlikely. Of the two of us, I would be more likely to recognize signs of his interference. With you . . ." He hesitated. "No offense, Vryce, but you're hardly well versed in demon recognition."

"He could fool you if he tried."

"But he'd have to work much harder at it. And I'm willing to bet that the Iezu, like men, prefer the path of least resistance."

"Yeah, but can we be sure of that?"

"No," he admitted. "It's a gamble. A last-ditch effort in a game where Calesta controls most of the pieces. I'm sorry I had to plan it alone, but sharing my fears with you would have meant sacrificing the effectiveness of the feint. And seeing how little we have going for us without it . . ." He shrugged. "I apologize, Vryce. You deserved better."

"No." He sighed heavily and raised up a hand to rub his temples. "Don't. You were right, as usual. Let's just hope it worked." He glanced toward the east, where the mountain cleft beckoned. "So what happens now?"

"If Calesta's paying attention to us right now, then he'll assign his local pawns to direct pursuit. But I don't think he is. I think that he's arrogant enough—and distracted enough—to believe that his current arrangements are sufficient."

"But we can't really know that, any more than we can know what his next move will be."

"There are four dozen men waiting for us right now at Gastine Pass," he said calmly. "That much is without question. Assuming my understanding of the situation is correct, I estimate two hours before Calesta realizes something is wrong, as that's how long it would have taken us to reach his little trap. At that point it will be too late for anyone from there to catch up with us. He'll have to make new plans, focusing on the western route."

"And then what? If he can motivate that many to come after us . . ." *Four dozen! God in Heaven!* "You said yourself that the towns bordering on the Forest would be ready and willing to protect their turf. What makes that region any safer for us?"

"Time, Vryce. Time." With a jerk he tightened the strap securing his horse's saddle. "He can give them all the dreams he wants, but few men will rise up out of bed at that instant to fight his battles. I'm willing to bet he can't muster a lynch mob until morning, and by then we should be far beyond their reach."

"Gerald." He put a hand to the saddle of his own horse. "It's more than a hundred miles to the pass from here. That's a hell of a ride in one night, even for horses that are endurance trained. Do you really think these two are going to make it?"

"All they have to do is get us there." His black cloak fluttered in the evening breeze as he mounted, like a vast pair of wings. "As for their endurance . . . I did what had to be done to assure that." He brought his animal about so that it faced their distant goal. "And no complaints from you this time. Two horses are a small enough sacrifice, if their expiration puts us ahead of their enemy."

Hand trembling slightly, Damien touched his horse's flank. He could feel no change in the animal's substance, but that didn't mean that nothing had been altered. How little effort would it take to refigure its equine biochemistry so that the beast devoured itself for energy, ignoring all signs of exhaustion? How many vital systems had the Hunter reWorked, so that the processes which would normally kill the beast were circumvented, redirected, thwarted? He felt sick as he swung himself up to his accustomed seat. He felt as if death itself were poised there between his legs, wanting only the proper hour to make its true aspect known. But what other option was there?

"No complaints," he muttered. Swinging his own horse around, so that they faced the looming Ridge. "I promise."

Full-out gallop: the rhythm of death.

He wondered if Calesta could hear it.

Hour melding into hour, knees aching as he gripped the animal beneath him. A short stop to dig food out of his pack, then hurried mouthfuls swallowed while riding. Trying not to feel sick over the decay that was taking place beneath him, only telling himself over and over that there was no choice. If they didn't make the western pass by morning, then Calesta would have the whole day to mobilize the valley folk against them.

Innocent blood on his sword, now wiped clean from all but his soul. . . .

Two horses are a small enough sacrifice. . . .

God help him, what had he become?

Closer and closer to the great ridge they rode, until its shadow blocked out the moon setting behind them, leaving only Casca's crescent to light their way. It was a vast mountain range, barren and forbidding, and its stark silhouette was as unlike the gentle rolling hills of the south as the cracked frozen surface of a glacier was unlike a cool mountain stream. A steep oceanic ridge birthed when this continent was at the floor of the ocean, it cut across the land like an immense wall, protecting the fertile human settlements from the winds and the poisons of the regions beyond. It was said there were similar mountains to the north, scoring the land in parallel welts like claw marks, but most were submerged in a frozen sea, and none but the Earth-ship had ever seen them. One was enough, as far as Damien was concerned.

They rode through its foothills—if that word could be applied to such a place—where the earth began its steep slope upward. The towns which had been built in this region were far to the south of them, clustered along the river that coursed down the valley's center. And for good reason, Damien noted. There was a temblor as they approached the ridge, and the cascade of sharp-edged rocks that came plummeting down the steep slope were an eloquent warning to any would-be traveler. Yet it was worth the risk for them, he thought, if it kept other people away. In this land where any human soul might be controlled by their enemy, isolation was a prerequisite for survival.

Mile after mile beat numbly into Damien's flesh, his horse's skin like fire between his legs, beneath his hands. God alone knew what was happening inside it, as the miles pounded underfoot one by one. Once he started to rein up to feed them, but Tarrant waved angrily for him to continue. *Not necessary,* his expression seemed to say. Or perhaps instead, *No point.* His heart cold, Damien obeyed. This ride would echo in his dreams for years to come, he knew, but not half so loudly as the ones he would have if they failed to get through the western pass before dawn.

Two horses is a small price. . . .

What's the third route to Shaitan's valley? he had asked Tarrant, when the two pulled up briefly so that Damien might relieve himself.

A tunnel from beneath my keep, that exits there.

From the Forest? Damien had asked, surprised.

The Hunter nodded. *I built it years ago, against the possibility that someday a human army might attack the keep itself. If I were to need an escape route, it stood to reason that it should be to a place where men would fear to follow. An unlikely event at best, but I pride myself on being prepared.*

There was an army in the Forest now. What would happen if Jahanna fell? Would it affect Tarrant's power, or only his mood?

None of that matters now, Damien told himself. *Nothing matters but Calesta's death.*

He hoped, as they rode, that the Hunter shared his sentiment.

"There it is."

They pulled up beside one another on a flat stretch of ground. Beneath them the horses had gone past sweat, past blood-flecked foam, to a state so painful and degraded that Damien flinched to note its symptoms. They were truly members of the living dead now, who wanted only Tarrant's approval to fall to the ground and expire. Damien hoped for their sake that the moment came soon.

Black Ridge Pass wasn't like its eastern sister in scope or configuration, but it promised a tolerable climb. A past earthquake had rent the ridge almost to its base, and time and weather had worked at the flaw, carving a u-shaped saddle into its slope. The approach was a steep climb, but not so impossible that horses couldn't manage it. He glanced down at his mount and shuddered. *Or whatever horses have become.*

Then Tarrant kicked his own mount into motion, and Damien had no choice but to follow. The fact that the Hunter made no attempt to Divine their odds of success, or to otherwise See what lay ahead, was a chilling reminder of their enemy's Iezu capacity. If there were some kind of ambush here, Tarrant knew they would never see it; no Working of his, no matter how well refined, could change that fact.

Trust to his planning, Damien told himself. *Trust to his under-*

standing of the enemy. But even as his mount's trembling feet bit into the harsh mountain slope, he couldn't help but remember what Tarrant had said before. It was a gamble. No more than that. And if Calesta had foreseen their latest move . . . Damien flinched as they climbed, half-expecting an arrow in the back at any moment. But none came. They were up a hundred feet above the valley floor, then two hundred, and still no one and nothing came at them. Four hundred. Eight. Still they climbed in safety, so far that Damien finally loosened his death grip on his weapon long enough to button the collar of his jacket closed. The wind this high up was fierce, sweeping as it did across the face of the ridge for hundreds of miles without obstacle, and every hundred feet the travelers gained in altitude cost them a few degrees of subjective heat. By the time they were high enough to see the whole valley spread out beneath them, Damien's teeth were chattering, and not wholly from fear. The sky above glittered with starlight, but despite that warning the horizon was still dark. They had some time left, then . . . but not much.

And then, with a lurch, Damien's dying steed managed to gain the coveted ground at the end of the climb. The pass itself was a narrow passage that cut through the ridge at an angle, with crumbled rock and a thin film of ice underfoot; the horses stumbled as they negotiated it, while Damien fought not to look up at the two peaks that flanked them, snow-clad sentinels that reared up ghost-pale in the moonlight at either side.

Suddenly, without warning, Tarrant's horse went down. The Hunter barely got clear of it before it began to convulse, horrific spasms coursing through its body in waves. Damien froze for a moment, horrified by the sight, and then quickly dismounted. It was not a moment too soon. Blood streaming from its nose and mouth, the animal that had faced death to bring him here went down on its knees, then screamed in terror and joined its fellow in dying. The sight of its suffering was too much for Damien. "Kill them!" he yelled at Tarrant. "You started this, damn you, you finish it!"

For once the Hunter didn't argue. Damien saw the unearthly chill of the coldfire blade blaze to life, and the ice on the mountains to both sides flickered with eerie silver-blue light as its work was done. Not until Tarrant was finished did he look at the horses again, and even in death their suffering was so apparent that it made him sick to his gut to see it.

There was a time when even that small act of mercy would have put Tarrant's soul in jeopardy, he realized. *Have we come so far beyond that, that such fine distinctions no longer disturb his unholy patron?* He watched for a moment as the Hunter worked at getting his saddlebags loose from his horse's body, then stooped beside his own mount's corpse to follow suit. *The Unnamed expects him to die,* he thought grimly. *In the face of that, what transgression has any meaning?*

The stars were bright overhead by the time they had their supplies freed, sorted, and repacked, but the horizon was still comfortably dark. That gave them at least an hour, Damien estimated, maybe more. Enough time get through the pass and find shelter, God willing. For the first time in days, he felt almost optimistic.

"Let's go," Tarrant urged, and he led the way north.

It was no easy path, that narrow divide. Mountain waters had dripped down the flanking slopes and frozen, making flat sections treacherous. Rockfalls had strewn the ground with thousands of knife-edged obstacles, some large enough to require climbing over, some small enough to lodge in the leather of a boot sole. It was a hard transition from twelve hours of hard riding to such a strenuous hike, and more than once Damien stumbled. But they had cheated time and Calesta both, and that knowledge gave him new strength with every step he took. The inhabitants of the valley would be less than happy about following them here, where the spirits of the dead were said to rule. Once they made it to the far side of the pass, Tarrant said, they would surely be safe.

And then they came around a turn and Shaitan's valley spread out before them, as suddenly as if they had lifted a veil to reveal it. Below them the earth swirled with a gray mist that seemed almost alive. No, not gray: thin streamers of silver, that glowed with an eerie phosphorescence. He could see figures within it that appeared almost human, but they were too far away for him to make out any details. "Shadows of the dead," Tarrant said quietly, following his gaze. Clouds hung low about the valley floor, their surfaces reflecting the stars as no real clouds should. And in the center of it all, rising up from the clouds and the mist like a mountain from the sea—

Shaitan. Its summit glowed with hot orange fire, and streams of that color cascaded down its flank, into the unnatural mist that obscured its base. Its steep cone reared up high into the sky, and the clouds of ash that surrounded seemed to glow with their own inner fire, so fiercely did they reflect its light. Above it the sky had been blanketed with ash, whose undersurface rippled with orange and red highlights as a sea might ripple with froth. It made Damien feel strangely light-headed to stare up at it, and he forced his eyes downward again, to a more comfortable terrain.

"Do the dead really live down there?" he asked Tarrant.

"Shadows of the dead," he confirmed, "which are not quite the same thing."

"What's the difference?"

"The real dead, if they survived separation from their flesh, would feed as other faeborn creatures do: upon the species that gave birth to them. While the shadows of the dead . . . do not feed. Do not hunger. Do not expire. They're like reflections in a mirror: perfect, but without real consciousness. The only world they know is the moment in which they died, and they only exist here, where the currents are so powerful that *thought* is practically the same as *being.*"

"They don't sound very dangerous."

Tarrant looked at him sharply. "Don't kid yourself."

"But if they don't need to feed—"

"They're perfect reflections, formed at the instant of death. Violent deaths mostly; those are the kind with the greatest power." He gazed out at the vista before him. "You think of what that would mean, to have a creature whose only memory of life is the one moment when it betrayed him . . . and then ally that image to *that* power, down there." A sweeping gesture encompassed it all: the mists, the volcano, the unseen currents that swept like tsunami across the earth. "I'd call that very dangerous indeed."

He glanced at the sky again, toward a place where it was clear, and saw the constellation of Arago rising over the top of the ridge. Why did that seem wrong to him? He shook his head as if to clear it, but the thought wouldn't come to him. It was still dark, at least. Starlight might serve as a warning of the coming dawn, but in and of itself it wouldn't hurt Tarrant—

And then there was someone else there beside them, someone who gestured sharply down the slope and bade them, "Come quickly!"

He half drew his sword, then sheathed it again when he saw who it was. "Karril?" he asked. Not quite believing.

"Come," the demon urged. Waving toward the slope behind him, taking a step in that direction as if to inspire them to follow. "There's not much time."

Damien looked back at Tarrant; the Hunter's expression mirrored his own hesitation. "The Iezu can't imitate one another," he said at last.

"And they can't kill humans either," the demon reminded him, "But don't bet your life on that." Again he gestured down the hillside, and whispered fiercely, "Trust me, old friend! If nothing else, you know I respect Iezu law. Come with me!"

Something in his words or his manner must have decided Tarrant, for the Hunter nodded and began to follow him. Damien trotted alongside, praying that neither would lose his footing on the treacherous ground.

—And then they were sliding down the vast slope, so quickly and so recklessly that Damien couldn't even pretend to control his descent. In what must have been no more than a handful of seconds, they dropped so far that Damien could no longer make out the pass above them, yet Tarrant continued to follow. Even when that meant descent through a grove of thorned brambles that tore at their clothing and skin as they forced their way through. Even when that meant dropping down from a ledge into utter darkness, trusting to the demon's judgment. A demon which could be no more than Calesta's newest illusion, and never mind that Iezu law forbade it ...

It was a ten-foot drop into darkness, and then there was earth to support their feet again. "This way," the demon urged. He showed them a dark space that led into the mountainside. "Quickly!" With only a second's pause to study his face—for motive, perhaps?—Tarrant passed within the cavern's mouth and was gone. Damien hesitated, then moved to follow. But Karril's hand fell on his arm, stopping him.

"It's over," the demon announced. Not to Damien. To the air above him ... or something in it. "You failed, brother! Give it up!"

—And the illusion was suddenly gone from Damien's eyes, the false backdrop of night that had blinded him to a deadly truth. To the east of him dawn blazed brightly—dawn!—and even as he watched the white sun breached the horizon, filling the valley beneath it with fatal, unforgiving light. Had Tarrant been shelterless right now ... He felt sick just thinking about it.

"This way," Karril said gently, and he led Damien into the cavern's darkness.

Immersion in the blackness of the underearth was blinding after such a vision; he fumbled for his lantern and lit it with trembling hands, praying that Karril wouldn't leave him behind while he did so. But the demon waited patiently, and not until he had the wick adjusted and the perforated door latched shut did he urge him onward, into the mountain's heart.

Two chambers later, safely beyond the reach of the sun's killing light, they found Tarrant. The adept was sitting with his back to stone, his eyes shut as if in pain.

"It's dawn," Damien said quietly.

"So I gather." The pale eyes slid slowly open, fixing first on Damien and then, at last, on Karril. "You saved my life," he whispered. "In defiance of Iezu law."

"He broke our law." The demon's tone was defiant. "Should I sit back and let him be rewarded for that?"

The Hunter shut his eyes again. Now that the illusion had been lifted, Damien could see that his face was reddened where dawn's light had fallen upon it. What kind of power did these Iezu wield, that could blind a man to his own pain?

Perceptual distortion, he mused. *That's all it is. A power more deadly than any other, if used without reservation.*

"Thank you," Tarrant whispered. Not to Karril alone, it seemed, but to both of them.

The demon hesitated. "I can give you dreams—"

"No. Leave me the pain." He lifted a hand to his face, wincing as the fingers made contact. "Let it be a reminder to me of what we're fighting."

The stars, Damien thought suddenly. The stars had been wrong. Arago shouldn't have risen that high until the sun was nearly up. He should have known the truth from that. He should have guessed.

"Don't," the demon said gently. *They can read what's in your heart.* "You couldn't have known. Not even we knew, until the dawn was well underway."

He looked sharply at the demon. "We?"

Karril nodded. "There are others here. Some as human as I am, others so alien in form even I can't speak to them. And the mother of us all is stirring, after so many centuries of inactivity that some of us thought she might be dead."

"Toward what end?" Damien asked sharply. "Will she get involved in this?"

The demon shrugged wearily. "Who knows? Those few of us who can speak to her use a language I don't understand. Most think that she'll respect her own law and stay out of it. But then, we also thought that Calesta would be punished long before this." He looked at Tarrant; his expression was grim. "I can't keep my brother from using his power to stop you, but I won't allow him to kill you directly. That much I can promise."

"Karril—"

"It's not much of an assurance, I know." His tone was frankly apologetic. "But it's the most I can offer right now. I'm sorry."

"Karril, please—"

But the demon had already begun to fade. A few seconds later only his voice remained, and a few precious words that lingered in the dark cavern air before they, too, dispersed into nothingness.

Whispered:

Good luck.

Thirty-four

The creature called Amoril ran through the halls of the Hunter's keep, howling out his frustration in a wild, inarticulate cry. Over the shapeless mounds of what had once been human flesh—the Hunter's servants, now half-eaten and left to rot—past curtains soaked in blood and urine, past golden sconces which had once held torches but which now, in deference to Amoril's new Master, held only darkness, he made his way to the Hunter's chapel, where an even greater Darkness awaited.

"Not fair!" he screamed. The human words felt strange to him, tattered remnants of another life. But his anger couldn't be vented without the proper words and so he remembered them, formed them, forced them out. "It's not fair!" he howled to the black space surrounding him. The smell of blood was thick in the air, and he could see crusted stains on the altar, left over from his nightly human sacrifice. "We made a deal!"

For a moment it seemed that he was truly alone in the room. If so, it would hardly be the first time. The dark forces which he had courted back in his human past didn't take an active role in his life; rather, having remade him so that he served their purpose, they preferred to sit back and feed in silence on the fruits of his labors. Now, however, something stirred. Its presence was pain and fear and insufferable hunger, and the thing called Amoril whimpered as it manifested itself.

Have patience, came the black whisper.

"You promised me the Forest," he choked out. "You said it would be mine!"

It will, a thousand voices assured him. *As soon as the Hunter is dead.*

"You said you were going to kill him!"

We said that he would die, the voices corrected. *And so he will, once the compact is broken. Soon.*

"There are men in the Forest," he growled. "Church men with weapons, coming here to the keep. The Forest should be stopping them, but it isn't. He still controls it!" Phlegm clotted suddenly in his throat and he spat it out onto the floor, a thick black mass. "Why would he let them come here? Why won't his Workings stop them?"

There was silence for a moment, such utter silence that for a moment he feared his Masters had deserted him. Then the voices returned, a sibilant whisper that filled the cold room.

The cause of that is irrelevant. Gerald Tarrant will be dead before the next sunrise, and the Forest will be freed from his control. You will have enough time to stop them.

"You said he would die before and he didn't," he accused. "Why should I believe you now?"

The answer was pain. Black pain, cold pain, that wrenched at his limbs and sent needles of ice stabbing down into his flesh. With a cry of anguish he fell to the floor, his body contorting into shapes no human form should ever adopt, racked by the Unnamed's punishment.

At last, whimpering, he lay on the floor like a beaten dog, echoes of the terrible pain scraping across his nerves like a rasp.

Your role is not to question, but to serve. The whispers had become one voice now, that filled the whole chamber with its venom. He trembled, knowing how merciless the owner of that voice could be. *Tarrant will not fight this death. He embraces it willingly, for the power it will give him.*

"Power?" he whispered weakly. Suddenly he was struck by a new and terrible fear: what if the Hunter, in his dying moment, struck out against the servant who had betrayed him? The man whose sacrifice had sent him to Hell? What then? He began to gasp out a question, but the sounds of it caught in his throat. What if the Unnamed perceived in that question further defiance? He whimpered softly and drew up his body into a tight ball, as if that simple posture could somehow save him. No. Better by far to say nothing. Better to bear this fear in silence.

But the voice must have heard his thoughts, for it answered him. *The power he invokes will be directed at another, not you.*

It took a minute for the words to sink in. "Thank you," he whispered. "Thank you."

But the voices were gone. He waited for a while longer in his huddled position, shivering with dread, but no new power assaulted him.

At last, very slowly, he unfolded his limbs. No response. Very carefully, very slowly, he raised himself up. Still nothing. With a whimper that was half fear and half relief, he finally got to his feet again. Still nothing. The Unnamed had truly gone.

One more day, he thought. He could taste the Forest's power on his lips, a heady tonic. *Just one more day, and then it'll all be mine. Won't you be sorry then, my brave little Churchmen!*

Then all the human words deserted him. Hungry, restless, the creature called Amoril set off at a frantic lope to find his pack.

Thirty-five

The Forest had changed.

Narilka had gone barely ten steps into it, and already she knew something was wrong. It wasn't a difference she saw as much as one that she felt, but she felt it so strongly that for a moment she just stopped, too shaken to move forward. She remembered the Forest from before. Not clearly, not willingly, but she remembered. The Hunter had set her loose in these woods and she had stumbled through its preternatural darkness like a terrified animal, not yet aware that the creature out of legend who followed her trail was a man, and would never hurt her. Now, as she breathed in the rotting stink that came and went like a breeze, she knew that something was wrong. As she gazed upon the necrotic mold that clung to the trunks of the Hunter's trees, she knew that no growth like that had been here before. And as she dared to reach out with her hopes and her fears into the heart of the Forest itself, struggling for some fae-borne sense of Andry's passage, the presence that she sensed within that realm of shadows was enough to make her draw back, sickened. Not a human presence, that. Not the clean demonic signature of the Hunter either, which she knew so well from their two brief encounters. This was something less than human, something so unclean that the Forest itself would surely vomit it up if it had the power to do so. What was going on here?

She reached out for a nearby tree—one of the few healthy ones—and shivered, trying to absorb it all. Had he changed also, the Forest's monarch? Was this transformation just a facet of his own soul's evolution, reflected in the trees and the earth of his homeland as a simpler man might be reflected in a mirror? If so . . . She shuddered. The monarch of the old Forest had declared her safe. Would his promise

hold in this transformed place? And what about Andrys' supposed invulnerability? Suddenly she felt very cold, and very alone. Until this
moment her quest had been like a dream, her way so brightly lit by
the flame of her love that she never got a close look at the shadows
which were gathering behind her. Now, suddenly, she felt smothered
by them.

With trembling hands she lit her lantern, so that its earthy light
might reassure her. As she adjusted the wick, she heard a sudden
sound behind her and she almost dropped it as she whipped about,
her free hand going to the hilt of the long knife which was sheathed
at her hip. But it was only a forager rooting in the dirt. Thank the
gods. For a moment she had thought it might be a soldier, and had
braced herself for a far more unpleasant confrontation.

The guard at the Church camp would be changing soon and they
would discover that she was gone. Or maybe it would take them
longer than that. Maybe they had enough duties to occupy their time,
so that each soldier would think another had attended to her. Maybe
hours would pass and the sun would set and darkness would fall
again before they realized that she had slipped away at dawn . . . and
by then it would be too late for them to stop her. Gods, let it be so!
She had wanted to circumvent the Church camp entirely, had even
turned her horse toward the east with the intention of cirling wide
about it and entering the Forest from another direction. Then it had
struck her just how foolish that plan would be. There were no roads
inside the Forest, and certainly no markers to measure distance or indicate direction. How could she hope to find Andrys unless she followed directly in his footsteps? So she had come back reluctantly to
Mordreth, her starting point, and taken the north road directly to the
Forest's edge. Where the Church had made its encampment. Where
the soldiers of the One God stood guard against all enemies, real and
imagined.

It had been easy enough for her to explain her presence to them.
A lifetime of having men make presumptions about her nature had
given her a feel for that game, even though the presumptions were
usually wrong. Perhaps she was lucky that men were on guard when
she rode into the camp. Surely women would have seen through her
subterfuge, and watched more closely for hints of what lay beneath.
Men rarely bothered.

She was afraid for her lover, she said as the guards confronted her.
She had spent too many sleepless nights and tortured, distracted days
thinking about the dangers he was facing, and at last she had decided
to follow him. That was what she told them, and certainly the words

were true enough. What was false was the manner in which she spoke them, and the conclusions she inspired the guards to draw. She appeared to be a weak woman, a confused child, a fragile creature who clearly had never considered the hard reality of battle when she set off to be with her loved one. Now, at the edge of the Forest, with these men explaining the true nature of war to her, she would of course understand that she couldn't ride into the Forest alone, that she didn't *want* to ride into the Forest alone, that the best thing for her to do was wait here, in this camp, until her lover finished his manly work and returned to her. They would be glad to protect her until then, they said. And their eyes added: *such a woman needs protection.*

Bullshit.

They let her use his tent for the night. That brought genuine tears to her eyes, to see the manner in which he had left his few possessions, to read his state of mind in their disarray. Belongings were strewn all about the interior, soap and razors, bits of clothing . . . and a tassel. She gasped when she saw that. It was a tiny thing, black silk with brass tinsel wound around the base, and she wouldn't have noticed it at all if it hadn't been so familiar. She'd owned a scarf with tassels on the ends, just like that. She remembered it. She'd worn it as a belt one night and then lost it. Later she'd thought that maybe she had left it at his place, but when she'd looked for it the next day, it wasn't there. Or so it had seemed.

Oh, Andrys. She shut her eyes tightly, and her hand clenched shut about the tiny thing. He must have hidden it among his possessions days in advance so that she wouldn't find it and reclaim it, more comfortable with the concept of theft than he was with the thought of asking her openly for a keepsake. There were tears coming to her eyes now and for a short while, in the privacy of his tent, she let them flow. Why had she let him come here alone? Why had she ceded to anyone—even his God—the authority to separate them?

Never again, she promised herself.

She'd spent that night in the Church camp, huddled among his possessions. In the morning it had rained, which was an event so fortuitous that she whispered a quick thanksgiving to Saris, just in case the goddess had been responsible for it. In the distance she could see the morning guard huddled in their rain capes, keeping watch on the paths that led to and from the Forest. Did they really think something from that darkbound realm would brave the sunlight to strike at them? Or were they more concerned that she might continue her journey, and compromise the purity of their faith-driven campaign with her presence? She had no doubt that they would stop her if they could, and so she planned her next move carefully, knowing that she would have only one chance to get past them.

There was a cape among Andry's belongings similar to theirs, and she put it on. Its bulk covered her clothing and her pack and its hood, drawn forward against the rainfall, cast her features into deep shadow. Clad thus, her booted legs imitating the stride of the soldiers as best she could, she made her way to the outskirts of the camp. There was another guard there—a man, she guessed by the height— and for a moment she thought he would recognize her despite her disguise. Heart pounding, she raised up a hand as if to acknowledge his presence, then set off with a firm stride toward the edge of the Forest. He didn't follow her. Nor did he raise an alarm. She knew that he would have done one or the other if he'd realized who she was; he could hardly allow the sanctity of his Patriarch's mission to be com- promised by the presence of a single pagan woman!

Remembering the Patriarch's rejection of her pleas, she shook her head sadly. *Is there so little to fear in this world that you have to make enemies out of your neighbors? Does your God have nothing better to do than pass judgment on the innocent?* But deep within her heart, where it hurt to look, she did indeed understand him. And she knew that in a way he was right. She had seen the Forest and she knew its power, and nothing short of the One God Himself was going to bring it down.

Quietly she slipped out of the rain cape and let it fall to the ground behind her. There was no need for it now that the rain had stopped, and its bulk might slow her down. A faint mist clung to the ground, but despite its clammy touch she was grateful for it, for it made the earth damp enough to hold the mark of footprints. If she could find the place where Andrys and his fellows had entered the Forest, she could surely follow their trail. It was too bad that her im- provised plan hadn't allowed her to bring her horse along; it would have made the journey easier. But if she had tried to bring it along with her the guards would surely have noticed, and therefore she must do without it.

As she traveled, searching the ground by lamplight for a promising sign, the Forest changed about her. Not in a neat progression, as one might expect, but in fits and starts. In one place the smell of rotting meat was so strong that it nearly choked her, and she held a damp cloth over her mouth in the desperate hope that it would keep out the worst of the stink. Ten steps later, that smell was gone. Unwhole- some growths clung to the tree trunks in one place, but left neighboring acres undisturbed. Wormlike creatures writhed at the foot of the great trees as tribes of smaller parasites slowly chewed their way through their skins, but twenty steps away no sign of worm or parasite was visible. She didn't remember the Hunter's realm being like that before. She couldn't imagine that the man who had shown her the glories of the night—fearsome and violent, yes, but ordered as the finest music is ordered, and pristine as the moonlight itself—would have condoned such a state of affairs.

And then she found it. She thought it was a riverbed at first, a trough scoured into the mud by some flash flood that had swept town from the mountains. But holding her lantern close, she saw the footprints that marked its bottom. They were horses' prints, the triune markings of an eastern breed. She had found the Church's trail at last.

A sense of relief so intense that it was almost painful welled up inside her. Not until this moment had she been willing to admit to her greatest fear, which was that the Hunter's realm might swallow all signs of Andrys' passage, so that no one could follow him. But these tracks were so clearly marked, so utterly mundane in form, that she felt a sudden rush of confidence, and even the sour stink of the Forest seemed to fade for a moment, as if to acknowledge, *This is it. This is right. Follow him.*

Turning up her lantern wick, she followed the soldiers' trail deep into the Forest. The lumps of horse droppings scattered here and there were still damp and pungent, which seemed to imply that they weren't far ahead of her. Thank the gods! She tried not to think about what her reception would be when she finally caught up with them. The Church soldiers would be furious, but Andrys . . . she could feel his need now, as though there were a cord connecting them. Andrys was all that mattered. And if his god truly meant to bring down the Hunter, surely he wouldn't let the love of a single woman stand in his way?

The region's thick darkness folded about her like a shroud as she walked, until the light of her lantern was all but smothered. Trembling, she kept her eyes on the ground before her, refusing to search for threats in the looming darkness at either side. If the Forest meant to attack her now, then it surely would do so, and no single lantern could stop it; she had gambled everything on the Hunter's promise, and now, with his words ringing in her ears like a prayer, she gave her whole attention over to following the trail before her. It wasn't easy. The earth was dryer this far into the Forest, which meant that the marks she was following were more shallow, less certain, easily confused with the scrabblings of local animals. It was so hard to see in the gloom that once she went down on one knee so that she might run a hand along the trail for a foot or two to confirm its presence by touch, but the sudden sense of something burrowing beneath the soil, something filthy and hungry and drawn to her heat, made her stand up quickly again. *It won't hurt me,* she told herself. Her heart was pounding; her hand felt clammy against the lantern's handle. *Nothing here will hurt me.* But despite that self-reassurance she moved quickly forward, whispering a prayer to her goddess that her feet might stay on the right path, even as she fled unseen horrors beneath the earth.

Hours passed, cold and immeasurable. She found a hump of rock and sat down on it, resting just long enough to catch her breath and wash down a bit of dried biscuit with a swallow of water. Had she truly run in this place once for three days and nights? She trembled to recall those hours of terror. Could Andrys sense the Hunter's constant presence here, or was that sensation reserved for the woman he hunted? For his sake, she prayed he was immune.

At last, her strength renewed by the meager meal, her courage somewhat bolstered, she lowered herself down from the rock and prepared to take up the Church's trail once more.

Then she heard the noise.

It wasn't like the other noises that surrounded her, although it would have been hard for her to describe the way in which it differed. A thousand creatures had skirted the edge of her lamplight since she had come here, and their scrabblings and slitherings had become an accustomed counterpoint to her own footsteps. This noise was different. This noise echoed with purpose. This noise, as it mirrored her own footsteps, warned of something intelligent, something focused . . . something dangerous. Something unbound by the Hunter's promise, that was free to sate its own hunger in these nightbound woods.

Her heart began to pound, but she forced her stride to stay even. Surely anything that belonged in this darkness could outpace her easily; the trick was not to run, not to provoke it. The Church soldiers couldn't be far ahead—right?—and if she could just get within hearing range of them, maybe the thing that was following her would be frightened off. Or maybe she could cry out and get someone to come to her, fast enough to keep it from moving in on her—

And then there was a sound ahead of her, and another to her side. She heard footsteps first, like those which followed her, and then a kind of snorting. She felt a chill crawl along her skin, and only the knowledge that displaying her fear would make things a thousand times worse kept her legs from locking up in terror beneath her. *Ev-*

erything in the Forest is his, she chanted silently. *Nothing of his will hurt me.* But what if her fears had manifested some new creature, some demonling not yet broken to the Hunter's ways? Would she still be protected then? There was rustling on both sides of her now, so loud that she knew it was deliberate; the things that echoed her steps were taunting her. *Goddess, help me. Please. . . .* Her legs were numb, her feet so heavy she could hardly move them. Could her pursuers smell her fear? Did it whet their appetite? *Oh, Andrys, what have I done!*

A figure moved into the path before her. At first it seemed to be some kind of animal and she took a step backward involuntarily, trying to put herself out of range of its teeth. But then it straightened up, and stretched somehow, and when she held the lantern up so that she might see it better, she saw that it was human in shape, human in countenance . . . but not human in substance. That much she saw with her heart, if not her eyes.

It was the white man, the Hunter's servant. But not as she remembered him from their meeting years ago, a slender, lithe creature with ghostly white skin that gleamed in the moonlight, feral hunger that gleamed in his eyes. This was a creature of plague and rot, a living manifestation of the malignance that had assailed the entire Forest. His hair—if hair it could be called—was a matted mass of dirt and slime that seemed to move of its own accord as he watched her. His body seemed somehow distorted, in posture if not in form, his clothing was torn and filthy and reeked of urine, and his eyes . . . those were the most horrible thing about him, she thought. Not human eyes at all, but pits that seemed gouged into his flesh, emptiness where eyes should have been, framed by a ring of flesh pulled back so hard against his bone that she could see black veins pulse beneath it.

"Ah," he whispered, and the sound was more a growl than any human utterance. "It seems we have company." His voice gurgled thickly in his throat, as if some growth within that passage made human speech a trial. "So rare, these days."

Stay calm. You know how to deal with him. Just stay calm and do it. She tried to reach a hand into her jacket pocket, but she was shaking so badly that she couldn't find the opening. Wolflike creatures were moving into the circle of light now, and like their master they were horribly deformed, filthy satires of a once-proud pack. If the Hunter's own servants could be so twisted, what did that imply about their master? She trembled to think about it. *Stay calm!* Then her hand slid into the pocket—finally—and she clutched the thing within it, grasping it like a lifeline. Even as he took a step toward her she jerked it out and held it up before him, wielding it as a warning, a weapon. The Hunter's token dangled in the lamplight, glints of gold along its edge warning back those demons who would defy his will. It had worked once before, when this creature meant to toy with her. Surely it would do so now.

The white man stared at her amulet for a long, silent moment.

Then he laughed.

Goddess! She felt her soul flinch as the sickening figure came toward her. *Help me!* She tried to back up, but something large and cold had come up behind her legs; it took all her remaining strength not to fall backward over it, into its waiting jaws.

"The Hunter isn't around right now," the white creature informed her. He grinned, displaying a mouth full of rotting and bloodstained teeth. "But don't worry. I'm sure we can manage to entertain you in his absence."

He reached for the amulet then and she tried to back away from him, but the beast behind her knees moved suddenly and she fell over it, her lantern hurtling to the ground far out of reach. She tried to regain her feet, but it was impossible; the beasts closed in on her even as she struggled to get to her knees, their jaws closing tight about her arms and legs, their rank weight forcing her down again.

She screamed. Hopeless effort! What did she think it would gain her, in this land where even the laws of sound would surely be warped by sorcery? But the cry welled up from a core of terror so stark, so primitive, that mere logic could not silence it. And the white man laughed. He laughed! The whole Forest was his now, not only its plants and creatures but the very air itself. Who could hear her, if he willed it otherwise?

And then his face bent down close to hers and his hands closed tightly about her wrists—icy flesh, dead and damned, that sucked out her living heat through the contact—and she could feel her frail grip on sanity giving way, the darkness of terror closing in about her brain even as the flesh of the albino's pack closed in around her body. Sucking her down into depths where was neither terror nor pain, only mindless oblivion.

Andrys! she screamed, as the darkness gathered in thick folds about her. The sound built up in her throat and left her mouth, but made no tremor in the air. *Andrys!*

He couldn't hear her. No one could. No one except the Hunter's servant, whose beasts even now were mauling her frozen flesh.

Oh, Andrys. . . .

Thirty-six

Sunset was sandwiched between earth and ash, its light like a wound in the darkening sky. Though the sun itself had disappeared behind distant mountains, its rays, stained blood red by a veil of ash, lit the bellies of the clouds like the fire of Shaitan itself. Now and then a wind would part the ash-cloud overhead and the light of the Core would lance through, but it was a fleeting distraction. The day was dying.

Pointedly not looking down at the landscape that spread out beneath his perch, Damien squeezed his way back into the shelter that Karril had found for them. The lantern he had left at the first turn was still burning, and he caught it up as he made his way back to the place where Tarrant waited. Unlike the Hunter, he needed light to see.

Tarrant was exactly as he had left him, resting weakly against the coarse wall of the cavern. By the lamp's dim light Damien could see that his burns hadn't healed, and that was a bad sign; a full day's rest should have restored him. His scar alone remained unreddened, and its ghostly white surface, framed by damaged flesh, reminded Damien uncomfortably of the scavenger worms of the Forest.

"Sun's gone," he said quietly. No response. He put down the lantern and lowered himself to the ground beside Tarrant, striving to maintain an outer aspect of calm when inside he was anything but. *Come on, man, we've got a long way to go and not a lot of time to get there!* But something about Tarrant's attitude scared him. Something that hinted that the worst damage wrought last night might not be that which was visible, but some wound inside the man that was still bleeding.

At last, unable to take the silence any longer, he ventured, "Gerald?"

The pale eyes flickered toward him, then away. Staring at something Damien couldn't see, some internal vista.

"We can't win," the Hunter said weakly. The pale lids slid shut; the lean body shivered. "I thought we could. I thought there must be limits to his power. I thought that human senses were complex enough to defy absolute control—"

"And you were right—" he began.

"No. They aren't complex at all. Don't you see? What we would call a *view of the sun* is no more than a simple pattern of response in the eye, which is translated into simple electrical pulses, which in turn pushes a handful of chemicals into place within the brain . . . there are so many places in which that flow of information can be interrupted, and with so little effort! Our enemy has that power, Vryce. One spark in the wrong place, one misaligned molecule . . ." He gestured up toward his ravaged face with what seemed like anger, but for once Damien didn't think the emotion was directed at him. "The only thing stopping him was Iezu custom. Now that he's willing to disregard the law of his own kind, what chance do we have?"

"First of all," Damien said, with all the authority his voice could muster, "It isn't that simple a process. You of all people should know that. Do you think all those molecules in your head are labeled clearly, so that it's easy to tell which one does what? Oh, *you* could probably figure it out—I wouldn't put too much past you—but I doubt if Calesta's got the patience or the know-how for that kind of work. Which means that he may have the power to screw with our heads, but he's not necessarily going to do it right every time."

"He did it well enough to—"

"Shut up and listen for once! Just once! All right?" He waited a moment, almost daring Tarrant to defy him. But the Hunter was too weak to spar with him like that . . . or perhaps he was simply too astonished. When it was clear that his outburst had had the desired effect, Damien told him, *"He didn't do it perfectly.* If you or I had known what to look for, we would have seen the signs, we would have known that trouble was coming, we could have taken precautions—"

"What the hell are you talking about?"

"The *stars,* Gerald. He could black out the sun from our sight, but he couldn't change every one of the stars so that its position was right!" He told him about the constellation he had noticed, that shouldn't have been so high in the sky until dawn was well underway. "Or maybe he just didn't bother with details," he concluded. "Maybe his arrogance was such that he imagined simple darkness would work the trick. Well, now it won't. Now we know how his Iezu mind works. And if he couldn't pull off that illusion perfectly, maybe all his work has flaws. Maybe, like an Obscuring, a Iezu illusion succeeds because men don't think to look at it too closly. Well, now we know to look."

"And do you imagine that we can remain so perfectly alert at every moment, that not a single detail out of place will escape our notice? Because that's what it would require, you know. Even if his illusions are less than perfect—and we don't know that for a fact—he's no fool. He'll wait until our guard is down, until we're being less than perfectly careful, and then what?" He raised up a hand to his face, wincing as the pale fingers traced the scar there. "I didn't feel my own pain," he whispered. "I could have died out there, and not until the final moment would I have understood what was happening."

"Karril said he'd protect us," Damien reminded him. "He can't stop Calesta from misleading us, or from making others try to kill us, but he won't let you walk into the sun. He promised."

The Hunter's voice, like his manner, seemed infinitely weary. "And what about Iezu law? What about the rule their creator set forth, that there was to be no conflict between brothers?"

"Maybe," he said quietly, "there are things that matter more to Karril than that."

"Like what?"

"Like friendship, for one."

He dismissed the possibility with a wave of his hand. "The Iezu aren't capable of friendship. Their venue is limited to one narrow range of emotion, and their only motivation is a hunger for—"

"Oh, cut the crap, Gerald! You know, you're a brilliant demonologist in theory, but when it comes down to facing facts you can be downright stupid." He leaned toward the man, as if somehow proximity could give his words more force. "Was it Iezu nature that made Karril take me down to Hell to rescue you? Where does *pleasure* fit into that? And was it Iezu nature to do what he did last night: defy the law of his creator to step into the midst of his brother's war, at the risk of angering the one creature on this planet who can kill him? He did that to save *you*, Gerald Tarrant. For no other reason. Just to save you." He leaned back on his heels. "That's friendship by any standard I know. To hell with who or what he is. I'd be damned proud to have a friend that loyal myself."

"You wouldn't have said that once. You'd have damned yourself for even entertaining such a thought."

"Yeah. Well. We're worlds away from that time now. I may not like that fact, but I accept it." He studied the Hunter—his wounds, his weakness—and then asked, "You need blood, don't you? Blood to heal."

The Hunter shut his eyes, leaning back against the stone. "I drank," he whispered.

"Warm blood? Living blood?"

Tarrant said nothing.

"I'm offering, Gerald."

Tarrant shook his head; the motion was weak. "Don't be a fool," he whispered hoarsely. You need your strength as much as I need mine."

"Yeah," he agreed. "The difference is that my strength can be renewed easily enough. Or don't you think that a Healer would know how to accelerate the production of his own blood?"

"You can't Work here," Tarrant told him. "Not even to heal yourself. Shaitan's currents would swallow you whole."

Damn. Damien drew in a slow breath, trying to think. Were there alternatives? "What about fear? I don't mean a nightmare this time. The real thing. Straight up." He managed to force a laugh. "God knows there's enough of it inside me right now for both of us."

But the Hunter shook his head, dismissing the thought. "Without an artificial structure? The channel between us isn't strong enough for that. That's why I used dreams."

The words were out before he could stop them. "Then make it stronger."

Slowly the Hunter looked up at him. Those chill eyes were black now, bottomless, as dark and cold as the fires of Shaitan were bright and hot. "And could you live with that?" he demanded. "Knowing what I am, understanding what such a channel would do to the two of us? Could you live with yourself, knowing that a part of me was in your soul, and would be until one of us died?"

"Gerald." He said it quietly, very quietly, knowing there was more power in such a tone than in rage. "I knew when we came here that we probably weren't getting out of this mess alive. So what are we really talking about? A day or two? I'll deal."

Tarrant turned away from him. Maybe the channel between them was already stronger than he thought, or perhaps Damien simply knew him well enough to guess at what he was feeling; he could feel the sharp bite of hunger as if it were his own, the desperate need not only to feed, but to heal. Damien reached out and grasped the man's arm, as if somehow that would lend his words more power. "Listen to me," he begged. "Deep inside there's a part of me so afraid I don't even like to think about it. It's in that place where you store hateful feelings and then bury them with lies and distractions, because you can't bear to face them head on. Because you know they'll eat you alive if you try." He whispered it, pleading; "Why waste that, Gerald? It's food to you, and the strength to heal yourself. Take it," he begged. "For both our sakes."

For a long, long time the Hunter was silent. Then, ever so slightly, he nodded. Just that.

Damien let go of his arm. His heart was pounding. "What do I have to do?"

Silence again, then a handful of words whispered so softly he could barely hear them. "Complete the bond."

"How?"

Slowly, the Hunter then reached into the pocket of his tunic for the knife he carried there. Not the same one he had used so long ago to open Damien's vein, establishing the channel between them in the first place—that had been lost in the eastern lands—but one very much like it, that he had purchased afterward. He opened the blade partway and then quickly, precisely, pressed its point into the flesh of his fingertip.

"Here," he whispered. Raising up his hand, so that the tiny drop of blood might be visible. Black, it seemed, and so cold that its surface glittered like ice. Or was that only Damien's expectation, playing games with his vision? "Only once in my long life have I offered this bond to another man . . . and that one betrayed me."

As vulnerable as this will make you, it will make me equally so. The words rose up out of memory unbidden, and for a moment Damien understood just how desperate the Hunter must be to offer such a bond. *You fear this more than I do,* he thought. Reaching out to touch the glistening drop, gathering its dark substance onto his own fingertip. *Damn Calesta, for making us do what we fear the most.*

As the Hunter had done to his first offering years ago, so now Damien did to this. Touching his tongue to the cold, dark drop. Forcing himself to swallow it, as one might a bitter pill. Forcing his flesh to take the Hunter's substance into itself, so that a deeper link might be forged—

—And the monster within him rose up with a roar from those hidden places where it had lain shackled, its bonds shattered, its howling triumphant. Fear: pure and terrible, agonizing, undeniable. Fear of dying in this place. Fear of surviving, but as less than a man. Fear of returning to a world in which he no longer had a purpose. Fear that Calesta would claim his soul, or else leave him unclaimed—the ultimate sadism!—to witness his final holocaust. Fear that the Church would fail and mankind would be devoured by the demons it had created . . . and fear that it would succeed, and the world would become something unrecognizable, that had no place for him. Those fears and a hundred more—a thousand more, ten times a thousand—roared through Damien's soul with such horrific force that he could do no more than lie gasping on the floor of the cavern, shaking as they exploded one after another in his brain.

Then, at last, after what seemed like an eternity, the beast's roar quieted. He could still hear it growling in the corners of his brain—it would never be wholly quiet again, not while Tarrant lived—but if he tried hard enough, if he focused on other things, surely he could learn not to hear it. Surely.

"You all right?"

He managed to open his eyes, amazed that his flesh still obeyed him. For a while it hadn't. "Just great," he whispered. It seemed there was an echo in the chamber, that it took him a minute to place. *Tarrant's perception.* The thought sent a chill down his spine. *I'm feeling him hear me.* Fear uncoiled anew in his gut, rising up to—

He choked back on it, hard. His whole body trembling, for a moment he could do no more than lie where he was, struggling to get hold of himself. Then slowly, very slowly, he rose up to one elbow. Tarrant offered him a hand for support, and he grasped it in his own. Not cold, that undead flesh, but comfortable in its temperature, comforting in its strength. That, too, made him shiver.

"It won't last long," the Hunter assured him.

"Yeah." He brushed himself off with shaking hands. "Only until one of us dies."

"As I said." The Hunter reached down to pick up his backpack, handed it to him. There was a strange kind of echo to the gesture, such that when Damien closed his hand about the leather strap it was as if he had just done so seconds before. Unnerving. "Not long at all."

He drew in a deep breath, then slipped his arms into the straps. It seemed to him that the air between them was warmer than before; was that some new faeborn sense, or just overheated imagination?

"The strangeness of it will fade," the Hunter promised. It seemed to Damien that he smiled slightly. And yet his mouth didn't change, nor any other part of his expression. Weird.

"How about you?" he asked. The Hunter's face, he saw, was back to its accustomed ghastly color. "Feel stronger?"

"Strong enough to send a Iezu to Hell." And he added: "Thanks to you."

For a moment there was an awkward silence. Not quite an expression of gratitude. Something stronger, and subtler.

"All right, then." Damien shifted the pack on his pack until its straps fell into their accustomed position, allowing him free access to his sword. Without further glance at Tarrant he started toward the exit, knowing that the Hunter followed. "Let's do it."

The valley was . . .

Different.

Where before a dark valley floor had served as backdrop for mist and moonlight, now an ocean of fiery power seethed and frothed, driving itself onto the rocks beneath them with such force that a spray of earth-fae, fine as diamonds, drizzled down the slope of the ridge. Where once vague tendrils of mist had curled about the crags and monuments of Shaitan's domain, now it was possible to see things stirring, snakes of mist that resolved into semihuman form and then, with a ghastly cry that Damien could feel in his bones more than he could hear, melted into mist once more. The whole of the valley floor was in motion, spewing forth malformed creatures and then swallowing them up again while Damien watched; the sight of it made him dizzy, and he leaned back against the ridge for support, afraid that he might lose his balance and fall into it.

And then that vision faded. Not utterly, though he would have liked that. Out of the corner of his eye he could still sense unearthly motion, and he knew that he wouldn't be able to walk along that ground without feeling the earth-fae twine about his flesh, without knowing that here every human thought became a thing with a face and a hunger and a chance to scream, before Shaitan's power swallowed it up again.

"A taste of my Vision," the Hunter said quietly. "Now that you can share it."

"Is that really what you see down there?"

The Hunter chuckled. "A faint shadow of it, no more. The most your human brain can handle. Here." He held out something to Damien. "Put this on."

It was a fist-sized bundle, soft and gleaming. Damien shook it out to its full length, nearly ten feet long. "A scarf?"

"Just so." The Hunter had taken out one of his own and was wrapping it about his head like a turban. The fine black silk was so thin that it seemed more like smoke than fabric, and when he drew a fold of it across his face and fixed it there, it gave his white skin a weird, ghostly quality. "Shaitan's breath is hard on the skin. You'll want to put on your gloves also."

"Not to climb down a mountain, I don't."

—and his hands are burning, corrosive mist eating into the flesh until the skin peels off in reddened bits, blood welling in the wounds—

"Okay, okay! Gloves it is!" He fumbled in his pack and retrieved them. "God." He put the wrong hand in the wrong glove and had to start over. "You're a lot of fun to travel with, you know that?"

"The fun," Tarrant assured him, "has not even started yet."

He looked down into the valley again. The ground was dark. The mist was just mist. It was comforting. Damien wrapped the black silk around his head as he had seen Tarrant do—it took three tries—and noted that it had a faint chemical odor, as if it had been treated with something. It did surprisingly little to affect his vision; perhaps it had also been Worked in that regard. *Tarrant's been here before*, he reminded himself. *He knows what he's doing.*

"Ready?"

The Hunter had brought a special rope for the descent, a thin line meant to steady them on the rubble-strewn slope, long enough to guide them down almost to the valley floor. He tied one end to a spire of rock and sent the other end, weighted, hurtling down into the darkness.

Damien sighed. "As ready as I'll ever be."

Tarrant led the way. Slowly, oh so carefully, they dropped down toward the valley floor and the dangers that made their home there. At times the Hunter would stop and signal for Damien to do the same, and they would grasp the thin rope to keep from sliding while he waited for whatever danger he had sensed to pass them by, or turn its attention elsewhere, or . . . whatever. Damien didn't want to know the details.

The rope gave out at last and they had to make their way without it. Gazing down at the ground by his feet, eerily lit by the orange fire of Shaitan in the distance, Damien couldn't help but notice the tendrils of mist that played about his feet, couldn't help but remember the vision that Tarrant had shared with him. When he made the mistake of looking too closely at the misty tendrils, they reared up like snakes and began to take on a more distinct form—but Tarrant ignored them, and just nudged him forward at a faster pace. Soon they were moving too fast to look at things closely, thank God. If you didn't look, did they leave you alone?

At last they reached a place where the ground seemed level enough, and Damien allowed himself a small sigh of relief. Thin orange highlights played along the earth, not enough to see by; with a glance at Tarrant to make sure it was all right, he took out his lantern and lit it. Golden light flickered upon the bellies of mist-clouds, outlining ghostly faces that formed and faded as he watched. "Those are no danger," Tarrant told him, when he seemed hesitant to move forward. "Come."

It was an eerie place, and the orange light from Shaitan, flickering and fading as its lava fields pulsed, did little to make it more comforting. Craggy monuments lined the valley floor, and the mist flowed between them like rivers. A handful of plants had tried to take hold on the rocky ground, but they were stunted things, pale reflections of a hardier species, and their leaves and bark had been eaten away in seemingly random patterns, fibers peeling back to reveal a core laced with channels and pockmarks. The very smell of the place was strange, as if the plants were struggling to create some kind of natural perfume but were too wounded to do it right; wisps of unnatural odor came and went with the breeze, mixed with the stink of ash and the omnipresent bite of sulfur in the air. The ground seemed solid enough, but what if that were just another of Calesta's illusions? *Karril said he would protect us,* Damien told himself as they walked. *He won't let Calesta kill us with illusions.* Yet there was a vast gap between *killing* and *being safe,* Damien knew that, and if Calesta believed that Tarrant had figured out a way to kill him . . . what would he do? Damien gazed up at the mists surrounding them, at the craggy monuments that reared high over their heads, and shivered. That Calesta would strike at them was not to be questioned. The only question was when, and how.

The bastard's afraid of us, he told himself. Trying to derive some satisfaction from the thought.

And then something drifted out at them from the mists, all too human in shape for his comfort. Tarrant said nothing, but urged him forward with a touch, and Damien obeyed silently, his stomach a tight knot of dread. They walked like you did with a mad dog, slowly, pretending not to notice its presence, while all the while your heart was pounding, and sweat was running down your face. The figure had come closer now, close enough to investigate, and it took everything Damien had not to turn and look at it. Were there other figures by its side, or was that only his fear making him see things? Or Calesta's power, turned against them at last? Damn it, if this place didn't give him a heart attack all by itself, waiting for the enemy to strike at them might just do it.

He was moving forward, watching the strange figure out of the corner of his eye, when suddenly Tarrant grabbed his arm and jerked him back. He felt cold air rush up against his face, and as he looked down he could see that there was no ground in front of him, not by a good fifty or sixty feet. He had almost walked right into it.

"God," he whispered.

Tarrant had turned to face their pursuer. His body was rigid with tension, which Damien found less than reassuring. With a last glance down at the chasm by his feet, Damien turned as well, and dared to look at the thing that had been following them. At first it seemed no more than a shadow, and then, as he gazed upon it, it took on form and substance. A man's head, gashed from nose to jaw. A man's throat, rubbed raw by rope. A man's body—

"My God," he choked out, turning away.

A man's body gutted open, intestines streaming down its legs like worms, heart twisting between the jagged shards of a shattered rib cage. He felt sickness welling up inside him and didn't know if he could hold it in. Was it better to vomit away from a ghost, or right on top of it?

"*Go.*" Tarrant's voice was no more than a whisper, but the power it bound made the figure's surface ripple like water. The Hunter put a hand to his sword and drew it out ever so slightly. The coldfire didn't blaze with its normal brilliance, but curled about his hand and wrist like tendrils of glowing smoke. "You have no business with us. Leave us alone, or . . ." He pulled the sword free another inch, to illustrate his intention.

The creature stared at them, and for a moment Damien was certain that it was going to move toward them. But then, with a snarl, it moved back a step. And another. Fading into the mist before their eyes, until its outline could no longer be seen.

Damien allowed himself the first deep breath in several long minutes. "A shadow?"

The Hunter nodded.

"Is it gone?"

"As much as such things ever are, in this place."

"You could have destroyed it, right?"

The sword snapped shut. The veiled gaze of the Hunter was cold and uncomforting. "Let's hope I don't have to try." He took a step closer to the precipice, and Damien dared the same. A river had cut into the plain before them, etching out a canyon that twisted back in hairpin turns on either side. Water glistened blackly at its bottom, and thick clouds of mist clung to its walls that all but obscured its details.

"The land is filled with these," Tarrant told him. "They make the plain into a veritable maze, and one wrong turn can leave a man trapped."

Until sunrise, Damien thought. That would be long enough, where Tarrant was concerned. "You said you've been to Shaitan before."

"Not by this route. From the tunnel that exits under my keep, which leads to much simpler ground. Not through this." He shook his head tightly, his frustration obvious. "I had hoped the canyons would be visible from above, so that I could sketch out a path for us before we descended. But the view—as you saw—was hardly that useful."

"So what now?"

He gazed out into the distance, narrowing his eyes as one might gazing into a bright light. "I can make out some of its pattern from here. Enough to guide us, perhaps."

Perhaps. How long was the day this time of year, ten hours, eleven? Not long enough to pick their way through a maze of this complexity. Damien looked up toward Shaitan's light in the distance—not so very far from them, but a world away for all that they could get to it—and then down into the depths again. "What about crossing it?" he asked. "I know it's a climb, but we've got the supplies for it, and even that seems preferable to trying to walk around it."

In answer the Hunter pointed down into the darkness. It took Damien a minute to figure out what he was pointing at, and then several minutes longer to make out what it was. When he did, he cursed softly.

Bones lay scattered across the floor of the narrow canyon, the skeletons of three men clearly visible. Shreds of fabric and flesh still clung to their upper portions, but their legs had been stripped and polished until nothing remained but lengths of bone as white as snow. Serpents of mist writhed in and out of the joints as Damien watched, like maggots on fresh meat.

He tried to think, at last ventured, "Acid?"

Tarrant nodded. "Shaitan's breath is venomous, and so is her blood. Or so the legend says. They should have listened to it."

"Is all the water here like that?"

He nodded. "It's leached out of the ash-clouds by rain, so that the very earth is soaked with it. That's why so few things live here . . . so few *natural* things, that is."

"Shit."

A faint smile flickered across the Hunter's face. "Aptly put, Vryce. As usual." He looked both ways along the length of the canyon, then nodded toward the left. "Shall we?"

"If you tell me we've got something better to go on than guess-work," Damien challenged. "Otherwise we'd be better off looking for that tunnel of yours, and heading to Shaitan from there."

"My Vision will afford us some guidance, at least for the nearer obstacles." In illustration of which he reached out a gloved hand to-wards Damien, and the channel that bound them flared to life; Damien could see with his own eyes how the currents of the earth-fae followed the lips of the canyon, their patterns reflected in the mist-clouds overhead. "As you see." In the distance it was just pos-sible to see a place where the canyon turned, perhaps giving access to the plain beyond. "And the path is no easier to my tunnel from here, I regret. Either way, the real risk . . ."

He didn't finish the thought. He didn't have to. *Either way, Calesta's what we have to worry about. He can make us see canyons that aren't there, or run from shadows that don't exist, or even make us walk over the edge of a chasm, thinking it solid ground. . . .* But no, Karril had said he would protect them from a move like that. If only their ally would expand his beneficence to encompass lesser strategies!

They set as good a pace they could along the rocky earth, moving sometimes by the light of the lantern and sometimes, when the mist cleared from overhead and the clouds were obliging, by the blood-colored fire of Shaitan. Ghostlike shapes wisped in and out of life on all sides of them, and occasionally Tarrant would lead Damien out of the range of one that was becoming too solid for comfort. Shadows, he called them. Reflections of the dead. Damien saw one whose head had been severed, and another whose ghostly blood flowed where its arms and legs should have been. Most of them seemed confused rather than dangerous, as befit spirits whose minds contained but one single moment of consciousness, but some were clearly hostile to liv-ing men, and while they had no interest in Tarrant, it was clear they considered Damien fair game. More than once the Hunter had to bluff them back, and one time, when a wretched creature with its skull split open proved itself determined to vent its undead wrath on Damien, Tarrant pulled his sword wholly free and let the coldfire blaze. The result was like a block of ice slamming into Damien's gut, that left him dazed and gasping and very nearly toppled him over into the canyon beside him.

"What the vulk was that?" he demanded, as the Hunter finally sheathed his sword. At least the hostile shadow was gone; one less threat to deal with. "I don't remember it doing anything like that before."

"The currents here are like a warped mirror, that reflects and distorts any Working. That's why I try not to use this," he explained, as he settled the sword back into place. "Or any other kind of power."

That's just great, Damien thought, as he struggled to get his breath back. *Another thing to worry about.*

Periodically Tarrant would gaze at the earth and sky with an almost desperate intensity, and Damien knew that the adept was searching their environment for any detail out of place—no matter how small or seemingly irrelevant—that would warn them of Calesta's power being used against them. But after each such stop Tarrant simply shook his head silently, frustrated, and then took up the march again. Were the canyons real, or illusions meant to mislead them? How easy it would be for Calesta to turn them aside from their proper path, or draw them toward a false one! If the demon's work lacked perfection in any detail, it could well be so subtle that no merely human eye was going to catch it. Or even Tarrant's.

If so, we're doomed. He didn't dare meet Tarrant's eyes, but through the newly intensified channel between them, he could taste the panic that was slowly taking root inside him. It matched his own. *If we can't find a way to tell what's real from what isn't, we don't stand a chance.* Standing by Tarrant's side, he stared out at the same daunting vistas, hoping against hope that his limited vision might reveal some secret detail the adept missed. But each and every canyon looked hopelessly real, and the bones that were scattered here and there along their bottom—and even at the top, where the two walked—were eloquent reminder of how deadly this land was, and how few travelers made it through.

At last, weary, they paused for a rest. Damien pulled a hunk of bread from his stores and chewed it dryly, careful to disturb the thin veil no more than he had to. Tarrant neither ate nor drank, but stared off into the darkness surrounding them as though somehow he might find an answer there. Through the link between them Damien could sense his state of mind, and it wasn't comforting.

At last the adept said, "I'm going to have to Work. There's no other way." He glanced up toward the sky, a reflexive action only; the ash cloud overhead would keep him from seeing the dawn until it was all but upon him.

"A Locating?"

The Hunter shook his head. "Too easy for our enemy to fake. Remember what he did in Seth? And besides, any precise Working is doomed in this place. Much in the same way that complex music loses its coherency in a hall with too many echoes. No, this Working must be in its purest unstructured form: a plea for the fae to accommodate our mission, however it sees fit. A single chord, pure and simple."

"Sounds damn vague to me."

"Anything more than that is doomed to failure, I assure you."

"And how do we know that Calesta won't vulk the results of this Working, too?"

The Hunter hesitated. And for a moment, just a moment, the channel between pulsed with fresh energy and Damien could taste the emotion inside the man. Thick fear, black and choking; it was hard to believe that a man could contain that kind of emotion inside himself and not let it show. "He'll no doubt try to," he admitted. "And we know all too well how adept he is at that game. But if my Working succeeds, then by definition it must offer us a tool over which he has no power."

"And what are the odds of that?"

The pale eyes met his. The voice betrayed not a tremor of fear. "Better than the odds if we don't try anything."

Working. Normally Tarrant could manage it with no more effort than a single moment of tension, perhaps a narrowed gaze if the matter was difficult, but now . . . Damien watched the adept brace himself, eyes shut tightly in concentration, and felt himself grow sick at what that implied. Then he drew out his sword from its warded sheath, and the fae bound to the sharpened steel seemed to glitter hungrily in Shaitan's bloody light. Damien felt the Working take shape and braced himself for the frigid bite of the Hunter's coldfire, but the power that surged through him when the moment came was like nothing at all familiar. It was a force that froze and burned all at once, that left his flesh shaking as if an entire storm system had squeezed through his veins. He didn't need Tarrant to tell him that wasn't all from the Working; the feeling of heat was a dead giveaway that some other power was involved. Tarrant had stated his Call, and the fae was reflecting it back at him with the accuracy of a funhouse mirror. God willing, the distortion would be minor. God willing they wouldn't conjure something worse than what they were already dealing with.

When he was done Tarrant resheathed his sword, and the coldfire faded. "Do you think—" Damien began, but the Hunter waved him to silence. The tension in the man was palpable now, and Damien had to turn away and not look at him, to keep from being sucked into it. He had enough fear of his own, thank you very much, and didn't need to absorb any one else's.

And then, in the mist before them, something stirred. He saw Tarrant take a half step forward, then stop. A shadow? An illusion? Or something else? Wisps of silver fog twined and gathered, and slowly took on a form that seemed human. Was this the fae's answer to their need, or simply another of the walking dead, drawn by their cry of desperation? As it slowly became distinct from the mist that surrounded it, Damien saw that its form was female, and that in life it must surely have been a beautiful woman, for even in death its features were graceful and pleasing—

Then Tarrant gasped, and stepped back as if struck. There was more fear in that one sound than Damien had ever heard him utter, and for a moment Damien was rooted to the spot. Then he took a step forward as if to—what, protect the man?—close enough to see the figure clearly, and make out its details.

She was a slender woman, delicately formed, with a thick corona of hair that still hinted at its living color, a soft red-gold. Her eyes were large and were fixed on Tarrant with such intensity that it was clear her living self had known him. A victim, perhaps? Her lips were full and likewise tinted with a trace of rouge, so alive in their aspect that Damien could almost imagine a human breath passing through them, and a heartbeat behind it. She wore a long gown of what must have been a fine wool, pale in color, and on it . . . he squinted, trying to bring it into focus. The folds of the gown shifted slowly as if in a breeze, and sometimes they seemed pure white, while others . . . he caught a flicker of color and tried to focus on it . . . thin tendrils of red running down between the folds, and a scarlet stain just where the heart would be.

And then Tarrant whispered, *"Almea."*

And he understood. *Dear God.* He understood.

"Your wife?"

"No." The Hunter shook his head. "Not my wife. A shadow, formed by the currents here. Not her."

He looked at the ghostly image, then back at Tarrant. It was hard to say which of the two was paler.

"Maybe it was formed in answer to—"

"No!" The figure was moving toward Tarrant; the Hunter backed away quickly. "It's Calesta's illusion. It must be. Or else a real shadow, drawn by our presence here. My God," he whispered. His voice was shaking. "If it's the latter . . ."

"It's your *wife*, Gerald."

"As she died!" The red lines on her body came into focus for a moment, and Damien could see the whole of her clearly: bloodstained, ravaged, tortured by a madman's blade . . . and then the white cloth folded in again, softly, gently, and the only pain visible was in her eyes. "Almea Tarrant as she was in her last living moments, with none of what came before! None of the love, none of the memories, none of the things that might mitigate her terror as she—as she—"

The shadow had stopped moving. Was watching him.

Damien dared, "I don't think she's here to hurt you."

"How can she be here for anything else? Remember what I did to her, Vryce!"

She was waiting, Damien thought. She expected something. What?

"You called for help," he offered.

He whispered: "I tortured her."

She was watching. Waiting. Not Tarrant's wife, but an isolated fraction of the woman. One instant of her living existence, frozen in time by the power of this place.

He drew in a deep breath, trying to sound calmer than he felt. "She's the first shadow here that hasn't gone after us. Maybe that means something."

Tarrant said nothing.

The figure turned. Not wholly away from them, but slowly moving in that direction. There was no hate in her eyes, Damien noted, nor anger, but a vast tide of pain. And maybe something else . . . something more.

"She loved you very much," he observed.

Tarrant shuddered. "This thing wouldn't remember love."

She had stopped. She was waiting. For them.

"Gerald," He said it gently, testing the words. "I think she wants us to follow her."

"For what? To help us? More likely to lead me deeper into this trap—"

He looked into the shadow's eyes, at the reflection of life that shimmered in their depths.

"I don't think so," he said quietly.

Tarrant looked at him in astonishment. "Why?" he demanded hoarsely. "Why would she help me, after what I did to her?"

"Maybe she wants to see you punished for what you did. You did say you expected to die on Shaitan, didn't you? Maybe she wants to lead you to your death." He drew in a deep breath. How could he word the next idea so that the Hunter would accept it? "Or maybe in that last moment what she wanted was to save you. Maybe she saw the man she had married being swallowed up by an evil so powerful that all her words, all her love, couldn't save him . . . and now he has one chance to redeem himself. The first real chance he's had in centuries." He waited a moment, then said softly, "You knew her, Gerald. You tell me."

The shadow was waiting.

"If she's an illusion—" Tarrant began.

"She isn't."

"How can you be sure of that?"

"Because for all of Calesta's subtlety, I don't think he could have created *this*." He gestured toward the shadow; did it smile sadly in response? "A reflection of pain, yes, and maybe hatred, and certainly a hunger for vengeance. Those are things he understands. But the rest?" Reading what was in her eyes, he shivered. *God, what a woman she must have been.* "Calesta knows nothing about human love; how could he mimic its form so perfectly?"

The Hunter turned to him. His pale eyes were so haunted, so tormented, that Damien had to fight not to look away. "Is that what you see in her?" he demanded.

"Among other things," he said quietly. "Enough that I think she might want to lead us where we're going. And we haven't got a whole lot of other options, have we? Unless you have something up your sleeve you haven't told me about."

"No."

"So?"

For a long time he just stood there. Damien waited. So did she.

"All right," he said at last. A whisper, barely audible. "All right."

They turned to where the ghostly figure stood, and saw that it had moved a few steps away. Damien waited until Tarrant had begun to walk toward her, then did so himself. His heart was pounding, with hope and fear both. Almea Tarrant's shadow would be immune to Calesta's illusory persuasions; the Iezu had no power over faeborn creatures. Which meant that she could probably lead them around the true obstacles, and save them the trouble of avoiding things that weren't really there.

If she wanted to. That was the catch. Watching her from behind, her ghostly substance trailing out into wisps of white smoke that were swallowed up by the omnipresent mist, he prayed that he had read her right. If not, they had so little hope. . . .

She led them away from the canyon they had been following, onto a stretch of plain with little to distinguish one mile from another. Damien glanced nervously at Tarrant, but there was no way of telling from the adept's expression if he could see anything useful, or if he was equally without a reference point. Soon the noxious mist closed in around them, sealing them in a shell of fog so thick that they could see no farther than the few steps ahead of them. Strange things moved within that mist, half-made creatures that pressed against its border like curious fish, but nothing came too close. Was that in response to Tarrant's power, or hers? Did the shadows of the dead respect each other's territory, so that no other creature would bother them while she was there? He stiffened as something with red eyes seemed to be coming straight at him, but it scattered like smoke before it could reach him. For now, for whatever reason, they seemed safe enough. God willing it would stay that way.

Step after step, mile after mile, they followed the shadow of Almea Tarrant across the poisoned earth. Skirting monuments of blackened rock, crushing malformed grasses beneath their feet, working their way around the shore of a tiny lake whose surface smoked like water about to boil. The smell that surrounded them was sometimes rotting, sometimes sickeningly sweet, but always backed by the sharp tang of sulfurous poisons. Thank God for the scarves Tarrant had Worked, which seemed to keep the worst of it out of their lungs. Damien reached up to his every now and then to make sure it was secure. He had traveled enough in volcanic regions to know how quickly your lungs could seize up once that stuff saturated them, and was doubly grateful to Tarrant for having prepared for it.

We're going to make it, he thought, even as his legs began to ache from the hike. His mouth was growing dry from thirst, as well, and he knew that should be dealt with. He struggled to get out his canteen without slowing his pace and fumbled the cap open, but when he lifted his veil to access its contents a sudden gust of sulfurous fumes hit him full in the mouth. Before he could stop himself, he had breathed some of it in, and though he dropped the veil right away, it set off a coughing fit so powerful that for a moment he couldn't walk at all. Over and over a deep hacking cough shook him, and he could only pray that the others would stop long enough for him to pull himself together. Did the Almea-shadow care if he reached Shaitan, or was she only concerned with her husband's fate? The thought of being abandoned in this place was truly terrifying, and he was overcome with relief when his eyes cleared at last and he saw that both Tarrant and the ghost were still with him. "You can drink through the veil," the Hunter told him. *Great. Just great.* He did so as they began to walk again, wincing as the bitter taste of some unknown chemical flowed into his mouth along with the water. *Thanks for warning me in advance.*

And then they came to a place where a canyon cut across their path, blocking their way. Deeply etched, steep-walled, it cut off the land to the right of them, forcing them to swing around to the left if they meant to continue their journey. But the shadow of Almea didn't go that way. It didn't move at all. It stood at the edge of the canyon as if judging the depth a man might fall, then looked back at them. Just for a second. And then, without a sound, it stepped forward, into the chasm itself.

Dear God . . .

She hung suspended above empty space, her feet pressed against the air as if she stood on solid ground. The far wall of the canyon was perhaps twenty feet away, but she didn't seem in any hurry to reach it. As casually as if it were real earth beneath her feet, she walked out to the middle of the empty space, then stopped and turned back to them. After a moment, when they didn't follow, she reached out a slender arm toward them. Bidding them forward.

"If she is an illusion—" Tarrant began.

"Then she can't kill us like this. Remember? Karril promised."

"Karril promised Calesta wouldn't kill us. I don't remember him saying anything about my wife."

Silent, she waited. Without her help there was no way to go on.

"Look," Damien said at last. "She hasn't got any reason to hate me, right? So I'll go first. If it's a trap for you, maybe . . ." He couldn't finish the sentence. *Maybe she'll take pity on an innocent man and warn me back.* "Maybe it'll be okay," he finished lamely.

He walked to the edge of the canyon and started to look down into it . . . and then forced his eyes up, fixing them on her. There was no way to read in her face what she intended, or how far she might go to entice Tarrant over that edge. Finally he drew in a deep breath and forced his right foot forward. He kept his eyes fixed on her as he moved, resolve like an iron fist around his heart. He moved his foot forward a few feet and down, to where open air seemed to be, and then he was stepping forward but there was nothing solid under him, nothing! and his survival instinct cried out in panic for him to throw himself back hard and fast, before his full weight was committed . . . but he knew that a good illusion would feel like that, too, and so he didn't. Eyes shut, cold sweat breaking out across his brow, he committed his full body's weight to his forward leg. And it held. Praise be to God, it held! He took another step forward, and then another. Slowly exhaling, he opened his eyes and looked down. It was a dizzying sight.

He turned back to where Tarrant stood and tried to force a smile to his face. "Well? You coming?" The Hunter hesitated, then approached the edge himself. Damien watched as the man made the same wary foray that he had, and saw how his face went white with shock as he felt the ground fall out from beneath him. But he, like Damien, persisted, and soon they both stood free on the ground that had been so effectively hidden from them, Calesta's illusion spread out beneath their feet.

"Apparently he hasn't forgotten us," the Hunter whispered.

The Almea-shadow led them onward, deeper and deeper into the maze of mist and acid. They skirted one canyon, turned away from another, and came to yet another which the shadow led them across. This time they followed her without hesitation. How many hours were passing while they fixed their attention on the next stretch of poisoned earth, sour odors rising from the mutated plants at their feet as if to welcome them? It seemed to Damien that the ground had begun to incline; how far from Shaitan's peak did the volcano's slope begin? His legs ached and his throat felt raw from breathing the sulfurous air, even through Tarrant's silken filter. Even as he prayed that it wasn't much farther to Shaitan's peak, he remembered the sight of that looming cone, and knew that his legs would hurt much worse before this was over.

And then there was a wall of rock before them, and Almea stepped into it and was gone. The two travelers looked at one another, and then Damien, holding his breath, followed her. For a moment it seemed as if he had indeed walked into a stone wall—and then that feeling was gone, and the illusion also, and the open plain stretched out before them, with Almea waiting just ahead.

"I do believe we found the right guide," he whispered. And he could have sworn that Tarrant smiled, albeit weakly.

The ground became rougher after that and walking slowed accordingly; the shadow set as fast a pace as she could, but she wouldn't leave them behind. It seemed to Damien that he could sense a growing tension in the air; Calesta's, perhaps? If the Iezu were truly worried about Tarrant reaching Shaitan, then he must be near panic now. What had the Hunter told him, that they had no power other than illusion? And he had clearly lost that hand. Good God, they might make it after all.

The gradual slope became a steep incline, and walking turned to climbing. Through the thin silk veil he could taste the biting sulfur of Shaitan's winds, the reek of foul gases vented up through the volcano's crust. Gouts of fire blocked their path, some whistling, some roaring, some burning in eerie silence. They skirted most, but some they simply walked through. All felt equally hot. Once Damien saw his pants catch fire, and the heat about his legs almost drove him to run for cool earth to roll it out. But *she* wasn't running and so he didn't either, and within minutes—as soon as Calesta realized that his newest gambit had failed—that vision faded as all the others had, into the stuff of memory.

Damien found that he was gasping for breath, and his heart had begun to pound so loudly in his chest that it drowned out the other sounds around him. The ground itself was trembling as if from an earthquake, but unlike an earthquake the motion was continual. It made for an oddly vertigous sensation, in which nothing about or beneath him felt solid. As he climbed, he could smell the dry heat of lava nearby, hopefully not too close to where they were. How high up did Tarrant need to go, to do whatever it was he had come here to do?

And then they came around a chest-high boulder, and saw that right ahead of them a thin stream of lava blocked the way. It had vented through the mountainside not thirty feet away, and though it was narrow enough to jump over, Damien wasn't sure that was the kind of exercise he wanted. "Is there another way?" he asked the ghost. She turned back to him slightly, just long enough to meet his eyes, then faced the stream and started toward it. But he didn't move.

"Vryce?"

Her eyes. It was only for a moment that he had looked at them, but that moment made him tremble. "Not the same," he whispered. He looked at the lava stream, so dangerously close, and began to back off. "We've lost her. . . ."

The shadow turned back to them. She was the same as before in all superficial aspects, but something indeed had changed within her. That hint of softness Damien had sensed, behind all the pain. That one emotion in her that didn't reek of hate. That thing which Damien had interpreted as *love*. . . .

"Damn!" he whispered. When had they lost the real one? He whipped about as if hoping that she was waiting there behind them, but all that was behind them was a pitted slope strewn with boulders. When and where had Calesta made the substitution? All that it would have taken was a moment of inattention, easy enough in this land where every shadow seemed threatening.

"If he means to hide her, then we won't be able to find her." Damien could hear the exhaustion in Tarrant's voice, of a soul wrung dry by fear. "We'll have to go on alone."

"No. We can't." He was remembering all the obstacles they had walked through, or walked over, or simply ignored. "We don't stand a chance without her guidance." *Think, man, think!* "What are the limits of his power?" he demanded. *Think!*

The dead thing that wasn't Almea watched as Tarrant considered. "He can create images that appear real. He can cause us not to see things that truly exist. He has some ability to affect the internal senses—hence our sensations of heat and of falling as we defied his illusions—but that ability must be limited, or else he could simply incapacitate us with pain."

Internal. That was the key. Was there some kind of internal link between Tarrant and his wife's shadow, that might help them find her? Evidently the Hunter had thought of the same thing, for he shook his head. "If it were really my wife, perhaps. But this isn't the woman I lived with, remember that. It's a construct of the fae, which contains no more of Almea Tarrant's true substance than would her reflection in a mirror. Believe me," he said, "under the circumstances I wish it were otherwise."

No help there, then. Damien looked desperately about the landscape as if seeking inspiration for some new line of attack . . . and he found it. It was streaming along the ground not ten yards from his feet.

"We might as well move forward, then." His heart was pounding with terror as he made his way toward the lava stream, but he knew that he didn't dare hesitate. "Because without your wife's shadow I think we're as good as dead here, don't you?" He had ten feet left to go, and he could smell the gases that were sizzling on the lava's surface. "Calesta's as good as killed us this time by hiding her, so why not take a chance?" *Walk into it,* he ordered his muscles. *Don't worry about whether it's real. Just do it.*

He was less than a step from the lava stream when something

reached out and stopped him. Thank God. He let it push him back from the molten rock, then reached up to wipe the sweat from his face. All he accomplished was to make the silk veil stick to his skin.

"You play a dangerous game," Karril growled.

He managed a dry smile. "Just holding you to your promise."

The Iezu took him by the shoulder and forced him back down to where Tarrant stood waiting. "There," he said. He didn't sound at all happy. "As I promised."

The real Almea-shadow was behind them, as clear as if no illusion had ever hidden her. The false one was gone, or maybe just invisible, which was almost as good.

"Would you have really walked into it?" Karril asked him. Damien said nothing. At last the demon sighed. "All right. If that's the way you want it." He glanced at Tarrant, and with a thin smile said, "Just remind me not to play poker with him."

"You and me both," the Hunter whispered, and it seemed to Damien that for a fleeting instant there was a smile on his face, too.

Up the slope they went, Almea gliding easily, the two men struggling behind. Much to Damien's surprise Karril stayed with them, and when he caught his breath long enough to question him about that choice the demon would only say gruffly, "Someone has to keep the two of you out of trouble."

We've won, he thought. But it was only the journey that was finished. Ahead of them lay Shaitan, and a Working so deadly that no man might attempt it and survive.

They climbed. In places the trembling of the ground was so subtle that they didn't hear it, only felt it beneath their feet and hands; in others it was like a genuine earthquake, and Damien's teeth chattered as he pulled himself higher and higher up the broken slope. Sometimes it felt like the very planet beneath them was about to crumble, and he had to shut his eyes and draw in a deep breath and summon all his self-control in order to ignore it. The shadow waited. And Karril climbed behind them. And inch by inch, foot by foot, they made their way toward their destination.

At last they came to a place where Karril signaled for them to stop. The Almea-shadow seemed content to obey, so Damien and Tarrant did likewise. The ground was so steep they could barely stand upright, but supported themselves by leaning against cracked boulders of congealed lava.

"It's over!" Karril cried out to the mist surrounding them. "You couldn't stop them from getting here, and now you can't stop them from doing what they came to do. Let them see it for themselves!"

For a moment it seemed to Damien that the whole world hesitated. The rumbling of the earth, the crackling and hissing of nearby lava, the pounding of his own heart . . . all quieted for a moment, as if waiting. Then, slowly, the mist surrounding them began to thin. White smoke gave way to thinner tendrils, and that in turn gave way to air clear enough that the side of the mountain could be seen.

With a gasp Damien leaned back hard against Shaitan's flank, and he saw Tarrant do the same. A hundred feet beneath them he could see clouds—real clouds—gathering about the mountain's peak like a flock of broad-winged birds. Between them the air seemed to stretch downward forever, until the flank of the mountain crumbled and flattened and merged into the valley floor so very, very far below. Had they really climbed that far up? he wondered. His eyes found it hard to believe, but his muscles were wholly convinced.

He turned his gaze upward, toward the peak of the great volcano. A short climb farther would bring them to its lip, a jagged rock line silhouetted by the orange glow of Shaitan's magmal furnace. The black clouds overhead seemed almost close enough that he could touch them, and their undersides flickered with all the colors of fire, reflected from the crater and its attendant vents. The entire sky seemed filled with fire, a universe of burning ash, and thank God that Almea had brought them up on the windward flank, because the stuff spewing forth from that crater looked hot enough and thick enough to choke even a sorcerer.

He looked back down at Tarrant and was startled to find yet another figure beside him. Black and sharp-edged and oh so very familiar. Instinct made him reach for his sword, even though he knew in his heart that steel would do no good against *that* kind. It was a gut response.

"Give it up," Calesta commanded.

Tarrant turned away from him and began to climb. From the crater above them a spray of fire seemed to spew forth, and a hail of molten pebbles clattered down around them. He kept going.

"You can't kill me!" the black demon cried defiantly. "All you can do is waste your own life, and throw away eternity. I can give you what you want!" Tarrant climbed on. A lump of rock directly ahead of him split open and lava began to pour forth—and then Karril cursed and muttered something and it was gone.

"I think he has what he wants," the god of pleasure told his brother. "Despite your help."

There were other figures appearing on the slope now, some human, most not. Shapes wrought of gold and smoke and writhing colors, that gathered on the smoking ground to watch Tarrant's ascent. Some were as fine as glass, and almost invisible to Damien's eyes. Others seemed to be made of flesh, as Karril was, and only a sorcerous feature or two hinted at nonhuman origins. One was made entirely of silver, neither male nor female but more beautiful than both combined.

"Family," Karril told him. And in answer to Damien's unspoken question, he added, "They won't interfere."

Up out of the crater itself something was rising now, that was neither lava nor smoke nor any volcano-born thing. A swirling of color, that lit the ash from beneath. A cloud of images, that blended one into another so quickly Damien had no time to make out details. Faces—planets—the softness of flowers—the faceted light of jewels . . . those images and a thousand more swirled in the center of a cloud of light, no more solid than a Iezu's illusion, no more lasting than a dream. Damien felt as if he were staring into a great mirror, that reflected back at him all the fragments of his life in no special order, with no special meaning: a chaos of consciousness. With a sudden burst of fear he realized what it was, what it must be . . . and he prayed that Tarrant wouldn't look up and see it, lest it drain him of the last of his failing courage.

"Is it—?" he breathed.

"As I said," Karril's voice sounded strained. "Family."

Tarrant had climbed as high as he could now, without trusting his weight to the last crumbling bit that might betray him. With effort he rose up to his feet, and the light of the Iezu's creator combined with the hot orange glow of Shaitan's furnace backlit him with a corona hardly less bright than the sun's.

"Hear me, Calesta!" His voice was strong despite his obvious physical exhaustion; reaching his goal had clearly renewed him. "I Bind you with sacrifice. With the Pattern that has served man since his first days on this planet. I bind you to me as a part of my flesh, a part of my soul, indivisible—"

"Go to hell!" the demon cried.

The Hunter drew his sword then, and its cold power blazed with furious light. Along the channel that bound them, Damien could feel the Hunter's will reaching out, the coldfire his source of fuel, his burning hatred a source of strength. *Come join with me,* the power urged. Damien tasted the Hunter's hunger, and his cruelty. He ran through the Forest in the Hunter's place, and tasted the sweet fear of women on his lips. The hot bouquet of blood filled his head like a heady wine, so that he had to put out a hand to steady himself. The

joy of killing, the pleasure of the hunt, the ecstacy of torture . . . they
surged through him like a flood tide and they surged through the demon also, a temptation too terrible to resist. Drawn by the power of
the unexpected feast, Calesta moved forward. A thousand figures cir-
cled about, human and otherwise, watching. It seemed to Damien
that the mother of the Iezu was watching also, and he prayed desperately that she wouldn't interfere with this.

"With this sacrifice," the Hunter pronounced, "I bind you to me."
And with that he heaved the sword up high, over the jagged rock edge
of the crater, into the hidden depths beyond. An explosion shook the
ground beneath Damien's feet, so powerfully that he thought the
earth might open beneath him. But it quieted, and over the beating of
his heart he could hear the sizzle of lava in the distance, the muffled
roar of fire. Shaitan had accepted Tarrant's offering.

Then the adept met his eyes—his alone—and the fear that shone
in those pale glittering depths was only matched by their determination. "You must understand, Vryce. I honestly believed that somewhere, somehow, I could find an answer. I believed that in the month
remaining to me I could discover a way to break my compact and survive, and ultimately cheat death anew . . . and I chose this instead.
This sacrifice of life, which is the ultimate altruism. The sacrifice of
eternity, made in the very face of Hell." He held out an arm to
Calesta, and it seemed to Damien that he smiled. "Come share it
with me, demon!"

And he opened himself up to the full force of Shaitan, the raw,
bloody power of Erna's wildest currents. For an instant Damien could
see the world through his eyes, could feel his agony as the fae roared
through him, too much force for any one man's soul to contain . . .
and he saw the hillside blaze with a heat so terrible that the sight of
it could burn out a man's brain, and he felt the Hunter's soul catch
fire as the man screamed—as *he* screamed—and through it all he
knew that it had *worked*, that Calesta had absorbed the full force of
Tarrant's altruistic sacrifice, that the terrible gamble had paid off—

And then the channel between them was gone, just as Tarrant had
promised it would be. Severed by the instant of his death as cleanly
as flesh might be severed by a knife. *Oh, Gerald.* The Hunter's body
lay crumpled and still, and when drops of burning dust fell upon it,
it didn't stir. The swirling colors that had hovered above the crater
had gathered over him now, but that didn't matter. None of it mattered anymore. The Hunter was dead.

May God be merciful to you, he prayed. *May he weigh this day
against the others of your life, so that in the balance He finds cause*

for forgiveness. May He acknowledge in His Heart that every gener-
ation born to His people from now on will have a chance to prosper
because of your sacrifice—

And then it was suddenly more than he could handle, all of it. He let himself down to the trembling earth, and he put his head between his hands, and he let down the barriers that had protected him for so long, from fear and sorrow both. Never mind if the Iezu saw him cry. Never mind. They would mourn, too, if they understood. Any sane creature would.

In the east, a new dawn was just beginning.

Thirty-seven

Andrys despaired, *I'm not going to make it.*

They had stopped their march to eat and to feed the horses. The men and women who shared his mission were trying to rest, to renew themselves for the next hour's march. He couldn't even pretend. How could you relax when all the demons of Hell were battering at your skull?

For a long time he remained on his horse, and though Zefila and a few others narrowed their eyes as they noticed him there, no one bothered him. But then the Patriarch came over and as usual didn't say anything—as usual, didn't have to say anything—and with a hot flush of shame he dismounted at last. The alternative was trying to explain that his gut churned at the mere thought of making contact with the Forest soil, and he couldn't do that. Flinching as his soles touched the damned earth, he tried not to let his terror show as he walked to the place where rations were being doled out. How could they know what the Forest was, or what it was doing to him? How could he explain to them that it wasn't just a collection of trees, or even a complex ecosystem, but a single creature, living and breathing in perpetual darkness, that seemed intent on swallowing him whole?

What good would it do to tell them? he despaired, as he received his allotment of food. The thought was not without bitterness. *They'd be happy if it devoured me.*

It was getting worse and worse as they went on. He had hoped that the hours of riding would dull his senses until all feeling ceased, but it had done just the opposite. Every hoofbeat that brought him closer to the heart of the Hunter's domain was like a nail driven into his flesh, and it was all he could do not to scream, not to beg them to turn back, turn back! and take him out of this place that was slowly remaking him, turning him into something he was never meant to be.

How could he explain to the Patriarch what was happening? He didn't understand it himself. Shutting his eyes, he remembered the moment when they had first come to the Forest's border, when he had stood so close to it that he could feel its power like a chill breath upon his neck. He had been afraid to go forward then, as any sane man would be, and for a moment it seemed to him that he would truly be unable to ride on. Then the Patriarch came up beside him, and he put his hand across the vast space separating them and clasped him upon the arm. Strength flowed through the contact, enough that Andrys could gasp out a few words.

"I can't," he whispered. "I don't have the strength."

The hand on his arm tightened for a moment, and he quailed at the thought of the anger that might now be directed at him. But the Patriarch's voice was quiet and level, with no condemnation in it. "Then trust in God, my son. He does."

Andrys looked at him, and for a moment their eyes locked. For a brief moment he sensed the deep well of strength in the other man, a reservoir so vast that all the trials of a lifetime could never empty it. *Give me one drop of that in my own soul,* he begged silently. *Let me taste it, just for a day.* Then the moment passed and he was on his own once more. Heart numb, he urged his horse forward, into the point position. Past the Patriarch. Past Zefila. Forward, step by step, into . . .

Temptation.

Oh, yes, there were horrors enough in the Forest to send any sane man running. Oh, yes, he was sickened by the foul odors of the place, nauseated by the aura of rot that clung to every tree, every stone in the place. Yes, he could feel the chill power of Gerald Tarrant battering at the gateway of his soul as the fae tried to pry his identity loose, to let *his* take its place. All those things and more were there, enough to freeze any man's blood. But there was something else, too. Something so unexpected that he could hardly absorb it. Something so horrifying in its implications—and so seductive in its form—that he dared not give voice to it, for fear the others would declare him mad.

He could *feel* the trees, as the Forest breeze caressed them. He could feel their coarse bark as if it were his own skin, and he winced at the sharp bite of parasites burrowing beneath it as if it were his own flesh they ate. High above him he could feel the thick night deepening, the faint sting of moonlight on his branches, the cold breath of a mountain wind stirring his leaves. Too much sensation for any one man to absorb . . . and yet only the gateway, he sensed, to an even greater vision.

Was he going crazy? Or was this simply a manifestation of Gerald Tarrant's own link with the Forest, a sign that it indeed recognized Andrys as part of itself? He was afraid to ask. He was afraid that somehow, by putting the experience into words, he would give it more power. He was afraid that his soul would drown, not in a sea of terror, but in a tidal wave of sensation so rich and so fascinating that no man could resist it.

There were birds in the trees, and he could taste their hunger lapping at his branches as they searched for the insects that were their chosen fare. And he was aware of those insects as well, a patter of frenzied movement punctuated by such stillness that it seemed the whole of the Forest was holding its breath. The bark of the trees was alive with tiny organisms, and if he shut his eyes he could sense the Forest as they did, overlapping images of food and hunger and fear and satiation and so many other sensations, alien yet familiar . . . he could lose himself in it, he knew. All too easily. He could lie down on the chill earth and let it take him, open up his soul until all the life of the Forest poured into him. Sweet, dark ecstacy! Unspeakably tempting to the hedonistic spirit in him, that craved sensation at any cost. Maddeningly tempting to the wounded shell of a man that he had become, desperately in need of escape. What narcotic could rival such an experience, or offer such total escape from the bleak reality that his life had become?

Shaken, he went back to his horse and fiddled with its saddle, as if seeking some weak point in the harness that needed his attention. His hands were trembling so badly he was afraid someone would notice, but the others were too intent on their own duties to bother. God, he needed a drink. How else did you drive out such a vision, which lapped at your brain like a woman's tongue, hinting at sensations beyond human bearing? Was this what the Hunter experienced every day? he wondered. Did he escape his own undead flesh to revel in the heat and the hunger of his creations? Or was that an experience reserved for a living Tarrant, which even the great Hunter might not share? The thought of it made his head swim. And the very real fear that he would be swallowed up by those new sensations made him clench his hands into fists so tightly that his fingers throbbed with pain, as if by doing so he could somehow control the source of the alien sensations, and drive the Forest out of his soul.

They ate quickly, remounted, rode on. Into a night so endless, a land so twisted and degraded, that its oppressive power strangled even whispered conversations among them. They had no means of measuring their path or of even chosing their direction. Their compasses had ceased to work long ago, cursed by their own fears into a state of inaccuracy so pronounced that finally, with a sigh, Zefila ordered them put away for good. The path they followed was serpentine, and it seemed to Andrys that several times they crossed their own tracks as they rode along it. No one else seemed to notice it, or at least, no one mentioned it. Was it just a hallucination, conjured by his fear? Or was it a true vision, visible only to those who saw with the Hunter's eyes?

The Forest was herding them, that much was clear, but to where? If their subterfuge worked, it should lead them to the black keep at the heart of the Forest. If not . . . then they might wander these dark woods forever until hope and supplies both ran out. Wasn't that how the Forest worked? Entrapping the men in a maze of wood and stone until they died, perhaps mere yards from a place where the sun was shining?

Don't think about that, he thought, pulling at his collar with a feverish finger. *You'll go crazy.*

After what seemed like an eternity on horseback, Zefila indicated that it was time to make camp for the day. When they came to an area that was clearer than most, they halted their horses and dismounted one after the other, as exhausted by the aura of futility that hung about their company as they were by the exertion of a long ride. *Time to sleep,* Andrys thought. Not a happy thought. God, he needed a drink. His throat was burning and his hands were shaking and he really didn't know how he was going to make it through the next hour, much less continue on like this for another day without fortification. He almost turned to the Patriarch and begged for a swallow from the metal flask the Holy Father had confiscated back at the beginning of their march. Almost. But in the end he lacked the courage to confront the man, or perhaps he was ashamed to admit to such weakness in front of him. Grimacing as he dismounted, he braced himself by remembering that there were times in the past when Samiel had locked up—or smashed—all the bottles of liquor in the keep, and he had made it through. Somehow.

Food was doled out: cold, uncomforting rations. He tried not to think about the predators circling the campsite just beyond the reach of their meager light, but his senses were more attuned to the Forest than before, and he could hear them treading warily about the camp, wanting only the right signal to attack. God willing, they'd keep their distance.

He stiffened suddenly. His nerves felt like someone had just screeched fingernails across a slate, right behind him.

Something was wrong.

He shook his head, wincing as a sharp bolt of pain shot through his temples. The animals had stopped their circling. The very night air seemed uncommonly still. He felt as if he were standing before a tidal wave, a vast bore of black water that was about to bear down on him.

"Mer Tarrant?" someone asked.

—And it struck him in his gut like a physical blow, so powerfully that he staggered backward, falling over a man who had been unpacking supplies behind him—falling over him and then still falling, down past the earth, down *into* the earth, falling into a chasm of darkness so absolute that there was no earth in all the universe, nothing to cling to, no one to scream to . . . it was a hot darkness, so hot that he could taste his skin charring, he could hear his hair sizzling, he could smell his blood boiling to vapor—

He screamed. Or tried to. God only knew if the sound had reality; in his world it echoed and echoed until it filled the dark, hot space with sound, until it deafened him to hear his own cries, his own terrified keening—

"Tarrant! What is it?"

He could feel a vast tremor run through the Forest then, a vibration that ripped loose ghost-white roots and sent the scavenger worms digging madly for cover. What was happening? Not an earthquake, but something infinitely more fearsome. He fought his way up from the darkness, struggling to focus on real things: the people around him, the horses stamping nervously on the ground, the sharp pain in his thigh where he had struck it against a rock in his fall. Focus. Think. Try to figure out what the hell is happening.

"Mer Tarrant?" a woman asked.

"I'm okay," he whispered hoarsely. Hearing his own words as if they were that of a stranger. There was something wrong in the Forest, so terribly wrong that he sensed his very life depended on being able to define it, yet its definition slithered from his mental grasp. The soldiers were in danger now, he realized, far more danger than they had ever been in before, far more danger than any of them could anticipate—

"Oh, my God," he whispered. Suddenly understanding. "No. Not that."

"What?" It was Jensing, an older man with a wife and children to go back to. "What is it?"

Andrys looked for the Patriarch, found him. Their eyes met.

"We're not safe any more," he gasped. "You have to do something—"

"Why?" the Holy Father demanded. His tone was utterly cool, incredibly controlled. Couldn't he sense the danger here?

"It broke," he gasped. "His link with it. Gone." He stared into those blue eyes, so maddeningly calm, and heard the terror rise in his own voice. "*It isn't his anymore.* Don't you understand what that means? I won't be able to—"

White-furred shapes erupted from the forest's edge. Sleek killers, lithe and powerful, with teeth that gleamed like pearls along their slathering jaws. They gave no warning, but burst from the stillness of the surrounding woods with a suddenness and a silence that seemed more demonic than bestial and they were upon the company so quickly that few could muster a defense. One man went down with a cry of anguish, sharp teeth ripping at his throat before he could manage to reach his sword. A woman screamed as two beasts bore down on her, their claws making short work of her face. Something pale and hungry leaped toward the group that was surrounding Andrys, and before anyone could react it had borne one woman down upon him, spattering him with blood as it tore through her throat mere inches from his face. There was screaming now—some battle cries, some howls of fear—and the mixed sound churned in Andrys's brain as he struggled to kick the dead weight of the woman off his chest, praying that the creature would go with it. Then someone managed to take up a weapon and spear the beast, forcing a blade through its gut while Andrys struggled to get his own weapon loose. Even that didn't stop the thing. He felt the teeth clamp shut around his leg as his sword slid free of his sheath and he kicked out wildly with his other foot, hoping to dislodge it before those powerful jaws slid around to the back of his steel greaves, or else crushed them utterly. Another sword hacked at the animal, blinding him with a spray of black, foul-smelling blood. He struggled to get away from the beast, and when at last he did he fought his way to his knees, and then to his feet. He was as ready to fight as he had ever been in his life, but he knew deep inside that even that wasn't enough. Ten years of civilized fencing bouts in an upper-class salon had hardly prepared him for *this.*

There were dozens of them in the camp now, and they were carving their way through the Church's troops with tooth and claw and sheer bestial savagery. Some of them were attacking the soldiers, but most of them were going for their mounts, as if they knew the saddled beasts to be unarmed. Amidst the rearing, squealing horses it was impossible to see how many animals there were, but the smell of blood was thick in the air and the few men who dared come near that battlefield were spattered in crimson.

As for the beasts who had chosen human prey ... with their strength, claws, and endurance they were five times as deadly as any equivalent human host would have been, and ten times more terrifying. Their powerful jaws cracked the shafts of the spears that were thrust through their flesh, and even the sharpened steel hooks of barbed spearheads that were left dangling from their flesh didn't slow them down. Their misshapen paws grasped at weapons with almost human dexterity, and jerked them out of the soldiers' hands with savage strength. They might have been devils for all that they acknowledged pain, and the worst of it all was that Andrys had no doubt that devils—true devils—would follow them. In one terrible instant the Forest had ceased to recognize him as its master, and now it was free to unleash all those horrors which it had been saving up since the moment they first violated its borders.

"Get together!" Zefila yelled, and somehow the order carried above the cacophony. Those men and women who were still standing began to fight their way toward each other, gathering together as herd beasts will do when surrounded by predators. Andrys struggled toward them, his own sword dripping a line of black blood along the ground, and relief washed over him as he got to the point where there was human flesh to put his back to, and sharp steel swords to protect his sides. Several of the soldiers had managed to take up their springbolts and now, with the protective efforts of their comrades buying them a precious second in which to aim, they launched their projectiles. Again and again, pausing only to reload from boxes at their feet, trusting to their brothers and sisters in battle to protect them as they did so. Bright quarrels bit into white fur, freeing blood as black as the night itself. A smell filled the clearing which was ten times more horrible than the rotting stink of the Forest, and Andrys felt bile rise up in the back of his throat with such revulsive power that for a moment he feared he would be overcome by it. Several of the soldiers were, and their comrades struggled to protect them while they doubled over, giving vent to their fear and their revulsion in a hot, fierce flow.

I'm going to die here, Andrys thought as he gouged one of the creatures with his sword; the creature leaped back with such force that it took everything he had to yank the weapon loose before it was pulled from his grasp. Was that Narilka's voice he heard, crying out his name in the midst of this madness? The delusion lent him strength, and he dared move forward far enough to stab at the creature's face. He didn't hit it himself, but in its effort to avoid him it impaled itself on another's spear. Good enough. *We're all going to die here.*

But the tide of battle was turning. The beasts who had feasted on horse flesh had left, carrying chunks of their booty away in blood-soaked jaws; their fellows were slowly losing ground. As their numbers diminished the humans spread out, extending their protective circle to include their fallen comrades. So many were dead, so many wounded . . . you couldn't look at them, Andrys discovered, or you'd stop fighting. You didn't dare think about what the battle had cost, or the sheer horror of it would paralyze you.

And then it was over. The last beast was dead, or dying, or fled into the night. Soldiers moved silently to slice each and every white-furred throat that remained, not wanting to be taken by surprise as they recovered the camp. Others moved quietly to where the fallen lay, and in a few corners of the battlefield soft weeping could be heard. That sound shook Andrys to his core. These were city folk, he realized, like himself, and for all their brave talk and macho posturing they had probably never seen more violence than a tavern brawl, or at best a temple riot. Nothing had prepared them for what they saw now. Nothing could.

Gerald Tarrant—you bastard!—you caused this! And so help me God, if I catch you, you'll pay for it. With a trembling hand he wiped blood from his eyes, hoping it wasn't his own. *First by my hand, and then in Hell.*

"You all right?"

It was Zefila. The blood smeared on her face was black, and it reeked of the beasts. He managed to nod and she turned away, evidently satisfied that he could take care of himself. Where had the Patriarch found a woman of such fortitude, he wondered? How had he known, when he interviewed hundreds for this quest, which ones would stand up to such horror?

The Patriarch. He started suddenly, aware that he hadn't seen the man since the battle started. Whipping about in sudden fright, he searched the battle-scarred campsite for him—and found him, to his relief, standing at the edge of the camp. His robes were spattered with blood and he seemed to be favoring his left leg, but he was alive. Thank God, Andrys thought. How could they have gone on without him?

"Bind up the wounded," Zefila ordered. "Get them on horseback, if the animals will have them. Move it! Those things may come back."

"What about the dead?" a woman demanded.

There was a pause. Several men stopped what they were doing, and all turned to look at the Patriarch. The cool blue eyes did not meet their gaze, but turned outward as if staring at some distant vista.

"We take them with us," he said at last. His tone was strangely bitter. "For as long as we have the horses to carry them." He looked over the battlefield, and his proud brow furrowed as if in pain. "Men who serve the One God with their lives deserve better than to rot in a place like this."

With a nod of approval, the man nearest him began to gather up the nearest body; others followed suit, handling the abandoned flesh of their fellow soldiers with a reverence that was born not only of love, but of fear. It could have been them. In another fight—perhaps in their next one—it might be.

The Patriarch walked slowly to where Andrys stood. His steps were heavy, as though he bore some great weight upon his shoulders. When he came within hearing, he said, very softly, "I shouldn't resent the time it will take, I suppose. Or remind myself that the flesh is but a shell, which has no real value once the spirit has abandoned it. Every minute we delay here puts us at greater risk, but the alternative. . . ." He shook his head in frustration. "It clouds too many futures. Fosters too many resentments. Let them do what comforts them."

He winced then, and reached out to a nearby tree for support. Andrys hesitated, then dared, "Are you all right?"

The Patriarch exhaled slowly. "I'm over seventy," he said at last. "Such exercise as this is hardly recommended at that age."

Then his sharp gaze fixed on Andrys, ice-blue, unwavering.

"You must help us," he said quietly.

Andrys felt his heart skip a beat. "I . . . I don't know what you mean."

"If the Forest is our enemy now, then it's only a matter of time before something else takes an interest in us. Judging from this experience . . ." He looked about the camp, his eyes narrow with foreboding. "We might survive another open assault, like this one, and persevere despite it . . . but not all the dangers of the Forest will be so obvious."

He remembered the sense he'd had of hungry things burrowing beneath the earth, and he nodded tightly.

"You have to find us a way through, Mer Tarrant. Either that—"

He drew in a sharp breath. "I can't—"

"—Either that, or we're doomed."

He opened his mouth to protest, but no sound came forth. Because the Patriarch was right, God damn it, and Andrys knew it. Shaking, the Prophet's descendant struggled to find courage within himself. There was so precious little of it to draw on! But they would all die if he failed them now, he knew that. And he would die as well. Not merely losing his life, as the others would do, but surrendering it to the very power he had come to destroy.

"How?" he whispered at last.

"I don't know," the Patriarch said quietly. "You tell me, Andrys Tarrant."

He was about to say something in response, but at that moment one of the supply officers came toward them, with a list of precious armaments lost in the struggle. As Andrys listened to the two of them discuss the amount of black powder lost with the horses, he felt a cold certainty crawl down his spine, to settle uncomfortably in his stomach. If the Forest were their enemy now, then there was only one thing to do. And only one man, he knew, who could attempt it.

He stared out into the Forest and shivered, sensing its power. Its hunger.

Only me.

He went to a far corner of the camp. It was as far as he dared go for privacy, while still being within the border of the light. Two soldiers flanked him silently, a man and a woman, and took up positions just out of his line of sight, but close enough to protect him if any new danger threatened. Respectful but determined: the man to whom they had sworn their fealty would not be allowed to die.

For a long time he just stood there, trying to work up enough courage to do what had to be done. His whole body was trembling. Was that the first manifestation of alcholic withdrawal, or a simple fear response? It frightened him that he could no longer tell the difference.

Calesta, help me.

It wasn't the first time he had prayed to his patron within the Forest, but this was the first time the demon didn't answer. That in itself was fresh cause for panic. While Calesta hadn't always answered his prayers in Jaggonath, it had been pretty clear that once this campaign was underway he would support Andrys. The thought that the demon might leave him on his own here was something so frightening he couldn't even consider it.

Calesta, he implored. *I need you!*

No answer.

Shaking inside, he drew in a deep breath and tried to steady himself. If the demon wasn't going to help him, then he would have to do this himself. There was no other option, right? People would die if he failed. *He* would die if he failed. Right?

Shivering, he shut his eyes and tried to clear his mind. It took no effort for him to establish contact with the Forest. The instant he stopped fighting to resist it, sensations slid into his brain, trees and birds and insects and microbes and even the earth itself—

Only it had changed. All of it.

He felt the trees throughout the Forest twitching, tension eating into their bark like acid. Hungry things that burrowed beneath the ground writhed blindly in their tunnels, unable to find their way to the surface. Sharp-toothed predators growled at their mates, and a white-furred scavenger ate her children while her packmates fell on one another in mindless rage. All throughout the Forest it was like that, fear and fury reigning where order had once held sway, and Andrys could feel the cause of it echo in his flesh: the loss and the shock and the pain of a wound that would never heal, a separation so unspeakable that the entire ecosystem reeled in despair.

He could feel his body staggering as he tried to absorb that knowledge and still maintain his own sense of identity. If he failed in that— even for a moment—he would never be able to return, he knew that. He struggled to establish some kind of focus, to narrow his senses in on the area surrounding the camp and the paths leading from it, in the hope of discovering . . . what? What did they want him to do?

You tell me, Andrys Tarrant.

He could feel the currents now, not just coursing about his feet but flowing through his very flesh. Chill currents, swift and powerful, they tugged at his body like a riptide and nearly pulled him off his feet. He could feel the earth-fae surging through the Forest, uniting all creatures within its confines even as it drew them inexorably toward the Center. Toward that place where the power was strongest, the earth-fae was deepest, the very heart of the region—

He felt his heart skip a beat, and for a moment nearly lost himself. How easy it would be to give in to that current, and let it sweep him toward the heart of the whirlpool! That was where all the energies of the Forest were focused, that was the heart and brain of Jahanna, and every living thing that drew strength from sorcery was drawn there, to commune with the Forest or to be devoured.

That was where the black keep would be.

Shaking, he forced the visions out of his brain. It took every ounce of his strength to do so, and even so he wasn't entirely successful. A faint echo of the Forest remained within him, as though somehow a seed of it had invaded his flesh. Dark and cold, he could feel it growing inside him, and he knew that if he nurtured it too much it would take root in him and flourish, until his own soul was strangled by it.

The Patriarch had come up beside him. He said nothing, waiting. For a long moment Andrys was silent, drawing strength from his presence.

Then, without looking at him, he said quietly. "I know the way."

For a moment there was no response. Then a firm, strong hand clasped his shoulder in silent support. It seemed to him that strength flowed through the contact, bolstering his own failing courage.

"It isn't easy to fight for one's soul," the Holy Father said. The hand remained a moment longer, then fell away. "I know that."

Something hard and cold touched his arm. He looked down, and to his astonishment saw the head of a silver flask. The sight of it shook him to his roots, and it took a moment before he could take the container from the Holy Father, a moment longer to uncap it.

Brandy. He savored its sweet smell like perfume, then tipped up the flask to drink from it. Alcohol burned in his throat as it went down, then spread out in warm waves from his stomach. One swallow. Two. Then he forced himself to put it down, even though his soul was screaming for more. He capped it, and handed it back to the Patriarch. His hands were no longer shaking as badly as they had been.

"You'll have to lead us," the Patriarch told him. "There's no other way."

He nodded. The older man clasped his shoulder once more, then turned away and left him. The two guards looked at him with half-veiled curiosity.

You'll have to lead us.

Warmed by the alcohol, Andrys Tarrant shivered.

Thirty-eight

Images cascading one into another, too fast and furious to separate. *Visions and sensations tangled together so tightly there is no way to pick one out from all the others, no means of absorbing the storm of images except as one chaotic whole.*

Stars.

Space.

Fire.

Blackness.

"What the vulk. . . ?" Damien's throat was raw and his lungs constricted from sulfur fumes. The words made it past his lips just long enough for him to hear them, then they, too, were drowned in a deluge of alien sensations.

Loss.

Despair.

Fear.

Desperation.

Oh, my children, my children. . . .

"Karril?"

No answer.

The ship hurtles through the blackness of space like a spark of life, its substance hot in the emptiness. Its walls are not flesh but a living equivalent, energies bound in the place of matter, the skin of a sentient creature that knows nothing of blood or of bone or even of material tools . . . but a creature nonetheless. Born for this mission, raised for it, trained for it, the creature-that-is-a-ship hurtles through the wasteland between the stars, her precious children gathered inside her. . . .

"Karril!"

Each child bred for a single purpose, focused and pure in its substance. One to read the stars and choose a course. One to gather up the thin energies of the void and make food from them. One to steer and one to record and one to dream and one—more precious than any other—to carry the patterns of inheritance of their race, so that when the time is right, a whole new world can be peopled with her children.

He had a spasm of coughing and for a moment the images scattered. His lungs were refusing to admit enough air. The images that reformed in his head when the spasm was done were swimming with black spots.

How fragile they are, her children, her crew! How they struggle to adapt to this new place, how they fight to serve her . . . all in vain. They were not made for this strange planet, where forces that have no name wreak havoc with every living process. First the seeker dies, and then the dreamer, and the gatherer, and so on through all their number. Child after child submitting in his turn, either to a natural death or to such mutation that she herself must kill them to keep the family pure.

The veil. It had fallen from his face, leaving him exposed to Shaitan's poisons. With a shaking hand he pushed it back into place, praying that it would ease the constriction of his lungs as well as protecting him from fresh assault. And it seemed to. Thank God, it seemed to.

The death of the breeder is the most devastating loss of all. Without his storehouse of reproductive patterns she will live out eternity on this hostile planet without hope, without purpose, her only comfort the memories that slowly fade as year fades into year, century into century. Periodically she wonders if it might not be more peaceful to follow them all into death, to end her suffering forever. But though the fantasy of suicide is tempting, it isn't really a choice for her. Like all her people she has been born for a purpose, and hers is to give life to others, not to take her own.

And then, when hope has been lost for so long that she's all but forgotten the flavor of it, she becomes aware of something new on the planet. Not a creature born to its hateful currents, but a stranger, like herself. A traveler. In joy she reaches out to it, to the thousands of individuals that make up its racial consciousness . . . and comes up with silence. Painful, hateful silence! The newcomers can't hear her. They lack the senses. The structure of their life is so different from her own that interface between them is all but impossible. Sur-

rounded by a host of creatures who would welcome her as a fellow explorer on this hostile planet, she is more alone than ever.

The images were all over him. Not only before his eyes, but in his brain as well. Images so alien that at first he could hardly interpret them, but one by one they sorted themselves out so that he could understand. And he trembled inside, as that understanding came.

She would try one last time. In the period before she came to this planet she had given birth to children who would serve her needs: she would do the same here, in order to reach these people. She had to wait long years for one to come close, for the place that best supported her own life was hostile to theirs. But at last one came, and she lifted the pattern of his soul from his flesh with a mother's sure skill, and used it to make a new kind of child. Half-breed, maverick, enough like her to understand her need, enough like this new species to communicate with it directly. Alas, though the theory was sound, the result was disappointing. Her first child was so like her that its father-species couldn't even see it. The second was the same. The third was apparent to them, but could find no common language with which to communicate. Again and again she tried, using those creatures that approached her resting place as templates for her experiments. She gave birth to children so like herself that they shared her own limitations, and to children so like their fathers that they lacked the ability to see her at all, and to dozens who had qualities of both, but never in the correct proportion. She gave them the ability to alter perception, so that they could bridge the vast conceptual gap between their parent races, but the ones who were strongest in that area had no real understanding of what she was, or why they had been born. Still she tried, over and over, each time new material made its way to her domain, hoping against hope that someday the right combination would be found. . . .

And it had been found, but not as she had imagined. Not in the soul of one child but in the presence of many, each one interpreting for the brothers most like him, taking her memories and her hopes and her fears and clothing them in a framework of alien understanding—of human *understanding—until at last, in the brain of a dying sorcerer, they were translated so that men might comprehend them—*

He pushed himself up onto his elbows and stared toward Shaitan's peak. The mother of the Iezu had completely enveloped Gerald Tarrant's body. Images played along her surface and throughout her substance, human and alien both. Stars, faces, mists and darkness, color and light and a thousand shapes without form or name. An attempt at some kind of visual language? Or perhaps simply the reflections of all the humans she had courted, as she plucked from each a single strand of consciousness to guide her procreative efforts.

He looked at Karril, kneeling by his side, and saw in the Iezu's expression such unadulterated shock that only one interpretation was possible. *He didn't know. None of them knew.*

"You're human," Damien whispered. The words made his throat burn.

The Iezu nodded slowly. "Half," he agreed, in a voice that trembled with awe. "And half . . ." He looked up at the mother. "Something else."

And then suddenly, with frightening clarity, Damien saw the last image again. This time the detail that had almost escaped him didn't.

. . . in the brain of a dying sorcerer . . .

He struggled to his knees; the motion set off a fit of coughing so violent that it almost knocked him down again. But that wasn't going to stop him. The living circuit the Iezu mother had described was clearly using a man's brain for its receiver, and since that wasn't him and there was only one other man present—

"He's alive?" He struggled to his feet as he gasped the question, and started to stagger toward Tarrant. "I felt him die!"

A hand grabbed his arm and pulled him back, roughly enough that he nearly fell. "And so he did. Does your kind never start up a man's heart once again, after it falters? Is the brink of death such an absolute place that no human soul is ever rescued from it?" Damien tried to pull loose from him, but the demon (no, not a demon, something strange and alien and terrible and wonderful, but not a demon) wouldn't let go. "Don't," Karril warned. "She saved him for her purposes, not yours. If you get in her way now, there's no telling what she'll do."

"So she can use him as a translating device? Is that her purpose?"

The Iezu shook his head. "She doesn't need him for that. Now that she understands the pattern, and her children know how to help her, any human will do."

"What, then?" He stared up at the mother's fluid form, trying to catch some glimpse of the man inside it. "What does she want him for?"

The Iezu turned his attention to the creature as well, and for a long moment said nothing. Damien saw that many of the other Iezu had gathered near the mother, as if to intensify their bond.

"She says that he killed her child." Karril found the words with effort; clearly the Iezu bond was less than a perfect translator. "She says that the right to do so is hers and hers alone, and not even an alien may take it from her."

"So she's punishing him? Is that it?"

But the Iezu shook his head. "Not punishing, exactly. More like . . . using him."

"For what?"

Karril hesitated. Damien could see his brow furrow in concentration as he struggled to find the proper words. "To replace what was destroyed," he said at last. "To make her family whole again."

To replace—?

Oh, my God.

Hundreds of men and women had come into this valley in past centuries, courting the wild power of Shaitan. From each she had taken one seed, one spark of consciousness, never realizing that a man was made up of a thousand such elements and her Iezu children inherited only one. What happened to those men? he wondered suddenly. Did Karril's human father leave this place in the same condition he had come to it, or did he leave behind him that capacity for pleasure which made human existence bearable? What would be left of Gerald Tarrant when the process of *replacement* was over?

As if in answer, the mother of the Iezu rose from Tarrant's body and withdrew to the lip of the crater. Damien had no eye for her, but made his way as quickly as he could to where the Hunter lay. *"Dying"* was the image the mother had chosen. Not *"alive,"* but *"dying."* That meant the man wasn't out of danger yet. Damien put a hand to Tarrant's face, and even through the silk veil he could feel its uncommon heat. Its *human* heat. *If he did die, even for an instant, then his compact is broken. He's free.* He put his hand above the man's mouth and felt, even though the silk, a thin stirring of breath. "You son of a bitch," he whispered hoarsely, "you're alive!"

The Hunter's eyes fluttered weakly open, and for a moment it looked as if he was going to say something typically dry in response. But then the strength left him and he shuddered and closed his eyes, never having made a sound.

"Karril!" He hauled Tarrant up by the shoulders until he was sitting upright, then wrapped one arm about him. Cinders that had fallen in his hair began to smoke as he cried out, "Help me get him out of here!"

For a moment Karril hesitated, and Damien wondered if he hadn't perhaps asked for more help than the Iezu could give. How solid was the body he wore, constructed of fae for convenience's sake and clad in an illusion of humanity? But then the Iezu began to climb, and when he reached Tarrant he went around to his other side, wrapping his arm about the man's torso so that together they could lift him. Clearly whatever served him for flesh was solid enough to function. Cinders smoked in their clothes and their hair as they struggled to carry the Hunter down from the deadly peak. Once Damien had to stop to beat out a burning spark that had taken hold of a fold of his shirt sleeve, and another time Karril called a halt in order to brush red-hot cinders from the Hunter's hair. Tarrant tried to help them by supporting his own weight, but the simple fact was that he was too weak to walk unaided.

At last, after a nightmare descent, they found shelter beside a cooled lava dome, a blister of rock whose position on the slope would protect them from the worst of the wind-borne ash. With a groan Damien lowered Tarrant to the ground so that his back was supported by the rocky protrusion, and then let go. The earth was trembling here, but it wasn't too warm, which was as good an omen as they were likely to get. There was, of course, no telling where Shaitan's fury would erupt next, and it could well be right beneath their feet . . . but that was such a mundane terror after all they had experienced that it had been strangely leached of power. With a sigh Damien lowered himself beside the Hunter, his legs throbbing with exhaustion as he stretched them out. How long had they been going without a real break now, ten hours, twelve? He rubbed a knot that was forming in his thigh, wincing as the tender flesh recoiled from the pressure. He wasn't going to make it much longer, that was certain. He squinted over toward the sun to get a sense of its position, then out at the Ridge. It seemed much closer to them than it had been before; Almea must have led them partway around the volcano's peak. Now they faced south, and the knife-edged mountain chain was close enough for him to make out details on its flank.

"There," he said, and he pointed in a direction where the ground seemed smooth and solid, where a clear path between the meandering acid streams could be determined. "We'll go that way."

"I don't think he's in shape to move."

Damien looked down at Tarrant, and for a moment was so lost in wonder that he could hardly concentrate on the issue at hand. There was sunlight falling across his face—sunlight!—seeping through the silk in bands of white to illuminate a face that had been in darkness for nearly a millenium. Sunlight glistened on the fine beads of sweat that were gathering on his forehead, and the skin beneath them was flushed with a hint of red, just like a living man's should be.

It hit him then, perhaps for the first time, just what had happened.

He had known the words before, but he hadn't felt their impact. Now he did.

God has given you a second chance, he thought in wonder, as he touched trembling fingers to the silk veil that protected Tarrant's face. *After so many centuries of evil that your soul must surely be black as jet.* He remembered the Binding that Tarrant had worked on Calesta, the horrific images of bloodlust and sadism that had risen up from the Hunter's core to overwhelm them both. That was all still inside the man, and it would take more than a single dose of sunlight to exorcise it. But now, for the first time, he was free to fight it. Now he was free to struggle against the accumulated corruption of his last nine hundred years, and reclaim his human soul. *God has given you a chance to redeem yourself. A second beginning.* "Don't you waste it," he whispered. The Hunter's eyes flickered open briefly, but he saw no comprehension in them. Finally he forced his gaze away, back to the path before them. "We can't stay here."

Karril nodded and moved to take up Tarrant's arm again, to support him. But Damien gestured for him to wait a minute. He pulled out his canteen from his pack, took a short drink—too short for comfort, but his supplies were running low—and then offered it to Tarrant. For a long minute the Hunter simply stared at it, and Damien wondered if he was too dazed to even realize what it was. But then he took it, his hand shaking slightly, and lifted it to his lips and drank. He seemed to wince as the water went down, but continued to drink nonetheless. *Thin stuff compared to what you're used to,* Damien thought dryly. He let him drink as much as he wanted, despite the dwindling supply, trusting to the man to know his own needs. At last Tarrant handed the canteen back to him, and it seemed to Damien that his grip was stronger than before. His pale eyes were open now, and glittered with something of their accustomed light. Even his breathing seemed less labored.

We're going to make it, Damien thought. Awed by the concept. *Both of us. We're going to get out of here alive, and make it back to the living world—*

Suddenly the ground heaved beneath them, as though something were stirring to life underneath it. "Time to move," Karril suggested, and Damien agreed. Hurriedly they caught up Tarrant again, helping him to his feet and then guiding him down the slope as fast as he could move. After a short distance Damien led them off to one side, so that if, God forbid, anything did come up out of the ground where they'd been sitting, they might stand a chance of not being hit by it. Down the slope they struggled, half walking, half sliding, and when they came to a smooth enough place they even forced Tarrant to a half-run, trying to cover as much ground as they could. Thank God, the Hunter seemed to be recovering his strength. And just in time. Thus far the wind had been in their favor, pushing the ash cloud east and north so that it didn't affect them, but Damien didn't want to bet his life on how long that would last. Down the slope they struggled, step by step, stumbling and sliding as the rocky ground became an avalanche of gravel, or as sections gave way entirely to reveal twisted gaps beneath the surface. At one point the ground split open behind them with a roar, venting a torrent of gases that Damien could smell even through his veil, and an avalanche of smoking rocks buried the path they been following mere moments before. Great. Just great. Here they had faced Hell and worse, vanquished the son of an alien life-form and rescued Tarrant from the ranks of the undead . . . all to be buried alive while they were on the way home? Not likely, he swore. Not if he could help it.

At last—finally!—the slope leveled off. The cracked surface of Shaitan gave way to the jagged monuments of her valley bed, and then—just when it seemed to Damien that he couldn't climb down another foot—to level ground. They stopped ever so briefly to take another sip of water, and Damien pressed a bit of food into Tarrant's hand, but he didn't want to stop even long enough to make sure that the adept ate it. There were shadows of the dead here, hungry for the pain of the living, and without Tarrant's help he knew he didn't stand a chance against them. He chewed his own portion as they started forward again, and prayed that Tarrant's body still remembered how to digest such solid nourishment.

Moving as quickly as they could, they made their way across the valley floor. The mists were thinner in this place and few shadows even noticed them. The very closeness of the ridge—so near that they could make out a few malformed trees on its flank—lent them a last burst of strength, past the point when their bodies might normally have failed them. *Just this one last hike,* Damien promised himself, *and then it's all over. You can make camp on the ridge somewhere and get some real sleep, and tomorrow you can head back and start your life over.* The thought of untroubled sleep was so enticing that for a moment he could think of nothing else, that sweet physical surrender as darkness and peace closed in around him, the sure caress of dreams. . . . He looked up sharply at Karril, who refused to meet his eyes. *Shit. I guess we all have to eat, right?*

By the time they finally reached the far side of the valley, the sun was well overhead, and the Core also. Their light had been so wholly eclipsed by Shaitan's ash-cloud that an eerie pseudo-night had fallen across the valley, blood red shadows sculpting rocky promontories in sharp relief. Tarrant was still walking, although his pace and his posture warned that his newfound strength was near to giving out. But they were going to make it, Damien thought feverishly. They were really going to make it.

Sleep. It beckoned to him from the slope up ahead, from that place where the mists of the valley gave way to the cold winds of the Ridge. That place where no lava could reach them, no demons would follow them, nothing and no one would disturb their peace. It seemed almost heaven compared to their recent travels, and he struggled toward it with all the energy he could muster. How long now since they had last rested, or eaten a real meal, or even paused to get their bearings? Incredibly, Tarrant kept going, and Damien didn't want to know whether the man's strength was genuinely improving or whether it was simply desperation that drove him. Some things were better left unquestioned.

And then they were there at last, high enough on the rocky slope to be safe. Damien remained standing just long enough to wrestle his pack off his back and remove his sword harness, then fell to the earth in exhaustion, Tarrant doing the same by his side. Never mind that the ground was sharp and uneven, and their flesh was bruised from the day's events. He was alive. Tarrant was alive! And as for the few threats remaining . . .

"I'll keep watch," the Iezu promised, and he nodded. Good. Yes. That would do it.

We made it, he thought. Numbed by the concept. *We really made it. We're going to live.*

And then sheer exhaustion closed in around him and all of it—the hope, the fear, the jubilation—gave way to darkness.

"Damien."

He was so sore it seemed he could hardly move. Someone was shaking him and it hurt. For a moment he cursed and tried to push the troublesome hands away, but they disappeared when he grabbed at them and reappeared elsewhere.

"Damien. I'm sorry. You need to get up."

Damn. Damn. What was it now? He forced his eyes to open, and discovered that even his eyelids hurt. There wasn't a part of his body that didn't pain him, and that included his bladder. Clearly he had slept longer than certain bodily processes would have liked. "Karril? What the hell is it?"

When the Iezu saw he was awake, he leaned back on his heels, letting him get up at his own pace. "It's Tarrant," he warned. "Something's wrong."

Shit. He forced himself up to a sitting position, despite the complaints from all muscles involved. *Not now, not after all we've gone through!* "What is it?"

"I don't know. I'm afraid—" He stopped himself then, as if he was afraid that by saying the wrong thing he might make the matter worse. "You're the Healer."

He crawled over to where Tarrant lay. Like himself the Hunter had wound up sprawled across the rocky ground with his head upslope, the only position in which one could sleep without tumbling down the steeply canted slope. Even as he approached, Damien could see that the man's breathing was labored, and his color looked bad, very bad. A day ago it wouldn't have mattered, that ghastly pallor. Now it was a sign that Death was tightening its grip on the one man arrogant enough to defy it.

"What is it?" Karril demanded.

Damien raised up his veil a bit, braced himself, and drew in a deep breath. Nothing happened. Reassured that they were now above the level of Shaitan's poisons, he freed Tarrant from his silken cocoon and watched as the man drew in short breaths, too quick and too shallow. He didn't have to hear the faint wheezing sound at the end of each one to know what was wrong, or see the fear in Tarrant's eyes to know just how wrong it was. The Prophet's color—and his medical history—made that all too clear.

"Damn," he whispered. "Not now, God. Couldn't you let us get home first?"

"What is it?"

"Heart attack." He could see Tarrant flinch as he spoke the words. "Or heart failure, more likely. He had the first incident right before he died, we know that." *And it drove him over the brink of sanity, so that he murdered his family and ransomed his own soul to the Unnamed. Must this end the same way, God? Have you no better purpose for him than that?* "Where's the cause?" he demanded of Tarrant. "Do you know? Did you try to fix it?"

The Hunter shook his head weakly. "Doesn't matter," he whispered. "You can't Heal here."

"Just tell me, damn you!"

He shut his eyes and trembled: it was clear that every word took effort. "Congenital damage to the arterial wall," he whispered. "Mitral valve . . ." He was struggling for each breath now, and Damien could hear the rasping wheeze behind each one. "Acquired. I tried. . . ."

When it was clear that he had lost the strength for further speech, Karril dared, "Can you do something?"

What was he supposed to say? That there was nothing harder than Healing a beating heart, because if your every effort wasn't perfectly attuned to that muscle's natural rhythm, you could bring it to a halt altogether? That was all irrelevant anyway, wasn't it? Damien couldn't Heal here. The currents would fry him alive before he even got started.

Think man, think. There had to be a way. He hadn't come this far to give up now. What tools were available to him? Tarrant was too weak to Work. He couldn't do it with this much fae around. The Iezu—

He drew in a sharp breath as it all came together. "Karril. Your kind can work with the fae, can't it?"

The Iezu hesitated. "Not as you do. We can't Work—"

"I know that! Sorcery's not what I meant." He struggled to find the proper words. "You can mold it, can't you? Like you did to make a body." He looked pointedly at the flesh Karril now wore, which he had used to support Gerald Tarrant. "I mean as a purely physical force. Can't you do that?"

The Iezu nodded.

"Can you block it off? Divert its flow, maybe?" The Iezu looked dubious. "Anything, Karril! The currents here are too strong for me to Heal with. Is there any way you can help? If not—" and he nodded toward Tarrant, "—he'll die."

The Iezu drew in a deep breath, deliberately melodramatic. "I can try," he said at last. "Although I can't promise—"

"Just do it!" Damien snapped. The Hunter's lips were faintly blue: a bad, bad sign. "And hurry!"

The Iezu disappeared. Not fading slowly, as he normally did, but snuffed out like a candle flame in a wind. Apparently to manipulate the fae he had to be in his natural form . . . whatever the hell that was. *Doesn't matter,* Damien thought grimly. *Whatever works.* He sat down by Tarrant's side and gripped the man's shoulder in reassurance. "You're not going to die," he whispered. "Not after all I went through to bring you here. You're going home, dammit." And then he saw the Hunter's eyes widen in surprise, and he knew by that sign that the currents had changed. For the better, he prayed, as he prepared himself for Working. If not, they would both be dead soon enough.

With a deep breath for courage he reached down into the currents, grasping hold of Shaitan's power—

Or rather, tried to. But there was nothing there. Had Karril failed him? Again he reached out with his mind, in the manner he had been taught, and again he utterly failed to make contact. But this time there was something there. A faint slithering of power, just enough to confirm that the currents were active. There was enough fae coursing around Tarrant's body to Heal him, but Damien couldn't seem to access it.

What the hell was wrong?

Again and again he tried, until a hot sweat broke out across his skin from the strain of his efforts. But the fae was like a wriggling eel, that slithered out of his mental grasp each time he tried to close in on it. Beside him Tarrant was gasping for breath, and his lips and eyes were shadowed with a deathly blue tint; he clearly didn't have much time left. Again Damien tried to tackle the elusive earth-power, pouring everything he had into the effort. And for an instant he seemed to make real contact with it. For an instant he could taste what was wrong, and though he didn't know its cause, the result was all too clear. The fae could be Worked, all right, but at a terrible price to the Worker. Was Damien Vryce willing to risk death to do this Healing, or was his own survival too precious for him to make such a commitment? He looked down at Tarrant, so very close to the gateway of death himself that his skin had taken on the color of a corpse, and felt an upwelling of cold determination in that place where the heat of fear might have taken root. *You were willing to give up your life on Shaitan to save mankind from Calesta. You were willing to face Hell for that. I can't let you die now, at the very threshold of salvation. I can't rob you of the chance to make your peace with God at last . . . not even to save my own skin.*

—And the fae roared into him, currents ten times more hot than any he had Worked before. For a moment it was all he could do not to drown in it, not to lose himself in the raging flow. Then, at last, he managed to take hold of it with his will and give it form. A Seeing. A Knowing. The tools he needed to see into Tarrant's flesh, to analyze it, to alter. . . .

The Hunter's heart took shape before him—no, *about* him—red muscle pounding out a feverish rhythm, a living sea that throbbed about his head as the spasms that drove it pulsed more and more desperately. He struggled to concentrate on the task at hand, and not let the hot sea sweep him away. *Mitral valve,* Tarrant had said. Damien searched for it, found it, and Knew it. The thin flap of tissue had thickened across most of its surface, and as he watched it struggle to close time and time again, he could see how the damage crippled it, how its failure to seal completely allowed blood to flow back the way it had come. That was his immediate target, clearly. He focused in his Knowing until he could see the individual cells of the valve itself, trying to judge the extent of the damage. It was indeed acquired, as Tarrant had said, which was a promising sign; beneath the thick layer of scar tissue was a valve that might do its work properly, if given half a chance.

Aware that every second counted, that even as he Worked in this scarlet realm its owner was dying, Damien nonetheless took a few precious moments to acquaint himself with the rhythm of the laboring heart muscle. Slowly, with a surgeon's fine precision, he began to pry away the damaged cells. Not too quickly, lest a bit of coherent flesh tear loose and provide deadly blockage in some lesser vein . . . but not too slowly either, lest the Hunter expire even as he Worked. Carefully but quickly he struggled to establish a middle ground, knowing that his every move had to be perfectly attuned to the heart's own rhythm or deadly fibrillations would set in. One clump of cells dissolved into the bloodstream, then another, then another. He struggled to break up the scar tissue into manageable bits, while all the while riding the motion of the valve as if he were part of it. Thank God the tissue underneath was sound, he thought. He could see it swaying in the red sea as he freed it up, graceful and fluid in its natural motion. And it was almost free now. He reached out with his Healing to dissolve the last piece of scar tissue, saw its cells swept away by the hot scarlet tide . . . and it was done. The valve was closing properly once more, and the heart was slowly calming. He allowed himself a moment of pure relief, knowing the worst was over. But there was still the congenital damage to be dealt with, which had caused the buildup in the first place. What had Tarrant said, something about an arterial wall? He searched for the damage and found it, a segment of muscle malformed in its making, whose thickened bulk cut short the flow of blood to vital areas. Unlike the scar tissue on the mitral valve, this was intrinsic to the muscle itself, and its removal would leave a gaping hole in a very dangerous place. Briefly he wished for a companion Healer with whom he could coordinate his efforts. And then, that futile prayer voiced, he plunged himself into the damaged flesh. Not just cutting loose this time but healing as well, forcing the surrounding cells to regenerate—and to do so properly—even as he cut the mutated part away. Shaving down the damaged tissue into small enough bits that the body could dispose of it safely, even as he forced its replacement. It seemed to take him forever, but at last that, too, was done.

For a short while he rested, his Vision maintained, watching as the whole system beat more perfectly than it had since its original creation. Then, when he felt his strength was up to it, he fashioned a diuretic out of the materials at hand and set that loose in the bloodstream, making sure that any waste products he created in the process would be safely expelled. And then, at last, it was time to withdraw. It wasn't without fear that he let his Knowing fade, and his Seeing, and all those other tools which he had conjured. He had been willing to die to Heal Tarrant; must that vow now be fulfilled? But there was no dark power waiting to devour him as he withdrew his senses from Tarrant's flesh, and nothing felt any different about his own body or its attendant consciousness. Unless it was the sudden need to urinate. That was pretty urgent. With a muttered curse he got to his feet and walked a few feet away, to where a sharp overhang looked out over the valley. Good enough. He added his bodily excretions to the realm of the dead, and then turned back to look at Tarrant.

The man was sitting up, albeit weakly, and already his color looked better. His breathing sounded labored but not nearly so bad as before, and Damien had faith that the diuretic he had created would dry his lungs out in short order. There had been no lasting damage to the heart muscle itself, which meant that as soon as his condition stabilized, he should be as good as new. Whatever the hell that meant.

"It seems," the Hunter whispered hoarsely, "that I owe you once again."

"Yeah." He shrugged off what promised to be an awkward expression of gratitude. "And you took me traveling to new and exciting places. Let's just call it even, okay?"

But there was a dark edge to Tarrant's expression that warned him something was seriously wrong. For a moment—just a moment—he wished he wouldn't tell him what it was. "I tried to watch you Heal," the Hunter said quietly. "I couldn't."

He shrugged. "You were in pretty bad shape. What did you expect?"

"That shouldn't have stopped me," the adept insisted. "I've Worked during worse." His voice was low, and tinged with fear. "Something's *wrong*, Vryce."

His first instinct was to dismiss that thought and any similar fears as a symptom of Tarrant's condition. It was a known fact that heart failure tended to bring on a sense of dread in its victims, and while that emotion normally focused on the event itself, there was no reason why it couldn't spill over into other areas. There was also a possibility that the adept had simply met his limit, and was so drained by his condition that not even Working was possible. That last was the most appealing explanation, and he tried hard to believe it. But honesty forced him to remember how much trouble he'd had accessing the fae for his own Working, and the feeling he'd had at the time that using the fae might cost him his life. "Maybe it's just the currents in this place," he offered. But he knew even as he spoke that it had to be something more.

The Hunter shook his head sharply. "The currents may be stronger here, but earth-fae is earth-fae. And I tried other Workings while you were busy." He nodded toward the overhang. "None had any effect at all. I've Worked the fae for nearly a thousand years, Vryce, and it never failed to respond like that. Yet *you* Worked it," he said; the words were almost an accusation.

"Yeah. Barely." He turned away, not wanting to meet Tarrant's eyes. That was one experience he didn't feel like sharing. "I'm not sure I could do it again." *Not unless I really wanted to,* he thought. *Not unless I was willing to pay a hell of a price for it.* "You may be right," he admitted. "But if so, then what—"

Tarrant began to shift position as he spoke, but a sudden spasm turned his words into a groan. It took no magician to know what that meant; Damien had been expecting it. "I Worked a diuretic to drain your lungs," Damien told him, "so you'll be voiding excess fluid pretty steadily for a while. May I recommend the view over that way?" He indicated the overhang, then couldn't resist adding, "You do remember how to piss, I assume?"

With a wordless glare the Hunter got to his feet and headed toward the scenic spot. Damien watched him for a moment, then—when he was satisfied that he was steady enough on his feet not to go tumbling down the mountainside—he looked at Karril. "Well?"

"Well what?"

"Your kind can see the fae, can't it? So I assume you saw what happened. Any guesses?"

"I was quite involved with my own assignment, thank you very much. You were the one who didn't want to be drowned in the local power, remember?—But yes, I saw what happened. And it was . . ." He hesitated. "Strange."

"In what way?"

"The fae responds naturally to humans, you know that. Every human thought, every dream, even a man's passing fancy will leave its mark on that power. Oh, sometimes there's no more than a quiver in the current—hardly enough to affect the material world—but the response is always there. *Always.* Except when you tried to Work before," he told Damien. "When you first tried to Heal Tarrant, there was no response at all. And he's trying to Work right now—" he looked pointedly at Tarrant, "—and it's the same as it was with you. No response at all."

Tarrant's concentration was focused on the ground at his feet, and he was clearly trying to mold the local currents to his will. His brow had tightened into a hard line. His eyes were narrowed to slits. He even cursed, perhaps the first time that Damien had ever heard him do so. Clearly, his chosen tests had failed.

With one last glance at the ruddy sunset to the west of them (and Damien didn't have to be psychic to know how much Tarrant wanted to study it longer, his first sight of the sun in over nine centuries) the adept rejoined them. "Something's changed, no doubt about it." His tone and his expression were both grim. "I can't tell for certain what happened without some more specific tests, but I don't think either you or I should count on being able to Work until we get out of here. Once we get back, I can figure out what happened, and hopefully discover a way to work around it."

Hopefully. There was a stress on that word, ever so subtle, which underscored a fear neither man would voice. If something had changed in the currents, what if that change were permanent? What if it turned out to be a problem not with the fae, but with them?

And then the other words hit him. So casually voiced, but they resounded in his brain all the more powerfully for their lack of emphasis. *Once we get back.* Such a simple, disarming phrase! As if *getting back* were something they had always expected to do. As if they hadn't thought they would die on this journey, and thus had made no plans for ever going home. Damien felt his heart lurch as he acknowledged that the possibility was suddenly very real. Tarrant was alive. The enemy they thought they could never vanquish was dead and gone. They were going home. . . .

Focus on that, he thought. Not the other thing. That was too terrifying to face, and they weren't likely to come up with answers until Tarrant had the strength and the leisure to investigate the matter. He forced himself to turn to Karril and he asked, "Will you come with us?" Not only because the Iezu would be a valuable guide in this land—doubly valuable if they really couldn't Work—but because, at that moment, Karril was part and parcel of their triumph, and he wanted him there.

The Iezu looked at Tarrant, and something unspoken seemed to pass between them. At last he shook his head. "I can't. I'm sorry. My family . . ." He gazed out into the valley, toward Shaitan, where the other Iezu gathered. "There are so many questions to be answered now. My place is with them for as long as I can stay here." He looked back at Tarrant, as if expecting him to say something, but the Hunter remained silent. "I'm sorry," he said again. "But you really don't need me now."

"I understand," Damien assured him. He turned to Tarrant, but the Hunter's eyes were fixed on Shaitan. "We can stay here a while if you think you need more rest, but we're low on supplies, so it can't be too long. You tell me." When Tarrant said nothing, he pressed, "Ready to go home yet?"

"Do what you think is best," the Hunter said quietly.

He knew that tone of voice. God damn it, he knew it all too well. He knew what it meant when the Hunter shifted from the plural pronoun to the singular, too, and damn it to Hell! This wasn't the place for that kind of game, or the time for it, or . . . or anything!

"We're going home, right?" His tone was half plea, half growl. "Calesta's dead. The Forest's so far gone by now that you can't change what happens there one way or the other. Right? The whole goddamn world's at peace and I didn't figure we'd both still be part of it, so I don't have the kind of food and water it would take for two people to go off and do something stupid. Whatever that stupid thing happened to be. —Are you listening to me, Gerald?"

The adept's eyes remained fixed on Shaitan, as if something there were so fascinating he dared not turn away even for a moment. "She's a *starfarer*," he breathed. "Not just the descendant of an alien species stranded on this world—like we are—but an individual born and bred on another planet, with memories of foreign stars and the technology needed to get to them." At last he turned away from that view and faced Damien again. "What was the point of all my work, if not to give us the stars? Why have men rallied to the Church's banner for the past thousand years, if not for that dream?" He turned back to Shaitan and inhaled deeply, as if tasting its potential in the air. "This place is a gateway. This creature, this mother of aliens . . . is mankind's future. Her technology may be too alien for us to use directly, but perhaps between us we can forge something that will serve both species."

"And her children will, no doubt, be happy to act as go-betweens to—" He saw the quick look that passed between Tarrant and Karril and felt something tighten in his gut. "What is it? What's wrong with that?"

Karril said quietly, "We can't stay here."

Tarrant nodded. "The Iezu were bred to interact with humans, and must do so for their own survival. There's no food here to sustain them, nor anything else that they require. And even if they could stay, what would become of the temples they're nurtured, the cults that have declared them gods, the human symbionts they must support? Oh, some of them will remain here for a time, but will those few be enough? When will the critical mass of this gathering be weakened enough that the mother's voice loses its coherency, and humanity loses its most valuable ally?"

Speechless, Damien turned to Karril for support. But the Iezu only nodded sadly, as if to say, *Yes, he's right. It's only a matter of time.* "So what?" he demanded. "You're going to stay here? There's no food here for you either, Gerald, do I have to remind you of that? And what the hell are you going to do for them, anyway?"

"I'm not going to stay," he said quietly.

He forced himself to breathe in deeply. "Well. That's something, anyway."

"Humanity will need a means of translation. So will the Iezu for that matter, at least the ones most human in aspect."

"So what do you propose to do? Work some kind of translating pattern? You know that's impossible right now. You said yourself that until you had a chance to test the currents you wouldn't know why they had failed to respond to us, much less be able to Work them again. So what then?"

"A Working isn't what's needed now. Not as much as a sound understanding of who and what the Iezu are, and how their mother's need was expressed through each of them. They are her true language, Vryce, her cries of desperation rendered in fae and flesh. What form did each one first appear in? What pattern did their learning take?" He looked at Karril. "At what point did they first express emotions outside of their aspect, and what prompted that change?"

"You're talking about a complete family history," Damien challenged. "Going back—what—nearly a thousand years?"

"Nearly that," Karril agreed.

"No one's going to have that kind of information just sitting around. If you want those kinds of facts, you'll have to do research, and for that you need to go back to where there are people and libraries and loremasters to help you." Ciani had kept notes on everything, he remembered suddenly. Perhaps other adepts did the same. "We can look for some sorcerer who specializes in demon lore—"

And then it hit him. Just like that. One moment blissful ignorance, and the next, stunning truth. "Shit," he whispered. "No."

Tarrant said quietly. "I'm afraid so."

"There's a *war* on in the Forest. Have you forgotten that? More enemies than you can count, all focused on your destruction—"

"And they mean to burn the Forest to the ground when they're done, and all my possessions along with it. Which means that in a few days' time my notebooks will be ash, and the Iezu's history lost forever."

"We can work a Remembering—" he began.

And then he remembered what the fae was like now. How hard it was to Work. And he knew that they dared not count on being able to use it in the future, not for a matter this complex.

"Shit," he muttered. "Shit."

"I told you I have a tunnel, Vryce. It comes in under my keep, to a chamber so well warded that even if my enemies gain access to the building itself, they will never find its entrance. We'll come in and take what we want and be gone again before the Church ever realizes we're there, I promise you."

"And do you know for a fact that your wards still work?" he demanded. "Have you thought of that?"

"I tested one which I carry, and its effect is unchanged. Apparently past Workings still maintain their power." His pale eyes glittered redly in the dying sunlight; even without the fae his gaze had tremendous power. "So what do you say, Vryce? Must I go there alone? Because with or without you, I cannot allow those notes to burn. Too much of mankind's future depends on them."

Shit.

He turned away from them both, struggling to think it out clearly. The last thing he needed now was a trek to the Forest, least of all while the Patriarch and his soldiers were tearing the place apart. The last thing Tarrant needed now was a fresh exertion, when his newly healed flesh was still struggling with the transition from undeath to life. The last thing anyone here needed was to risk all that they had won for a handful of books—*books,* God damn it! Even if those books were the key to humanity's future, and that of the Iezu. Even if those books might allow both species to return to the stars.

Shit.

He raised a hand to his head and rubbed his temples wearily. He didn't have a headache yet, but one was surely on the way. The body had to do something to protest such utter lunacy.

It's safe, right? Doors locked and warded. Books safely hidden. One quick visit and then it's all over. And Tarrant would go with or without him, that much was clear. Did Damien want that newborn soul running head-on into the Patriarch's troops without someone there to support him? Such a confrontation could well send him spiraling down into darkness again. And after all the time and effort he had put into saving the man, he could hardly allow that. Could he?

"All right," he muttered. Sighing heavily. "What the hell. Let's do it."

Tarrant nodded. "I thought you might feel that way." He sounded relieved, Damien thought. As well he should.

It could be worse. At least we don't have to get on a boat again.

Shaitan rumbled in the distance.

Thirty-nine

Calesta was gone.

At first Andrys tried to deny it. He told himself a hundred reasons why the demon might be unwilling to respond to him, or unable to respond to him, and he managed to half-believe one or two. But then, as hours passed and his desperate entreaties brought no response, fear began to take hold. He fought the emotion off as long as he could, but now, hours later—days later, perhaps, who could judge time in this place?—certainty set in, and with it a dread so cold that he shivered inside his blood-spattered armor, not knowing how he could go on.

Calesta was gone, without question.

Andrys was on his own.

They were forging through a hostile Forest now, and every turn held new threats. More than once they were attacked by creatures that called the Forest their home, and if thus far those assailants were too few or too weak to pose any real danger, that was just the luck of the draw. The next time they were attacked it might be the white pack again . . . or worse.

More than half the horses had been lost in that battle, either killed or maimed or run off in terror. The tethers of those that fled had been burned through in some cases, cut through cleanly in others, as if somehow their fear had managed an equine Working and freed them. More likely it was the fears of their riders which had done exactly that. Before they left the battle site the Patriarch had led them in prayer for a few minutes, trying to focus their energies in a positive manner, but how much good was that going to do? In the back of all their minds was a new awareness of the power of the Forest's fae, and a growing fear that it would betray them. What happened to tethers could just as easily happen to explosives.

A good portion of the remaining horses were now carrying the wounded, with the result that all had to take their turn at walking. Andrys preferred it. His role as pathfinder required continued sensitivity to the Forest's fae, a terrifying immersion in its power; he used the act of walking as a focus for his sanity, the pain of his blistered feet as an anchor to the world of solid things. Though the Hunter was no longer actively mated to the Forest, yet his essence still permeated it, and if the younger Tarrant relaxed his guard even for an instant, the chill power of that corrupt soul would come pouring into him, drowning out the warmth of his living spirit and replacing it with something in its own dark image. Step by step he fought its influence, but despair was growing inside him. How long could he keep this up, without some kind of assistance? What hope did he have of coming out of this sane, if Calesta had truly abandoned him?

His only comfort lay in a black silk scarf, now wound about his waist beneath the armor. *Her* scarf. He still felt shame about stealing it from her and, in fact, had tried to bring himself to ask for it on at least three separate occasions, but each time his courage had failed him. Was he afraid she would withhold such a gift? That she would laugh at him for wanting it? Or was it that putting such a request into words would be as good as admitting that he lacked the strength within himself to succeed in this mission without such a token? Now that scarf was his only comfort, and the sweat-soaked silk tugged at his waist with every movement, reminding him of the brief time they had spent together.

Hour after hour, mile by mile, they fought their way through the Hunter's domain. Even the plant life seemed determined to resist them now, and more than once they had to hack their way through a tangle of thorn bushes and tree limbs in order to move forward. It hadn't been like that before, Andrys noted. When they stopped for a meal and the ground began to stir beneath their feet, forcing them to move on, that was new, too. Clearly whatever power he had provided as the company's talisman was at an end, now that the Hunter was no longer in control here. And that was a terrifying thought indeed.

They broke march three more times to water the horses and see to their own bodily needs—always in rocky areas, where the underground scavengers couldn't reach them—and once to rest in short shifts, restless and fearful. Try as he might, Andrys couldn't sleep; he wondered how many could. These weren't soldiers, trained to pursue combat in the face of enervating exhaustion, but simple men and women whose concept of exertion before today was a short stint in a gym, followed by a hot bath and dinner. Not this.

His own strength was wearing thin from exhaustion, and his nerves, continually stretched to the breaking point, were beginning to give way at last. How much longer could he last?

Calesta, help me! I can't make it alone. I'm not strong enough.

No answer.

Rats. There were rats. She could hear them scrabbling in the darkness, searching for food along the muddy floor. Periodically one would come up to her to see if she was food. Sharp teeth would nip her skin and she would kick out wildly, hysterically, and maybe she hurt it or maybe it just went away. For a while. They all came back.

She didn't know how long she had been in this place. It was long enough for her to have crawled along the length and breadth of her prison and explored with her fingers every inch of its surface. The walls were of roughly carved stone, wet with slime, and the muddy water that pooled on the floor was ankle-deep in places, barely a film in others. There was no sign of a door that she could make out, and as for the soft lumps she landed on as she moved, several of which squirmed underfoot . . . she'd rather not know.

She was hungry now, so hungry that even her terror had weakened, and though her mouth was parched, she dared not drink from the water that was available, or even lick the moisture that clung to the wall by her side. She had wept until she had no more strength left with which to weep, and now she curled up in the dank puddle, shivering, and tried to accept her fate.

Oh, Andrys. . . .

She'd only wanted to help him. She would have done anything to accomplish that, would willingly have accepted any fate in order to make his burden easier. But now she was here and he was gods knew where and every time she dozed off from exhaustion, something sharp or slimy would crawl across her and she would start slapping it away hysterically before sleep had even fully released her—

It was just a nightmare, she told herself. Some nightmares happened while you dreamed and some happened while you were awake, but they all ended sometime, right? She licked at her lips with a dry tongue, wondering how long she would last. Was this all the white man had wanted her for, to waste away in this foul pit without even knowing where she was? Was he feeding on her de-

spair, or on some other part of her emotional substance? She wouldn't give him that pleasure, she decided. For as long as she had the strength to dream, she would relive memories of life, and of love. She would fantasize about Andrys Tarrant until his image was so set in her brain that even in her last moments, even while the rats and lizards gnawed at her dying flesh, her soul would still be joyful. Let that albino bastard feed on her love if he wanted to; it would probably give him heartburn.

Something stirred overhead, where there had been no motion during all her imprisonment. She sat up weakly, bracing herself against the slimy wall. There was a scraping noise and then it seemed to her that something moved. There was a line of darkness forming that was less black than that which surrounded, dim and insubstantial, but yes, it might even be called light. She blinked hard as she stared at it, not quite believing.

"Time to come out." It was the white man's voice, no longer wholly human but a strange gurgling sound; she had trouble making out the words. Something came down from the darkness and splashed to the floor by her side. She reached out a tentative hand to see what it was, and felt a smooth wooden shaft pointing upward. A ladder. He had lowered a ladder.

"Up," he growled. "Now!"

Narilka hesitated. Whatever was waiting for her up that ladder could be even worse than her current misery, which she had almost come to terms with. She remembered the foul breath of his pack, the pain of their teeth in her flesh. No. Better the darkness than that.

When he saw that she wasn't moving, he howled in fury, a sound more animal than human. She heard scrabbling as his beasts ran toward him, and with a sick feeling in her heart she realized that the things she feared most might simply come down into the darkness and drag her out; her obstinacy would gain her nothing. Slowly, her hands shaking, she forced herself to climb. The creatures up ahead of her were growling, and the white man also. When her head cleared the opening, he reached out and grabbed her long hair, hauling her up by it. Stars of pain danced behind her eyes.

"I need you," he hissed. His hand tangled in her muddy hair, savagely pulling her head back. "Don't fight me. I'll let them eat you if you do, you understand me? I'll hurt you!"

She didn't have the strength to nod. She couldn't summon the voice to answer.

Snarling, he dragged her away.

The flat Forest earth gave way to rocky ground, to the gentle slope of hills, to the steep incline of a mountainside. That was a good sign, the Patriarch told them. Vryce's notes made it clear that the Hunter's keep was in the mountains, therefore they were headed in the right direction.

Then there came a point at which the horses could no longer manage the steep climb, and had to be left behind. Given the choice between staying with them or making the climb with their company, the wounded chose to struggle onward. Andrys didn't blame them. In a place this hostile, where the darkness might erupt with new dangers at any moment, a handful of wounded men and women wouldn't stand a chance by themselves.

The dead were unloaded and buried in a makeshift cairn. It seemed a waste of time to Andrys. Didn't the Church teach that dead flesh was only an empty shell? Wouldn't their companions want them to hurry on their way, rather than risk a delay to attend to such a meaningless ritual? But once more, the Patriarch insisted. To leave the dead unhonored now would "poison too many futures," he said. Whatever the hell that meant.

They climbed. Bearing their supplies upon their backs, foodstuffs and explosives lashed side by side. Upward they climbed, higher and higher, tramping out a switchback path along the rocky slope. At times the way was so steep that they had to cling to the very vines which meant to hinder them, and men who failed to get a handhold slid back two steps for every one they gained. Andry's wounds burned like fire, but he was willing to bet that was nothing compared to the Patriarch's own pain, or that of the other wounded soldiers. The currents had become so powerful that he could hear them now without even trying; their roar drowned out all other sounds, making speech impossible. So strong was the pull on his flesh that he had to fight step by step not to be dragged down to the earth, where its power—and Gerald Tarrant's—could drown him. How much longer could he hold on?

At last the ground leveled out a bit. Andrys leaned against a tree to catch his breath, then jerked back violently as a serpent hissed mere inches from his face. Did this damned place never let up? One by one his companions joined him, and though none dared to say it, clearly all hoped that the worst of the climb was over. They were carrying not only their supplies and their weapons, but a share of the equipment which had been on the horses, and that load on their backs made every step hurt tenfold.

Now, he sensed, the enemy was near. Whatever dark power had been trying to stop them, whatever creature now sat at the heart of the Forest and wove black webs of hate to entrap the living, it was here, right before them. He could taste its presence in his mouth, bitter and repulsive. He could smell it on the wind, a stink so foul that several men and women had wrapped scarves about their noses and mouths in the desperate hope of keeping it out. He could hear it echoing in his brain, a presence so unclean that the Hunter's own power seemed pristine by comparison.

There was a ridge ahead of them that blocked their view. Zefila sent out scouts to explore. From where he waited, Andrys could see them tense up as they rounded the natural barrier. At last, after what seemed like an endless wait, the men returned and signaled for the others to join them. Andrys and Zefila went first, with the Patriarch limping behind them. They came to the end of the ridge and crept around it—

And stopped. And stared.

Ahead of them, looming up into the night itself, was a castle. The trees which cloaked so much of the Forest gave way in this place, and Andrys could see it clearly by the light of Prima's crescent. It was a black structure, gleaming black, with a surface that might have been made of rippling water, so did it seem to move when the light shimmered over it. He heard the others gasp as they came around the turn, but their surprise couldn't possibly equal his own. Nor could they feel the horror that he did, gazing upon the citadel that his undead ancestor had built.

It was Merentha Castle. His own home keep, down to the last finely worked detail. Cast in black volcanic glass, a mockery of the home which had sheltered him. There, in that window, Samiel had watched for him; there, in that doorway, Betrise had scowled. There, in that courtyard . . . he started toward it, drawn by his own horror. Would that be the same as well, down to the last black flagstone?

"Tarrant!" Zefila grabbed him from behind, nearly jerking him off his feet as she pulled him roughly backward. "Stay with us, damn it!"

Silently, wary, they entered the courtyard. There were bodies all over the place. Human bodies, half-devoured and now rotting. Mounds of horseflesh in similar condition. Soldiers prodded a few just to make sure they were really dead, then fanned out, springbolts at the ready. Where was the danger? Andrys could feel it, but he couldn't define it. Something was waiting for them. Where?

"There's no one here," a woman dared.

"Make sure of it," Zefila ordered. She nodded toward a pair of men, who started toward the building—

And white shapes appeared along the wall of the courtyard, where moments ago there had been nothing. Of course, Andrys thought darkly. A simple Obscuring, the most basic of all Workings. In a war defined by sorcery, they should have expected it.

The white animals—identical to those which had attacked them earlier—were spaced out at regular intervals along the wall. There were a hell of a lot of them, Andrys noted grimly. But they would have to come down from the wall and cross a good part of the court-yard to get to them. With enough springbolts and a good dose of luck the soldiers might just survive this.

As if in response to that very thought another figure appeared. This one was human, and as it moved to the edge of a parapet it pulled another figure with it. A shaft of moonlight fell across them, illuminating a ghastly albino visage above, a pale and a hollowed face beneath—

Andrys' heart nearly stopped beating as he realized who it was the albino held as hostage. The whole world seemed to stop for a moment, frozen in that single instant of horror.

"Church-man!" The albino cried out the title in defiance, but it seemed to Andrys that there was a tremor of fear in his voice. "I have your girl! Do you see?" He shoved her forward, into the moonlight, his other hand holding a knife to her throat. "Back off now with all your men, or I'll cut her throat right in front of you!"

He could see her clearly now, her terrified eyes pleading with him. The albino held her by the hair with one hand, and he jerked at it as he snarled, "I'm waiting." Andrys saw her wince from pain, but she made no sound. No doubt the albino, like his master, would take pleasure in her cries.

It had to be an illusion, he thought desperately, some kind of evil Working. Narilka couldn't be here. Could she?

As if sensing his thoughts, the white man pressed his blade into the throat of his prisoner; a jewel of red welled up at its point. "Tell him," he hissed.

"Andrys." Her voice was weak, but not nearly as fearful as he would have expected. "Please."

"You see?" the albino demanded. "Do you need to hear more?"

He looked back at the Patriarch in panic. The Holy Father's expression was grim, but he shook his head. Some vision had clearly shown him that this was not the time for him to wield his power. Which meant that Andrys was on his own. He looked about desperately for Zefila, but she wasn't about to interfere without some signal from the Patriarch.

"Leave this place now," the albino growled. "Or her blood will be on your hands."

Why wasn't the man attacking them? His pack was in position. There were enough of the beasts to paint the courtyard red with blood. Did he fear that here, in the heart of the Hunter's realm, Andrys could tap into his ancestor's power? Did he imagine that open battle might tip the scale and turn Andrys into an enemy he couldn't defeat? With sudden inspiration, the younger Tarrant realized just how intense the man's fear of the Hunter still was. And the reality of his own helplessness was all the more painful for being contrasted against the albino's expectations.

His soul knotted in anguish, he looked up at Narilka. How helpless she seemed, that fragile body bent back to meet the knife! Fragile unless you knew her inner strength, fragile unless you had seen her defend herself, fragile unless you'd heard stories of the men who had taken her for a victim, only to be taught otherwise. . . .

He looked into her eyes then, and he knew. He saw the message that was in them, and he understood.

"Your choice," the albino snarled, in a voice so bestial it was barely comprehensible.

Give me a chance, her dark eyes begged. Not trembling with fear, but with another kind of tension. *Just one chance.*

He saw the albino's knife arm tense; the moment of choice was at hand. There was only one thing he could think of that would give her a chance, only one distraction that would work. Though his soul quailed at the mere thought of it, he dared not hesitate. He had failed her in so many ways in the past . . . he would not do so again.

He opened himself to the Forest. Not slowly, not carefully, but all at once, casting aside the defenses he had nurtured during their march, ready to die if that was what it took to save her. And power came welling up inside him with stunning force. Not any force of his own conjuring but a dark power, a cold power, that bore a hated signature. Undead, unclean, Gerald Tarrant's essence coursed through his blood in a flood tide, tearing loose the last fragile moorings of his human identity. Spreading through his flesh like a poison, remaking every organ, every cell, wrapping icy fingers about his soul and squeezing, squeezing—

With a gasp he opened his eyes. The ground was alive with silver light. The moonlight shivered with music. The walls of the castle glowed with a power that was centuries in the making, his to use at will. But he didn't need it. It was enough that the essence of Gerald Tarrant looked out through his eyes; it was enough that the man's power and ruthless confidence echoed in his voice.

"Release her," he commanded.

The albino's eyes went wide with shock. Or was it terror? Andrys saw him flinch as he realized just what manner of power his adversary had summoned, and in that moment his hand wavered ever so slightly as it held the knife—

Narilka moved. Reaching up to grab his knife arm with both of her hands, kicking out behind her as she pulled herself forward and down, struggling to keep the blade from her throat as she forced him over her body The move was so unexpected that he was thrown utterly off balance. Levered forward over her back, he slammed into the edge of the parapet. The knife clattered down to the courtyard as he grabbed for the edge of the low stone wall with his free hand; his other remained tangled in her hair, and for a moment it seemed as if he might use that as a lifeline to pull himself to safety. But she rammed the heel of her hand into his face hard, so hard that Andrys could hear bone crack; he lost his grip on the edge of the wall and began to slide. For one chilling moment it seemed that he might drag her down with him, but she braced herself against the wall with all the strength she had left and was rewarded a second later when the handful of hair still wrapped about his hand finally tore loose. Down he plummeted, twisting as he fell, and when he struck the hard flagstones beneath, the soldiers were ready for him.

Shivering, Andrys fell to his knees. He could see Narilka up on the parapet, he could see the albino being hacked to pieces on the ground before him, but he couldn't connect to any of it. His human emotions had been devoured, and now only a ravenous darkness remained. Andrys Tarrant himself was lost, a mere whisper of human memory fading in the endless blackness; the Forest's fae was taking its place, claiming the body and soul that had fought it for so long. Currents of power roared through his flesh, until the sounds of the real world were drowned out by the thunder of it. Moonlight scoured his skin like acid as the power of the forest began to remake his flesh, molding it according to the patterns which Gerald Tarrant had established.

She was alive, he thought as the darkness claimed him. That was all that mattered. The Forest had given her what she needed and now it was time to pay the price for it.

Andri—

The roots of the trees sucked at his vitality. The earth lapped at his living heat. He was spiraling down into death, but in the Forest death wasn't an end. Eternity beckoned, frigid and lightless.

Andri, talk to me. Please.

A thousand voices chittered about him. Sounds of the living, they meant nothing to the creature he now was. But one voice echoed down into the darkness, and it made his soul shiver to hear it.

Andri!

A human memory stirred in the darkness. Some tiny spark deep inside him began to struggle. The voice drew him like a magnet, pulling him up through the darkness, up against the currents, up to the surface that was so very far away.

Please, wake up. Please, Andri.

The last wounded vestige of Andrys Tarrant reached for the sound of her voice with all the strength he had. Feeling the warmth of flesh on his body, of hands—of *her* hands—touching him, drawing him back.

"Narilka?" he gasped.

She fell upon his chest, holding him, weeping. Where her tears touched him, the coldness faded from his flesh. Her voice was a balm, that brought him back to the world of the living. The heat of her life burned him, but it was a welcome pain.

"I'm all right," he whispered. It took everything he had to move his arm, to lift it up, to place it around her shoulders. For a moment he just lay there, exhausted by the effort. The Forest was still alive in his soul, but its grip was weakening. Soon he would move again. Soon he would get to his feet. Every human act, even one as simple as walking, would reinforce his dominion over his own flesh.

"I love you." He whispered it into her hair, oblivious to the filth which caked it. In his eyes she was pure and beautiful. "Don't ever leave me."

The wolves were gone. Had they been mere illusions all along, which vanished when their maker died? Or had the animals simply turned and run, fearful of doing battle without a sorcerer by their side? From where he lay, he could see soldiers moving into the castle, searching the grounds, unpacking explosives. Soon the real work would begin. By dawn the Hunter's citadel would be rubble, and all the power that it conjured as a symbol of evil would be scattered to the winds. Too bad the Hunter himself hadn't been there. . . .

He stiffened. A cold chill wafted up his spine. His arm about Narilka tightened.

"Andri?"

He struggled up to a sitting position. She helped him. Though the Forest's power no longer flowed freely through his soul, a fragile vestige yet remained. A hint of awareness that made his skin crawl, a whisper of . . . what?

"What is it?" she asked him. "Tell me."

Slowly, her arm supporting him, he got to his feet. The act of breathing felt alien to him; his lungs ached as though they had gone unused for centuries. What was this new thing that he sensed, this threat that he couldn't put a name to? It was close, very close. He could taste it.

And then he knew. He stared at the castle, he sensed what was inside it, and *he knew*.

"Oh, my God," he whispered.

"Andri?" Her voice was soft, but he could sense the fear behind it. "What's wrong?"

Calesta wasn't here now, but Calesta wasn't needed. Memories returned of their own accord. Samiel. Betrise. Abechar. His own home castle, drenched in blood.

A dark strength filled him. The love that had warmed his soul gave way to hate.

"The Hunter's here," he whispered.

Forty

The tunnel seemed to go on forever. Maybe it did, Damien thought. Maybe this was the true Hell, and they would spend the rest of eternity trudging through this stifling darkness, heading toward a destination that didn't even exist. If so, it would serve Tarrant right.

But it was hard to be angry at a man who was so clearly having a hard time of it. His battered mortal flesh needed mortal things to heal itself—food and water in quantity, safety from stress, adequate sleep—and on this trip it wasn't likely to get any of them. He knew what the Hunter had been capable of, but what were the limits of this living man who walked by his side? He couldn't begin to guess. Yet despite the flush which bore witness to painful exertion, and the increasing stiffness of his stride, Tarrant refused to slow down for any reason. *That* was the old Hunter, Damien knew. He only hoped the new one was up to past standards.

When they slowed down for a moment to dig out a portion of their dwindling supplies, or stopped completely—miracle of miracles—to relieve themselves of meals long since processed, Damien took a moment to study his companion. Tarrant was limping now, and the manner in which he walked hinted at blisters near the breaking point, but despite that obvious pain his spirit was unflagging. Whatever the Iezu mother had taken from him, it wasn't affecting either courage or endurance. What kind of child had the Hunter's soul given birth to, that would now walk the land with a mind of its own and the ability to orchestrate detailed illusions? He kept looking for a sign of something missing in Tarrant, some facet of his personality that had been drained of substance, but thus far in their journey he had been unable to identify it. Perhaps he had been wrong about the process, and the conception of a new Iezu would cost its father nothing. God willing.

They had walked for hours now, too many to count, and when Damien raised up his lantern to look at Tarrant's face, he could see a brief flicker of pain tense across his brow with each step. It did no good to suggest that such pain would only intensify if he refused to pace himself properly. The one or two times that Damien even dared to hint at such a truth, Tarrant glared at him with a venom that would have done his old self proud, as if the suggestion that they take a few minutes to recoup were not only foolish, but deeply offensive.

"Look," the ex-priest said at last, when they paused once more to eat a portion of his dwindling supplies. "They can't find this secret place of yours, right? And they're not going to burn the Forest until they're safely out of it, which'll take days at best." He leaned back against the cold stone wall, his muscles throbbing painfully as he shifted his weight. "So we've got a little time to pace ourselves. We can spare a few minutes to rest. Just long enough to get a second wind." And he added dryly, "Living people do that kind of thing, you know."

Tarrant stared at him for a long moment, then silently upended the canteen and swallowed one more precious bit of its contents. It was their last such container, Damien noted; somewhere they were going to have to find more water, and soon. Tarrant capped the canteen with meticulous care and hung its strap about his shoulder, for once not assuming that Damien would carry it.

"They intend to blow up the keep," he said. And he began to walk down the tunnel again with a quick, lopsided stride.

"Blow up?" For a minute he was too shocked to move. Then he had to run a few steps to catch up to Tarrant, and for a moment that left him no breath for words. "You mean, as in explosives?"

"That is the usual procedure."

He grabbed Tarrant by the arm, jerking him to a stop. "Are you telling me that while we're in there sorting through your notebooks the entire keep is going to come crashing down on our heads?"

A faint ghost of a smile flitted across his face. "I do hope our timing will be better than that."

"These are *books* we're going after." His voice was low but his tone was fierce. "Books, Gerald! I appreciate how important they are, but that doesn't make them worth dying for. I don't mind risking my life to save a life—or even to preserve an ideal—but to risk something like that for a pile of *books*—"

"*Those books are a gateway to the future,*" he said sharply. "A dictionary of translation between our own species and that of the Iezu's maker, which will allow us take a step our Terran ancestors never even dreamed of. And if you're correct about the changes in the fae . . . if, in fact, humans will not be able to Work to gain knowledge . . . then that gateway might never be accessible again. Ever. If we let those books be destroyed now, our descendants will be doomed to centuries of trial-and-error guesswork. And who can tell how much that will net them? The knowledge we sacrifice today may be lost forever—"

"And you'd be willing to risk death for that?" he demanded. "For knowledge?"

"I did once before," he pointed out. "Perhaps the second time is easier."

He smoothed the fabric of his sleeve where Damien had crushed it, but bound no fae with the gesture; the wrinkles remained. "Stay here, if you like. The way out will be safe soon enough." He dropped the canteen strap off his shoulder and let the metal container fall to the floor; in the smooth-walled tunnel the impact echoed like a gunshot. "I'll go alone."

"Like hell you will." Damien reached down to catch up the canteen. Tarrant was moving quickly; he had to jog to catch up with him. "Who'll get you out of trouble next time if I'm not there?"

The Hunter made no answer.

The tunnel began to slope upward at last, hinting at an end. Damien's legs hurt so badly as he forced himself up the angled floor that he feared they would lock up from exhaustion and refuse to carry him; he didn't even want to think about what Tarrant was feeling. How long had they been walking now—one day? Two? If they did get blown up they'd have a chance to rest, at least. It didn't sound all that bad right now.

At last, just when it seemed that neither of them could manage another step, they came to the base of a staircase carved into the mountain's stone. Without even pausing for breath, the Hunter began to ascend. Damien saw him stagger once and he braced himself to catch him from behind, but the Hunter put out a hand against the wall of the tunnel for balance, paused long enough to draw in one long, shaky breath, and began to climb once more. The man's determination was inhuman, Damien observed as he climbed unsteadily behind him. And why should that surprise him? This was a man who had once bested Death by sheer force of will; why should a little detail like physical pain slow him down?

They climbed two flights' worth of stairs, maybe more. At the top there was a small landing where they paused to catch their breath, and a heavy alteroak door barring the way beyond. Thick iron braces were clearly meant to hold a wooden bar that would lock it from this side, but—thank God—that wasn't in place. Damien wasn't sure he could have lifted it. Without asking for help, Tarrant grabbed hold of the nearer brace and began to pull; when it was clear that his effort wasn't enough, Damien grabbed hold of the other one and added his strength to the effort. Together, inch by inch, they pulled the massive door open. Its hinges made a creaking sound loud enough that Damien flinched, and a foul smell gusted through the opening, right into his face. It was an odor of rotting meat and bodily waste and at least a dozen other things that he didn't care to identify, and for a minute or two it was all he could do not to vomit. What the hell was going on here?

If Tarrant noted the smell, he made no mention of it. When the door was open far enough to admit a man, he slipped through, and Damien followed. As he did so, he turned up the wick of his lantern a bit so that they could see the space they were entering. It was a small chamber, crudely carved, with little in the way of comfort or decoration. There was a large slab table in its center, carved whole from the same gray stone, and his lantern's dim light picked out several objects that lay upon its surface. Damien took a few steps closer, trying to make out what they were. Chains. Manacles. Feces of some sort, possibly human, that had been smeared across the table's surface. The latter smelled pungently recent.

"Do I want to know what this place is?"

"No," Tarrant stared at the mess on the table for a few seconds, his eyes narrowed to slits. God alone knew what he was thinking. "Suffice it to say that I kept it somewhat cleaner."

He moved to the far corner of the room, where a lighter door swung open easily at his touch. As they passed through this one, Damien could hear faint sounds from above, murmurs and impacts transmitted down through the layers of rock. The soldiers of the Church must be very close.

"My wards will hold," the Hunter said quietly, as if sensing his thoughts. As they walked on blistered feet through the fetid darkness, Damien wondered which of them he was trying to convince. Then suddenly the Hunter drew himself up, as if alerted to a hostile presence. Damien stiffened and drew his sword, ready for action. But

Tarrant's eyes were fixed upon the ground, where the earth-fae would be bright and rich with meaning; it was knowledge that had alerted him, not some foreign presence.

At last Tarrant said, in a voice that was still and cold, "He's dead."

"Who?"

"Amoril. My apprentice." The pale eyes narrowed. "My betrayer."

"Are you sure?"

He seemed to hesitate. Were the messages of the fae less clear to him now that he had no Working to interpret them? "Yes," he said at last. "He lived—and ruled here—long enough to leave his mark upon the currents. That stink is his as well, no doubt . . . or that of his animal familiars. He never was fastidious." The thin mouth curled in distaste. "That he's gone now is equally clear, and there's only one way to explain that." He looked at Damien; his expression was grim. "If they've truly killed him, then we have very little time left."

They moved on, through a space that was more cavern than tunnel, in whose distant recesses water dripped with agonizing slowness. Now and then a noise would drift down to them, echoing through some flaw in the stone overhead. Soldiers' voices, issuing orders. Animals' howls, the cries of the dying. It was good that they could hear such things, Damien told himself. It was when the noises stopped that they would be in real trouble.

They came to another door, this one so finely worked that it seemed out of place in the rough stone corridor. Tarrant touched a ward at its center, which may have been meant to unlock it; the polished wood pushed easily inward, and the two men moved into the room beyond. Damien's lantern light revealed a modest chamber, shelf-lined, which might have been a library in another age. Tarrant's workshop, no doubt.

Utterly devastated.

He could feel the sight of the destruction strike Tarrant like a physical blow, and he flinched himself as he gazed about the room. Books had been hurled down from the shelves and mangled. Manuscripts had been shredded and wadded up like garbage. Leather covers, ripped from their volumes and scored with claw marks, reeked of urine and decay. He could hear the Hunter's indrawn breath as he gazed upon the wreckage of his storehouse of knowledge, and he sensed that in some bizarre way this pained him more than Amoril's other betrayals, or even the loss of the Forest itself.

You believed that knowledge like this would be sacred, he thought. *You thought that even the Evil One, being man-made, would respect its value.* He shook his head sadly. *Welcome to the real world, Gerald.*

There was a large trestle table in the center of the room, now overturned. Silently Tarrant moved to one end and reached down for a handhold; Damien put down his lantern and hurried to the other end to do the same.

"At least your people hate fire," he offered, as they righted it. "If they'd burned the place there'd be nothing left at all."

Tarrant made no comment. Reaching down into the mess that was under his feet, he brought up a single page, torn and crumpled and crusted with something brown. For a long time he stared at it, and Damien sensed that he was watching how the fae clung to the paper, how the current responded to the words that were on its surface. Then his hand clenched tightly, crushing it.

"We'll never find the right pages in time," he muttered. Damien could hear the exhaustion in his voice. "Not without a Locating."

"Of course we will. We have to, right?" He spotted several whole notebooks on one of the shelves and pulled them out. "Hell, my desk in Ganji looked worse than this."

For a moment Tarrant's eyes met his. For a moment he could sense the utter despair welling up inside the man, not a product of this one moment or even of several moments past, but of everything he had experienced since they'd started on this God-forsaken mission. Even the Hunter's indomitable spirit had its limits, he realized. And there was no sorcery left to sustain him now.

In the distance there was a louder sound; voices arguing, it seemed to Damien, and the impact of metal on stone. It seemed uncomfortably close.

"Come on," he urged. He put the notebooks down on the table and began to search for more. "We've got a lot to go through here."

He didn't look at Tarrant again, but focused on the shelves surrounding him. Whoever had ravaged the hidden library might have worked with enthusiasm, but he lacked efficiency; there were several dozen volumes still intact, and he pulled them free and shook them off and brought them to the table. There Tarrant searched through them page by page, sorting through the diaries of his undead centuries to find the notes he needed. God willing, Damien thought, they'd be somewhere in these intact volumes. Otherwise . . . he looked at the mess on the floor and shook his head, trying not to think about what that search would be like. Or how damned long it would take.

There were voices even closer now. Too close. He looked at Tarrant.

"My wards will admit no one but myself or Amoril to this chamber," he said, responding to Damien's unspoken question. "And Amoril being dead—"

"What if they carry his body with them?"

"Even if they think to do that—and I doubt they have so much insight—it won't work. The wards respond to a man's vital essence, not to dead flesh." But despite his assurance it seemed to Damien that he turned the pages faster than before, and his eyes darted up occasionally to ascertain that the door to the library was indeed still shut.

Then footsteps resounded, heavy and purposeful and clearly headed in their direction. "Shit," Damien muttered, putting down the book he held in order to draw his sword. The Hunter rose, swaying slightly as he did so; clearly his exhausted muscles were less than enthusiastic about the concept of a fresh workout. Damien's own muscles ached like hell, but that didn't matter now. Whatever had gotten past the Hunter's wards was damned likely not to be friendly.

And then the door opened and the light of an unshuttered lantern blinded him for an instant. He took a step backward and squinted against the light, fighting to make out details of a figure that seemed to glow with all the power of the sun—

"Oh, my God," he whispered. Almost dropping his sword. "Who the hell. . . ?"

The figure in the doorway was wearing armor cast in silver and gold, that captured his lamplight and reflected it a thousand times over, making the golden sun upon his breastplate blaze like the star of Earth itself. After hours spent in the semi-darkness, the light was blinding. But that wasn't what stunned Damien so. He was a seasoned enough warrior not to be unmanned by simple pyrotechnics, and even the sight of the Prophet's famous armor come to life, just as it had been painted on the Cathedral's high wall, was something he could come to terms with. It was the sight of the man who wore the armor that utterly unnerved him, so that his grip upon his sword grew weak and the familiar steel blade nearly fell from his hand.

The man was Gerald Tarrant.

No, Damien thought. Fighting the power of the image. This man's skin was tan, where Gerald's was pale. This man's eyes were darker, and deeper set. He was slightly shorter than the Hunter, and maybe a little bit stockier, and his hair wasn't quite the same length. But except for those minor details the resemblance was amazing. Unnerving. Even—given the circumstances—terrifying.

This was how Gerald Tarrant must have looked in his first lifetime, when the heat of life still surged in his veins, when the passions of mortal existence still blazed in his eyes. Even the man's wounds bore witness to his living state: a livid red scratch mark swelling across his brow, a hot purple bruise along the line of his jaw. And the look in his eyes ... there was a hate so hot in them that Damien could feel it like a flame upon his face; even the hate-wraiths that wisped in and out of existence about the man were red and gold and orange, fire-hues that sizzled in the keep's chill air.

The burning eyes fixed on him, then on Tarrant. There was madness in them, and an echo of pain so intense that Damien flinched to see it. With bruised hands the newcomer put down his lantern and then swung a hefty springbolt into firing position, aiming at the Hunter's chest. But Damien stood between the two of them, close enough to foul a clean shot.

"Get back," the man rasped. There was a hysterical edge to his voice, the sound of a soul pushed almost to the breaking point. Damien had seen enough men in that state to know how very dangerous it was. "Get out of the way!"

He couldn't move. He didn't dare. *A knife in the heart is as fatal to an adept as it is to any other human.* Who had said that? He couldn't remember. "Who are you?" he managed. Not because he thought the man would answer him, just to buy a precious moment's delay.

To his surprise it was the Hunter who responded. "Andrys Tarrant." Was that a tremor of fear in his voice? "Last living descendant of my family line."

"You killed them!" the newcomer cried hoarsely. His hand on the springbolt was shaking; the dried blood on his face was streaked with sweat. "God damn you to Hell for it." He reached up with his left hand to wipe away what might have been a tear, or maybe just a drop of sweat, then quickly returned it to the barrel of his weapon. "I don't know who you are," he snapped at Damien, "and I don't care. But I've got two bolts loaded and so help me God, if you don't move out of my way, one of them's for you."

There was nowhere to run to. No way to Work a defense. One slender wooden shaft was all it would take, to pierce a heart that had only just started to beat again. In this strange new world they were in, there was no way to stop it.

God, don't let it end like this. Please. Give him a chance to come back to You.

The Hunter's manner gave no sign of his desperation, but Damien knew him well enough to hear it in his voice."It's over," Tarrant said quietly. "You've won."

"Shut up!" the man shouted. He raised the weapon higher, and cursed as he confirmed the fouled sightline along the barrel. In a voice that edged on hysteria, he shouted at Damien, "Move!"

"The Forest is dead," Gerald persisted. His voice was low and even; Damien could sense the monumental self-control required to keep it that way. "That's what you came to do, isn't it? The Forest and its current master are dead, and its past master. . . ." He let the sentence trail off into eloquent silence, as if daring his enemy to complete it. "Isn't that what you wanted, Andrys? To destroy all my work, so that I would have nothing left?" How much did he know about the man from past Knowings, Damien wondered, how much could he read in the currents now, how much was he guessing? His very life depended on those skills. *"You won. It's over. Go back to your life."*

"I have no life, you son of a bitch." The man's voice was shaking. "Not while you're alive."

The finger on the trigger tensed. Damien's muscles were ready to move, wound taut as the steel springs inside that killing weapon.

"Calesta is dead," Gerald Tarrant said quietly.

The newcomer's face went white. He reeled slightly as if struck, and his finger moved a precious inch or two back from the trigger.

"You bound yourself to him," Gerald pressed. "Didn't you? What did he promise you? Forgetfulness? Purging? An orgy of vengeance?" He paused. "Did he tell you what the cost of that would be? Did he tell you that you would lose your soul if you served him?"

"That doesn't matter," he whispered.

"He was my enemy long before you were involved." Damien could see the newcomer flinch as each word hit home, forcing him to reconsider a relationship he had clearly taken for granted until this moment. "Did you know that? He'd use any tool that was available to accomplish his ends. Even my own flesh and blood. Or did you think when he offered his power to you that it was only for your benefit?" He shook his head sharply, tensely. His whole body was poised like that of an animal about to bolt for cover, or launch itself at its prey. "He lived for pain and pain alone. Not only mine, but yours. Killing me wouldn't be enough for him, not unless I knew in my last dying moment that he had also destroyed those things I valued most. The Forest. The Church. And now you."

"You *value* me?" He spat the words out in disbelief, almost unable to voice them. "What kind of bullshit is that? How stupid do you think I am?"

"You're my own flesh and blood," the Hunter said icily. "Not the proudest member of my line, certainly not the strongest, but right now you're all that's left. When he claims your soul, he will debase a history that stretches back nearly a thousand years." The pale eyes were an icy flame that chilled whatever they gazed upon. "That will be his true triumph, Andrys Tarrant. Not my death. Your corruption."

"If Calesta's dead, then he has no power now—"

"Doesn't he?" the adept demanded. "Do you know what will happen if you kill me now? That spark of Calesta's hate which lies like a dormant seed within you will take root and grow, until it strangles all within you that is still human. *That's* his vengeance, Andrys Tarrant. Not your paltry campaign, not even the rigors of Hell itself, but the knowledge that as you pull that trigger, you commit yourself to *his* world, in which the only joy is suffering."

The man reeled visibly, as if the words had been a physical blow. "No," he whispered hoarsely. "You're just trying to talk yourself out of a—"

"Look within yourself, then! Imagine the hatred taking hold, *Calesta's* hatred taking hold, the embrace of vengeance consummated at last . . . and then ask yourself how you'll return to the real world after that. Or did you think it would all end when you pulled that trigger? Did you think your soul would be magically cleansed at the moment of my death?" He shook his head sharply. "This is just the beginning. The easy part."

"You killed them," he whispered. Raising up the weapon again, aligning it with his eye once more. "My brothers, my sister, all of them! God damn you to Hell! You deserve to die!"

"Then pull the trigger," the Hunter dared him. "And destroy us both."

Andrys Tarrant blinked hard; sweat ran redly down the side of his face. "I don't . . . I can't. . . ." His hands were shaking. Suddenly he gestured toward Damien with the springbolt. "Go," he whispered hoarsely. "Get out of here."

"I think—" he began.

"This isn't your fight! It's between him and me. Whoever the hell you are, just get out of here! Now!"

Damien hesitated, then looked at Gerald. The Hunter nodded ever so slightly. "He's right, Damien." His voice was quiet but strained. "There's nothing more you can do here."

"Gerald—"

The Hunter shook his head. Damien's protest died in his throat.

"Go," Gerald Tarrant whispered.

He swallowed hard, trying to think of something to do, something to say, anything that could change this moment. He imagined himself in Andrys Tarrant's place, and sensed how very easy it would be to fire. How many times had he dreamed of putting an end to the Hunter so quickly, so easily? But now the issue was no longer that simple. Now the Hunter had become . . . something else.

Hadn't he?

You killed my family, the younger Tarrant had accused.

He forced himself to move as indicated. Andrys took a few steps into the room to give him a wide berth in case he intended to attempt a last minute rescue . . . and indeed he might have, if there had been an opening. But there wasn't. And then he passed through the door and it slammed shut behind him, and he knew that one way or another a man was going to die.

You killed my family.

It was justice, surely. Long overdue. Generations would celebrate the death of a man who was every bit as evil as Calesta, whose heart was so like the Iezu's in its core that when he had beckoned to his enemy with the full force of the Hunter's sadism, Calesta had come to him like a lover.

He needed time, God. A man can't contain that kind of evil and then be rid of it overnight. But he would have come back to You.

His heart heavy, his feet like lead, he ascended the winding staircase that led to the upper levels. Up he climbed, toward the black halls he remembered so well. Up to where the soldiers of the Church were laying down explosives and fixing fuses in place. Up to the living world, where the Forest was dying so that new things might be born, where the legend of the Hunter would give way to other things fearsome and terrible, but none so full of despoiled brilliance, or of courage. . . .

There were tears in his eyes, blinding him. Hot tears.

He kept walking.

They had built a bonfire in the courtyard. He watched as they carried the pieces of Amoril's body over to it and threw them one by one onto the flames. He watched the pieces char and sizzle and lose their human coherency, and he sensed the relief among the soldiers as it was guaranteed, by that burning, that no undead resurrection would bring their enemy back.

Distantly he watched, as if from another world. No one disturbed him. Not the soldiers whom he knew, not the Patriarch . . . no one. Surrounded by a cocoon of darkness he watched as the flames danced, feeling their heat upon his face, an alien thing in the Forest night.

And then there was a stirring in the main portal of the keep, and a figure emerged from the shadows within it. One man, clad in armor of silver and gold, bloodstained sword gripped tightly in one hand. There was a dark-haired girl in the crowd who ran toward him, but something in his manner made her stop before she had reached him. The Patriarch rose up from where he sat and took one step toward him, but then Andrys Tarrant's gaze—haunted, bloodshot—froze him in place.

Slowly he raised his other hand, along with the trophy it held. His bloodied fingers gripping it by the hair, he raised up the severed head of Gerald Tarrant so that all could see it. Damien shut his eyes, but the image was already burned into his brain and he couldn't shut it out. That white skin, truly bloodless now. Those silver eyes, emptied of all intelligence. That life which was ever so much more than a mere human life, smothered out like a candleflame. . . .

He mourned. God would condemn him for it, perhaps, but he mourned. The man who had once been called Prophet deserved that much, surely.

Five steps brought Andrys Tarrant to the edge of the fire. For a second he paused, as if giving those about him a chance to fix the moment in their minds Then he cast the head onto the pyre—that tortured face, so like and unlike his own—and cried out as the first flames licked at it, as if feeling their bite on his own flesh. He fell then, and the dark-haired girl ran to him, and she dropped to her knees and held him and wept. The Patriarch came up beside them and offered his own words of comfort. *God has led us to triumph,* perhaps. Or something like that. Some ritual prayer that couldn't possibly do justice to this moment, or to the man whose death had made it possible.

No one noticed Damien Vryce as he left the courtyard. No one saw him slip into the shadows of the Forest, away from the light of the flames. Away from the keep, and its storehouse of knowledge. Away from . . . everything.

In the silence of the Forbidden Forest, in the darkness that the Hunter had called home, Damien prayed for God's forgiveness, and for the peace of his friend's soul.

Forty-one

They blew up the black keep at solar noon, when the hot white light of day set the finials ablaze and the glass stones shimmered like quicksilver. It had taken them all morning to prepare for the act, exposing all the rooms of the keep before a single fuse was lit, so that there was no chamber, no closet, no corner in which a shadow of the Hunter's power might remain to sabotage their efforts. Amidst the towering, thickly thatched trees of the Forest that had meant waiting until day was well under way, for dawn, like sunset, lacked the angular power to breach the lower windows. In the meantime they mixed the materials they had brought to the Forest with meticulous care and constant prayer, and laid their fuses to the sound of Churchchants. Every grain of powder was tamped down in the One God's name; every precious fiber was dedicated to His purpose. In a world where one man's doubts might skew a host of enterprises, one couldn't be too careful.

They were following a plan set down by the first settlers, in the days when the ravaged colony had struggled to record all of Earth's knowledge. Inner walls first, and supporting columns, then the outer structure of the keep. On Earth such a pattern would have guaranteed a controlled infall of debris, minimizing the risk to those who watched. On Erna, where there was no guarantee that any of the fuses would fire properly, much less any fantasy that all the explosions could be timed—call it a dream. Call it an act of faith.

It went off perfectly.

They heard the first blast from down the mountainside, and felt the ground tremble beneath them. The second followed seconds after, and then the third, and a barrage that was more deafening than all three combined. With a sound like thunder the black walls shattered, some blowing outward, most falling inward. Floors collapsed beneath the weight of ceilings, fell to the floors below, collapsed again. The mountain shook. The sun was obscured by smoke. Fragments of obsidian, sharp as arrow points, fell to the ground like rain.

After the smoke cleared, the Hunter's keep was gone.

Some monuments still remained, spared by the conquerors' lack of adequate explosives, or else by the limits of their book-learned skill. A single buttress arched up against the sky, seemingly defiant. A segment of the courtyard wall jutted up from the ground, its base buried in rubble. There were parts of walls still standing within the keep, against which debris had drifted like sand, or snow; vast dunes of wreckage that promised frustration to any man or beast that might dare to brave the site in search of buried knowledge, or some key to power.

They said prayers over the rubble, as soon as the dust had settled. Prayers and sunlight would expose and destroy any remnant of power clinging to the ancient stone. No one doubted the power of that combination. No one doubted that the Hunter was now gone forever. No one doubted that a great and terrible age had finally been brought to a close, with this single act that would reverberate through history. Such was the power of symbols in men's minds, they told each other. Such was the power of their Patriarch.

And Damien alone, sitting apart from all the others, removed from their celebration, saw what was within the Patriarch's soul that day. Not joy, but a dark and terrible anxiety. Not relief, but a fresh determination. Damien alone, knowing his Church, knowing the Patriarch—but most of all, knowing his fellow men—understood the cause of that anxiety.

And knowing, he mourned.

Forty-two

The Holy Father walked out carefully upon the rocks, booted feet wary on the slippery surfaces. Thick brush tangled about his ankles, not the twisted, perverted vines of the inner Forest, but the rich green life of a region that was daily bathed in sunlight. After days in that stifling domain, their smell was a heady tonic.

He stood where the rocks went out into the river listening to the waters of the Lethe rush about his feet. Fish darted quicksilver beneath the gleaming surface, and a red crab scuttled out of the way as his shadow fell upon its hunting ground.

He looked at the place—its sun and its water and its rich, teeming life—and he looked at the currents of earth-fae which were bright beneath his feet, and he gazed into a plethora of possible futures, so tangled together now that his best efforts could barely pull loose a single thread. He shut his eyes and let them seep into him, and when he was sure that he liked the feel of them, he nodded and said quietly, "This is the place."

The soldier who had accompanied him on his search beat his way back through the bushes that lined the river, hurrying back to tell the others. For a short, precious time the Patriarch was alone.

Give me courage, God. Lend me Your strength.

His left leg hurt so badly that he could barely stand on it. There was a good chance that it had broken back when the white beasts attacked them, but he hadn't told anyone. There could even be an infection by now, if a shard of bone had broken through the skin. No matter. He had managed the tortuous climb despite it, wincing at every step, almost crying out when a misplaced footfall caused his wounded leg to jar against the earth. But he knew that if he'd told them what was wrong, they would have stopped then and there to tend to him, increasing the risk to all at least tenfold. And maybe deep inside, in that hidden place where a man least wanted to look, he was afraid that if he sat down and gave in to the pain, if he offered exhaustion that opening, he would never rise up again.

His body ached from a fatigue so terrible that it was only raw faith that kept him standing. Raw faith and the knowledge that if he gave in now, if his soldiers had to carry him back, the Church would lose more than any campaign could ever restore. Now was the crux, the focal point of a thousand futures; now was the moment when loss must be turned to gain, when the hundreds of futures in which his Church succumbed to the temptation of easy violence must be cut short, so that brighter fates could flourish.

There was a rustling behind him, and then a man appeared in the waist-high brush. He bowed deeply to the Patriarch, as one might bow to a god. That hurt him more than the pain in his leg and all his exhaustion combined. Didn't they see what they were doing? Didn't they comprehend the risk?

They never do, his conscience assured him. *Which is why the Church must lead them.*

As he must lead the Church.

With careful steps he waded across the shallow river. The water was ice-cold, mountain drainage, and within a few steps his feet were so numb he could hardly feel them. Good, he thought. At least they wouldn't hurt. With all of the burdens he bore today, he deserved a few square inches of flesh that didn't pain him.

There was a crowd gathered on the bank of the river by the time he reached the other side, and more were coming. The wounded were helped into place by their fellows, foliage trampled flat as dozens of men and women sought a place to stand or sit. That a place as beautiful as this should exist a mere stone's throw from the Hunter's mountain was a gift of God, he mused; he prayed that it would recover once they had left.

He took up a position on a rock on the far side of the river, staggering slightly as he fought for balance on its slippery surface. Two of the men started toward him to help, but he waved them back. For this he needed them in one place, so that his speech would have full effect.

Past where he stood, the water flowed into the Forest proper, nourishing all life forms within that darkened realm. Past where he stood, the currents of earth-fae on which all power depended, even the creative power of prayer, flowed directly toward his people. Overhead the sun was bright, washing the light gap clean of any lingering malignance, burning away the fears and sorrows which might otherwise create new demons in these volatile currents. Good. That was as it should be. A handful of dark futures dissipated as he watched, and it seemed that several promising ones took their place. Many of the futures now emerging were similar, he noted with satisfaction, their potentials converging upon this moment like animals at a water hole. Soon, soon, he would nourish his chosen few, banishing the others forever.

He drew in a deep breath and gazed upon his people. Blood-stained, muddied, they waited on the opposite shore for the words that would seal their victory. He counted them silently, making sure that all were there. Zefila had taken up a position behind and above the others, he saw. Andrys Tarrant was off to one side, as if doubtful that the rest of the company would accept him. He had his pagan girlfriend with him, the Patriarch noted. There were so many futures tangled about that pair that he couldn't pick any one out, but it seemed to him that the balance, on the whole, was positive. Let her share in this moment, then. Let her see what kind of courage the One God inspired in its faithful.

Only Damien Vryce was missing, and for a moment—one terrible moment—the Patriarch feared that he wouldn't show up at all. He didn't know why it was so important that the ex-priest be present—indeed, he would much rather never look at him again—but his faeborn visions had convinced him that Vryce's presence would increase the odds of success here a hundredfold. How ironic—and unfair!—that God would reward such a man with that kind of importance.

And then the flurry of futures that swirled around him resolved to a mere hundred or so, as Damien Vryce beat his way through the underbrush and took up a place on the riverbank. He looked toward the Patriarch, but didn't dare meet his eyes. Nor did he look at the other soldiers, or Andrys Tarrant. That was probably best, the Patriarch mused. He had kept far enough apart from the others that none had asked him why he was there, or what part he had played in the battle between faith and sorcery, but every man knew that he had come out of the black keep, and that was condemnation enough. If the Holy Father hadn't made a show of tolerating his presence, they probably would have run him out of camp. Or worse.

Watch now, he bade Vryce silently. *Gaze upon true faith, in all its fearsome glory.*

He raised up a hand to still the group, and dozens of whispered conversations ceased. In the silence that resulted, it seemed to him he could hear their hearts pounding . . . and maybe, with the fae underscoring his every thought with power, he could. An adept's damnation.

"Praised be God," he pronounced, "who has brought us to this day of triumph." He could see waves of power spreading out from where he stood, echoing the rhythm of his speech. "Praised be the courage of the fallen, who gave all that they had to defend their fellows." Had it always been thus, and he had simply lacked the power to See it? He watched as the shimmering futures shifted in response to those fae-waves, and he shivered inwardly. How could a man live with such vision, and still remain a man?

He led them in the Prayer for the Dead, a recitation crafted ages ago by some anonymous hand. It was beautiful, it was comforting, it was a somber reminder that their victory had cost them dearly. He wondered if the Prophet had written it.

When they were done, he gave them a moment to revel in their pride, taking the time to draw in a deep breath, trying to still the trembling of his flesh so that they would see only the image he wanted them to see, a leader serene and confident. Not a man overcome by hesitancy, remorse . . . and yes, he had to admit it, fear. Not the truth.

"There comes a time," he began at last, "when a man is tested. Sometimes the test is of his courage, or his strength, or his endurance. Sometimes it is of his inner conviction, his faith." He drew in a deep breath. "Sometimes it is of his judgment. That is the most difficult test of all, my children . . . and it can be the most painful.

"Like the father who steals a loaf of bread to feed his starving child, daring the vengeance of the law because he feels that the law of life is more pressing, we each make our choices when we must. Who can judge a man in such an instance, or say with certainty that the course of his heart is wrong? What is the will of government, when contrasted against a man's innate morality?

"Such are the ways of the laws of man, which are by definition imperfect. But human governments come and go, and statutes change daily in response to circumstance. The Law of the One God is a different thing. Written by God's own Prophet, affirmed by generations of priests, it was meant to be an absolute Law, which would endure for all time. A reflection of God's own Spirit, whose wisdom would be unquestionable. A pathway to salvation.

"Decry violence, the Law instructs. Reject sorcery. Resist, above all else, corruption of the human spirit."

His throat was dry. He drew in a deep breath, and wished he could reach down into the water and draw up a handful to cool his mouth. But his wounded leg throbbed and his muscles felt weak, and he thought that if he tried he might not rise up again.

"It came to pass that an Evil was born into our world, so great that faith alone could not do battle with it. We tried, my children, we tried. Five centuries ago we marched against the Forest with an army vast enough to tame a continent, with standards and with sorcery and with a host of weapons . . . and we lost. We *lost*. We suffered a defeat so devastating that in the five centuries since we haven't managed yet to recover, in numbers or in faith.

"What would have happened after that war, if the soldiers of the One God had succeeded? Would those men and women have gone back to their homes and their families and enjoyed the rewards of their success? Or would they have sought out other enemies, other Evils, so that now, five hundred years later, you and I would live in a world in which *faith* and *violence* were all but synonymous? A world in which constant war drained man of all his vital energies, so that nothing was left to devote to higher aspirations?

"Such were the questions I asked myself as I saw this Evil growing. Such was my torment of faith that nightly I prayed for guidance. While all about me temples fell, blood was shed, the souls of my people were made black by intolerance." He looked pointedly at the handful of soldiers who had been involved in the temple riots, and he saw them flinch as the accusation struck home. "The man in me longed to respond in kind to this Evil. The leader in me knew the cost of such action.

"Will you let Your people perish? I asked God. *Is it truly Your will that mankind surrender to this darkness, rather than risk one transgression of Your Law? Would you rather we die now, blindly obedient, than survive to serve You?*

"Then one night, I saw a vision. Say perhaps that God sent it to me, responding not to one man's prayers but to the pain and the fear of all His people. Or say instead that it welled up from the depths of my soul, from that secret place where *conscience* resides. What I saw was a creature of light, so bright and so beautiful that it hurt my eyes to look upon it. Its voice was not one voice but a choir, and as it spoke, its words echoed in my soul with a power that made me tremble.

"The Lord God of Earth and Erna is perfect, it said to me, *but the world of men is not, nor are the creatures who inhabit it. Therefore are human choices uncertain, and full of strife. If given a choice between one man's sin and the destruction of a nation, what leader*

would choose the latter! But remember this if you choose to trans-gress, it warned me. *Like the father who steals bread for his child, knowing it to be against the law, you must be prepared to pay the price for your actions. Thus alone can you save the child and still uphold the Law."*

He lifted up to his hands toward the heavens in an age-old attitude of prayer; futures flitted about his head like restless birds, bright and agitated. "Hear me, oh, my God," he prayed. "Hear me, Lord of Earth and Erna, creator of humankind, now made King of this Forest. In or-der to serve my people, I have trangessed against Your greatest Law. I have committed bloodshed, and sanctified violence, and encouraged in my people a fever of destruction which runs counter to Your every teaching. Let the sin be mine alone, not theirs. If any soul is to suffer corruption, let that soul be mine. Forgive these people, repair their spirits, replenish their souls' inner strength, make them as innocent in their faith as they were before my call urged them to violence. On my head and mine alone is the fault for any wrong we have commit-ted. On my soul sits the weight of your judgment, my God."

All eyes were upon him, unwavering. He could see in their depths a ghost of doubt now, a quiver of fear. Good. Let them question what they had done here and they might yet be saved.

"In acceptance of Your Will," he drew out a slender knife from his sleeve, turning its blade so that it glittered in the sunlight, "and in recognition of the righteousness of Your most holy Law, do I offer You this sacrifice." Quickly he placed the knife against his palm and cut downward with it, hard. There was little pain, for the blade was sharp, but something stabbed his heart as the blood began to flow free. Fear? Regret? Those emotions had no place here, he thought fiercely. He raised up his hand in a gesture of benediction, so that all might see what he had done; a thin crimson waterfall splashed down into the river, and it seemed to him that the fae itself was stained red as it coursed outward from him.

"May You cleanse this land forever of the darkness which once ruled here," he prayed. Thin streamers of red were unfurling in the water, reaching toward the stunned men and women who stood upon the opposite bank. "May You cleanse my people of the darkness which has gripped their souls, so that in this new world which they have made they may be worthy of salvation. In Your Name, Lord God of Earth and Erna."

Earth-fae. It would give his words tenfold power, and adhere his message to the souls of his people. With his new sight he could see the power of his sacrifice spreading out in waves from the falling blood, and as each wave touched the future-images surrounding him they shimmered and shifted, taking on new patterns of potential. Some were more positive than before, but not enough. Not enough! God in Heaven, was he offering up his life for nothing?

And then Damien Vryce moved forward. Hesitantly at first, his eyes never leaving the Patriarch, then with firm conviction as he stepped into the river. He walked forward until he was near the river's center, knee-deep in the mountain water, then reached down with his hand and touched it. A thin stream of red curled about his fingers, almost invisible now as the Patriarch's blood thinned in the river's swift current. With a muttered prayer he brought up his hand to his forehead and touched it, leaving a drop of water on his brow. As he bowed to the Holy Father, another man staggered forward, following his lead. And another. And another. In the waters of sacrifice they baptized one another, and he could see the futures that gathered about them shifting tenor as they accepted, by that ritual, the gesture he had made. Scenes of violence dissipated even as he watched, and he felt tears come to his eyes as he saw them replaced by visions of hope, and peace, and reverence.

It wasn't all in vain, then.

No one saw him raise up the knife again, to a point some six inches down from where he had cut before. No one saw him press its slender point into his flesh, or twist it deep between the bones, or cup his hands so that the sudden spurt of arterial blood might be disguised as something less vital.

I accept Your judgment, God of Earth and Erna, and give myself into Your Hands.

He saw Andrys Tarrant step into the water, then turn back to see if his lover was following. Did she know that for a thousand years the Tarrant men had refused to marry except within the Church? After a moment—a long moment, fraught with obvious indecision—she nodded, and stepped into the water beside him, accepting the hand that he offered her.

One more soul for God, he thought. That was how you won a world. Step by step. Infinite patience. . . .

The world began to waver in his vision. The futures—so many favorable now!—began to fade. How long would it be before they realized what he had done? He tried to step down from his perch, but the water surrounding it was deeper than he remembered and he went down heavily, his damaged leg slamming into the river bed hard enough to send spear points of pain shafting up into his groin and beyond. He groaned, and for a moment almost fell. One or two of his people started toward him, but he waved them back. His wounded arm hung down now, where none could see it, and it seemed strangely distant now, not like part of his own flesh at all. From somewhere came the sound of splashing, as if of a body approaching, but that, too, seemed distant, a sound from another world. He drew in a deep breath and swayed, his strength ebbing out into the cold river current that swirled about his thighs. *The efficacy of sacrifice is in direct proportion to the value of that which is destroyed.* Or so the Prophet had written. What could possibly be of more value to this Patriarch, whose greatest dream had been to live long enough to see his world change? "I have nothing more precious to give," he whispered to his God. Darkness was closing in about his vision like a tunnel. The river's murmur had become a roar that filled his ears and drowned out all other sound. He could feel himself drifting off, could feel his soul's linkage to the flesh that housed it separating like a frayed cord, and he struggled to remain upright as long as possible. Best to die with dignity, he thought, to give this symbol power. Best to hold out long enough that no one tried to save him, until he was finally past all saving.

And then he felt a touch at his side, human warmth, a powerful grip. He managed to focus clearly enough to make out a face, bearded and scarred and furrowed with concern. Vryce. At first he thought the man was going to try to help him, but then he saw the truth, that Vryce understood—not only what he was doing, but the necessity for doing it—and he let the man support him as the last of his worldly strength left him. Upright unto the end, his lifeblood staining his robes and Vryce's jacket as it streamed off into the river, to cleanse the Forest with its power.

Unto your judgment, my God. For Love of You.

In the darkness that was gathering now he saw a vision slowly take shape. A hazy point of light shimmered, shivered, then expanded into the shape of a planet, complete and perfect before his eyes. Erna. He could sense the rhythms of its tides, the heat of its life, the immeasurable beauty of its potential. He sensed the peace of a planet in utter harmony, where all life and all of nature were bound together by a power that flowed around and through everything. . . .

. . . and he felt the presence of Man on Erna, an alien intrusion, abhorrent. He saw the tides of fae respond to the invader's presence, struggling to absorb him, to adapt. He heard the voice of one man rising above that of three thousand, offering Erna a key, a channel, a Pattern for contact.

Sacrifice.

Loss as a link; destruction as a creative force. Casca's madness re-shaped the currents, carving out a niche of violence and mourning for his species to inhabit. And mankind thrived. The children of the col-onists spread out across the planet, until their numbers were so great that no one man might command that kind of power again. Only something greater than a man, that served as the focus of a thousand souls. Something like a Church. A crusade.

A legend.

He saw a mountain crowned with smoke, whose slopes spewed forth gouts of fire, whose base was ringed by ghosts. He saw a man climb up that slope—but no, not a man, not *merely* a man. This was a legend incarnate, figurehead for a nation of fear. The Hunter trailed nightmares in his wake, that linked him to a million souls across the face of the planet. And when he raised up his sword and bound the fae to serve him, when he offered up the most valuable thing that any man possessed, the very currents shook with the force of his conjur-ing. From the ground at his feet shock waves swept across the planet, and the Patriarch saw that when they passed, the currents of the fae shifted, as if accepting some new message into their substance. A new Impression, more powerful than Casca's. A new Pattern for con-tact, that would change the face of sorcery forever.

He saw his own body as if from a great height, Vryce now wholly supporting its weight. He saw men wading across the river in panic as they realized what he had done, but it was too late now for them to save him. The deed was done, the Pattern consummated. A new set of futures was taking shape, brighter and clearer than any he had seen before, and in them he could see the force of his own sacrifice encircling the globe, reflected and magnified in the souls of his faith-ful like sunlight in fine crystal. Such power, he saw, could change Erna forever. The Hunter had already paved the way, establishing a new channel for the currents to follow. He, with his death, would confirm that Pattern, and set it upon the face of the planet forever.

Self-sacrifice.

How many sorcerers would practice their Art when death was the price of a Working? How many men would be willing to part with their lives as casually as they had once parted with books, or arti-facts, or even the lives of others? Those few who might dare to Work wouldn't be men of greed or cowardice now; the new rules would scare those away. Perhaps one man in a million would dare to pay the price the fae demanded, to serve a higher goal. Perhaps. As for the rest, they would observe that the fae was now a distant force, un-Workable . . . and slowly the fae would respond to that belief, and become so in truth. As it had changed after Casca's sacrifice, so it would change again.

Bright futures exploded before his eyes, blinding in their brilliance. He saw a sky peppered with colorful explosions, winged carriages that flew like birds, a thousand and one precious legends of Earth come alive before him. There were things he didn't know the name for and things whose purpose he couldn't begin to guess at, but oh, the overall pattern was clear. Tears came to his eyes as future after future unfolded before him, not all of them perfect, but so full of hope! He saw what must have been a spaceship—how smooth it was, how plain in design, how unlike anything he would have imagined a spaceship to be!—and then the visions began to fade, pictures bleeding into a field of light, sensations into a numbing warmth—

"Thank You, Lord," he whispered. Voicing the words within his soul, not knowing or caring if they ever reached his lips. "Thank You for giving me this."

Slowly, peacefully, the Patriarch let loose his hold on life, and slid down into the embrace of his God.

Dawn

Forty-three

The wedding was held in Merentha, beneath suitably sunny skies. There were storm clouds to the west, but no one saw them. There was a faint whiff of ozone in the air, harbinger of trouble to come, but no one smelled it. There were even a few drops of rain that fell upon the crowd during the ceremony itself, but no one noticed them, and the spots of wetness that lingered for some time afterward went likewise unregarded. All in all, despite the true weather, it seemed a beautiful day.

From his vantage point at the edge of the milling crowd, Karril grinned at the figure by his side. "Nice going, Sis."

Saris smiled.

There were flowers strewn about the ancient estate in such profusion that the air was a heady perfume, the scents of roses, carnations, lilacs, and a dozen other varieties all mingling in the afternoon breeze. True Earth-flowers, all of them, rushed to Merentha from gardens and hothouses all over the continent. They were gathered in pots by the front of the house, they twined up the trellis supports of the bridal canopy, they festooned the silk canopy itself in carefully orchestrated profusion. On the great wall they had been arranged so as to cover the sections of new mortar and stone which had recently been added, making it seem that the antique barrier was as perfect on this day as it had been when erected, nearly five hundred years ago. And if the scent of the flowers lacked perfect balance in any one place, if the cloying sweetness of one bloom interfered with the delicate fragrance of another . . . well, that was one problem easily corrected. It paid to have Iezu among the wedding guests.

"How many of us are here, do you think?" Saris whispered.

Karril looked over the multitude and ventured a quick count.

"Ten that I can see. Maybe more. Hard to pick them out in this crowd."

"All in human form," she mused. Her tone that made it clear that she found the thought incredible.

"Of course." He chuckled. "Wouldn't want to detract from the proceedings, would we?" He patted her gently on the shoulder—flesh-toned, not silver, and as flawless in texture as one would expect from a Iezu of her aspect—and whispered, "It's more fun this way, isn't it?"

"*Fun* is your department, not mine." But she smiled as she said it, and he sensed her relaxing at last into the unfamiliar masquerade.

A bridal canopy had been raised in the middle of the courtyard, in accordance with some ancient Earth-custom whose purpose had been forgotten even as its aesthetic details were faithfully preserved. Sunlight shone through the fine white silk, rendering it aglow against the azure brilliance of the afternoon sky. White was the color of weddings, according to Earth tradition, and despite the fact that most of Erna preferred more festive colors, the Tarrant clan had always been Earth-reverent in its practices. Today was no exception.

And Andrys Tarrant looked fine in white, there was no doubt about that. White velvet ribbed in white satin cording for a jacket, full white sleeves of a silk so light that it fluttered in the breeze like fine gauze, white leather gloves and boots so supple that they clung to his body like a second skin, fringed and embroidered with silken threads of the same hue. Against such a background his skin, normally so pale in aspect, took on the bronze sheen of a healthy tan, and the sun picked out Core-gold highlights in his newly trimmed hair. He looked good and he knew it, and his self-confidence, as always, was irresistible to those who surrounded him. Karril chuckled as waves of lust rose from the crowd that gathered around him, mostly (but not all) from women. As for the ladies he had courted and seduced in the past, there were dozens of them here today, and not all had come to wish him well. For the most part they crowded around the wedding lawn with an impatient mixture of curiosity and resentment, waiting to see the waiflike foreigner who had stolen the prize they had so coveted.

She was beautiful, there was no doubt of that. There was no Iezu illusion active here, nor any need for it. The soft silk gown of graduated layers, Revival-inspired, made her slender form seem almost wraithlike, angelic, and her jet-black hair, hanging loose about her shoulders, cascaded down her back like a second veil. When the wedding crowns were placed upon their heads (of her own design, it was whispered, sculpted and polished by those same slender hands that now offered and received a pair of rings) the fine silver filigree glittered against the jet-black strands like stars on a clear night.

"Flat as a board," one woman whispered, drawing up her own considerable endowment into a position of prominence. "Pale as a ghost," another observed, lightly stroking her own cocoa skin. "Won't last a week," a third muttered, and they all nodded their agreement that yes, they knew Andrys Tarrant's taste in women, and no, this stick of a ghost-child wasn't going to keep him amused for long.

It was a priest of the One God who bound the two together, and Saris nodded her approval as the second rings were exchanged, the bonds of Earth joining those of secular marriage in a tradition as ancient as the Tarrant name. She had known, as Narilka had not, the tradition of that family, and as much as she would miss the girl as a worshiper she knew there were times that even a "goddess" had to give way to fate. *Would she have signed on to his faith so willingly if I hadn't released her back then, when all this started?* she wondered. Either way, she had no regrets. The difference between a true godling and a Iezu was that the latter wasn't dependent upon worship. And love, besides, was a very special kind of beauty.

"Come on," Karril urged, nudging her forward. "We'll miss the fun."

A reception line was forming now, and it stretched across the courtyard and back again; officials first, then neighbors, friends, and whoever else cared to greet the host and hostess of the afternoon's festivities. In that Andrys Tarrant was claiming the ancient title of *Neocount* with all its prerogatives and responsibilities, there were more than a few men and women of local importance who had seized this opportunity to introduce themselves. Most of them clearly had their doubts about the situation—a few even had the bad manners to mutter that it would have been better for them all if Samiel had survived, rather than this irresponsible playboy—but one by one, as they shook Andrys' hand, they saw in his eyes an indefinable *something* which said that yes, this man had changed, and if they would give him a chance, he might surprise them. That, too, was a Iezu gift, but one so subtle that neither side noticed its oddness.

"I don't understand—" Saris began, and Karril whispered, "Shhh!"

There were past lovers coming to the head of the line now, buxom women with temptation in their gait and a knowing sparkle in their eyes. Coolly the first one took Narilka's hand and offered her congratulations, her eyes never leaving those of Andrys. *Acknowledge me,* they urged him, *if you dare.* To her delight he caught up her hand and kissed it, his manner as flirtatious as ever, and introduced her to his bride in a way that made it clear he still found her utterly desirable. Smugly she glanced at the new bride, her face warm with triumph. *You can marry him if you like, my dear, but you'll never change him. And when he tires of your meager pleasures, we'll have him back again, and teach him just how poor his judgment was when he bound himself to you.* But if she expected the black-haired girl to respond with embarrassment, or (even better) with jealousy, she was to be disappointed. The bride greeted her graciously, even gladly. Amazing! Was she that blind to her husband's proclivities, or was she simply living in a fantasy in which marriage, like a magical spell, would suddenly and completely alter his behavior? But then she looked at Andrys again, and she saw the way he regarded his bride, and a flush rose to her own cheeks as the truth hit home. The habits of a lifetime could not be shed in a single afternoon, and thus it was with this playboy's surface mannerisms. But deep within his eyes an adoration glowed that put all his former lovers to shame. And his bride, however young, however inexperienced, understood that. She endured his flirtation because she knew it for what it was: a habit, no more, now empty of meaning, no more to be criticized in him than the way he walked, or the casual elegance with which he dressed. It was all show without substance now, and she was too savvy to feel threatened by it. Andrys' former lover slunk away with chastened mien, and another, eyes glowing with anticipated triumph, took her place.

"You're a voyeur," Saris accused.

Karril chuckled. "No argument there."

Tables were set out laden with rich foods, a lavish spread such as only the rich could conjure. Karril walked behind the tables while servants doled out portions to the guests, checking the quality of each offering, prepared to intervene should any one item come up short. But it was all perfect, from hors d'oeuvres to wine to the inevitable wedding cake, and at last he retired in the shade of a tree to feast himself on the enjoyment of those who were eating.

"They're gone," Saris noted.

"What?" He followed her gaze toward the main gate of the keep, then chuckled anew as he realized what she meant. "Their guests are satisfied. The requisite ceremony's been performed. Why not sneak off for a few minutes to celebrate in private, while attention is fixed elsewhere?" He shot her an appraising glance and noted, "You don't hang out with humans a lot, do you?"

"This is the first time I've put on a really human form."

"It looks good."

"Thank you," she said, startled.

He leaned back against the tree trunk and crossed his arms, to all appearances a well-sated guest who was waiting for his food to digest. "There'll be more of that now, you know. Curiosity will win out over fear in all but a few of our kind. New emotions to learn, new experiences to court . . . we might even try that one in time," he said with a smile, nodding toward the keep where the two lovers had disappeared.

"What? You can't mean—" She looked at him in astonishment. "It's just an illusion, Karril, you know that. The fact that this time you chose a male form and I chose a female—"

"I didn't meant that," he said quickly. "Obviously we're not human; in fact, that goes without saying. But think about it, Saris: surely our mother did more than spawn a few random demons when she conceived us. She meant to create a *species*, according to the rules of life as she knew them. Clearly she wanted us to be self-sustaining. Doesn't that imply some kind of reproductive capacity? And doesn't that in turn imply some kind of . . . interactive potential?"

She stared at him in disbelief, unable to muster words. At last she laughed, a silver sound. "You're incredible, you know that?"

He grinned. "It's been said."

"You've spent too many hours in human form. It's addled your mind."

"And you're too mired in your aspect for your own good. Break loose! Experiment! I promise you'll enjoy it."

"I have a religion to run. Worshipers to entertain—"

"You think they'll complain if we give them a new godling? Ah, Saris, think of it! What kind of a child would the gods of beauty and ecstasy produce? I shiver just to imagine the possibilities."

She looked at him in amazement. "Is that a proposition?"

He chuckled. "I guess it is."

"You don't even know what reproduction entails, for us."

"No," he admitted. "But I think that figuring it out could be a lot of fun." He winked at her. "Reproduction usually is."

"That's your aspect, not mine."

"Ah, Saris!" He caught up her hand in his; through the veil of fine flesh he could feel the throb of living energy, the true substance of the Iezu. " 'Aspect' is just preference, not a prison. Don't you see that? We're the children of living creatures, with the capacity to be just as versatile as our parents. Why not give it a try?"

"I don't see you reaching outside your aspect in this experience."

With a soft laugh he let loose her hand, and struck at his chest as though marking the entrance point of an arrow. "Touché."

A sudden commotion among the guests drew their attention. Someone was proposing a toast, it seemed, raising a glass of perfect wine to catch the sunlight, in dedication to the newlyweds. Others joined in, and the fine wine was sipped and savored. A hundred souls resonating in perfect unison, relishing the moment: a symphony of pleasure. Karril leaned against the tree in contentment, drinking it in as a toast of his own, and shut his eyes as the waves of human enjoyment washed over him.

She watched him for a moment, observing his reaction, and then a faint smile softened her expression. She relaxed a bit and leaned against the tree beside him, watching the guests as they feasted.

"I'll think about it," she promised.

Forty-four

The shop was in a quiet part of town, and despite the fame it had quickly earned since opening—or one could say, the *notoriety*—its facade was modest and unassuming. HUNT SHOPPE, the sign said, its typeface and proportion suggesting a modest business. There was a display of fishing rods in one corner of the window, bows and crossbows in the other. In the center a finely tanned skin served as backdrop for all the accoutrements of the hunter's art: compasses and maps, backpacks and canteens, and a selection of heavy-bladed knives guaranteed (so the sign read) to gut with a simple twist of the wrist, and skin with the ease of slicing butter.

The man looked in the window a long, long while, and wondered about why he had come here. He'd never cared for the sport much in general, and the thought of gutting a living animal—or at least one very recently dead—made his stomach turn. For a moment he almost turned back and went home. Then he remembered how lonely it was there, how empty the spacious house was without the sound of other voices. And he drew himself up and pushed open the heavy wooden door, bracing for what was inside.

The shop's interior was larger than he would have guessed, and every inch of it was filled with hunting apparati. There were other customers there, half a dozen of them, and he watched for a moment while a man hefted a brass-butted springbolt to his shoulder, testing its balance. Another bent the length of a fishing rod in a wide U-shape and harrumphed that yes, it would probably do.

Once more, he almost turned and left. Almost.

"Can I help you?"

The clerk was a young man, about his own height and build. Nondescript, just as he was. For a moment he hesitated. "Riven Forrest?"

It couldn't be him, could it? Surely a man capable of helping him would be more . . . more . . . well, more *something*.

To his relief the clerk nodded toward a door at one side of the shop. "Probably in the office. Just go on through, you'll find him."

The door led to another room, smaller than the first, less crowded. There were paintings in this room and other forms of art as well, all depicting objects of the hunt. Skerrels, nudeer, lynkesets . . . some were wandering through their native habitat in a wholly natural mode, the kind of nature-loving art that would be hung over the couch in a family room, or by the fireplace. Others were less natural, and oddly disturbing. A marmosa frozen atop a fallen log, its large ears cocked forward with desperate intensity, its eyes wide and anxious. Nudeer crouching in the high grass, preparing to bolt for their lives. And a waterfowl of some kind, floating on the rippled surface of a lake. He couldn't put his finger on what it was about that last one that bothered him so, until at last he realized that the shadow of an armed human loomed over the water, its reflection barely visible among the reeds. Animals caught in their last living moments; the passion of the hunt as seen through the eyes of those who must die to consummate it. He felt uncomfortable viewing those paintings, but it was hard to look away. Involuntary voyeurism: the fascination of Death. For the first time coming here, he believed that he might be in the right place after all.

There were rooms beyond that one, small corridors that twisted back on themselves, even a walk-in closet that had been made to house a Hunt Shoppe display. There were tools he didn't recognize, and restraining devices that seemed better proportioned to human limbs than to any animal he had ever seen. There were traps of all shapes and all sizes, deadly and humane, and wax images demonstrating how some of them were meant to be used. There was a lot more art, and not only of animals. One lithograph, finely rendered, depicted the final showdown between the Selenzy Slasher and the police who ran him down; the bright red ink was particularly effective. Another showed the last moments of Karth Steele as he plunged through the southern swamps, the head of his latest victim still in his hands. Convicts and torturers, criminals turned prey . . . he felt somehow unclean as he viewed their last moments on Erna, as if something voyeuristic had awakened in his soul that he would far, far rather pretend wasn't there in the first place.

At last, with effort, he forced himself away from those pictures and through the next doorway. Beyond it was a small room, unmistakably outfitted as an office. He felt a wave of relief wash over him, as if he, too, had been fleeing from some unseen pursuer, and had finally, here, found sanctuary. Even the furniture was normal, and the only painting—a portrait of an attractive man hung over the small fireplace—was blessedly unthreatening.

The man behind the desk said nothing as he entered, but looked up at him and waited. He was pale of skin, dark-haired, and his sharp, angular features reminded the man of a predatory bird. His eyes might have been a human color—brown or gray or maybe even a dark blue—but in the hooded lamplight which was the room's only illumination they appeared black, a limitless black that sucked in the lampglow and swallowed it whole.

"Forrest?" he stammered, finding his voice at last. "Riven Forrest?"

The man behind the desk nodded, and indicated a chair by his visitor's side. It was a welcome offering, and he fell into it heavily.

"I'm Riven Forrest. And you are?"

He started to speak his name, then hesitated. *Gods, this is crazy. He can't help you if he doesn't know who you are, now can he?* "My name is Helder. Allen Helder." He had to force the words out; beads of sweat were beginning to form on his brow. "I have a . . . an unusual problem. I was told you might be able to help me."

Crazy, crazy, crazy. If this man turns me in, then what do I do? The law doesn't take kindly to this kind of thing.

But Forrest was utterly calm; his voice, when he spoke, was more suggestive of casual visitation than of secretive negotiations. "I'm familiar with your problem, Mer Helder. I believe we may be able to do business." He leaned forward on the desk, steepling his fingers. "Why don't you give me the details?"

He knew, the man thought wildly. He knew! That meant that the person who had given him Forrest's name must have also told him . . . how much? Oddly, the thought didn't inspire panic, only a strange sort of calm. He was committed now. Forrest knew his business. What could he do under such circumstances, other than proceed?

"My wife and I divorced two years ago." He said the words quickly, forcing them out before he could think about them. Before the pain could take hold again. "We had three children. I got custody. A girl, Sofie, and two boys, Rori and Tonio. I have all the particulars here. . . ." He reached into his jacket and brought out a small packet of papers; he cradled it in his hands as he spoke as if it were itself some precious living thing. "My wife was . . . abusive. Not toward me, but when she was angry, or when she was frustrated, she used to take it out on the kids." He paused, biting his lip. Gods, how the memories hurt! "I had to prove that to get custody of all three. I had to . . . there were bruises . . . I had to discuss some things. . . ." He shook his head, feeling the tears come again. Hating himself for being that weak in front of a stranger. "She was furious about the judgment. She spent a year trying to fight it in court, then finally gave up and left Jaggonath. I don't know where she went. Things were so bad between us then . . . we couldn't talk. Not about anything. She was so bitter. So angry." He looked up and found the black eyes fixed on him; hungry, hungry eyes. "I don't know what happened," he whispered. "I was so careful. . . ."

"You think she kidnapped your children."

His eyes squeezed shut as he remembered. The empty house. The closets and drawers in disarray, so obviously ransacked for supplies. The open door, swinging in the wind. "I know it," he choked out. "I'd left them in Toni's care—he was so proud of being old enough to take care of the others, a little man of the family!—and then, when I came home . . . nothing! What else could have happened? He would never have opened the door to a stranger. There wasn't any sign of a struggle. Who could have done it, other than her?"

The pale man regarded him as he reached for a cup by his side. His eyes never leaving the man's, he sipped from it, then set it aside. "You've gone through legal channels."

"Oh, yes. First the police. They were no help at all. I've been through three private investigators, and they keep coming up with promising leads, but each time they get to a place they find out that she just left it. Once, it turned out she was never there at all."

Forrest nodded thoughtfully. "She's running. And she has the sense to set a false trail, or at least make an effort at it."

"They can't help me," he stammered. "I was told . . . maybe you can. I'll do *anything*," he added quickly. "Just get them back for me, and you can name your price. If I have it, it's yours."

For a long time Forrest looked at him. In the silence the man could hear his own heart pounding; did he look as desperate as he felt? *If you fail me now,* he thought, *what other hope is there?* But he didn't dare move. He didn't dare speak. The black gaze had him frozen, like a nudeer in a predator's jaws.

"I can track her," Forrest said at last. "I can get your children and bring them back to you. I can see that she never interferes in your life again. The price is one hundred fifty a day, plus expenses. Do you care if your ex-wife is injured?"

"I—" For a moment the words wouldn't come; he had to force them out. "I'd rather not. If that's possible."

"One hundred and sixty, then. Payment due in full when the children are returned to you."

He offered his hand. The man stared at it for a moment, then took it. And shook it, hard.

"Thank you," he whispered. "Thank you."

"Thank me when the work is done, Mer Helder."

He indicated the packet of papers in his hand. "I have all the information written down here, including the reports of the men I hired. Charcoal portraits of the children—"

"Leave it," Forrest said quietly. "I'll go through it tonight. For now, go home. Forget you ever came here. The next time you see me will be when I bring you your children. If you seek me out before that, I'll consider our contract null and void. Do you understand that?"

"I understand," he whispered. Trying not to think about what special techniques this man must employ, that he took such care to keep his workings secret.

"It's been a pleasure doing business with you, Mer Helder." Forrest nodded what was obviously a dismissal.

But the man didn't move. "Do you think—" he dared. "I mean, can you—"

"Prey is prey," he said. "The fact that it's human in this case makes the game more interesting, but not necessarily more difficult. Intelligence, like instinct, can be anticipated. Manipulated." He took another sip from the cup, his gaze never leaving the man. "If your children are still alive, then I guarantee results. If not . . . then you haven't spent anything, have you?" The black eyes glittered; in the lamplight they seemed strangely inhuman. "Good night, Mer Helder."

He managed to get to his feet and head toward the door, even though he longed to beg for better reassurance. Was there really a chance for him to be reunited with his children? Could this strange man succeed where so many had failed? But it was clear from Forrest's manner that he was no longer welcome in the office, and so he hurried out. The last thing he wanted to do was anger the only man who could help him.

He'll get them for me, he thought desperately. *He will. I know it.*

Repeating that thought like a mantra, he made his way out of the strange shop, and started the long walk home.

For a long time after his visitor left, the man called Riven Forrest was still. Waiting for the air to clear, it seemed. Waiting for the psychic dust to settle. At last, when he judged that the atmosphere was right, he reached out and put his hand on the packet the man had left behind. Just that. He could breathe in its contents in images, which was faster and far more satisfying than reading. What were words, anyway? At best they only hinted at the exhilaration of the hunt; at worst, they muddled and obscured it.

Leaning back, he shut his eyes and envisioned the task at hand. She would be afraid even now, after all these months. He would dissect that fear. Fear was what made animals run, and the shape of that fear was what you used to divine their path. Do it right, and the fae itself would vibrate in harmony with your pursuit. There was no escape after that. Not when the planet itself was your collaborator, and every living thing on it an extension of your will.

At last, when he was satisfied that he had absorbed the emotional essence of this new case, he smiled. Plans were already forming in his brain. Patterns were already being sketched out, tested, and adjusted within him, in a process far more natural than breathing. He was in his element now, and he loved every minute of it. Was there any sweeter challenge to court than the hunt of intelligent prey?

He picked up the cup before him. The liquid inside was thick and red, and carefully heated to body temperature. He liked it best that way. Traditional.

The painting which loomed over the fireplace was a portrait of the Hunter. With a smile, the creature called Riven Forrest raised the cup up toward it; the red liquid sloshed thickly inside.

"Here's to you, Dad," he whispered.

And he drank.

Forty-five

Damien thought, *I can't believe he's dead.*

People were shouldering their way past Damien in anxious haste, as if afraid that the world might change again before they could profit from it. Newsmongers and merchants and sorcerers and tourists and even one or two who labeled themselves "Earth scientists," going from south to north in search of new knowledge, or north to south seeking profit for what they had already gleaned, or else staying here, at the midpoint of the journey, to sell their fellow travelers whatever they'd be willing to buy. Human enterprise at its best.

Let it go, Vryce. Just let it go.

The first week he had been here he'd told himself it was because he didn't know what else to do with himself. In a way, that was true. The priesthood was closed to him, not because he couldn't get himself reinstated if he wanted to—the Holy Mother in the West would surely respond positively to a heartfelt appeal—but because the Patriarch had been right, damn him. The clarity of faith which had once been Damien Vryce's hallmark was gone now, and what had taken its place might be made to serve the Church in a thousand ways, but it wasn't appropriate for a priest. There were other things he could do, of course, such as bodyguarding couriers and explorers or taking on such commissions himself. For all that the fae was "tame" now, there were enough demons left over from the time before that it would be quite a few generations before anyone felt safe traveling alone. In token of which . . . he half rose out of his seat as something dark and winged swept down from the smoke-filled sky, swinging his springbolt up as he thumbed off the safety—but it pulled up sharply into the thin winds and was lost behind a cloud before he could track it and fire. Lucky beastie. Between his own sure aim and the handful

415

of trigger-happy tourists who fished for demons in the smoke-filled valleys, damn few things made it through. He had shot down over a dozen himself this week, and collected a fair bounty on each from the tavern's owner. A good deal, all around. That and the free ale made it possible for him to put off certain decisions that he would rather not make ... like what he going to do with himself when this was all over. Like when the hell he was going to acknowledge that it *was* all over, and get his shit together and start living again.

With a sigh he emptied the mug of ale, and waved away the server who offered to bring him another. Black Ridge Tavern. He looked about it in amazement, at walls and chairs and beer-taps that would have been unthinkable mere weeks before. The place was crowded as always, and the rough space was filled with the smell of fire, sweat, and sawdust as tourists and tabloid artists and self-appointed ambassadors to the Iezu made their best attempt at conversation. Overhead roof beams were being nailed in place even now, and the sounds of saw and hammer added to the overall din. With a sigh he finally rose up from his seat, and made his way out of the crowded common room. Onto the deck which wound over and about the mountain's crest, offering men a firm path where once even horses feared to tread.

Black Ridge Pass. Once it had been a windswept corridor from one world into the next, known only to those who cared about such desolate places. Now it was a veritable hothouse of human activity. On the northern flank of the ridge there were already three inns finished and two more under construction, and never mind that the walls weren't painted yet and the indoor toilets weren't working. How many people got to hike past a live volcano on their way to the outhouse? On the south side there was little permanent construction, for the most interesting part of the view wouldn't last more than a few months at best, but a narrow wooden deck had been constructed that led half a mile along the sloping mountainside, so that tourists could drink their fill of the spectacle at hand before it died down forever.

The Forest was burning. Its enemies had waited until the dry season prepared it properly, then set fire to it in a dozen places along its border, so that the purifying conflagration would work its way inward from all sides at once. That way only, they explained, could man be certain that all the degenerate life-forms within the Forest died forever, rather than fleeing to accompanying regions. It was a good plan, and it would almost certainly succeed, and if Damien Vryce took a moment to mourn the loss of the Hunter's prize horses, or the fact that no man would ever again wield the kind of power that would

make it possible to evolve new ones . . . well, that was his own human weakness speaking. Progress had its price. In the long run mankind would benefit from this act of destruction, and that was what
mattered.

Wasn't it?

He walked to where the narrow deck began and leaned against its
railing, watching as the great fire miles away lit up the land with
roaring brilliance, clouds of ash whipping about its head with whirlwind fury. For two weeks now it had burned that brightly, and the
winds in the Raksha Valley had roared west instead of east, sucked in
by its insatiable hunger for oxygen. A massive thunderhead cloud had
reared up from the fire, impossibly high, a vast mushroom of water
and ash that towered over the Black Ridge's walkways like God's own
vengeance made manifest. The great cloud blotted out the sun at
times, at other times filtered its light so that dense, bloody shadows
played across the walkways. The tourists loved it. The scientists
were in seventh heaven, explaining to anyone who would listen—and
many who wouldn't—that this was *fire weather*, a natural phenomenon, wholly predictable by their Earth-born art. He watched them
drink themselves into joyful oblivion over the fact that they now
lived in a world where such things could be measured, understood,
predicted—while later that night a sorcerer cast himself from off the
very place where Damien now stood, unable to adapt to a world that
now declared his kind powerless.

He understood how a man could do that. He didn't share the
man's despair, exactly—no matter what the Patriarch might have
thought, he had never been that addicted to power—but in the secret
recesses of his heart he nursed his own, gentler regret. He wanted to
See the fae again. Just once more. He wanted to See the corrupt Forest currents surge beneath that cleansing fire, and taste their essence
as they came out the other side. He wanted to See what the currents
of the shadowlands looked like now that the Mother of the Iezu was
active there, now that her children were meeting with journalists on
the very trails he and Gerald Tarrant had forged. The loss of his Vision was like a wound that refused to heal, doubly painful because he
had done it to himself . . . and yes, he knew that what they had done
was good, and necessary, even if they hadn't understood all the implications at the time . . . but that didn't quell the longing inside him.
He was, after all, only human.

*How would you be dealing with all this, Gerald? They say that
adepts can still see the fae, although they can no longer Work it;
would you come to terms with that as the price of man's salvation,*

or rage against the bonds that your own sacrifice forged for us? Or would you find some new way around the rules, carving out a niche for yourself in this new world as surely as you did in the old?

He wanted the man to be here now, to see all this, to witness the bad and the good and pass judgment on it all with cool sardonic indifference. He had seen him die, but he still couldn't accept it. Maybe that was what was keeping him here. Maybe until he came to terms with the Hunter's death—no, with *Gerald Tarrant's* death, which was a different thing entirely—he wouldn't be free to start his own life moving again.

Something dark moved against the clouds, that didn't follow the pattern of ash and wind; without thinking he drew up his springbolt to the ready and prepared to fire—

And there was a crack right by his ear, as loud as if the very mountainside had split open beside him. Startled, he missed the shot. Someone else didn't. An unseen projectile slammed into the winged thing, hard enough that its scaled wings nearly snapped off as it was thrown back from them. A moment later it exploded into a mist of blood and fire, to the delight of those tourists who had been present to see the shot. Some of them applauded.

His left ear ringing, he turned around to see who the marksman was. A young man nodded back at him, not warmly but apologetically, as one damned well should after firing off a pistol that close without warning. For a moment he almost said something sharp, but he managed to swallow the words before they came out. Never mind that the guy looked like some spoiled brat from a rich house, out to play with explosives now that he could do so without risking his own pretty skin; there was nothing inherently wrong about using a pistol, or killing demonlings, and Erna wasn't experienced enough in firearms etiquette to make deafening one's neighbors a mortal offense. He managed to nod stiffly himself and hoped it looked forgiving, then turned back to the view. On both sides of him tourists were gathering at the rail now, straining to see down into the depths below. He wondered how many of them understood the significance of the killing they had just witnessed. Like legions of demonlings killed in the past this creature was now dead and gone, but unlike its predecessors, it would never be replaced. The minds of men no longer had the power to give life to such creatures. Which meant that someday, when enough demons and wraiths and hate-constructs had been dispatched, there would come a time when men and women could walk about safely in the night, as they did on other planets.

It was an awesome thought, and an oddly unnerving one. He wondered if he would recognize that world as his own.

Tarrant would.

He shut his eyes, trying not to feel that loss. The tourists at the rail had kept their distance from him, thank God, perhaps sensing the darkness of his mood. He could hear them chattering on all sides of him, but the sound had no meaning to him. In this one spot, in this one single moment in time, he was alone with his memories. Just him and the Forest.

"Hard to believe that he's gone, isn't it?"

Startled, he turned back to see the young man watching him. "What?"

"The Hunter." The youth resheathed his pistol in a worked leather holster that hung from his belt. Both pieces looked expensive. "I assume that's who you're thinking about."

He shook his head, unable to believe the man's audacity. "You assume a hell of a lot."

"You don't act like one of the tourists. You've been here too long to be an ambassador to the Iezu, self-declared or otherwise, and you don't talk to the news service people." He nodded toward the fire beneath them. "Why else would a man be here, if not to contemplate the Hunter's demise?"

Arrogant, he thought, *as well as spoiled.* He judged the man to be twenty-two, if that, and from the look of him he had never done anything more strenuous than clean and oil Daddy's firearms collection. Smooth olive skin, without pockmark or blemish, was molded into features that were delicate, unseasoned. Untested. Thick black hair, nearly waist-length, was caught up in a braid at the back of his neck so perfect that there must surely be some expensive pomade keeping it all in place. A body shorter than Damien's own—but not by much—served as a lean and elegant frame for an outfit of expensive finery. Pants of glove-soft black leather. Knee high riding boots. A doeskin vest embroidered in layers of gold—probably the real thing— and a shirt of fine crimson silk that more than one exotic caterpillar had given its life for. All of that was topped off by dark eyes, thick-lashed, that languidly gazed upon the world as if they owned it—

Not twenty-two, he reassessed suddenly. Something in the youth's gaze made him shiver inside, but he was careful not to let it show. *Not that young by a long shot.*

"They say you were there," the youth said quietly.

"So what? You want my autograph?" He turned back to the face the fire, wishing the man would go away. "I have better things to do with my time." *And I don't need new mysteries.*

"They say you saw him burn."

That did it. He needed this scene like he needed another trip to Hell. "They say a lot—" he began angrily.

And then he stopped. Because it was wrong, the whole conversation was *wrong*. Who the hell *was* this guy? No one up here knew what Damien had done; he had kept it a secret precisely because he didn't want to go through this kind of interrogation. He hadn't even given out his proper name, lest someone figure out where that name had been recently and what it had done. The result was that no one here knew who he was, or what he had done. *No one.*

"Who the vulk are you?"

A faint glimmer of a smile ghosted across the youth's face. "One who has an interest in legends." He nodded toward the fire. "Come to see the heart of all legends burn."

"Yeah, well, The view's free." He turned back toward it himself, and wondered just what it would take to make this intruder go away. Maybe if he ignored him.

"They say you saw him die."

He sighed, and shut his eyes. *What the hell.* "I saw."

"They burned his head."

The memory was surprisingly vivid. "I saw that."

"And you're certain it was his?"

Andrys Tarrant holds the grisly trophy aloft, fingers clasped about its golden hair, and holds it still for all to see. For all to identify. "Whose else would it be?"

"Any man's, if the illusion were right."

He snorted derisively. "There is no more illusion."

"There are the Iezu."

He shook his head. "I asked them. Or rather, I asked one of them who I think would have given me an honest answer. They wouldn't interfere, he said. Their Mother forbade it."

"There is always sorcery," the youth said quietly.

"No." His hand fisted tightly about the rail. Damn it, did he have to go through all this again, as if he had never done so the first time? The Hunter was dead. He had seen him die. He had *felt* him die, as the channel between Vryce and the Hunter was severed by Andrys Tarrant's bloody sword. Wasn't that enough? "There's no more sorcery—"

"No more *easy* sorcery," the youth agreed. "But for a man willing to give up enough, there's still a Pattern to follow."

"He'd have to give up his life then, in order to fake his death. What the hell kind of sense does that make?"

"Perhaps not his life," the youth suggested. "Perhaps only part of it."

A shaft of Corelight breached the great mushroom cloud and reached the platform where they stood. Damien heard tourists murmur in delight as the brilliant light, stained crimson by the cloud, edged the rough wooden walkway in fire.

"What are you suggesting?" he demanded.

"What if the Hunter wanted to stage his own death? What if his would-be killer agreed that that was the best course? What if it was enough for both of them that the *Hunter* died—the legend—but something of the man at its core survived? That would be death of a kind, wouldn't it? Surely the sacrifice of one's identity could be seen as a kind of suicide. Perhaps enough to wield some power even in this altered forum. Think about it," the youth urged. "It would have to be a sacrifice that came from the soul itself, not just a surface gesture. A true death, from which there could be no resurrection. The body that walked away from that night might never lay claim to its true name again, or connect itself to its previous life in word or deed." He paused. "It couldn't even discuss its own fate in any manner except the most impersonal. To do otherwise would be to join itself to the part that had died, and thus consummate the destruction of the whole."

It took Damien a minute to find his voice. The thought was so incredible. . . . *But no,* he thought, *not incredible at all. Not if you knew Gerald Tarrant, and what he was capable of.*

He asked it quietly: "Do you believe that's what happened?"

The youth shrugged. "I merely suggest a course the Hunter might have followed. Who can say what the truth is? Think of it as an exercise for the imagination, if you like. I thought that as a fellow sorcerer—" he smiled faintly, "—or rather, as a fellow *ex*-sorcerer, you might find it . . . amusing."

A gust of wind blew toward them from the Forest, carrying on it a dusting of ash. As it blew across them it dusted featherweight fragments across the youth's shoulder and hair. Slim gloved fingers rose up and brushed at the soft bits as soon as they landed, in a gesture as reflexive as that of a cat licking its soiled fur. A minimal gesture, chillingly familiar, that should have trailed fae in its wake. It would have, once.

He looked into those eyes—dark, so dark, and not a young man's at all, not by a long shot—and managed, "Your name." Finding his voice somewhere, managing to shape it into words. "You never did tell me what it was."

For a long, silent time the youth looked at him. Just looked at him. As if the look was a kind of dare, Damien thought. As if he wanted to give him time to try to see another man in his eyes, to superimpose another man's life over his own.

"No," he said at last. Glancing once more toward the burning Forest, as if the answer were there. "I didn't, did I?" Once more a faint smile touched the corner of his lips; the fleeting minimalism of the expression was so familiar that Damien didn't know how to respond. Did one celebrate such a resemblance, or mourn what it implied? "Does it matter?"

"No," he whispered. "Not really."

An expression that Damien couldn't begin to read flickered across the youth's face. Something strange, intensely human, an emotion that would have been ill-suited to the Hunter's former mien. Affection? Regret? "Good-bye, Damien Vryce." The youth bowed ever so slightly, his eyes never leaving Vryce's own. "Good luck."

And then he turned with easy grace and began to walk back toward the pass, silken sleeves fluttering in the wind. Damien almost ran after him. There were things he needed to say, farewells and gratitudes and hopes for the future that he'd never had a chance to express in the Hunter's lifetime. But he didn't go after him. Nor did he call out the name that was on his lips, though it took all his self control not to. Because if what the youth said was true, then such words could prove fatal. Instead he watched the young man walk away in silence as if he were truly a stranger, feeling something inside himself twist into a knot as the distance between them grew. Not until a little girl brushed against the stranger, leaving a smear of dirt on that crimson sleeve—not until a gloved hand rose up to brush off the offending stain, and once more came short of succeeding—did a new thought, a startling thought, take shape within Damien's brain.

If the Hunter *had* made a bid for life (he reasoned), and if he *had* talked Andrys Tarrant into going along with it . . . if he *had* sacrificed himself in the way this youth suggested, and done so successfully, so that he now walked the earth as another man, no longer a sorcerer because the Patriarch's sacrifice had stripped them all of power . . . then that man, if he happened to get dirty now, would have to take a bath to get himself clean. Just like everybody else.

In the dawn of a new world, Damien Vryce smiled.